LOVE'S THEATER

LOVE'S THEATER

Edited by
Esther Selsdon

Carroll & Graf Publishers, Inc.
NEW YORK

Carroll & Graf Publishers, Inc.
260 Fifth Avenue
New York
NY 10001

This collection published in the UK by
Robinson Publishing Ltd 1995

First Carroll & Graf edition 1995

ISBN 0–7867–0157–9

Printed and bound in the United Kingdom

10 9 8 7 6 5 4 3 2 1

CONTENTS

SUBMISSION

LOVE

❧

EMPOWERMENT

INTRODUCTION

This is not a book of sexual arousal, it is a book about the female description of it. Since throughout history even the experience of personal fulfilment, let alone its subsequent expression, has been hugely proscribed for women, they have, whether consciously or subconsciously, been forced to channel their energies into either, at best, indirect means of description or, at worst, totally different fields.

Where sex scenes in novels by men often revolve around the kind of fantasies in which enigmatic (and always nameless and personality-free) women turn up unexpectedly in hotel bedrooms etc. and, immediately and quite anonymously, emerge as outlets for the gratification of self-centred and masturbatory male fantasies, literature written by women does not, as a whole, follow this trend. Whilst male creativity has an unerring tendency to revolve around the self, women's creativity has, in literary terms, historically had a tendency to revolve around the other. Female descriptions of relationships almost inevitably include a specific male as an integral part of the story. He is a character as well as an object of desire and his feelings for the heroine are generally a necessary part of the sense of satisfaction.

This tradition has, of course, sprung from an interlinked social and literary tradition. Women desired what they were brought up to desire or to admit that they desired and they could, therefore, only ever hope to describe their desires within these male-dictated terms – which did not ever mean that they did not feel desire in exactly the same way as men. Thus there grew up a creative female universe in which women used only those possible channels of expression open to them – whatever these might be. During the Middle Ages, almost the only permissible means of self-expression for a female was religion and women like Julian of Norwich used this 'displacement' activity to satisfy themselves as best they could and set about describing what can only be termed arousal but in the form of love for their god and religious fervour. This tradition continued well into the nineteenth century with women like the Brontës manifesting their desires, not as personal, internalized passions but as uncontrollable and externalized storms on dark, torrid Yorkshire moorland. As late as the 1950s, Margaret Laurence's heroine in *A Jest of God* releases her frustrations in much the same terms as Julian of Norwich, only here at a local gospel meeting.

In the twentieth century, when women have had much greater expectations as well as freedoms of behaviour and expression, their variety of self-expression has grown likewise. Whilst they can now look forward to what might happen ('**anticipation**'), the descriptions in literature of romantic relationships once they have happened, fall loosely into either an expression of profound affection for another, highly characterized, individual ('**love**') or a series of descriptions in which the idea of sexual activity is such anathema to the female central character that it is not so much the male who is objectified as the female herself ('**alienation**'). It would seem that the prime literary description of experience of sex without affection is, for women, a distancing from oneself and not pure pornographic fantasy as a man's would tend to be. And with alienation, naturally, come deconstruction and humour – the women look at themselves from the outside and realize the utter ludicrousness of what they are doing. Many of the scenes in this category are the funniest in the collection but almost all of them also express a search for some answer to ultimate loneliness – since this is how the disconnection from the partner is perceived. It is the woman who is marginalized by the the pure sexual act; the man retains his full personality at all times.

On the odd occasion when women write precisely in order to describe their specific sexual arousal, the resulting descriptions, whether because of social conditioning or biological determination, tend to come out in much the same terms as men's – '**submission**'. *The Story of O*, one of the most famous erotic novels by a woman, is characterized by the total subjugation of the female identity to male desire. And, even in Pat Califia's alternative lesbian writing, the prime female erotic fantasy is blind obedience and devotion to a sexual dominator. The only slight variation on the traditional male fantasy of the totally subservient female is that the female fantasy generally incorporates a response (some kind of devoted love) to a very specific other, rather than an egotistical desire for devotion from an interchangeable and characterless devotee.

Finally, and only in the late 1990s, women have started using reverse sexual imagery to its full logical conclusion – 'empowerment'. Once again, the sex scene has begun to be used not to describe arousal but, politically, to transform traditional views of women's sexuality and to make females the possessors of power. But, when the women wield such sexual domination, it is a precise and determined political act and not a merely individual erotic one: Eurudice's penis-chomping, free-roaming vaginas wander in packs through Central Park, waiting to pounce and castrate.

This book is, by its very nature, a random selection. Many of the pieces might lie just as happily under another or, indeed, most of the other headings. I have merely tried to identify some of the features that they have in common.

ES

DISPLACEMENT

❧

The humanity of Christ, understood as including his full participation in bodiliness, was a central and characteristic theme in the religiosity of late medieval women. Often it had erotic or sensual overtones. For example, Margery Kempe was so intensely attracted to Christ's maleness that she wept whenever she saw a male baby; in her visions she cuddled with Christ in bed and was bold enough to caress his toes. Angela of Foligno, Adelheid Langmann and Catherine of Siena, among others, married Christ in eucharistic visions. Underlining the extent to which the marriage was a fusion with Christ's physicality, Adelheid received the host as a pledge rather than a wedding ring, while Catherine received, not the ring of gold and jewels that her biographer reports in his bowdlerized version, but the ring of Christ's foreskin.

Caroline Walker Bynum,
Holy Feast and Holy Fast (Chapter 8)

EMILY BRONTË

From *Wuthering Heights*

Emily Brontë was born in 1818 and grew up in a parsonage in the town of Haworth in the middle of the Yorkshire Moors, alongside her sisters, Charlotte and Anne and her brother Branwell, children of an Irish clergyman. Their mother died when Emily was only three years old, leaving the children to grow up in a dark and isolated world in which they had to depend entirely on their own imaginative resources for entertainment. Though they all read every piece of literature available to them, this meant, in fact a staple diet of Romantic work written by men (Byron, Walter Scott etc.) and a vast collection of what Charlotte called 'mad Methodist magazines', packed to the brim with miracles, heinous sins and hideous retributions. Emily's limited world was bordered entirely by this narrow range of personal experience and extensive but emotionally charged reading.

Wuthering Heights, Emily's only novel, was written in 1847 when she was 29 and could not but be a mirror of this life. Realistic domestic detail is turbulently mixed together with a larger than life hero and a beautiful, wild heroine. Heathcliff is tall, dark and handsome and has only one name – he is a symbol of all that is wild and passionate and, being something that will bring Cathy such pleasure, his suit cannot succeed. Cathy, though she longs to be with Heathcliff, will deny herself the one thing in life that she cares about beyond the boundaries of reason and sensible behaviour, because the notion of women allowing themselves these 'selfish' acts of satisfaction is unthinkable. Cathy therefore marries the weedy and wealthy Linton whilst Heathcliff, thwarted, becomes a hard-hearted devil and seduces Linton's sister.

Heathcliff returns and, in this extract, forces a final interview with Cathy. He accuses her of having betrayed her own heart and Cathy, realizing that this is true, for once in her life does what she wants and allows Heathcliff to stay – a scene actually located in her bedroom. The significance of the setting is hardly hidden even to a nineteenth-century readership. Mutual declarations of love in such environments, however, were not to be allowed – the sexual implications were too awful. Emily Brontë had no choice at this point other than to kill off her heroine and Cathy expires and dies shortly afterwards.

Isabella, Linton's sister and Heathcliff's wife, writes home and asks, 'Is Heathcliff a man . . . and, if not, is he a devil?' Well, actually, neither. He is a fellow consumed by desire and, not being allowed to direct his sexual passions in the way he wishes, he takes the only route open to male characters – not by dying, like Cathy, but by becoming brutish, villainous and woman-hating.

[Chapter 15]

Another week over – and I am so many days nearer health, and spring! I have now heard all my neighbour's history, at different sittings, as the housekeeper could spare time from more important occupations. I'll continue it in her own words, only a little condensed. She is, on the whole, a very fair narrator, and I don't think I could improve her style.

IN THE evening, she said, the evening of my visit to the Heights, I knew, as well as if I saw him, that Mr Heathcliff was about the place; and I shunned going out, because I still carried his letter in my pocket, and didn't want to be threatened, or teased any more.

I had made up my mind not to give it till my master went somewhere; as I could not guess how its receipt would affect Catherine. The consequence was, that it did not reach her before the lapse of three days. The fourth was Sunday, and I brought it into her room, after the family were gone to church.

There was a man servant left to keep the house with me, and we generally made a practice of locking the doors during the hours of service; but on that occasion, the weather was so warm and pleasant that I set them wide open; and to fulfil my engagement, as I knew who would be coming, I told my companion that the mistress wished very much for some oranges, and he must run over to the village and get a few, to be paid for on the morrow. He departed, and I went upstairs.

Mrs Linton sat in a loose, white dress, with a light shawl over her shoulders, in the recess of the open window, as usual. Her thick, long hair had been partly removed at the beginning of her illness; and now she wore it simply combed in its natural tresses over her temples and neck. Her appearance was altered, as I had told Heathcliff, but when she was calm, there seemed unearthly beauty in the change.

The flash of her eyes had been succeeded by a dreamy and melancholy softness: they no longer gave the impression of looking at the objects around here; they appeared always to gaze beyond, and far beyond – you would have said out of this world. Then, the paleness of her face – its haggard aspect having vanished as she recovered flesh – and the peculiar expression arising from her mental state, though painfully suggestive of their causes, added to the touching interest which she awakened; and – invariably to me, I know, and to any person who saw her, I should think – refuted more tangible proofs of convalescence and stamped her as one doomed to decay.

A book lay spread on the sill before her, and the scarcely perceptible wind fluttered its leaves at intervals. I believe Linton had laid it there, for she never endeavoured to divert herself with reading, or occupation of any kind; and he would spend many an hour trying to entice her attention to some subject which had formerly been her amusement.

She was conscious of his aim, and in her better moods, endured his efforts placidly, only showing their uselessness by now and then suppressing a wearied sigh, and checking him at last, with the saddest of smiles and kisses. At other times, she would turn petulantly away, and hide her face in her hands, or even push him off angrily; and then he took care to let her alone, for he was certain of doing no good.

Gimmerton chapel bells were still ringing; and the full, mellow flow of the beck in the valley came soothingly on the ear. It was a sweet substitute for the yet absent murmur of the summer foliage, which drowned that music about the Grange, when the trees were in leaf. At Wuthering Heights it always sounded on quiet days, following a great thaw or a season of steady rain – and, of Wuthering Heights, Catherine was thinking as she listened; that is, if she thought, or listened, at all; but she had the vague, distant look I mentioned before, which expressed no recognition of material things either by ear or eye.

'There's a letter for you, Mrs Linton,' I said, gently inserting it in one hand that rested on her knee. 'You must read it immediately, because it wants an answer. Shall I break the seal?'

'Yes,' she answered, without altering the direction of her eyes.

I opened it – it was very short.

'Now,' I continued, 'read it.'

She drew away her hand, and let it fall. I replaced it in her lap, and stood waiting till it should please her to glance down; but that movement was so long delayed that at last I resumed –

'Must I read it, ma'am? It is from Mr Heathcliff.'

There was a start, and a troubled gleam of recollection, and a struggle to arrange her ideas. She lifted the letter, and seemed to peruse it; and when she came to the signature she sighed; yet still I found she had not gathered its import for upon my desiring to hear her reply, she merely pointed to the name, and gazed at me with mournful and questioning eagerness.

'Well, he wishes to see you,' said I, guessing her need of an interpreter. 'He's in the garden by this time, and impatient to know what answer I shall bring.'

As I spoke, I observed a large dog, lying on the sunny grass beneath, raise its ears, as if about to bark, and then smoothing them back, announce, by a wag of the tail that some one approached whom it did not consider a stranger.

Mrs Linton bent forward, and listened breathlessly. The minute after a step traversed the hall; the open house was too tempting for Heathcliff to resist walking in: most likely he supposed that I was inclined to shirk my promise, and so resolved to trust to his own audacity.

With straining eagerness Catherine gazed towards the entrance of her chamber. He did not hit the right room directly; she motioned me to admit him; but he found it out, ere I could reach the door, and in a stride or two was at her side, and had her grasped in his arms.

He neither spoke, nor loosed his hold for some five minutes, during which period he bestowed more kisses than ever he gave in his life before, I dare say; but then my mistress had kissed him first, and I plainly saw that he could hardly bear, for downright agony, to look into her face! The same conviction had stricken him as me, from the instant he beheld her, that there was no prospect of ultimate recovery there – she was fated, sure to die.

'O, Cathy! Oh, my life! how can I bear it?' was the first sentence he uttered, in a tone that did not seek to disguise his despair.

And now he stared at her so earnestly that I thought the very intensity of his gaze would bring tears into his eyes; but they burned with anguish, they did not melt.

'What now?' said Catherine, leaning back, and returning his look with a suddenly clouded brow – her humour was a mere vane for constantly varying caprices. 'You and Edgar have broken my heart, Heathcliff! And you both come to bewail the deed to me, as if you were the people to be pitied! I shall not pity you, not I. You have killed me – and thriven on it, I think. How strong you are! How many years do you mean to live after I am gone?'

Heathcliff had knelt on one knee to embrace her; he attempted to rise, but she seized his hair, and kept him down.

'I wish I could hold you,' she continued, bitterly, 'till we were both dead! I shouldn't care what you suffered. I care nothing for your sufferings. Why shouldn't you suffer? I do! Will you forget me – will you be happy when I am in the earth? Will you say twenty years hence. "That's the grave of Catherine Earnshaw. I loved her long ago, and was wretched to lose her; but it is past. I've loved many others since – my children are dearer to me than she was, and, at death, I shall not rejoice that I am going to her, I shall be sorry that I must leave them!" Will you say so, Heathcliff?'

'Don't torture me till I'm as mad as yourself,' cried he, wrenching his head free, and grinding his teeth.

The two, to a cool spectator, made a strange and fearful picture. Well might Catherine deem that heaven would be a land of exile to her, unless, with her mortal body, she cast away her mortal character also. Her present countenance had a wild vindictiveness in its white cheek, and a bloodless lip, and scintillating eye; she retained, in her closed fingers, a portion of the locks she had been gasping. As to her companion, while raising himself with one hand, he had taken her arm with the other; and so inadequate was his stock of gentleness to the requirements of her condition that on his letting go, I saw four distinct impressions left blue in the colourless skin.

'Are you possessed with a devil,' he pursued, savagely, 'to talk in that manner to me, when you are dying? Do you reflect that all those words will be branded in my memory, and eating deeper eternally, after you have left me? You know you lie to say I have killed you; and, Catherine, you know that I could as soon forget you, as my existence! Is it not sufficient for your infernal selfishness, that while you are at peace I shall writhe in the torments of hell?'

'I shall not be at peace,' moaned Catherine, recalled to a

sense of physical weakness by the violent, unequal throbbing of her heart, which beat visibly, and audibly, under this excess of agitation.

She said nothing further till the paroxysm was over; then she continued, more kindly –

'I'm not wishing you greater torment than I have, Heathcliff. I only wish us never to be parted – and should a word of mine distress you hereafter, think I feel the same distress underground, and for my own sake, forgive me! Come here and kneel down again! You never harmed me in your life. Nay, if you nurse anger, that will be worse to remember than my harsh words! Won't you come here again? Do!'

Heathcliff went to the back of her chair, and leant over, but not so far as to let her see his face, which was livid with emotion. She bent round to look at him; he would not permit it; turning abruptly, he walked to the fire-place, where he stood, silent, with his back towards us.

Mrs Linton's glance followed him suspiciously: every movement woke a new sentiment in her. After a pause, and a prolonged gaze, she resumed, addressing me in accents of indignant disappointment.

'Oh, you see, Nelly! he would not relent a moment to keep me out of the grave! *That* is how I'm loved! Well, never mind! That is not *my* Heathcliff. I shall love mine yet; and take him with me – he's in my soul. And,' added she, musingly, 'the thing that irks me most is this shattered prison, after all. I'm tired, tired of being enclosed here. I'm wearying to escape into that glorious world, and to be always there; not seeing it dimly through tears and yearning for it through the walls of an aching heart; but really with it, and in it. Nelly, you think you are better and more fortunate than I; in full health and strength – you are sorry for me – very soon that will be altered. I shall be sorry for *you*. I shall be incomparably beyond and above you all. I *wonder* he won't be near me!' She went on to herself. 'I thought he wished it. Heathcliff, dear! you should not be sullen now. Do come to me, Heathcliff.'

In her eagerness she rose, and supported herself on the arm of the chair. At that earnest appeal, he turned to her, looking absolutely desperate. His eyes wide, and wet, at last, flashed fiercely on her;

his breast heaved convulsively. An instant they held asunder; and then how they met I hardly saw, but Catherine made a spring, and he caught her, and they were locked in an embrace from which I thought my mistress would never be released alive. In fact, to my eyes, she seemed directly insensible. He flung himself into the nearest seat, and on my approaching hurriedly to ascertain if she had fainted, he gnashed at me, and foamed like a mad dog, and gathered her to him with greedy jealousy. I did not feel as if I were in the company of a creature of my own species; it appeared that he would not understand, though I spoke to him; so, I stood off, and held my tongue, in great perplexity.

A movement of Catherine's relieved me a little presently: she put up her hand to clasp his neck, and bring her cheek to his, as he held her: while he, in return, covering her with frantic caresses, said wildly –

'You teach me now how cruel you've been – cruel and false. *Why* did you despise me? *Why* did you betray your own heart, Cathy? I have not one word of comfort – you deserve this. You have killed yourself. Yes, you may kiss me, and cry; and wring out my kisses and tears. They'll blight you – they'll damn you. You loved me – then what *right* had you to leave me? What right – answer me – for the poor fancy you felt for Linton? Because misery, and degradation and death, and nothing that God or man could inflict would have parted us, *you*, of your own will, did it. I have not broken your heart – *you* have broken it – and in breaking it, you have broken mine. So much the worse for me, that I am strong. Do I want to live? What kind of living will it be when you – oh, God! would *you* like to live with your soul in the grave?'

'Let me alone. Let me alone,' sobbed Catherine. 'If I've done wrong, I'm dying for it. It is enough! You left me too; but I won't upbraid you! I forgive you. Forgive me!'

'It is hard to forgive, and to look at those eyes, and feel those wasted hands,' he answered. 'Kiss me again; and don't let me see your eyes! I forgive what you have done to me. I love *my* murderer – but *yours*! How can I?'

They were silent – their faces hid against each other, and washed by each other's tears. At least, I suppose the weeping was on both sides; as it seemed Heathcliff *could* weep on a great occasion like this.

I grew very uncomfortable, meanwhile; for the afternoon wore fast away, the man whom I had sent off returned from his errand, and I could distinguish, by the shine of the westering sun up the valley, a concourse thickening outside Gimmerton chapel porch.

'Service is over,' I announced. 'My master will be here in half an hour.'

Heathcliff groaned a curse, and strained Catherine closer – she never moved.

Ere long I perceived a group of the servants passing up the road towards the kitchen wing. Mr Linton was not far behind; he opened the gate himself, and sauntered slowly up, probably enjoying the lovely afternoon that breathed as soft as summer.

'Now he is here,' I exclaimed. 'For Heaven's sake, hurry down! You'll not meet any one on the front stairs. Do be quick; and stay among the trees till he is fairly in.'

'I must go, Cathy,' said Heathcliff, seeking to extricate himself from his companion's arms. 'But, if I live, I'll see you again before you are asleep. I won't stay five yards from your window.'

'You must not go!' she answered, holding him as firmly as her strength allowed. 'You shall not, I tell you.'

'For one hour,' he pleaded earnestly.

'Not for one minute,' she replied.

'I *must* – Linton will be up immediately,' persisted the alarmed intruder.

He would have risen, and unfixed her fingers by the act – she clung fast, gasping; there was mad resolution in her face.

'No!' she shrieked. 'Oh, don't, don't go. It is the last time! Edgar will not hurt us. Heathcliff, I shall die! I shall die!'

'Damn the fool! There he is,' cried Heathcliff, sinking back into his seat. 'Hush, my darling! Hush, hush, Catherine! I'll stay. If he shot me so, I'd expire with a blessing on my lips.'

And there they were fast again. I heard my master mounting the stairs – the cold sweat ran from my forehead; I was horrified.

'Are you going to listen to her ravings?' I said, passionately. 'She does not know what she says. Will you ruin her, because she has not wit to help herself? Get up! You could be free instantly. That is the most diabolical deed that ever you did. We are all done for – master, mistress, and servant.'

I wrung my hands, and cried out; and Mr Linton hastened his

step at the noise. In the midst of my agitation, I was sincerely glad to observe that Catherine's arms had fallen relaxed, and her head hung down.

'She's fainted or dead,' I thought; 'so much the better. Far better that she should be dead, than lingering a burden and a misery-maker to all about her.'

Edgar sprang to his unbidden guest, blanched with astonishment and rage. What he meant to do, I cannot tell; however, the other stopped all demonstrations, at once, by placing the lifeless-looking form in his arms.

'Look here!' he said. 'Unless you be a fiend, help her first – then you shall speak to me!'

He walked into the parlour, and sat down. Mr Linton summoned me, and with great difficulty, and after resorting to many means, we managed to restore her to sensation; but she was all bewildered; she sighed, and moaned, and knew nobody. Edgar, in his anxiety for her, forgot her hated friend. I did not. I went, at the earliest opportunity, and besought him to depart, affirming that Catherine was better, and he should hear from me in the morning, how she passed the night.

'I shall not refuse to go out doors,' he answered; 'but I shall stay in the garden; and, Nelly, mind you keep your word tomorrow. I shall be under those larch trees, mind! or I pay another visit, whether Linton be in or not.'

He sent a rapid glance through the half-open door of the chamber, and, ascertaining that what I stated was apparently true, delivered the house of his luckless presence.

KATE CHOPIN

From *The Awakening*

When Kate Chopin wrote The Awakening *it more or less damned her socially and professionally for the rest of her putative career. Though she was, by all accounts, a happily married woman, the world outside considered that such inflammatory work must be, to some extent, autobiographical and that Mrs Chopin, was, thus, as much a personal threat to their stated social systems as her work.*

Born in 1850 in St Louis, Missouri, of Irish and Creole parentage, Kate's childhood was largely dominated by female influences. Her mother, grandmother and great-grandmother were all independent widows who lived at home and had not remarried. Kate herself married an unsuccessful businessman who died in 1882 leaving Kate to pay off his debts and support six children. Two years later she began to write.

Though there had been a tradition of American women writers of bestselling novels, such as Harriet Beecher Stowe's Uncle Tom's Cabin, *women in general were considered best suited to fulfilling the growing demand for sentimental fiction. Kate Chopin's entire output consists of three collections of short stories, a first novel about divorce, a second which no longer exists and then* The Awakening. *She was so discouraged by its reception that she never wrote again and five years later she died of a brain haemorrhage.*

The novel most commonly compared, both in milieu and in plot, to The Awakening *is Flaubert's* Madame Bovary. *Charged with disseminating offensive literature* in 1837, Flaubert was considered a rather exciting man all-round and his novel sold out within days of his court appearance. The scandal which surrounded a woman writing about adultery fifty years later but in the United States, meant that both she and her book were condemned to oblivion. The heroine's concern for self-fulfilment at the expense of her husband and children was considered by contemporary critics to be 'trite and sordid' and containing a 'current of erotic morbidity'.

The plot compares a woman called Edna Pontellier and her closest friend, a fine Southern belle named Adele Ratignolle. Adele is obsessed with pregnancy and sewing and is, generally, languid and content. Edna begins to realize that unlike Adele she cannot live through her children's achievements alone. In the first extract, when the women are at their summer house on the beach, she knows that once she has come to this realization, she cannot turn back. Chopin is limited to expressing herself through alternative means – although the touch and movement of water is hardly a well-hidden metaphor, it is Edna's first point of contact with herself. Though this minor moment of sensuality may seem an insignificant one today, it was, as noted by contemporary reviewers, considered dangerously hedonistic in the late nineteenth century and about as explicitly sexual as Chopin could be. In the second extract, during which Edna's beau stays for dinner, passion is expressed by the merest of touches and is followed by discussion of another minefield of self-expression – gambling.

[Chapter 7]

E DNA PONTELLIER could not have told why, wishing to go to the beach with Robert, she should in the first place have declined, and in the second place have followed in obedience to one of the two contradictory impulses which impelled her.

A certain light was beginning to dawn dimly within her – the light which, showing the way, forbids it.

At that early period it served but to bewilder her. It moved her to dreams, to thoughtfulness, to the shadowy anguish which had overcome her the midnight when she had abandoned herself to tears.

In short, Mrs Pontellier was beginning to realize her position in the universe as a human being, and to recognize her relations as an individual to the world within and about her. This may seem like a ponderous weight of wisdom to descend upon the soul of a young woman of twenty-eight – perhaps more wisdom than the Holy Ghost is usually pleased to vouchsafe to any woman.

But the beginning of things, of a world especially, is necessarily vague, tangled, chaotic, and exceedingly disturbing. How few of us ever emerge from such beginning! How many souls perish in its tumult!

The voice of the sea is seductive; never ceasing, whispering, clamoring, murmuring, inviting the soul to wander for a spell in abysses of solitude; to lose itself in mazes of inward contemplation.

The voice of the sea speaks to the soul. The touch of the sea is sensuous, enfolding the body in its soft, close embrace.

. . . .

When, a few days later, Alcée Arobin again called for Edna in his drag, Mrs Highcamp was not with him. He said they would pick her up. But as that lady had not been apprised of his intention of picking her up, she was not at home. The daughter was just leaving the house to attend the meeting of a branch Folk Lore Society, and regretted that she could not accompany them. Arobin appeared nonplused, and asked Edna if there were any one else she cared to ask.

She did not deem it worth while to go in search of any of the fashionable acquaintances from whom she had withdrawn herself. She thought of Madame Ratignolle, but knew that her fair friend did not leave the house, except to take a languid walk around the block with her husband after nightfall. Mademoiselle Reisz would have laughed at such a request from Edna. Madame Lebrun might have enjoyed the outing, but for some reason Edna did not want her. So they went alone, she and Arobin.

The afternoon was intensely interesting to Edna. The excitement came back upon her like a remittent fever. Her talk grew familiar and confidential. It was no labor to become intimate with Arobin. His manner invited easy confidence. The preliminary stage of becoming acquainted was one which he always endeavoured to ignore when a pretty and engaging woman was concerned.

He stayed and dined with Edna. He stayed and sat beside the wood fire. They laughed and talked; and before it was time to go he was telling her how different life might have been if he had known her years before. With ingenuous frankness he spoke of what a wicked, ill-disciplined boy he had been, and impulsively drew up his cuff to exhibit upon his wrist the scar from a sabre cut which he had received in a duel outside of Paris when he was nineteen. She touched his hand as she scanned the red cicatrice on the inside of his white wrist. A quick impulse that was somewhat spasmodic impelled her fingers to close in a sort of clutch upon his hand. He felt the pressure of her pointed nails in the flesh of his palm.

She arose hastily and walked toward the mantel.

'The sight of a wound or scar always agitates and sickens me,' she said. 'I shouldn't have looked at it.'

'I beg your pardon,' he entreated, following her; 'it never occurred to me that it might be repulsive.'

He stood close to her, and the effrontery in his eyes repelled the old, vanishing self in her, yet drew all her awakening sensuousness. He saw enough in her face to impel him to take her hand and hold it while he said his lingering good night.

'Will you go to the races again?' he asked.

'No,' she said. 'I've had enough of the races. I don't want to lose all the money I've won, and I've got to work when the weather is bright, instead of – '

'Yes; work; to be sure. You promised to show me your work. What morning may I come up to your atelier? Tomorrow?'

'No!'

'Day after?'

'No, no.'

'Oh, please don't refuse me! I know something of such things. I might help you with a stray suggestion or two.'

'No. Good night. Why don't you go after you have said good night? I don't like you,' she went on in a high, excited pitch, attempting to draw away her hand. She felt that her words lacked dignity and sincerity, and she knew that he felt it.

'I'm sorry you don't like me. I'm sorry I offended you. How have I offended you? What have I done? Can't you forgive me?' And he bent and pressed his lips upon her hand as if he wished never more to withdraw them.

'Mr Arobin,' she complained, 'I'm greatly upset by the excitement of the afternoon; I'm not myself. My manner must have misled you in some way. I wish you to go, please.' She spoke in a monotonous, dull tone. He took his hat from the table, and stood with eyes turned from her, looking into the dying fire. For a moment or two he kept an impressive silence.

'Your manner has not misled me, Mrs Pontellier,' he said finally. 'My own emotions have done that. I couldn't help it. When I'm near you, how could I help it? Don't think anything of it, don't bother, please. You see, I go when you command me. If you wish me to stay away, I shall do so. If you let me come back, I – oh! you will let me come back?'

He cast one appealing glance at her, to which she made no response. Alcée Arobin's manner was so genuine that it often deceived even himself.

Edna did not care or think whether it were genuine or not. When she was alone she looked mechanically at the back of her hand which he had kissed so warmly. Then she leaned her head down on the mantelpiece. She felt somewhat like a woman who in a moment of passion is betrayed into an act of infidelity, and realizes the significance of the act without being wholly awakened from its glamour. The thought was passing vaguely through her mind, 'What would he think?'

She did not mean her husband; she was thinking of Robert Lebrun. Her husband seemed to her now like a person whom she had married without love as an excuse.

She lit a candle and went up to her room. Alcée Arobin was absolutely nothing to her. Yet his presence, his manners, the warmth of his glances, and above all the touch of his lips upon her hand had acted like a narcotic upon her.

She slept a languorous sleep, interwoven with vanishing dreams.

JULIAN OF NORWICH

from *Revelations of Divine Love*

Most information about Julian of Norwich is drawn from the autobiographical details contained in the written account of her visions. She claimed to be an illiterate anchoress (contemplative nun living a solitary, hermit-like existence in a bare, empty cell) but she had a fairly wide vocabulary and clearly knew some Latin and French.

Though very little is known about Julian, it is beyond dispute that she had, at some stage, made a threefold request of God which would, in her words, enable her 'to serve him more fully and to know him more intimately'. The first was to have 'mind of his passion', the second was 'bodily sickness' and the third was to have 'God's gift of three wounds' – in order that she might be more of 'true mind' with Christ and suffer with him bodily. In May 1373 she became very ill and believed that she would die but, having already received the last rites, she then experienced sixteen spiritual visions and made a total recovery.

In Julian's mind, it was not merely enough to praise God – she had to see what he saw, feel what he felt and even experience near-death and resuscitation, just as she believed that Christ had done. This total identification with the figure of God, which she describes with graphic detail in her description of her recovery, is a comparable phenomenon to what we think of nowadays as obsession. Julian does not want merely to worship the Lord, she wants to be him. This is remarkably similar in tone to Cathy's declaration to Nelly the maid in Wuthering

Heights *that*, '*My love for Heathcliff . . . [is]*
. . . a source of little visible delight, but necessary. Nelly,
I am Heathcliff.'

[Chapter 15]

The seventh revelation: the recurring experience of delight and depression; it is good for man sometimes not to know comfort; it is not necessarily caused by sin

AFTER THIS he treated my soul to a supreme and spiritual pleasure. I was filled with an eternal assurance, which was powerfully maintained, without the least sort of grievous fear. This experience was so happy spiritually that I felt completely at peace and relaxed: nothing on earth could have disturbed me.

But this lasted only a short while and I began to react with a sense of loneliness and depression, and the futility of life; I was so tired of myself that I could scarcely bother to live. No comfort or relaxation now, just 'faith, hope, and charity'. And not much of these in feeling, but only in bare fact. Yet soon after this our blessed Lord gave once again that comfort and rest, so pleasant and sure, so delightful and powerful, that no fear, or sorrow, or physical suffering could have discomposed me. And then I felt the pain again; then the joy and pleasure; now it was one, and now the other, many times – I imagine quite twenty. When I was glad I was ready to say with St Paul, 'Nothing shall separate me from the love of Christ', and when I suffered, I could have said with St Peter, 'Lord, save me; I perish!'

I understood this vision to mean that it was for their own good that some souls should have this sort of experience: sometimes to be consoled; sometimes to be bereft and left to themselves. The will of God is that we should know he keeps us safely, alike 'in weal or woe'. For his own soul's good a man is sometimes left to himself. This is not invariably due to sin, for certainly I had not sinned when I was left alone – it happened all too suddenly. On the other hand I did not deserve to have this experience of blessedness. But our Lord gives it as and when he pleases, just as he sometimes permits us to know its opposite. Both are equally his love. For it is God's will that we should know the greatest happiness we are capable of, for this bliss is to last for ever. Suffering is transient for those who are to be saved, and will ultimately vanish completely. It is not God's will therefore that we should grieve and sorrow over our present sufferings, but rather that we should leave them at once, and keep ourselves in his everlasting joy.

[Chapter 16]

The eighth revelation: the pitiful suffering of Christ as he dies, his discoloured face, and dried-up body

It was after this that Christ showed me something of his passion near the time of his dying. I saw his dear face, dry, bloodless, and pallid with death. It became more pale, deathly and lifeless. Then, dead, it turned a blue colour, gradually changing to a browny blue, as the flesh continued to die. For me his passion was shown primarily through his blessed face, and particularly by his lips. There too I saw these same four colours, though previously they had been, as I had seen, fresh, red, and lovely. It was a sorry business to see him change as he progressively died. His nostrils too shrivelled and dried before my eyes, and his dear body became black and brown as it dried up in death; it was no longer its own fair, living colour.

For at the same time as our blessed Lord and Saviour was dying on the cross there was, in my picture of it, a strong, dry, and piercingly cold wind. Even when the precious blood was all drained from that dear body, there still remained a certain moisture in his flesh, as was shown me. The loss of blood and the pain within, the gale and the cold without, met altogether in his dear body. Between them the four (two outside, two in) with the passage of time dried up the flesh of Christ. The pain, sharp and bitter, lasted a very long time, and I could see painfully drying up the natural vitality of his flesh. I saw his dear body gradually dry out, bit by bit, withering with dreadful suffering. And while there remained any natural vitality, so long he suffered pain. And it seemed to me, that with all this drawn-out pain, he had been a week in dying, dying and on the point of passing all that time he endured this final suffering. When I say 'it seemed to me that he had been a week in dying' I am only meaning that his dear body was so discoloured and dry, so shrivelled, deathly, and pitiful, that he might well have been seven nights in dying. And I thought to myself that the withering of his flesh was the severest part, as it was the last, of all Christ's passion.

[Chapter 17]

The dreadful, physical thirst of Christ; the four reasons for this; his pitiful crowning; a lover's greatest pain

And the words of Christ dying came to mind, 'I thirst.' I saw that he was thirsty in a twofold sense, physical and spiritual – of this latter I shall be speaking in the thirty-first chapter. The immediate purpose of this particular word was to stress the physical thirst, which I assumed to be caused by drying up of the moisture. For that blessed flesh and frame was drained of all blood and moisture. Because of the pull of the nails and the weight of that blessed body it was a long time suffering. For I could see that the great, hard, hurtful nails in those dear and tender hands and feet caused the wounds to gape wide and the body to sag forward under its own weight, and because of the time it hung there. His head was scarred and torn, and the crown was sticking to it, congealed with blood; his dear hair and his withered flesh was entangled with the thorns, and they with it. At first, when the flesh was still fresh and bleeding the constant pressure of the thorns made the wounds even deeper. Furthermore, I could see that the dear skin and tender flesh, the hair and the blood, were hanging loose from the bone, gouged by the thorns in many places. It seemed about to drop off, heavy and loose, still holding its natural moisture, sagging like a cloth. The sight caused me dreadful and great grief; I would have died rather than see it fall off. What the cause of it

was I could not see, but I assumed that it was due to the sharp
thorns, and the rough and cruel way the garland was pressed
home heartlessly and pitilessly. All this continued awhile, and
then it began to change before my very eyes, and I marvelled. I
saw that it was beginning to dry, and therefore to lose weight, and
to congeal around the garland. And as it went right round the
head, it made another garland under the first. The garland of
thorns was dyed the colour of his blood, and this second garland
of blood, and his head generally, were the colour that is congealed
and dry. What could be seen of the skin of the face was covered
with tiny wrinkles, and was tan coloured; it was like a plank when
it has been planed and dried out. The face was browner than the
body.

The cause of dryness was fourfold: the first was caused by his
bloodlessness; the second by the ensuing pain; the third by his
hanging in the air, like some cloth hung out to dry; the fourth was
due to his physical need of drink – and there was no comfort to
relieve all his suffering and discomfort. Hard and grievous pain!
But much harder and more grievous still when the moisture
ceased, and all began to dry!

The pains experienced in that blessed head were these: the first
was known in the act of dying, while the body was still moist, and
the other was that killing, contracting drying which, with the
strong wind blowing, shrivelled and hurt him with cold more than
I could possibly imagine. And there were other pains beyond
power to describe – for I recognize that whatever I might say
about them would be quite inadequate.

This showing of Christ's pain filled me with pain myself. For
though I was fully aware that he suffered only once, it seemed as if
he wanted to show it all to me, and to fill my mind with it as
indeed I had asked. All the while he was suffering I personally felt
no pain but for him. And I thought to myself, 'I know but little of
the pain that I asked for', and, wretch that I am, at once repented,
thinking that had I known what it would have been I should have
hesitated before making such a prayer. For my pains, I thought,
passed beyond any physical death. Was there any pain like this?
And my reason answered, 'Hell is a different pain, for there there
is despair as well. But of all the pains that led to salvation this is
the greatest, to see your Love suffer. How could there be greater

pain than to see him suffer, who is all my life, my bliss, my joy?'
Here it was that I truly felt that I loved Christ so much more than
myself, and that there could be no pain comparable to the sorrow
caused by seeing him in pain.

[Chapter 18]

*The spiritual martyrdom of our Lady, and others of Christ's
lovers; all things suffer with him, good and bad alike*

Because of all this I was able to understand something of the
compassion of our Lady St Mary. She and Christ were so one in
their love that the greatness of her love caused the greatness of
her suffering. In this I found an example of that instinctive love
that creation has to him – and which develops by grace. This sort
of love was most fully and supremely shown in his dear Mother.
Just because she loved him more than did anyone else, so much
the more did her sufferings transcend theirs. The higher, and
greater, and sweeter our love, so much deeper will be our sorrow
when we see the body of our beloved suffer. All his disciples and
real lovers suffered more greatly here than at their own dying. I
felt quite certain that the very least of them loved Christ much
more than they loved themselves, and quite beyond my power to
describe.

Here too I saw a close affinity between Christ and ourselves – at
least, so I thought – for when he suffered, we suffered. All
creatures capable of suffering pain suffered with him; I mean, all
creatures that God has made for our use. Even heaven and earth
languished for grief in their own peculiar way when Christ died. It
is their nature to know him to be their God, from whom they
draw all their powers. When he failed, then needs must that they
too most properly should fail to the limit of their ability, grieving
for his pains. So too his friends suffered pain because they loved
him. Speaking generally we can say that all suffered, for even
those who did not know him suffered when the normal conditions

of life failed – though the mighty, secret keeping of God did not fail. I am thinking of two kinds of people, exemplified by two quite different types: Pilate, and St Denis of France, who at that time was a pagan.

MARGERY KEMPE

from *The Book of Margery Kempe*

Born into a middle class family in Norfolk c.1373, Margery Kempe's mystical life began after the birth of her first child. At that time she had a vision of Christ and also suffered from temporary insanity, possibly caused by post-natal depression. After the birth of her fourteen th child, she persuaded her husband to join her in a vow of chastity. This, as she saw it, release from conjugal duties, meant that she was enabled to travel throughout Europe and the Holy Land, visiting holy shrines and religious figures – intellectual pursuit becoming here a direct substitute for sexual activity.

The autobiography that she dictated towards the end of her life (she died c.1440), and which is the earliest known autobiography in the English language, reveals the mind of a woman totally committed to the worship of Christ through devotion to his actual physical embodiment. Her adoration is written in highly erotic and emotive language and her passionate fervour often resulted in hysterical weeping and intense fasting. Christ's physical presence was very real to Margery and although she, by her own account, had what we would term a high libido, she believed that this was much better channelled into spiritual worship of Christ. The anxious and nervous condition induced by this state of affairs even served to validate her argument. Just as with Julian of Norwich, whom Margery met, the actual experience of passive suffering and the fighting of her erotic instincts, encouraged Margery to believe more fervently in her vocation.

Margery's mystical union with Christ offered her a direct link to God that put her outside the control of the church. Margery did not remain cloistered, nor did she join an established group of women religieuses within her community, rather she travelled as she wished and argued stubbornly with male clerics. Although a religious life provided one of the very few opportunities for female independence, Margery's highly vocal and visible relationship with Christ drew sharp criticism from the clergy. Whether or not her erotic and extraordinary mystical union with Christ was a conscious or unconscious effort towards independence on her part is debatable; it did however provide Margery Kempe with opportunities rarely enjoyed by women of the late fourteenth and early fifteenth centuries.

[Chapter 3]

ONE NIGHT, as this creature lay in bed with her husband, she heard a melodious sound so sweet and delectable that she thought she had been in paradise. And immediately she jumped out of bed and said, 'Alas that ever I sinned! It is full merry in heaven.' This melody was so sweet that it surpassed all the melody that might be heard in this world, without any comparison, and it caused this creature when she afterwards heard any mirth or melody to shed very plentiful and abundant tears of high devotion, with great sobbings and sighings for the bliss of heaven, not fearing the shames and contempt of this wretched world. And ever after her being drawn towards God in this way, she kept in mind the joy and the melody that there was in heaven, so much so that she could not very well restrain herself from speaking of it. For when she was in company with any people she would often say, 'It is full merry in heaven!'

And those who knew of her behaviour previously and now heard her talk so much of the bliss of heaven said to her, 'Why do you talk so of the joy that is in heaven? You don't know it, and you haven't been there any more than we have.' And they were angry with her because she would not hear or talk of worldly things as they did, and as she did previously.

And after this time she never had any desire to have sexual intercourse with her husband, for paying the debt of matrimony was so abominable to her that she would rather, she thought, have eaten and drunk the ooze and muck in the gutter than consent to intercourse, except out of obedience.

And so she said to her husband, 'I may not deny you my body, but all the love and affection of my heart is withdrawn from all earthly creatures and set on God alone.' But he would have his will with her, and she obeyed with much weeping and sorrowing because she could not live in chastity. And often this creature advised her husband to live chaste and said that they had often (she well knew) displeased God by their inordinate love, and the great delight that each of them had in using the other's body, and saw it would be a good thing if by mutual consent they punished and chastised themselves by abstaining from the lust of their bodies. Her husband said it was good to do so, but he might not yet – he would do so when God willed. And so he used her as he had done before, he would not desist. And all the time she prayed to God that she might live chaste, and three or four years afterwards, when it pleased our Lord, her husband made a vow of chastity, as shall be written afterwards by Jesus's leave.

And also, after this creature heard this heavenly melody, she did great bodily penance. She was sometimes shriven two or three times on the same day, especially of that sin which she had so long concealed and covered up, as is written at the beginning of this book. She gave herself up to much fasting and keeping of vigils; she rose at two or three of the clock and went to church, and was there at her prayers until midday and also the whole afternoon. And then she was slandered and reproved by many people because she led so strict a life. She got herself a hair-cloth from a kiln – the sort that malt is dried on – and put it inside her gown as discreetly and secretly as she could, so that her husband should not notice it. And nor did he, although she lay beside him every night in bed and wore the hair-shirt every day, and bore him children during that time.

Then she had three years of great difficulty with temptations, which she bore as meekly as she could, thanking our Lord for all his gifts, and she was as merry when she was reproved, scorned or ridiculed for our Lord's love, and much more merry than she was before amongst the dignities of this world. For she knew very well that she had sinned greatly against God and that she deserved far more shame and sorrow than any man could cause her, and contempt in this world was the right way heavenwards, for Christ himself chose that way. All his apostles, martyrs, confessors and virgins, and all those who ever came to heaven, passed by the way of tribulation, and she desired nothing as much as heaven. Then she was glad in her conscience when she believed that she was entering upon the way which would lead her to the place that she most desired.

And this creature had contrition and great compunction, with plentiful tears and much loud and violent sobbing, for her sins and for her unkindness towards her maker. She reflected on her unkindness since her childhood, as our Lord would put it into her mind, very many times. And then when she contemplated her own wickedness, she could only sorrow and weep and ever pray for mercy and forgiveness. Her weeping was so plentiful and so continual that many people thought that she could weep and leave off when she wanted, and therefore many people said she was a false hypocrite, and wept when in company for advantage and profit. And then very many people who loved her before while she was in the world abandoned her and would not know her, and all the while she thanked God for everything, desiring nothing but mercy and forgiveness of sin.

[Chapter 4]

For the first two years when this creature was thus drawn to our Lord she had great quiet of spirit from any temptations. She could well endure fasting – it did not trouble her. She hated the joys of the world. She felt no rebellion in her flesh. She was so strong – as she thought – that she feared no devil in hell, for she performed such great bodily penance. She thought that she loved God more than he loved her. She was smitten with the deadly wound of vainglory and felt it not, for she desired many times that the crucifix should loosen his hands from the cross and embrace her in token of love. Our merciful Lord Christ Jesus, seeing this creature's presumption, sent her – as is written before – three years of great temptations, of one of the hardest of which I intend to write, as an example to those who come after that they should not trust in themselves nor have joy in themselves as this creature had – for undoubtedly our spiritual enemy does not sleep but probes our temperament and attitudes, and wherever he finds us most frail, there, by our Lord's sufferance, he lays his snare, which no one may escape by his own power.

And so he laid before this creature the snare of lechery, when she thought that all physical desire had been wholly quenched in her. And so she was tempted for a long time with the sin of lechery, in spite of anything she might do. Yet she was often shriven, she wore her hair-shirt, and did great bodily penance and wept many a bitter tear, and often prayed to our Lord that he should preserve her and keep her so that she should not fall into temptation, for she thought she would rather have been dead than consent to that. And in all this time she had no desire to have intercourse with her husband, and it was very painful and horrible to her.

In the second year of her temptations it so happened that a man whom she liked said to her on St Margaret's Eve before evensong that, for anything, he would sleep with her and enjoy the lust of his body, and that she should not withstand him, for if he might not have his desire that time, he said, he would have it another time instead – she should not choose. And he did it to test what she would do, but she imagined that he meant it in earnest and said very little in reply. So they parted then and both went to hear evensong, for her church was dedicated to St Margaret. This woman was so troubled with the man's words that she could not listen to evensong, nor say her paternoster, nor think any other good thought, but was more troubled than she ever was before.

The devil put it into her mind that God had forsaken her, or else she would not be so tempted. She believed the devil's persuasions, and began to consent because she could not think any good thought. Therefore she believed that God had forsaken her. And when evensong was over, she went to the said man, in order that he should have his will of her, as she believed he desired, but he put forward such a pretence that she could not understand his intent, and so they parted for that night. This creature was so troubled and vexed all that night that she did not know what she could do. She lay beside her husband, and to have intercourse with him was so abominable to her that she could not bear it, and yet it was permissible for her and at a rightful time if she had wished it. But all the time she was tormented to sin with the other man because he had spoken to her. At last – through the impor-tunings of temptation and a lack of discretion – she was overcome and consented in her mind, and went to the man to know if he would then consent to have her. And he said he would not for all the wealth in this world; he would rather be chopped up as small as meat for the pot.

She went away all ashamed and confused in herself, seeing his steadfastness and her own instability. Then she thought about the grace that God had given her before, of how she had two years of great quiet in her soul, of repentance for her sins with many bitter tears of compunction, and a perfect will never again to turn to sin but rather, she thought, to be dead. And now she saw how she had consented in her will to sin. Then she half fell into despair. She thought herself in hell, such was the sorrow that she had. She thought she was worthy of no mercy because her consenting to sin was so wilfully done, nor ever worthy to serve God, because she was so false to him.

Nevertheless she was shriven many times and often, and did whatever penance her confessor would enjoin her to do, and was governed according to the rules of the Church. That grace God gave this creature – blessed may he be – but he did not withdraw her temptation, but rather increased it, as she thought.

And therefore she thought that he had forsaken her, and dared not trust to his mercy, but was troubled with horrible temptations to lechery and despair nearly all the following year, except that our Lord in his mercy, as she said to herself, gave her every day for the most part two hours of compunction for her sins, with many bitter tears. And afterwards she was troubled with temptations to despair as she was before, and was as far from feelings of grace as those who never felt any. And that she could not bear, and so she continued to despair. Except for the time that she felt grace, her trials were so amazing that she could not cope very well with them, but always mourned and sorrowed as though God had forsaken her.

. . . .

[Chapter 11]

It happened one Friday, Midsummer Eve, in very hot weather – as this creature was coming from York carrying a bottle of beer in her hand, and her husband a cake tucked inside his clothes against his chest – that her husband asked his wife this question: 'Margery, if there came a man with a sword who would strike off my head unless I made love with you as I used to do before, tell me on your conscience – for you say you will not lie – whether you would allow my head to be cut off, or else allow me to make love with you again, as I did at one time?'

'Alas, sir,' she said, 'why are you raising this matter, when we have been chaste for these past eight weeks?'

'Because I want to know the truth of your heart.'

And then she said with great sorrow, 'Truly, I would rather see you being killed, than that we should turn back to our uncleanness.'

And he replied, 'You are no good wife.'

And then she asked her husband what was the reason that he had not made love to her for the last eight weeks, since she lay with him every night in his bed. And he said that he was made so afraid when he would have touched her, that he dared do no more.

'Now, good sir, mend your ways and ask God's mercy, for I told you nearly three years ago that you[r desire for sex] would suddenly be slain – and this is now the third year, and I hope yet that I shall have my wish. Good sir, I pray you to grant what I shall ask, and I shall pray for you to be saved through the mercy of our Lord Jesus Christ, and you shall have more reward in heaven than if you wore a hair-shirt or wore a coat of mail as a penance. I pray you, allow me to make a vow of chastity at whichever bishop's hand that God wills.'

'No,' he said. 'I won't allow you to do that, because now I can make love to you without mortal sin, and then I wouldn't be able to.'

Then she replied, 'If it be the will of the Holy Ghost to fulfil what I have said, I pray God that you may consent to this; and if it be not the will of the Holy Ghost, I pray God that you never consent.'

Then they went on towards Bridlington and the weather was extremely hot, this creature all the time having great sorrow and great fear for her chastity. And as they came by a cross her husband sat down under the cross, calling his wife to him and saying these words to her: 'Margery, grant me my desire, and I shall grant you your desire. My first desire is that we shall still lie together in one bed as we have done before; the second, that you shall pay my debts before you go to Jerusalem; and the third, that you shall eat and drink with me on Fridays as you used to do.'

'No, sir,' she said, 'I will never agree to break my Friday fast as long as I live.'

'Well,' he said, 'then I'm going to have sex with you again.'

She begged him to allow her to say her prayers, and he kindly allowed it. Then she knelt down beside a cross in the field and prayed in this way, with a great abundance of tears: 'Lord God, you know all things. You know what sorrow I have had to be chaste for you in my body all these three years, and now I might have my will and I dare not, for love of you. For if I were to break that custom of fasting from meat and drink on Fridays which you commanded me, I should now have my desire. But, blessed Lord, you know I will not go against your will, and great is my sorrow now unless I find comfort in you. Now, blessed Jesus, make your will known to my unworthy self, so that I may afterwards follow and fulfil it with all my might.'

And then our Lord Jesus Christ with great sweetness spoke to this creature, commanding her to go again to her husband and pray him to grant her what she desired: 'And he shall have what he desires. For, my beloved daughter, this was the reason why I ordered you to fast, so that you should the sooner obtain your desire, and now it is granted to you. I no longer wish you to fast, and therefore I command you in the name of Jesus to eat and drink as your husband does.'

Then this creature thanked our Lord Jesus Christ for his grace and his goodness, and afterwards got up and went to her husband, saying to him, 'Sir, if you please, you shall grant me my desire, and you shall have your desire. Grant me that you will not come into my bed, and I grant you that I will pay your debts before I go to Jerusalem. And make my body free to God, so that you never make any claim on me requesting any conjugal debt after this day as long as you live – and I shall eat and drink on Fridays at your bidding.'

Then her husband replied to her, 'May your body be as freely available to God as it has been to me.'

This creature thanked God greatly, rejoicing that she had her desire, praying her husband that they should say three paternosters in worship of the Trinity for the great grace that had been granted them. And so they did, kneeling under a cross, and afterwards they ate and drank together in great gladness of spirit. This was on a Friday, on Midsummer's Eve.

Then they went on to Bridlington and also to many other places, and spoke with God's servants, both anchorites and recluses, and many other of our Lord's lovers, with many worthy clerics, doctors and bachelors of divinity as well, in many different places. And to various people amongst them this creature revealed her feelings and her contemplations, as she was commanded to do, to find out if there were any deception in her feelings.

. . . .

[Chapter 36]

'Fasting, daughter, is good for young beginners, and discreet penance, especially what their confessor gives them or enjoins them to do. And to pray many beads is good for those who can do no better, yet it is not perfect. But it is a good way towards perfection. For I tell you, daughter, those who are great fasters and great doers of penance want it to be considered the best life; those also who give themselves over to saying many devotions would have that to be the best life; and those who give very generous alms would like that considered the best life.

'And I have often told you, daughter, that thinking, weeping, and high contemplation is the best life on earth. You shall have more merit in heaven for one year of thinking in your mind than for a hundred years of praying with your mouth; and yet you will not believe me, for you will pray many beads whether I wish it or not. And yet, daughter, I will not be displeased with you whether you think, say or speak, for I am always pleased with you.

'And if I were on earth as bodily as I was before I died on the cross, I would not be ashamed of you, as many other people are, for I would take you by the hand amongst the people and greet you warmly, so that they would certainly know that I loved you dearly.

'For it is appropriate for the wife to be on homely terms with her husband. Be he ever so great a lord and she ever so poor a woman when he weds her, yet they must lie together and rest together in joy and peace. Just so must it be between you and me, for I take no heed of what you have been but what you would be, and I have often told you that I have clean forgiven you all your sins.

'Therefore I must be intimate with you, and lie in your bed with you. Daughter, you greatly desire to see me, and you may boldly, when you are in bed, take me to you as your wedded husband, as your dear darling, and as your sweet son, for I want to be loved as a son should be loved by the mother, and I want you to love me, daughter, as a good wife ought to love her husband. Therefore you can boldly take me in the arms of your soul and kiss my mouth, my head, and my feet as sweetly as you want. And as often as you think of me or would do any good deed to me, you shall have the same reward in heaven as if you did it to my own precious body which is in heaven, for I ask no more of you but your heart, to love me who loves you, for my love is always ready for you.'

Then she gave thanks and praise to our Lord Jesus Christ for the high grace and mercy that he showed to her, unworthy wretch.

This creature had various tokens in her hearing. One was a kind of sound as if it were a pair of bellows blowing in her ear. She – being dismayed at this – was warned in her soul to have no fear, for it was the sound of the Holy Ghost. And then our Lord turned it into the voice of a little bird which is called a redbreast, that often sang very merrily in her right ear. And then she would always have great grace after she heard such a token. She had been used to such tokens for about twenty-five years at the time of writing this book.

Then our Lord Jesus Christ said to his creature, 'By these tokens you may well know that I love you, for you are to me a true mother and to all the world, because of that great charity which is in you; and yet I am cause of that charity myself, and you shall have great reward for it in heaven.'

MARGARET LAURENCE

from *A Jest of God*

In Canada Margaret Laurence is regarded as one of the most important of first-generation feminist writers. She was born in 1926 and grew up in a provincial prairie town. She got married, had two children, divorced and went to live in England, where she wrote A Jest of God *in 1966. She received the Governor General's Award, the first woman ever to do so, for this novel, which was part of the Manawaka series – a quintet of novels portraying life in the small-minded prairie town where she grew up.*

A Jest of God is narrated by Rachel, who is a rather genteel and repressed Manawaka resident and local school teacher, painfully still unmarried and living with her mother at the age of thirty-four. Her world, like the world of most of the people and more particularly most of the women around her, is limited both geographically and, more importantly, in expectation. She rarely goes outside Manawaka and when she does it is on an excursion to the wild river with her new and clandestine lover and thus clearly symbolic, not only of the dangers of extending beyond your own small world, but also of the idea that this extension leads away from the constructed environment and into the natural and uncontrolled.

One of the novel's most dramatic scenes is in this early chapter where Rachel is invited by a teacher friend at school to go with her to the tabernacle. Rachel is an immensely frustrated woman but one who does, in spite of this, have emotions which move very strongly and just below the surface. Once again, the very notion of

doing something for oneself, purely for self-gratifica-
tion, is rather shameful and almost certainly dangerous.
This inner turmoil is clearly related to a nascent,
disturbing consciousness of sensuality – a fact drawn to
the reader's attention quite clearly by the events at the
end of the chapter.

I'M TO MEET Calla at the Tabernacle. I told Mother we were going to a movie. If I had said Calla's place, she might have phoned.

I'm sorry it's raining this evening. It means that hardly anyone is out. That's stupid – even if I did meet someone I know, how could they tell where I'm going? What about at the door of the Tabernacle, though? That's what bothered me most the last time. If anyone sees, it is certain to be one of Mother's bridge cronies, and the information will be relayed back at sonic speed, and there will be the kind of scene I dread, with Mother speaking more in sorrow than anger, as she's always claimed she was doing.

Japonica Street is deserted. The sidewalks are slippery and darkly shining like new tar with the rain, and the leaves on the maples are being pulled and torn like newspaper in the wind. The lawns have that damp deep loam smell that comes with the rain in spring.

This raincoat is the only new thing I've bought this season. I'm glad I got white. It looks quite good, and I thought that on a black night such as this it would be almost luminous, more easily seen by a driver if I'm crossing a badly lighted street.

Reaching River Street and passing the locked and empty stores, I can see myself reflected dimly, like the negative of a photograph, in the wide glass of display windows. The white coat stands out, but not as handsomely as I'd hoped. To my passing eyes it looks now like some ancient robe around me, and the hood, hiding my hair, makes my face narrow and staring. As in the distorting mirrors at a fair, I'm made to look even taller than I am. I have to pass myself again and again, and see a thin streak of a person, like the stroke of a white chalk on a blackboard.

At the foot of River Street, past the shopping part and down the slow curve of the hill, the old olive-green house stands high and angular, encrusted with glassed-in porches, pillars with no purpose, wrought-iron balconies never likely to have been used except in the height of summer, a small turret or two for good measure, and the blue and red glass circle of a rose-window at the very top. It was built by some waistcoated gent who made good, and then made tangible his concept of paradise in this house.

Whatever family once owned it, they've moved now, shrugged it thankfully off their shoulders, I expect. The sign extends the full width of the house, and is well lighted. The crimson words are plain to see.

Tabernacle of the Risen and Reborn.

People are going in, knots and clusters of them. I haven't seen a soul I know, thank God. But I can't go in. I won't. Now I want to turn and run. But Calla is beside me.

'You're looking very smart tonight, Rachel, in spite of the rain.'

'Oh – thanks. I'm glad you think so.'

'Well, c'mon,' she says encouragingly, taking my arm, 'let's go inside. I feel like a drowned rat. What a filthy night, eh? Never mind, we'll soon be in the warm. This way, kiddo.'

The room is larger than I remember it, almost as large as though the place had been a proper church. The chairs are in semi-circular rows, the same straight, thickly varnished chairs one used to find in every school auditorium, but replaced there now with lighter ones which can be stacked up, and the old ones probably sold to establishments such as this. The painted walls are heavy with their greenish blue, not the clear blue of open places but dense and murky, the way the sea must be, fathoms under. Two large pictures are hanging, both Jesus, bearded and bleeding, his heart exposed and bristling with thorns like a scarlet pincushion. There is no altar, but at the front a kind of pulpit stands, bulky and new, pale wood blossoming in bunches of grapes and small sharp birds with beaks uplifted. The top of the pulpit is draped with white velvet, like a scarf, tasselled with limp silver threads, and on the velvet rests a book. The Book, of course, not jacketed severely in black but covered with some faintly glittering cloth or substance impersonating gold, and probably if the room were dark it would glow – or give off sparks.

'Let's sit near the back.'

'Oh, okay, if you like.' Calla is disappointed, but willing to make any concessions because she's actually got me here. We push our way past feet, past coats containing people whose faces can't be seen because their heads are bowed. Then we're sitting in the middle of the row, and although I would have preferred the end, I can't move now.

I can't move, that's the awful thing. I'm hemmed in, caught. On one side of me sits Calla, bunched up in her gaberdine trenchcoat, and on the other side an unknown man, middle-aged, or so I'd guess from his balding head. He is leaning forward, head down, his large-knuckled hands clenched on his knees. He is a farmer, I think, for the back of his neck is that brick red that gets ingrained from years of sun and never fades, not even in the winter.

I must focus my mind on something, and not think of this meeting hall and everything around me. I must go away, pretend it isn't. When I first came back to Manawaka, Lennox Cates used to ask me out, and I went, but when he started asking me out twice a week, I stopped seeing him before it went any further. We didn't have enough in common, I thought, meaning I couldn't visualize myself as the wife of a farmer, a man who'd never even finished High School. He married not long afterwards. I've taught three of his children. All nice-looking kids, fair-haired like Lennox and all bright. Well.

The two ceiling bulbs are bare, and can't be more than forty watts. The light seems distant and hazy, and the air colder than it can really be, and foetid with the smell of feet and damp coats. It's like some crypt, dead air and staleness, deadness, silence. The scuffing of incoming shoes has stopped. They are all assembled now. Perhaps they are praying.

How can Calla sit there, head inclined? How can she come here every week? She is slangy and strident; she laughs a lot, and in her flat she sings with hoarse-voiced enjoyment the kind of songs the teenagers sing. She can paint scenery for a play or form a choir out of kids who can't even carry a tune – she'd take on anything. But she's here. Don't I know her at all?

Will there be ecstatic utterances and will Calla suddenly rise and keen like the Grecian women wild on the hills, or wail in a wolf's voice, or speak as hissingly as a cell of serpents?

Stop. I must stop. This is only anticipating that worst which never happens, at least not in the way one imagines. Nothing will happen. Yet my hands are clasped together more tightly than those of the quiet man beside me. What is he thinking? I wouldn't want to know.

A man has risen. A stubby man, almost stunted, an open candid face, nothing menacing, nothing so absurd that it can't be borne. He goes to the pulpit. He welcomes one and all, he says, one and all, spreading brown-sleeved arms and smiling trustingly. Now I'm ashamed to be here, as though I'd gate-crashed, come in under false pretences.

Singing. We have to stand, and I must try to make myself narrower so I won't brush against anyone. A piano crashes the tune. Guitars and one trombone are in support. The voices are weak at first, wavering like a radio not quite adjusted, and I'm shaking with the effort not to giggle, although God knows it's not amusing me. The voices strengthen, grow muscular, until the room is swollen with the sound of a hymn macabre as the messengers of the apocalypse, the gaunt horsemen, the cloaked skeletons I dreamed of once when I was quite young, and wakened, and she said 'Don't be foolish – don't be foolish, Rachel – there's nothing there.' The hymn-sound is too loud – it washes into my head, sea waves of it.

> *Day of wrath! O day of mourning!*
> *See fulfilled the prophet's warning!*
> *Heaven and earth in ashes burning!*

I hate this. I would like to go home. Sit down. The others are sitting down. Just don't be noticeable. Oh God – do I know anyone? Suddenly I'm scanning the rows, searching. Seek and ye shall find. Mrs Pusey, ancient arch-enemy of my mother, tongue like a cat-o'-nine-tails, and Alvin Jarrett, who works at the bakery and old Miss Murdoch from the bank. How in hell can I get out of this bloody place without being seen?

Rachel. Calm. At once. This isn't like you.

The lay preacher is praying, and I can't hear the words, somehow, only his husky voice, his voice like a husky dog's, a low growling. Beside me, the hulked form of the farmer sits crouched over. They all seem to be crouching, all of them, all around me, crouching and waiting. They are (of course I know it) praying. It's not a zoo, not Doctor Moreau's island where the beastmen prowled and waited, able to speak but without comprehension.

Then the lay preacher's voice forms into words in my hearing and I realize what he's talking about. The prayer is over, and he's addressing the congregation.

'Soon, very shortly, my brethren, I am going to read to you

from The Book of Life, The Counsel of Heaven, the true words written by Him on High, He the sole Author. All things shall be made clear, and the doubts of the doubters shall be laid low. We have doubted, yes. We have been infirm, yes. We have failed to trust the gifts given freely and fully by the Spirit. Did not Saint Paul chide the Corinthians for the same weakness? And it is through his letter to these people, these Corinthians, that marvellous first epistle, that thrilling document of the holy word of God that all our doubts shall pass away and we shall enter the peace of His spiritual fullness, for in the words of Saint Paul, that great and mild apostle, *God is not the author of confusion but of peace, as in all the churches of the saints.*'

His voice is creamy as mayonnaise. He makes Paul sound like a fool. What – Paul, mild? When he says *thr-ill-lling* it sounds like a Technicolor movie, one of those religious epics.

'The church of the apostles, the church of Peter, the church of Paul, the church of Philip who converted Simon the sorcerer, this very church, the church of the ancients, our brothers in faith, this church did indeed practise and enjoy to the fullest extent every gift of the Spirit. This church did in all knowledge know there was a place, and a holy place, for all the gifts of the Spirit, each and every one of the gifts of the Spirit. *Now there are diversities of gifts, but the same Spirit. For to one is given by the Spirit the word of wisdom – to another the word of knowledge – to another the gifts of healing – to another prophecy – to another divers kinds of tongues –*'

My hands are slippery with perspiration. Around me, the people stir – uneasily? Calla's face is withdrawn, absorbed, not her outgoing look, something fixed and glazed, and I cannot look at her any more. Will she? Imagine having to see someone you know, someone you are known to be friends with, rise in a trance and say – what? What would she say? I cannot bring myself to think.

The preacher has grown in stature. He actually seems taller. The pulpit has another step, maybe, and he has mounted it. Can that be it? He is all fervour now, and yet his voice is not loud. His arms are stretched, as though he knew there were something above and if he strained he might reach it – or else pull it down to his level. His voice no longer growls – it reaches out like arms of strength, to captivate. I must leave. I cannot stand this. But I cannot move. I see myself having to say 'Excuse me – pardon me', scraping and bumping past the other people in this row, feeling them glare at my discourtesy, having to push past this boulder of a man next to me, past his solid pillars of legs and the huge unmoving hands clenched there. I can't.

'Saint Paul advises moderation – of this we are well aware. And that the gift of tongues should not replace the more usual forms of worship – of this we are well aware. But if we speak of ecstatic utterances, my friends, we must ask – ecstatic for whom? In the early Church, the listeners were ecstatic. Yes, the listeners as well as those gifted by the Spirit. Thus can we all participate – yes, participate – in the joy felt and known by any one of our brothers or sisters as they experience that deep and private enjoyment, that sublime edification, the infilling of the Spirit – '

I feel so apprehensive now that I can hardly sit here in a pretence of quiet. The muscles of my face have wired my jawbone so tightly that when I move it, it makes a slight clicking sound. Has anyone heard? No, of course not. Their minds are on the preacher and – the hymn. The hymn? I can't stand. I seem to be taken to my feet, born ludicrously aloft, by the sheer force and weight of the rising people on either side of me.

> In full and glad surrender,
> I give myself to Thee,
> Thine utterly and only
> And evermore to be.

Can we at least sit down again, at last? Thank God. But someone will utter now. I know it. How can anyone bear to make a public spectacle of themselves? How could anyone display so openly? I will not look. I will not listen. People should keep themselves to themselves – that's the only decent way. Beside me, Calla sighs, and I can feel my every muscle becoming rigid, as though I hoped to restrain her by power of will.

A man's voice. Suddenly, into the muffled foot-shuffling and the half silence, a man's voice enters, low at first, then louder. I don't know where he is. I can't see him. He hasn't risen. He is sitting somewhere in the blue-green depths of this room, and he is speaking. His voice is clear, distinct, measured, like the slow careful playing of some simple tune. He speaks the words like a child learning, imitating. Slowly, stumblingly, then gaining momentum, the pace and volume increasing until the entire room, the entire skull, is filled with the loudness of this terrifyingly calm voice. For an instant I am caught up in that voice.

I see him. He is standing now. He is not old. His face is severe, delicate, and his eyes are closed, like a blind seer, a younger Tiresias come to tell the king the words that no one could listen to and live. The words. Chillingly, I realize.

Galamani halafaka tabinota caragoya lal lal ufranti –

Oh my God. They can sit, rapt, wrapped around and smothered willingly by these syllables, the chanting of some mad enchanter, himself enchanted? It's silly to be afraid. But I am. I can't help it. And how can anyone look and face anyone else, in the face of this sinister foolery? I can't look. I can only sit, as drawn in as possible, my eyes willing themselves to see only the dark-brown oiled floorboards.

He has stopped. I can't stand for a hymn. I'll stay sitting. But that would be too obvious. The decision is taken out of my hands as once again I'm lifted by the unasked-for pressure of elbows.

> *Rejoice! Rejoice! Emmanuel!*
> *Shall come to thee, O Israel!*

All I can visualize are the dimly remembered faithful of Corinth, each crying aloud his own words, no one hearing anyone else, no one able to know what anyone else was saying, unable even to know what they themselves were saying. Are these people mad or am I? I hate this hymn.

Celebrate confusion. Let us celebrate confusion. God is not the author of confusion but of peace. What a laugh. Let the Dionysian women rend themselves on the night hills and consume the god.

I want to go home. I want to go away and never come back. I want –

Are we seated? There is a kind of hiatus, a holding of breath in the lungs, a waiting. The quiet man beside me moans, and I'm shocked by the sound's openness, the admitted quality of it. Has his pulse been quickened or made infinitely slow? Impossible to tell. But I can see the vein in one of his wrists. Throbbing.

Calla is holding herself very still. I can feel the tension of her arm through our two coats. If she speaks, I will never be able to face her again. I can feel along my nerves and arteries the squirming and squeamishness of that shame, and having to walk out of the Tabernacle with her afterwards, through a gauntlet of eyes.

Silence. I can't stay. I can't stand it. I really can't. Beside me, the man moans gently, moans and stirs, and moans –

That voice!

Chattering, crying, ululating, the forbidden transformed cryptically to nonsense, dragged from the crypt, stolen and shouted, the shuddering of it, the fear, the breaking, the release, the grieving –

Not Calla's voice. Mine. Oh my God. Mine. The voice of Rachel.

'Hush, Rachel. Hush, hush – it's all right, child.'

She is crooning the words softly over me. We are in her flat. The chesterfield is covered with an old car rug, green and black plaid, and it is on this that I am lying. I remember only vaguely our getting here, walking through the streets and the wind, the rain pelting against me and I hardly noticing it at all. As for the rest, I remember everything, every detail, and will never be able to forget, however hard I try. It will come back again and again, and I will have to endure it, over and over.

The crying has stopped now. Calla hands me a handkerchief and I blow my nose.

'How long did it go on?'

'You mean – crying? You started in the Tabernacle, and I took you out right away, and – '

'No. I didn't mean that. I meant – the other.'

'Oh. Only a minute. Less, probably.'

'You don't have to be kind. How long?'

'I've told you,' Calla says. 'But if you won't believe me, what can I do?'

'Was it – was I – was it very loud?'

'No,' Calla says. 'It wasn't loud at all.'

I have no way of knowing whether she is telling me the truth or not. She is looking at me closely and questioningly, as though trying to decide whether to say something.

'Look – it's okay,' she says at last. 'I know it wasn't – well, you know – a religious experience, for you.'

I feel absolutely cold and detached from everything. My voice sounds flat and expressionless, nearly a monotone.

'I guess it's a good thing you realize that, anyway.'

'I'm not,' she says with unexpected bitterness, 'entirely lacking in all forms of understanding.'

'I didn't say you were.'

'No, but you think I'm a crank for going there. Maybe I am. I wanted you to go so you'd see it wasn't faked. And now look what's happened, what I've done. Oh, Rachel, I'm sorry – honestly I am. I should never – '

'*You're* sorry?' I can't understand this. 'I was the one who – '

I can't go on. I won't think of it. Calla is looking at me with a pity I can't tolerate.

'If only you didn't feel that way about it,' she says.

'Do you know what I detest more than anything else? Hysteria. It's so – slack. I've never done anything like that before. I'm so ashamed.'

'Child, don't. Don't be so hard on yourself.'

'I can't be hard enough, evidently. What will I do next, Calla? I'm – oh, Calla, I'm so damn frightened.'

She is kneeling beside the chesterfield, and the grey fringe of her hair is almost brushing against my face. She puts an arm around my shoulders and I realize from the rasping of her breath that she is actually crying. What has she got to cry about?

'Rachel, honey,' she says, 'it practically kills me to see you like this.'

Then, as though unpremeditated, she kisses my face and swiftly afterwards my mouth.

My drawing away is sharp, violent. I feel violated, unclean, as though I would strike her dead if I had the means. She pulls away then, too, and looks at me with a kind of bewilderment, a pleading apology, not saying a word. How ludicrous she looks, kneeling there, her wide face, her hands clasped anxiously. My anger feels more than justified, and in some way this is a tremendous relief.

It takes me less than a minute to get to the front hall and put on my coat and hood.

'Rachel – listen. Please. It was just that – '

I can't listen. I won't slam the door. I must shut it very quietly. Once I am outside, I can begin running.

E. ARNOT ROBERTSON

From *Cullum*

Cullum *was E. Arnot Robertson's first book and was published in 1928 when she was just twenty-four, and a young married woman. It was an immediate success and by far her most successful work. Robertson's own life was not a radical one in feminist terms. According to her friends, she could do nothing without her husband's assistance and relied on him totally in her everyday cares. Shortly after he drowned at the age of seventy, she committed suicide, aged fifty-eight. She, it seems, believed very strongly that women could not live independently without men and was quoted on a number of occasions as having stated that women had a smaller range of intellectual interests than men. Cullum – based apparently on Robertson's own experience of a failed love affair – belies the notion, however, that women have a smaller range of physical interests.*

It is the fairly straightforward story of the affair between a real cad, called Cullum, and a young woman named Esther. The love affair, related in hindsight by Esther, leaves a bitter rather than a romantic aftertaste. Though tame by today's standards, the fact that the couple are assumed to have had sex at all, would have been perceived as shocking to contemporary readers – that Cullum claims to have been thinking about another woman whilst having sex with Esther would have been thought an extraordinary breach of decorum for a woman writer.

Earlier in this scene, following Esther's first encounter with the dashing Cullum, she is very over-excited, and describes him enthusiastically to her older friend and mentor, Janet. Later that same day the scene which follows here takes place. Whether Esther does not recognize that her feelings are physical, or whether this is the only means available to Robertson to reveal that fact, is almost irrelevant. For the reader there can be no mistaking the displaced interest that Esther shows in her horses.

LYING AWAKE in bed that night I played with the idea, growing hot and disturbed at the thought of what this might mean. All things lovely and fantastic seem credible on spring nights; what might it not mean?

It was so still in my room that through the open window I could hear Jenny whinnying in the stables, and Osiris answering her across the yard. My room overlooked the stables, I could always tell my mare's high whinny from that of any of the other horses, and she and Osiris had called to each other so often these last few nights that I was beginning to recognize his deeper tone as well.

Urgent life, drowsy in autumn, asleep through winter, was awake and possessing the earth; the horses were troubled by the spring.

I slid out of bed and knelt at the window, where I could catch the sound of rustling straw as the horses moved restlessly in the stalls. Twice I heard a heavy thud, muffled by the thickness of the stable doors, as Jenny reverted to her old bad habit of kicking the partition. If she went on with it, she would be lame in the morning, I knew.

It was eerily still. Tenuous, unmoving clouds covered the moon, but the light percolated through, spreading itself dimly over a desiring world. There was a feeling of ancient savagery abroad, of unconquerable forces stirring. Mare and stallion whinnied again, wanting each other in this night of earth's excitement. Leaving the window, I felt hurriedly for shoes and a coat, moved by an impulse I did not wait to define.

Each board creaked as I crept downstairs, and I felt the black shadows of the house closing in like living presences behind me while I groped my way to the back door, whispering reassuringly to Justice who was chained there. If she had not recognized me, and had barked, waking the household, I should have had to explain what I was doing, and I realized suddenly that the explanation would sound idiotic at that time of night, or, indeed, at any other time, to practical people. Running my hand along the dresser shelf I knocked down a cup before I found the stable keys. The noise echoed as if the house were empty. Outside, it did not matter so much that the key of Jenny's stable grated loudly; no other bedroom looked this way. The straw crackled in the warm darkness as I went into the stable and then nothing moved for a few seconds. I knew that she was straining her head round to see the intruder. I took a deep breath to steady myself; Jenny, being nervous was likely to kick if she could not make out who it was. I talked to her and edged into her stall, feeling along the twitching body till I reached her head. She let me slip her halter and turned round of her own accord, squeezing me painfully against the partition and luckily just missing my felt-slippered feet with her hoofs. I could only trust to luck to avoid being trodden on until we were out in the yard, clattering over the cobbles.

'I say, Shades of my Ancestors,' I appealed, knowing that on Father's side they had been Scandinavian horses and cattle thieves, 'give us a hand, and for goodness' sake don't let this noise be heard!'

My estimation of them went up that night. Stout fellows they must have been to get away with strange horses by night; it is exceedingly difficult, I found, to move a horse quietly in the darkness, and this was a horse that knew me well. Jenny was trembling, and starting at every shadow, and it seemed to my anxious ears that we were making a tumult of sound.

I let her into Osiris's loose box, knowing that she was too eager to lash out at the stallion then, as blood mares do.

'You fool, Esther!' I whispered, laughing at myself as I went back to bed, where I shivered luxuriously in returning warmth, 'what did you do that for?'

No reason that I cared to recognize came forward to defend the impulse; but I dropped to sleep happily and was up two hours before anyone else, to return Jenny to her proper stall. I was glad that she had had Osiris when she wanted him, in a night when it seemed wrong that anyone should control the desire of another creature. She was officially mated, in the usual cold-blooded manner, two days later. Moon and I were, so to speak, best man and bridesmaid at the ceremony and when Moon was not looking I punched her in the ribs, coarsely.

KATHERINE MANSFIELD

Mr Reginald Peacock's Day

Katherine Mansfield was born in Wellington, New Zealand, in 1888, though she spent most of her life in England, where she was sent to school in 1903. Her first, and possibly best known, work In a German Pension *was published in 1911 and in 1912 she began to write for a literary magazine called* Rhythm *which was edited by a literary critic called John Middleton Murry. Theirs was a stormy relationship but she eventually married him in 1918, a year after she had been diagnosed as suffering from tuberculosis.*

Female frustration, isolation and male selfishness all play a strong part in her work, much of which consists of short stories. Though 'Mr Reginald Peacock's Day' is ostensibly the story of Reginald's frustration, it is clear that the women pupils are also desperately longing for some kind of satisfaction – though the only means available to them to assuage this longing (a displacement activity called 'the singing lesson') is ultimately, and ironically, controlled by Reginald himself. It is Reginald, therefore, who retains not only the central focus of power but, and perhaps more significantly still, the actual (male) way of seeing the world, since it is through his eyes that the story is told.

IF THERE WAS one thing that he hated more than another it was the way she had of waking him in the morning. She did it on purpose, of course. It was her way of establishing her grievance for the day, and he was not going to let her know how successful it was. But really, really, to wake a sensitive person like that was positively dangerous! It took him hours to get over it – simply hours. She came into the room buttoned up in an overall, with a handkerchief over her head – thereby proving that she had been up herself and slaving since dawn – and called in a low, warning voice: 'Reginald!'

'Eh! What! What's that? What's the matter?'

'It's time to get up; it's half-past eight.' And out she went, shutting the door quietly after her, to gloat over her triumph, he supposed.

He rolled over in the big bed, his heart still beating in quick, dull throbs, and with every throb he felt his energy escaping him, his – his inspiration for the day stifling under those thudding blows. It seemed that she took a malicious delight in making life more difficult for him than – Heaven knows – it was, by denying him his rights as an artist, by trying to drag him down to her level. What was the matter with her? What the hell did she want? Hadn't he three times as many pupils now as when they were first married, earned three times as much, paid for every stick and stone that they possessed, and now had begun to shell out for Adrian's kindergarten? . . . And had he ever reproached her for not having a penny to her name? Never a word – never a sign! The truth was that once you married a woman she became insatiable, and the truth was that nothing was more fatal for an artist than marriage, at any rate until he was well over forty . . . Why had he married her? He asked himself this question on an average about three times a day, but he never could answer it satisfactorily. She had caught him at a weak moment, when the first plunge into reality had bewildered and overwhelmed him for a time. Looking back, he saw a pathetic, youthful creature, half child, half wild untamed bird, totally incompetent to cope with bills and creditors and all the sordid details of existence. Well – she had done her best to clip his wings, if that was any satisfaction for her, and she could congratulate herself on the success of this early morning trick. One ought to wake exquisitely, reluctantly, he thought, slipping down in the warm bed. He began to imagine a series of enchanting scenes which ended with his latest, most charming pupil putting her bare, scented arms round his neck and covering him with her long, perfumed hair. 'Awake, my love!' . . .

As was his daily habit, while the bath water ran, Reginald Peacock tried his voice.

> 'When her mother tends her before the laughing mirror,
> Looping up her laces, tying up her hair,'

he sang, softly at first, listening to the quality, nursing his voice until he came to the third line:

> 'Often she thinks, were this wild thing wedded . . .'

and upon the word 'wedded' he burst into such a shout of triumph that the tooth-glass on the bathroom shelf trembled and even the bath tap seemed to gush stormy applause . . .

Well, there was nothing wrong with his voice, he thought, leaping into the bath and soaping his soft, pink body all over with a loofah shaped like a fish. He could fill Covent Garden with it! '*Wedded*,' he shouted again, seizing the towel with a magnificent operatic gesture, and went on singing while he rubbed as though he had been Lohengrin tipped out by an unwary Swan and drying himself in the greatest haste before that tiresome Elsa came along, along . . .

Back in his bedroom, he pulled the blind up with a jerk, and standing upon the pale square of sunlight that lay upon the carpet like a sheet of cream blotting-paper, he began to do his exercises – deep breathing, bending forward and back, squatting like a frog and shooting out his legs – for if there was one thing he had a horror of it was of getting fat, and men in his profession had a dreadful tendency that way. However, there was no sign of it at present. He was, he decided, just right, just in good proportion. In fact, he could not help a thrill of satisfaction when he saw himself in the glass, dressed in a morning coat, dark grey trousers, grey

socks and a black tie with a silver thread in it. Not that he was
vain – he couldn't stand vain men – no; the sight of himself gave
him a thrill of purely artistic satisfaction. '*Voilà tout!*' said he,
passing his hand over his sleek hair.

That little, easy French phrase blown so lightly from his lips,
like a whiff of smoke, reminded him that someone had asked him
again, the evening before, if he was English. People seemed to find
it impossible to believe that he hadn't some Southern blood. True,
there was an emotional quality in his singing that had nothing of
the John Bull in it . . . The door-handle rattled and turned round
and round. Adrian's head popped through.

'Please, father, mother says breakfast is quite ready, please.'

'Very well,' said Reginald. Then, just as Adrian disappeared:
'Adrian!'

'Yes, father.'

'You haven't said "good morning".'

A few months ago Reginald had spent a week-end in a very
aristocratic family, where the father received his little sons in the
morning and shook hands with them. Reginald thought the practice charming, and introduced it immediately, but Adrian felt
dreadfully silly at having to shake hands with his own father every
morning. And why did his father always sort of sing to him
instead of talk? . . .

In excellent temper, Reginald walked into the dining-room and
sat down before a pile of letters, a copy of the *Times* and a little
covered dish. He glanced at the letters and then at his breakfast.
There were two thin slices of bacon and one egg.

'Don't you want any bacon?' he asked.

'No, I prefer a cold baked apple. I don't feel the need of bacon
every morning.'

Now, did she mean that there was no need for him to have
bacon every morning, either, and that she grudged having to cook
it for him?

'If you don't want to cook the breakfast,' said he, 'why don't
you keep a servant? You know we can afford one, and you know
how I loathe to see my wife doing the work. Simply because all the
women we have had in the past have been failures and utterly
upset my régime, and made it almost impossible for me to have
any pupils here, you've given up trying to find a decent woman.

It's not impossible to train a servant – is it? I mean, it doesn't require genius?'

'But I prefer to do the work myself; it makes life so much more peaceful . . . Run along, Adrian darling, and get ready for school.'

'Oh no, that's not it!' Reginald pretended to smile. 'You do the work yourself, because, for some extraordinary reason, you love to humiliate me. Objectively, you may not know that, but, subjectively, it's the case.' This last remark so delighted him that he cut open an envelope as gracefully as if he had been on the stage . . .

Dear Mr Peacock,

I feel I cannot go to sleep until I have thanked you again for the wonderful joy your singing gave me this evening. Quite unforgettable. You make me wonder, as I have not wondered since I was a girl, if this is *all*. I mean, if this ordinary world is *all*. If there is not, perhaps, for those of us who understand, divine beauty and richness awaiting us if we only have the *courage* to see it. And to make it ours. . . . The house is so quiet. I wish you were here now that I might thank you in person. You are doing a great thing. You are teaching the world to escape from life!

Yours, most sincerely,

Ænone Fell

P.S. I am in every afternoon this week . . .

The letter was scrawled in violet ink on thick, handmade paper. Vanity, that bright bird, lifted its wings again, lifted them until he felt his breast would break.

'Oh well, don't let us quarrel,' said he, and actually flung out a hand to his wife.

But she was not great enough to respond.

'I must hurry and take Adrian to school,' said she. 'Your room is quite ready for you.'

Very well – very well – let there be open war between them! But he was hanged if he'd be the first to make it up again!

He walked up and down his room and was not calm again until he heard the outer door close upon Adrian and his wife. Of course, if this went on, he would have to make some other arrangement. That was obvious. Tied and bound like this, how could he help the world to escape from life? He opened the piano and looked up his pupils for the morning. Miss Betty Brittle, the Countess Wilkowska and Miss Marian Morrow. They were charming, all three.

Punctually at half-past ten the door-bell rang. He went to the door. Miss Betty Brittle was there, dressed in white, with her music in a blue silk case.

'I'm afraid I'm early,' she said, blushing and shy, and she opened her big blue eyes very wide. 'Am I?'

'Not at all, dear lady. I am only too charmed,' said Reginald. 'Won't you come in?'

'It's such a heavenly morning,' said Miss Brittle. 'I walked across the Park. The flowers were too marvellous.'

'Well, think about them while you sing your exercises,' said Reginald, sitting down at the piano. 'It will give your voice colour and warmth.'

Oh, what an enchanting idea! What a *genius* Mr Peacock was. She parted her pretty lips and began to sing like a pansy.

'Very good, very good, indeed,' said Reginald, playing chords that would waft a hardened criminal to heaven. 'Make the notes round. Don't be afraid. Linger over them, breathe them like a perfume.'

How pretty she looked, standing there in her white frock, her little blonde head tilted, showing her milky throat.

'Do you ever practise before a glass?' asked Reginald. 'You ought to, you know; it makes the lips more flexible. Come over here.'

They went over to the mirror and stood side by side.

'Now sing – moo-e-koo-e-ii-e-a!'

But she broke down and blushed more brightly than ever.

'Oh,' she cried, 'I can't. It makes me feel so silly. It makes me want to laugh. I do look so absurd!'

'No, you don't. Don't be afraid,' said Reginald, but laughed, too, very kindly. 'Now, try again!'

The lesson simply flew and Betty Brittle quite got over her shyness.

'When can I come again?' she asked, tying the music up again in the blue silk case. 'I want to take as many lessons as I can just now. Oh, Mr Peacock, I *do* enjoy them so much. May I come the day after tomorrow?'

'Dear lady, I shall be only too charmed,' said Reginald, bowing her out.

Glorious girl! And when they had stood in front of the mirror, her white sleeve had just touched his black one. He could feel – yes, he could actually feel a warm, glowing spot, and he stroked it. She loved her lessons. His wife came in.

'Reginald, can you let me have some money? I must pay the dairy. And will you be in for dinner to-night?'

'Yes, you know I'm singing at Lord Timbuck's at half past nine. Can you make me some clear soup with an egg in it?'

'Yes. And the money, Reginald. It's eight and sixpence.'

'Surely that's very heavy – isn't it?'

'No, it's just what it ought to be. And Adrian must have milk.'

There she was – off again. Now she was standing up for Adrian against him.

'I have not the slightest desire to deny my child a proper amount of milk,' said he. 'Here is ten shillings.'

The door-bell rang. He went to the door.

'Oh,' said the Countess Wilkowska, 'the stairs. I have not a breath.' And she put her hand over her heart as she followed him into the music-room. She was all in black, with a little black hat with a floating veil – violets in her bosom.

'Do not make me sing exercises to-day,' she cried, throwing out her hands in her delightful foreign way. 'No, to-day, I want only to sing songs . . . And may I take off my violets? They fade so soon.'

'They fade so soon – they fade so soon,' played Reginald on the piano.

'May I put them here?' asked the Countess, dropping them in a little vase that stood in front of one of Reginald's photographs.

'Dear lady, I should be only too charmed!'

She began to sing, and all was well until she came to the phrase: 'You love me. Yes, I *know* you love me!' Down dropped his hands from the keyboard, he wheeled round, facing her.

'No, no; that's not good enough. You can do better than that,' cried Reginald ardently. 'You must sing as if you were in love. Listen; let me try and show you.' And he sang.

'Oh yes, yes. I see what you mean,' stammered the little Countess. 'May I try it again?'

'Certainly. Do not be afraid. Let yourself go. Confess yourself. Make proud surrender!' he called above the music. And she sang.

'Yes; better that time. But I still feel you are capable of more. Try it with me. There must be a kind of exultant defiance as well – don't you feel?' And they sang together. Ah! now she was sure she understood. 'May I try once again?'

'You love me. Yes, I *know* you love me.'

The lesson was over before that phrase was quite perfect. The little foreign hands trembled as they put the music together.

'And you are forgetting your violets,' said Reginald softly.

'Yes, I think I will forget them,' said the Countess, biting her underlip. What fascinating ways these foreign women have!

'And you will come to my house on Sunday and make music?' she asked.

'Dear lady, I shall be only too charmed!' said Reginald.

> 'Weep ye no more, sad fountains,
> Why need ye flow so fast?'

sang Miss Marion Morrow, but her eyes filled with tears and her chin trembled.

'Don't sing just now,' said Reginald. 'Let me play it for you.' He played so softly.

'Is there anything the matter?' asked Reginald. 'You're not quite happy this morning.'

No, she wasn't; she was awfully miserable.

'You don't care to tell me what it is?'

It really was nothing particular. She had those moods sometimes when life seemed almost unbearable.

'Ah, I know,' he said; 'If I could only help!'

'But you do; you do! Oh, if it were not for my lessons I don't feel I could go on.'

'Sit down in the arm-chair and smell the violets and let me sing to you. It will do you just as much good as a lesson.'

Why weren't all men like Mr Peacock?

'I wrote a poem after the concert last night – just about what I felt. Of course, it wasn't *personal*. May I send it to you?'

'Dear lady, I should be only too charmed!'

By the end of the afternoon he was quite tired and lay down on a sofa to rest his voice before dressing. The door of his room was open. He could hear Adrian and his wife talking in the dining-room.

'Do you know what that teapot reminds me of, mummy? It reminds me of a little sitting-down kitten.'

'Does it, Mr Absurdity?'

Reginald dozed. The telephone bell woke him.

'Ænone Fell is speaking. Mr Peacock, I have just heard that you are singing at Lord Timbuck's to-night. Will you dine with me, and we can go on together afterwards?' And the words of his reply dropped like flowers down the telephone.

'Dear lady, I should be only too charmed.'

What a triumphant evening! The little dinner *tête-à-tête* with Ænone Fell, the drive to Lord Timbuck's in her white motor-car, when she thanked him again for the unforgettable joy. Triumph upon triumph! And Lord Timbuck's champagne simply flowed.

'Have some more champagne, Peacock,' said Lord Timbuck. Peacock, you notice – not Mr Peacock – but Peacock, as if he were one of them. And wasn't he? He was an artist. He could sway them all. And wasn't he teaching them all to escape from life? How he sang! And as he sang, as in a dream he saw their feathers and their flowers and their fans, offered to him, laid before him, like a huge bouquet.

'Have another glass of wine, Peacock.'

'I could have any one I liked by lifting a finger,' thought Peacock, positively staggering home.

But as he let himself into the dark flat his marvellous sense of elation began to ebb away. He turned up the light in the bedroom. His wife lay asleep, squeezed over to her side of the bed. He remembered suddenly how she had said when he had told her he was going out to dinner: 'You might have let me know before!' And how he had answered: 'Can't you possibly speak to me without offending against even good manners?' It was incredible, he thought, that she cared so little for him – incredible that she wasn't interested in the slightest in his triumphs and his artistic career. When so many women in her place would have given their eyes . . . Yes, he knew it . . . Why not acknowledge it? . . . And there she lay, an enemy, even in her sleep . . . Must it ever be thus? he thought, the champagne still working. Ah, if we only were friends, how much I could tell her now! About this evening; even about Timbuck's manner to me, and all that they said to me and so on and so on. If only I felt that she was here to come back to – that I could confide in her – and so on and so on.

In his emotion he pulled off his evening boot and simply hurled it in the corner. The noise woke his wife with a terrible start. She sat up, pushing back her hair. And he suddenly decided to have one more try to treat her as a friend, to tell her everything, to win her. Down he sat on the side of the bed and seized one of her hands. But of all those splendid things he had to say, not one could he utter. For some fiendish reason, the only words he could get out were: 'Dear lady, I should be so charmed – so charmed!'

ANTICIPATION

'Then stay with me a little longer,' Madame Olenska said in a low tone, just touching his knee with her plumed fan. It was the lightest touch but it thrilled him like a caress.

'Yes, let me stay,' he answered in the same tone, hardly knowing what he said.

Edith Wharton, *The Age of Innocence* (Chapter 8)

GEORGE ELIOT

From *Middlemarch*

George Eliot was born Mary Ann Evans, the daughter of an estate manager and his second wife, Christiana Pearson, in 1819. She began writing fiction when she formed a relationship with George Henry Lewes, who was married but separated at the time. Adam Bede *appeared in 1859 and established her firmly as a leading novelist of the day. She started writing* Middlemarch, *described by Virginia Woolf as 'one of the few English novels written for grown-up people', in 1871.*

From notes that Eliot wrote whilst working on the novel it is clear that it started out in 1869 as a story with the character of Lydgate at its heart. Work on this novel progressed very slowly and she began to lose interest, starting work on a new novel with Dorothea as its central character in 1870. It then seems to have struck her that the two books were, in fact, very similar in theme and situation, and she decided to merge them. Following the advice of Lewes, the new composite novel, which would now be an extremely long one, was published in bi-monthly parts, starting in December 1871. It was not actually completed until 1872.

Dorothea, the heroine, is an innocent idealist, anxious to be philosophical and to do good works. She considers that she is doing right when she is intellectually seduced into marriage with the academically advanced but emotionally deformed Casaubon. It is immediately clear to the reader that this is a bad choice. Sterile learning is simply not enough – Casaubon will never finish his redundant and unnecessary oeuvre, though he believes that he has, in this endeavour, found his true vocation, the search for which provides the novel with one of its main themes. Dorothea believes that hers is to learn, within a strict moral framework.

Then Dorothea meets the artistically inclined and somehow foreign, Will Ladislaw. From the very beginning, the reader wills them to recognize that they should love each other and only the two protagonists cannot see this. Will's otherness, his social unacceptability, the fact that he has come into Dorothea's world from an unknown outside, make his and Dorothea's union seemingly impossible and thus each encounter is full of tension and highly charged emotion. But Casaubon has to die and Dorothea go through a lengthy process of self-discovery before she can conceive of a romance with Ladislaw. She must first realize that her reforming zeal is laced with egotistical motivations and, in a world in which the individual is inextricably linked with the social, it is only when Dorothea discovers the real meaning of selflessness that she can appreciate Ladislaw. Much to the reader's frustration, this does not take place until some 900 pages into the novel.

We know, however, that this choice is the right one since Dorothea, for once, is inarticulate and lost for words. The storms rage and lightning flashes – once you have learnt your true social worth, you can experience real passion at last.

THE LITTLE OLD lady, whose bonnet hardly reached Dorothea's shoulder was warmly welcomed, but while her hand was being pressed she made many of her beaver-like noises, as if she had something difficult to say.

'Do sit down,' said Dorothea, rolling a chair forward. 'Am I wanted for anything? I shall be so glad if I can do anything.'

'I will not stay,' said Miss Noble, putting her hand into her small basket, and holding some article inside it nervously: 'I have left a friend in the churchyard.' She lapsed into her inarticulate sounds, and unconsciously drew forth the article which she was fingering. It was the tortoise-shell lozenge-box, and Dorothea felt the colour mounting to her cheeks.

'Mr Ladislaw,' continued the timid little woman. 'He fears he has offended you, and has begged me to ask if you will see him for a few minutes.'

Dorothea did not answer on the instant: it was crossing her mind that she could not receive him in this library, where her husband's prohibition seemed to dwell. She looked towards the window. Could she go out and meet him in the grounds? The sky was heavy, and the trees had begun to shiver as at a coming storm. Besides, she shrank from going out to him.

'Do see him, Mrs Casaubon,' said Miss Noble, pathetically: 'else I must go back and say No, and that will hurt him.'

'Yes, I will see him,' said Dorothea. 'Pray tell him to come.' What else was there to be done? There was nothing that she longed for at the moment except to see Will: the possibility of seeing him had thrust itself insistently between her and every other object; and yet she had a throbbing excitement like an alarm upon her – a sense that she was doing something daringly defiant for his sake.

When the little lady had trotted away on her mission, Dorothea stood in the middle of the library with her hands falling clasped before her, making no attempt to compose herself in an attitude of dignified unconsciousness. What she was least conscious of just then was her own body: she was thinking of what was likely to be in Will's mind, and of the hard feelings that others had had about him. How could any duty bind her to hardness? Resistance to unjust dispraise had mingled with her feeling for him from the very first, and now in the rebound of her heart after her anguish the resistance was stronger than ever. 'If I love him too much it is because he has been used so ill': there was a voice within her saying this to some imagined audience in the library, when the door was opened, and she saw Will before her.

She did not move, and he came towards her with more doubt and timidity in his face than she had ever seen before. He was in a state of uncertainty which made him afraid lest some look or word of his should condemn him to a new distance from her; and Dorothea was afraid of her own emotion. She looked as if there were a spell upon her, keeping her motionless and hindering her from unclasping her hands, while some intense, grave yearning was imprisoned within her eyes. Seeing that she did not put out her hand as usual, Will paused a yard from her and said with embarrassment, 'I am so grateful to you for seeing me.'

'I wanted to see you,' said Dorothea, having no other words at command. It did not occur to her to sit down, and Will did not give a cheerful interpretation to this queenly way of receiving him; but he went on to say what he had made up his mind to say.

'I fear you think me foolish and perhaps wrong for coming back so soon. I have been punished for my impatience. You know – every one knows now – a painful story about my parentage. I knew of it before I went away, and I always meant to tell you of it – if we ever met again.'

There was a slight movement in Dorothea, and she unclasped her hands, but immediately folded them over each other.

'But the affair is matter of gossip now,' Will continued. 'I wished you to know that something connected with it – something which happened before I went away – helped to bring me down here again. At least I thought it excused my coming. It was the idea of getting Bulstrode to apply some money to a public purpose – some money which he had thought of giving me. Perhaps it is rather to Bulstrode's credit that he privately offered me compensation for an old injury: he offered to give me a good income to make amends; but I suppose you know the disagreeable story?'

Will looked doubtfully at Dorothea, but his manner was gathering some of the defiant courage with which he always thought of this fact in his destiny. He added, 'You know that it must be altogether painful to me.'

'Yes – yes – I know,' said Dorothea, hastily.

'I did not choose to accept an income from such a source. I was sure that you would not think well of me if I did so,' said Will. Why should he mind saying anything of that sort to her now? She knew that he had avowed his love for her. 'I felt that' – he broke off, nevertheless.

'You acted as I should have expected you to act,' said Dorothea, her face brightening and her head becoming a little more erect on its beautiful stem.

'I did not believe that you would let any circumstance of my birth create a prejudice in you against me, though it was sure to do so in others,' said Will, shaking his head backward in his old way, and looking with a grave appeal into her eyes.

'If it were a new hardship it would be a new reason for me to cling to you,' said Dorothea, fervidly. 'Nothing could have changed me but – ' her heart was swelling, and it was difficult to go on; she made a great effort over herself to say in a low tremulous voice, 'but thinking that you were different – not so good as I had believed you to be.'

'You are sure to believe me better than I am in everything but one,' said Will, giving way to his own feeling in the evidence of hers. 'I mean, in my truth to you. When I thought you doubted of that, I didn't care about anything that was left. I thought it was all over with me, and there was nothing to try for – only things to endure.'

'I don't doubt you any longer,' said Dorothea, putting out her hand; a vague fear for him impelling her unutterable affection.

He took her hand and raised it to his lips with something like a sob. But he stood with his hat and gloves in the other hand, and might have done for the portrait of a Royalist. Still it was difficult to loose the hand, and Dorothea, withdrawing it in a confusion that distressed her, looked and moved away.

'See how dark the clouds have become, and how the trees are tossed,' she said, walking towards the window, yet speaking and moving with only a dim sense of what she was doing.

Will followed her at a little distance, and leaned against the tall back of a leather chair, on which he ventured now to lay his hat and gloves, and free himself from the intolerable durance of formality to which he had been for the first time condemned in Dorothea's presence. It must be confessed that he felt very happy at that moment leaning on the chair. He was not much afraid of anything that she might feel now.

They stood silent, not looking at each other, but looking at the evergreens which were being tossed, and were showing the pale underside of their leaves against the blackening sky. Will never enjoyed the prospect of a storm so much: it delivered him from the necessity of going away. Leaves and little branches were hurled about, and the thunder was getting nearer. The light was more and more sombre, but there came a flash of lightning which made them start and look at each other, and then smile. Dorothea began to say what she had been thinking of.

'That was a wrong thing for you to say, that you would have had nothing to try for. If we had lost our own chief good, other people's good would remain, and that is worth trying for. Some can be happy. I seemed to see that more clearly than ever, when I was the most wretched. I can hardly think how I could have borne the trouble, if that feeling had not come to me to make strength.'

'You have never felt the sort of misery I felt,' said Will; 'the misery of knowing that you must despise me.'

'But I have felt worse – it was worse to think ill – ' Dorothea had begun impetuously, but broke off.

Will coloured. He had the sense that whatever she said was uttered in the vision of a fatality that kept them apart. He was silent a moment, and then said passionately –

'We may at least have the comfort of speaking to each other without disguise. Since I must go away – since we must always be divided – you may think of me as one on the brink of the grave.'

While he was speaking there came a vivid flash of lightning which lit each of them up for the other – and the light seemed to be the terror of a hopeless love. Dorothea darted instantaneously from the window; Will followed her, seizing her hand with a spasmodic movement; and so they stood, with their hands clasped, like two children, looking out on the storm, while the thunder gave a tremendous crack and roll above them, and the rain began to pour down. Then they turned their faces towards each other, with the memory of his last words in them, and they did not loose each other's hands.

'There is no hope for me,' said Will. 'Even if you loved me as well as I love you – even if I were everything to you – I shall most likely always be very poor: on a sober calculation, one can count on nothing but a creeping lot. It is impossible for us ever to belong to each other. It is perhaps base of me to have asked for a word from you. I meant to go away into silence, but I have not been able to do what I meant.'

'Don't be sorry,' said Dorothea, in her clear tender tones. 'I would rather share all the trouble of our parting.'

Her lips trembled, and so did his. It was never known which lips were the first to move towards the other lips; but they kissed tremblingly, and then they moved apart.

The rain was dashing against the window-panes as if an angry spirit were within it, and behind it was the great swoop of the wind; it was one of those moments in which both the busy and the idle pause with a certain awe.

Dorothea sat down on the seat nearest to her, a long low ottoman in the middle of the room, and with her hands folded over each other on her lap, looked at the drear outer world. Will stood still an instant looking at her, then seated himself beside her, and laid his hand on hers, which turned itself upward to be clasped. They sat in that way without looking at each other, until the rain abated and began to fall in stillness. Each had been full of thoughts which neither of them could begin to utter.

But when the rain was quiet, Dorothea turned to look at Will. With passionate exclamation, as if some torture-screw were threatening him, he started up and said, 'It is impossible!'

He went and leaned on the back of the chair again, and seemed to be battling with his own anger, while she looked towards him sadly.

'It is as fatal as a murder or any other horror that divides people,' he burst out again; 'it is more intolerable – to have our life maimed by petty accidents.'

'No – don't say that – your life need not be maimed,' said Dorothea, gently.

'Yes, it must,' said Will, angrily. 'It is cruel of you to speak in that way – as if there were any comfort. You may see beyond the misery of it, but I don't. It is unkind – it is throwing back my love for you as if it were a trifle, to speak in that way in the face of the fact. We shall never be married.'

'Some time – we might,' said Dorothea, in a trembling voice.

'When?' said Will, bitterly. 'What is the use of counting on any success of mine? It is a mere toss up whether I shall ever do more than keep myself decently, unless I choose to sell myself as a mere pen and a mouthpiece. I can see that clearly enough. I could not offer myself to any woman, even if she had no luxuries to renounce.'

There was silence. Dorothea's heart was full of something that she wanted to say, and yet the words were too difficult. She was wholly possessed by them: at that moment debate was mute within her. And it was very hard that she could not say what she wanted to say. Will was looking out of the window angrily. If he would have looked at her and not gone away from her side, she thought everything would have been easier. At last he turned, still resting against the chair, and stretching his hand automatically towards his hat, said with a sort of exasperation, 'Good-bye.'

'Oh, I cannot bear it – my heart will break,' said Dorothea, starting from her seat, the flood of her young passion bearing down all the obstructions which had kept her silent – the great tears rising and falling in an instant: 'I don't mind about poverty – I hate my wealth.'

In an instant Will was close to her and had his arms round her, but she drew her head back and held his away gently that she might go on speaking, her large tear-filled eyes looking at his very simply, while she said in a sobbing childlike way, 'We could live quite well on my own fortune – it is too much – seven hundred-a-year – I want so little – no new clothes – and I will learn what everything costs.'

JANE SMILEY

From *One Thousand Acres*

Jane Smiley was born in Los Angeles and now teaches and lives in Iowa. With One Thousand Acres *she won both the Pulitzer Prize and the National Book Critics Award. It is a modern reworking of* King Lear, *with an ageing and irascible farmer in Iowa attempting to retire and share out his land between his three daughters. This is an unrelenting, insular world in which family secrets are rife and feuds run bitterly for generations.*

The two older daughters, Rose and Ginny (Regan and Goneril), are here the unfortunates who stayed behind and married local farmers whilst the youngest daughter, Caroline, got away thanks to an education and her sisters' determination. Rose and Ginny, who have put their whole lives into the drudgery of everyday farming, now have little to show for their selfless dedication to others. When Jess Clark, the son of a rival farmer, arrives home after long wanderings in the world outside, he represents all that is exciting and dynamic and barely possible when opposed to the domestic, the banal and the plain dull. Writing in 1991, Jane Smiley can express what this chance for life might mean to the two women in sexual terms. Rose's comparison of the inadequacies of Ty, her husband, are brutally contrasted to the forces of attraction she feels when she encounters Jess. She anticipates the wider possibilities of life and these are expressed in the most elemental of terms.

I LAY AWAKE in the hot darkness, naked and covered by the sheet. Every so often, I lifted the sheet and looked under it, at my blue-white skin, my breasts, with their dark nipples, the fore-shortened, rounded triangles of my legs, my jutting feet. I looked at myself while I thought about having sex with Jess Clark and I could feel my flesh turn electric at these thoughts, could feel sensation gather at my nipples, could feel my vagina relax and open, could feel my lips and my fingertips grow sensitive enough to know their own shapes. When I turned on my side and my breasts swam together and I flicked the sheet for a bit of air, I saw only myself turning, my same old shape moving in the same old way. I turned onto my stomach so that I wouldn't be able to look, so that I could bury my face in the black pillow. It wasn't like me to think such thoughts, and though they drew me, they repelled me too. I began to drift off, maybe to escape what I couldn't stop thinking about.

Ty, who was asleep, rolled over and put his hand on my shoulder, then ran it down my back, so slowly that my back came to seem about as long and humped as a sow's, running in a smooth arc from my rooting, low-slung head to my little stumpy tail. I woke up with a start and remembered the baby pigs. Ty was very close to me. It was still hot, and he was pressing his erection into my leg. Normally I hated waking in the night with him so close to me, but my earlier fantasies must have primed me, because the very sense of it there, a combination of feeling its insistent pressure and imagining its smooth heavy shape, doused me like a hot wave, and instantly I was breathless. I put my hand around it and turned toward it, then took my hand off it and pulled the curve of his ass toward me. But for once I couldn't stand not touching it, knowing it was there but not holding it in my hand. Ty woke up. I was panting, and he was on me in a moment. It was something: it was deeply exciting and simultane-ously not enough. The part of me that was still a sow longed to wallow, to press my skin against his and be engulfed. Ty whis-pered, 'Don't open your eyes,' and I did not. Nothing would wake me from this unaccustomed dream of my body faster than opening my eyes.

Afterward, when we did open our eyes and were ourselves again, I saw that it was only ten-fifteen. I moved away, to the cooler edge of the bed. Ty said, 'I liked that. That was nice,' and he put his hand affectionately on my hip without actually looking at me. His voice carried just a single quiver of embarrassment. That was pretty good for us. Then I heard the breeze start up, rustling the curtains, and then I heard the rattle of hog feeders and the sound of a car accelerating in the distance. The moon was full, and the shadows of bats fluttered in the moonlight. The sawing of cicadas distinguished itself, the barking of a dog. I fell asleep.

With Jess Clark in that old pickup bed in the dump the next afternoon, it was much more awkward. My arms and legs, stiff and stalklike, thumped against the wheel well, the truck bed, poked Jess in the ribs, the back. My skin looked glaringly white, white like some underground sightless creature. When he leaned forward to untie his sneakers, I felt my cheeks. As clammy as clay. Jess eased me backward. I didn't watch while he unbuttoned my shirt. He said, 'All right?'

I nodded.

'Really?'

'I'm not very used to this.'

He pulled back, away from me, the look on his face unsmiling, suddenly cautious.

'Yes,' I said. 'Please.' It was humiliating to ask, but that was okay, too. Reassuring in a way. He smiled. That was the reward.

Then, afterward, I began all at once to shiver.

He pulled away and I buttoned three buttons on my shirt. He said, 'Are you cold? It's only ninety-four degrees out here.'

'Maybe t-tt-t-terrified.'

But I wasn't, not anymore. Now the shaking was pure desire. As I realized what we had done, my body responded as it hadn't while we were doing it – hadn't ever done, I thought. I felt blasted with the desire, irradiated, rendered transparent. Jess said, 'Are you okay?'

I said, 'Hold me for a while, and keep talking.'

He laughed a warm, pleasant, very intimate laugh and said something about let's see, well the Sears man would be out tomorrow, at last, and I came in a drumming rush from toes to

head. I buried some moans in his neck and shoulder, and he
hugged me tightly enough to crack my ribs, which was just tightly
enough to contain me, I thought. He kept talking. Harold was
feeling a little sheepish and making Loren tuna-and-mushroom-
soup-with-noodles casserole for dinner. Jess had promised to put
it in the oven at four-thirty; what time was it now? The farmer
near Sac City had called him back, four hundred and seventy acres
in corn and beans, only green manures and animal manures for
fertilizer, the guy's name was Morgan Boone, which sounded
familiar, did it sound familiar to me? He said Jess could come any
time. Jess held me away from him again and gazed at me for a
long minute or two. I looked at the creases under his eyes, his
beaky nose, his serious expression. His face was deeply familiar to
me, as if I'd been staring at it my whole life. I took some deep
breaths and lay back on his shoulder. The sky was steel blue, the
sun caught in the lacy leaves of the locust trees above us. I wanted
to say, what now, but that was a dangerous temptation for sure,
so I didn't. I said, 'What time is it? Did we ever figure that one
out?'

'Three-fifteen.'

'I left the house at one.'

'It seems like a lifetime ago.'

'Is that true?' But I found it hard to believe that such episodes as
this weren't fairly routine for a good-looking guy on the West
Coast. I tried to sound joking. 'You've done this before.'

'Well, I've slept with women before. I haven't done this before.'

I said, 'I haven't slept with men. I've slept with Ty.'

'I know, Ginny. I know what that means.'

'Maybe you do. Maybe not.' I thought of saying, last night was
the best ever with Ty, last night when I dreamt I was a sow. I
could ask someone like Jess, someone good-looking and experienced, what that meant. Someone like Jess might be able to tell
me.

I sat up and reached for my underpants. The world had an odd
look, as if it were not itself, but a panoramic, 360-degree photograph of itself. I glanced at Jess again, then lay down on his
shoulder. He said, 'I trust you. I've trusted you since the first time
I saw you again at that pig roast. That's part of what draws me
back here.'

'Oh,' I said. 'That.'

Jess laughed, but didn't pursue it. I sighed, wondered when Ty and Harold and Daddy and Pete would be back. Rose, too, had gone off, to Mason City with the girls. I could feel myself disengaging from Jess. It was a natural will-less process, an ebbing that was more reassuring than anything else, since it seemed to mean that I could be satisfied as well as full of longing. My nose itched, and I sat up and wiped it on the tail of my shirt. Jess sat up, too. We smiled at each other, another degree of ebb. When he leaned forward to reach for his shirt, he ran his hand down my shin and said, 'You have nice ankles. I keep noticing them.' Then, 'May I ask you a question?'

'Sure.'

'You are such a nice person. How come you and Ty don't have any kids?'

'Well, I've had five miscarriages.'

'Jesus. Oh, Ginny.'

'Ty only knows about three. He couldn't stand it after that, so I've sort of kept the fact that we're still trying to myself.' A harsh look crossed Jess's face, and I felt another jolt of fear. I reached for my jeans, saying, 'Well, of course I shouldn't deceive him. I know – '

'It's the fucking water.'

'What?'

'Have you had your well water tested for nitrates?'

'Well, no.'

'Didn't your doctor tell you not to drink the well water?'

'No.'

He stood up and started pulling on his jeans, then sat down and put both his socks on without speaking. I could tell he was very upset. I said, 'Jess – '

He exploded. 'People have known for ten years or more that nitrates in well water cause miscarriages and death of infants. Don't *you* know that the fertilizer runoff drains into the aquifer? I can't believe this.'

'It wasn't that. It just hasn't worked. Rose drank the water – '

'It's not uniform. It doesn't affect everyone the same, and not all wells are the same. Yours might be closer to the drainage wells.'

'I don't know.'

'Are you still trying?'

We looked at each other, both contemplating the absurdity of this question in the circumstances, and smiled. 'Not today,' I said. 'I put in my diaphragm.'

'Hey – ' he reached into his pocket and pulled out a blue plastic capsule. I said, 'What's that?'

'A condom. Except that I forgot I remembered to bring it.' I took it and rolled it around in the palm of my hand. It was comforting, his forethought. I handed it back to him and he jumped out of the truck bed, then helped me down. We kissed, tenderly and thoughtfully, the way, maybe, people do when they have become unafraid to kiss one another, and then I ducked around the wild rosebushes and headed for home without looking back. I felt distinctly calm, complete and replete, as if I would never have to do that ever again.

At the supper table, after telling me about his trip to Sebulon Centre, who he saw and how my father acted, Ty said, 'Say, Gin, were you protected last night?'

I looked up from my plate and then pushed it away from me. It knocked against the water glass. I said, 'Well, not exactly. But I just finished my period. It's all right.'

'You sure?'

I snapped. 'Does that question mean you doubt my knowledge or my truthfulness? Which one?'

He snapped back, 'It means that there are things I'm not ready for yet.'

'It's been almost two years.'

'It's been almost three years.'

He was right. It was the fourth one I'd been thinking of. I could feel my face get hot. I raised my voice. 'All right, then. It's been almost three years. That proves my point even more.'

He got up and left the kitchen, closing the screen door carefully behind him. I watched him out the door without moving from the table. He stepped into the road and turned toward the corner of 686 and Cabot Street Road. I watched him stride away, and listened to the thin sound of his boots on the blacktop. I sat there for a long time, staring out the door, struck for the first time at what I had done and thought and felt that day, how, to the eyes of almost any outsider, it would look like I had become my own enemy and the enemy of all my family and friends. That was when the fear settled over me for good. After a while I went upstairs and took out my diaphragm and washed it and put it in its case.

CHARLOTTE LENNOX

From *The Female Quixote*

*Both the author's date and place of birth are obscure,
though she is believed to have been born in about 1725
in Gibraltar, where her father was an army officer. In
1739 he was sent to New York, to which the whole
family moved, and which means that she is on occasion
referred to as the first American novelist. Her father died
in 1743 and she returned to England alone and, not
knowing what else to do, started writing and got
married to a man called Alexander Lennox. He was a
fellow Scot and worked for a printer but made little
money. Charlotte appears to have considered him a
dead loss and the couple split up in the 1790s, when she
went to live with the sister of Sir Joshua Reynolds. In
1802, as a result of dire need, Charlotte was granted an
allowance of one guinea a week from the Royal Literary
Fund, but she died just a year later.*

*She was a great self-publicist and Samuel Johnson
arranged an all-night party for the launch of her first
novel,* Harriot Stuart. *It was through him that she met
Samuel Richardson, who had just published what was
to become the best-selling English novel of the
eighteenth century,* Clarissa. *Richardson acted as her
adviser and agent on* The Female Quixote *and introduced her to such luminaries as Henry Fielding.*

The title of the novel The Female Quixote *alludes to
the famous novel by Miguel de Cervantes,* Don Quixote
*(1605). In that book the eponymous hero insists on
behaving in a way entirely conducted by his knowledge
of chivalric romances. He acts out the role of a knight as*

defined by his reading of romantic adventures. Written in 1752, The Female Quixote *became one of the first novels in the English language to comment on the effects of too much novel reading. Arabella, the heroine, has also learned everything she knows from books. But this is because she is a female and protected by her father, lives closeted in a country castle where she has been brought up, with no one for company save a rather stupid and obliging maid and a collection of romances, once owned by her mother who is now dead. It is interesting to note here that Arabella's only inheritance from her female parent is a dangerous and silly one but, nonetheless, one in which she can imagine herself to play a central role.*

In reality she lives in a world controlled by men, most particularly her father, who decides that she shall marry her cousin. If she does not, she will lose a large part of her estate. By choosing to maintain her independence, she loses her means to remain independent. Finding herself cornered in this way, Arabella has no defences save those inculcated by the fictional, and only, world she knows. She imagines herself the victim of a multitude of rapes and kidnappings, in fantasies that become more and more absurd. The most attractive woman in the book, she is also the furthest away from any real concerns, the most rooted in the ridiculous.

But Arabella is truly strong-willed. She is so firmly fixed in her world-view that the only way for other characters to get what they want is by humouring her. Her cousin, Glanville, who does really want to marry Arabella, persuades his father to fall into line with Arabella's demands. It is because Arabella imagines she can assume the powers that a noblewoman in a fictional romance would possess, that she actually becomes the only woman who can assert power of her own. She speaks at great length, permits herself to interview men alone in her chamber, and instructs the males around her, when according to contemporary mores, she should do nothing but remain silent and be instructed herself.

Of course, though a woman may achieve some element of power and impose her will on a situation temporarily, in reality, the end of Arabella's story must involve marriage and, with it, a cessation of all power. In the meantime, as in this extract, she continues to hold centre stage and to anticipate her own romantic climax.

M R GLANVILLE had just finished her eulogium, when Arabella appeared; joy danced in his eyes at her approach; he gazed upon her with a kind of conscious triumph in his looks; her consummate loveliness justifying his passion, and being in his opinion, more than an excuse for all her extravagances.

[Chapter 11]

In which our heroine, as we presume, shows herself
in two very different lights

Arabella, who at her entrance had perceived some traces of uneasiness upon Miss Glanville's countenance, tenderly asked her the cause; to which that young lady answering in a cold and reserved manner, Mr Glanville, to divert her reflections on it, very freely accused himself of having given his sister some offence. 'To be sure, Brother,' said Miss Glanville, 'you are very vehement in your temper, and are as violently carried away about things of little importance as of the greatest; and then, whatever you have a fancy for, you love so obstinately.'

'I am obliged to you, Miss,' interrupted Mr Glanville, 'for endeavouring to give Lady Bella so unfavourable an opinion of me – '

'I assure you,' said Arabella, 'Miss Glanville has said nothing to your disadvantage: For, in my opinion, the temperament of great minds ought to be as she represents yours to be. For there is nothing at so great a distance from true and heroic virtue, as that indifference which obliges some people to be pleased with all things or nothing: Whence it comes to pass, that they neither entertain great desires of glory, nor fear of infamy; that they neither love nor hate; that they are wholly influenced by custom, and are sensible only of the afflictions of the body, their minds being in a manner insensible –

'To say the truth, I am inclined to conceive a greater hope of a man, who in the beginning of his life is hurried away by some evil habit, than one that fastens on nothing: The mind that cannot be brought to detest vice, will never be persuaded to love virtue; but one who is capable of loving or hating irreconcilably, by having, when young, his passions directed to proper objects, will remain fixed in his choice of what is good. But with him who is incapable of any violent attraction, and whose heart is chilled by a general indifference, precept or example will have no force – and philosophy itself which boasts it hath remedies for all indispositions of the soul, never had any that can cure an indifferent mind – Nay,' added she, 'I am persuaded that indifference is generally the inseparable companion of a weak and imperfect judgment. For it is so natural to a person to be carried towards that which he believes to be good, that if indifferent people were able to judge of things, they would fasten on something. But certain it is that this lukewarmness of soul, which sends forth but feeble desires, sends also but feeble lights; so that those who are guilty of it, not knowing any thing clearly, cannot fasten on any thing with perseverance.'

Mr Glanville, when Arabella had finished this speech, cast a triumphing glance at his sister, who had affected great inattention all the while she had been speaking. Sir Charles in his way, expressed much admiration of her wit, telling her, if she had been a man, she would have made a great figure in Parliament, and that her speeches might have come perhaps to be printed in time.

This compliment, odd as it was, gave great joy to Glanville, when the conversation was interrupted by the arrival of Mr Selvin, who had slipped away unobserved at the time that Arabella's indisposition had alarmed them, and now came to enquire after her health; and also if an opportunity offered to set her right with regard to the suspicions she had entertained of his designing to pay his addresses to her.

Arabella, as soon as he had sent in his name, appeared to be in great disturbance; and upon his entrance, offered immediately to withdraw, telling Mr Glanville, who would have detained her, that she found no place was likely to secure her from the persecutions of that gentleman.

Glanville started, and looked strangely perplexed at this speech; Miss Glanville smiled, and poor Selvin, with a very silly look –

hemmed two or three times, and then with a faltering accent said, 'Madam, I am very much concerned to find your ladyship resolved to persist in –'

'Sir,' interrupted Arabella, 'my resolutions are unalterable. I told you so before, and am surprised, after the knowledge of my intentions, you presume to appear in my presence again, from whence I had so positively banished you.'

'Pray, niece,' said Sir Charles, 'what has Mr Selvin done to disoblige you?'

'Sir,' replied Arabella, 'Mr Selvin's offence can admit of no other reparation than that which I required of him, which was a voluntary banishment from my presence: And in this,' pursued she, 'I am guilty of no more severity to you, than the Princess Udosia was to the unfortunate Thrasimedes. For the passion of this prince having come to her knowledge, notwithstanding the pains he took to conceal it, this fair and wise princess thought it not enough to forbid his speaking to her, but also banished him from her presence; laying a peremptory command upon him, never to appear before her again till he was perfectly cured of that unhappy love he had entertained for her – imitate therefore the meritorious obedience of this poor prince, and if that passion you profess for me –'

'How, sir,' interrupted Sir Charles, 'do you make love to my niece then?'

'Sir,' replied Mr Selvin, who was strangely confounded at Arabella's speech, 'though I really admire the perfection this lady is possessed of, yet I assure you, upon my honour, I never had a thought of making any addresses to her; and I can't imagine why her ladyship persists in accusing me of such presumption.'

So formal a denial after what Arabella had said, extremely perplexed Sir Charles, and filled Mr Glanville with inconceivable shame –

Miss Glanville enjoyed their disturbance, and full of an ill-natured triumph, endeavoured to look Arabella into confusion: But that lady not being at all discomposed by this declaration of Mr Selvin's having accounted for it already, replied with great calmness.

'Sir, 'tis easy to see through the artifice of your disclaiming any passion for me – upon any other occasion questionless, you would

rather sacrifice your life, than consent to disavow these sentiments, which unhappily for your peace you have entertained. At
present the desire of continuing near me, obliges you to lay this
constraint upon yourself; however you know Thrasimedes fell
upon the same stratagem to no purpose. The rigid Udosia saw
through the disguise and would not dispense with herself from
banishing him from Rome, as I do you from England – '

'How, madam!' interrupted Selvin amazed –

'Yes, sir,' replied Arabella hastily, 'nothing less can satisfy what
I owe to the consideration of my own glory.'

'Upon my word, madam,' said Selvin, half angry, and yet
strongly inclined to laugh, 'I don't see the necessity of my quitting
my native country, to satisfy what you owe to the consideration of
your own glory. Pray, how does my staying in England affect your
ladyship's glory?'

'To answer your question with another,' said Arabella, 'Pray
how did the stay of Thrasimedes in Rome, affect the glory of the
Empress Udosia?'

Mr Selvin was struck dumb with this speech, for he was not
willing to be thought so deficient in the knowledge of history, as
not to be acquainted with the reasons why Thrasimedes should
not stay in Rome.

His silence therefore seeming to Arabella to be a tacit confes-
sion of the justice of her commands, a sentiment of compassion
for this unfortunate lover, intruded itself into her mind; and
turning her bright eyes, full of a soft complacency upon Selvin,
who stared at her as if he had lost his wits –

'I will not,' said she, 'wrong the sublimity of your passion for
me so much, as to doubt your being ready to sacrifice the repose of
your own life to the satisfaction of mine: Nor will I do so much
injustice to your generosity, as to suppose the glory of obeying my
commands, will not in some measure soften the rigour of your
destiny – I know not whether it may be lawful for me to tell you,
that your misfortune does really cause me some affliction; but I
am willing to give you this consolation, and also to assure you,
that to whatever part of the world your despair will carry you, the
good wishes and compassion of Arabella shall follow you – '

Having said this, with one of her fair hands she covered her face
to hide the blushes which so compassionate a speech had caused –

holding the other extended with a careless air, supposing he would kneel to kiss it, and bathe it with his tears, as was the custom on such melancholy occasions, her head at the same time turned another way, as if reluctantly and with confusion she granted this favour. But after standing a moment in this posture, and finding her hand untouched, she concluded grief had deprived him of his senses, and that he would shortly fall into a swoon as Thrasimedes did: and to prevent being a witness of so doleful a sight, she hurried out of the room without once turning about, and having reached her own apartment, sunk into a chair, not a little affected with the deplorable condition in which she had left her supposed miserable lover.

[Chapter III]

The contrast continued

The company she had left behind her being all, except Mr Glanville, to the last degree surprised at her strange words and actions, continued mute for several minutes after she was gone, staring upon one another, as if each wished to know the other's opinion of such an unaccountable behaviour. At last Miss Glanville, who observed her brother's back was towards her, told Mr Selvin in a low voice, that she hoped he would call and take his leave of them before he set out for the place where his despair would carry him –

Mr Selvin in spite of his natural gravity, could not forbear laughing at this speech of Miss Glanville's, which shocked her brother, and not being able to stay where Arabella was ridiculed nor entitled to resent it, which would have been a manifest injustice on that occasion, he retired to his own apartment to give vent to that spleen which in those moments made him out of humour with all the world.

Sir Charles, when he was gone, indulged himself in a little mirth on his niece's extravagance, protesting he did not know what to do with her. Upon which Miss Glanville observed, that it was a pity there were not such things as Protestant nunneries; giving it as her opinion, that her cousin ought to be confined in one of those places, and never suffered to see any company, by which means she would avoid exposing herself in the manner she did now.

Mr Selvin, who possibly thought this a reasonable scheme of Miss Glanville's, seemed by his silence to assent to her opinion; but Sir Charles was greatly displeased with his daughter for expressing herself so freely; alleging that Arabella, when she was out of those whims, was a very sensible young lady, and sometimes talked as learnedly as a divine. To which Mr Selvin also added, that she had a great knowledge of history, and had a most surprising memory; and after some more discourse to the same purpose, he took his leave, earnestly entreating Sir Charles to believe that he never entertained any design of making his addresses to Lady Bella.

In the mean time, that lady after having given near half an hour to those reflections which occur to heroines in the same situation with herself, called for Lucy, and ordered her to go to the dining-room, and see in what condition Mr Selvin was, telling her she had certainly left him in a swoon, as also the occasion of it; and bid her give him all the consolation in her power.

Lucy, with tears in her eyes at this recital, went down as she was ordered, and entering the room without any ceremony, her thoughts being wholly fixed on the melancholy circumstance her Lady had been telling her; she looked eagerly round the room without speaking a word, till Sir Charles and Miss Glanville, who thought she had been sent with some message from Arabella, asked her both at the same instant, what she wanted? –

'I came, sir,' said Lucy, repeating her lady's words, 'to see in what condition Mr Selvin is in, and to give him all the solation in my power.'

Sir Charles, laughing heartily at this speech, asked her what she could do for Mr Selvin? To which she replied, she did not know; but her lady had told her to give him all the solation in her power.

'Consolation thou would'st say, I suppose,' said Sir Charles.

'Yes, sir,' said Lucy curtesying.

'Well, child,' added he, 'go up and tell your lady, Mr Selvin does not need any consolation.'

Lucy accordingly returned with this message, and was met at

the chamber-door by Arabella, who hastily asked her if Mr Selvin was recovered from his swoon: To which Lucy replied that she did not know, but that Sir Charles bid her tell her ladyship, Mr Selvin did not need any consolation.

'Oh heavens!' cried Arabella, throwing herself into a chair as pale as death, 'He is dead, he has fallen upon his sword, and put an end to his life and miseries at once – Oh! how unhappy am I,' cried she, bursting into tears, 'to be the cause of so cruel an accident – was ever any fate so terrible as mine – was ever beauty so fatal – was ever rigour so unfortunate – how will the quiet of my future days be disturbed by the sad remembrance of a man whose death was caused by my disdain – but why,' resumed she after a little pause. 'Why do I thus afflict myself for what has happened by an unavoidable necessity? Nor am I singular in the misfortune which has befallen me – Did not the sad Perinthus die for the beautiful Panthea – did not the rigour of Barsina bring the miserable Oxyatres to the grave – and the severity of Statira make Oroondates fall upon his sword in her presence, though happily he escaped being killed by it – let us then not afflict ourselves unreasonably at this sad accident – let us comfort ourselves with the thought that we have only acted conformable to our duty.'

Arabella having pronounced these last words with a solemn and lofty accent, ordered Lucy, who listened to her with eyes drowned in tears, to go down and ask if the body was removed, 'For,' added she, 'all my constancy will not be sufficient to support me against that pitiful sight.'

Lucy accordingly delivered her message to Sir Charles and Miss Glanville, who were still together, discoursing on the fantastical turn of Arabella, when the knight, who could not possibly comprehend what she meant by asking if the body was removed, bid her tell her lady he desired to speak to her.

Arabella, upon receiving this summons, set herself to consider what could be the intent of it. 'If Mr Selvin be dead' said she, 'what good can my presence do among them? Surely it cannot be to upbraid me with my severity, that my uncle desires to see me – No, it would be unjust to suppose it. Questionless my unhappy lover is still struggling with the pangs of death, and for a consolation in his last moments, implores the favour of resigning up his life in my sight.' Pausing a little at these words, she rose from her seat with a resolution to give the unhappy Selvin her pardon before he died. Meeting Mr Glanville as he was returning from his chamber to the dining-room, she told him, she hoped the charity she was going to discover towards his rival, would not give him any uneasiness; and preventing his reply by going hastily into the room, he followed her dreading some new extravagance, yet not able to prevent it, endeavoured to conceal his confusion from her observation – Arabella after breathing a gentle sigh told Sir Charles, that she was come to grant Mr Selvin her pardon for the offence he had been guilty of, that he might depart in peace.

'Well, well,' said Sir Charles, 'he is departed in peace without it.'

'How, sir,' interrupted Arabella, 'is he dead then already? Alas! why had he not the satisfaction of seeing me before he expired, that his soul might have departed in peace! He would have been assured not only of my pardon, but pity also; and that assurance would have made him happy in his last moments.'

'Why, niece,' interrupted Sir Charles staring, 'you surprise me prodigiously: are you in earnest?'

'Questionless I am, sir,' said she, 'nor ought you to be surprised at the concern I express for the fate of this unhappy man, nor at the pardon I proposed to have granted him; since herein I am justified by the example of many great and virtuous princesses, who have done as much, nay, haply more than I intended to have done, for persons whose offences were greater than Mr Selvin's.'

'I am very sorry, madam,' said Sir Charles, 'to hear you talk in this manner; 'tis really enough to make one suspect you are – '

'You do me great injustice, sir,' interrupted Arabella, 'if you suspect me to be guilty of any unbecoming weakness for this man: if barely expressing my compassion for his misfortunes be esteemed so great a favour, what would you have thought if I had supported his head on my knees while he was dying, shed tears over him, and discovered all the tokens of a sincere affliction for him?'

'Good God!' said Sir Charles lifting up his eyes, 'Did any body ever hear of anything like this?'

'What, sir?' said Arabella, with as great an appearance of surprise in her countenance as his had discovered, 'Did you say you never heard of any thing like this? Then you never heard of the Princess of Media, I suppose?'

'No, not I, madam,' said Sir Charles peevishly.

'Then, sir,' resumed Arabella, 'permit me to tell you, that this fair and virtuous princess condescended to do all I have mentioned for the fierce Labynet, Prince of Assyria; who though he had mortally offended her by stealing her away out of the court of the King her father, nevertheless, when he was wounded to death in her presence, and humbly implored her pardon before he died, she condescended as I have said, to support him on her knees, and shed tears for his disaster – I could produce many more instances of the like compassion in ladies almost as highly born as herself, though perhaps their quality was not quite so illustrious, she being the heiress of two powerful kingdoms. Yet to mention only these – '

'Good heavens!' cried Mr Glanville here, being quite out of patience, 'I shall go distracted – '

Arabella surprised at this exclamation, looked earnestly at him for a moment – and then asked him whether any thing she had said had given him uneasiness?

'Yes, upon my soul, madam,' said Glanville so vexed and confused that he hardly knew what he said –

'I am sorry for it,' replied Arabella gravely, 'and also am greatly concerned to find that in generosity you are so much exceeded by the illustrious Cyrus; who was so far from taking umbrage at Mandana's behaviour to the dying prince, that he commended her for the compassion she had shown him. So also did the brave and generous Oroondates when the fair Statira – '

'By heavens!' cried Glanville rising in a passion, 'there's no hearing this. Pardon me, madam, but upon my soul, you'll make me hang myself.'

'Hang yourself,' repeated Arabella, 'sure you know not what you say? – You meant, I suppose, that you'll fall upon your sword. What hero ever threatened to give himself so vulgar a death? But pray let me know the cause of your despair, so sudden and so violent.'

Mr Glanville continuing in a sort of sullen silence, Arabella raising her voice went on:

'Though I do not conceive myself obliged to give you an account of my conduct, seeing that I have only permitted you yet to hope for my favour; yet I owe to myself and my own honour the justification I am going to make. Know then, that however suspicious my compassion for Mr Selvin may appear to your mistaken judgment, yet it has its foundation only in the generosity of my disposition, which inclines me to pardon the fault when the unhappy criminal repents; and to afford him my pity when his circumstances require it. Let not therefore the charity I have discovered towards your rival, be the cause of your despair, since my sentiments for him were he living, would be what they were before; that is, full of indifference, nay, haply disdain. And suffer not yourself to be so carried away by a violent and unjust jealousy, as to threaten your own death, which if you really had any ground for your suspicions, and truly loved me, would come unsought for, though not undesired – for indeed, was your despair reasonable, death would necessarily follow it; for what lover can live under so desperate a misfortune. In that case you may meet death undauntedly when it comes, nay, embrace it with joy; but truly the killing one's self is but a false picture of true courage, proceeding rather from fear of a further evil, than contempt of that you fly to: for if it were a contempt of pain, the same principle would make you resolve to bear patiently and fearlessly all kind of pains; and hope being of all other the most contrary thing to fear, this being an utter banishment of hope, seems to have its ground in fear.'

[Chapter IV]

In which Mr Glanville makes an unsuccessful attempt upon Arabella

Arabella, when she had finished these words, which banished in part Mr Glanville's confusion, went to her own apartment, followed by Miss Glanville, to whom she had made a sign for that purpose; and throwing herself into a chair, burst into tears, which greatly surprising Miss Glanville, she pressed her to tell her the cause.

'Alas!' replied Arabella, 'have I not cause to think myself

extremely unhappy? The deplorable death of Mr Selvin, the despair to which I see your brother reduced, with the fatal consequences, which may attend it, fills me with a mortal uneasiness.'

'Well,' said Miss Glanville, 'your ladyship may make yourself quite easy as to both these matters; for Mr Selvin is not dead, nor is my brother in despair that I know of.'

'What do you say, Miss,' interrupted Arabella, 'is not Mr Selvin dead? Was the wound he gave himself not mortal then?'

'I know of no wound that he gave himself, not I,' said Miss Glanville. 'What makes your ladyship suppose he gave himself a wound? Lord bless me, what strange thoughts come into your head.'

'Truly I am rejoiced to hear it,' replied Arabella, 'and in order to prevent the effects of his despair, I'll instantly dispatch my commands to him to live.'

'I dare answer for his obedience, madam,' said Miss Glanville smiling.

ALIENATION

'What are you doing?' she asked him again and again.
'I'm shoving my cock in your cunt,' he replied.

Nina Fitzpatrick, *The English Disease*

VIRGINIA WOOLF

From *Orlando*

Born in 1882, the third of four children, Virginia was educated at home. After her father's death in 1904 and her second serious mental breakdown, Virginia published her first piece of work, a review in The Guardian *newspaper, and went to live in Bloomsbury, where she met and married Leonard Woolf and founded the Hogarth Press. With various family members and other contemporary artists, they became central figures in what was termed 'the Bloomsbury set' – leaders of the avant-garde in a variety of art forms. Mental illness plagued Virginia throughout her life and, in March 1941, by which time she was a major figure in the literary world, she drowned herself near her home in Sussex.*

Orlando, of all her novels, is the one which most closely deals with gender and sexuality. She begins it with the eponymous central character as a man in Elizabethan England but one day, having travelled through both time and space, he wakes up during the siege of Constantinople, as a woman.

'"Praise God that I'm a woman!" she cried, and was about to run into the extreme folly . . . of being proud of her sex, when she paused over the singular word, which, for all we can do to put it in its place, has crept in at the end of the last sentence: Love.'

In this extract Orlando, now a woman, returns to England and begins to explore her new position and its implications on her romantic life.

'A PLAGUE ON women,' said Orlando to herself, going to the cupboard to fetch a glass of wine, 'they never leave one a moment's peace. A more ferreting, inquisiting, busybodying set of people don't exist. It was to escape this Maypole that I left England, and now' – here she turned to present the Archduchess with the salver, and behold – in her place stood a tall gentleman in black. A heap of clothes lay in the fender. She was alone with a man.

Recalled thus suddenly to a consciousness of her sex, which she had completely forgotten, and of his, which was now remote enough to be equally upsetting, Orlando felt seized with faintness.

'Laa!' she cried, putting her hand to her side, 'how you frighten me!'

'Gentle creature,' cried the Archduchess, falling on one knee and at the same time pressing a cordial to Orlando's lips, 'forgive me for the deceit I have practised on you!'

Orlando sipped the wind and the Archduke knelt and kissed her hand.

In short, they acted the parts of man and woman for ten minutes with great vigour and then fell into natural discourse. The Archduchess (but she must in future be known as the Archduke) told his story – that he was a man and always had been one; that he had seen a portrait of Orlando and fallen hopelessly in love with him; that to compass his ends, he had dressed as a woman and lodged at the Baker's shop; that he was desolated when he fled to Turkey; that he had heard of her change and hastened to offer his services (here he teed and heed intolerably). For to him, said the Archduke Harry, she was and would ever be the Pink, the Pearl, the Perfection of her sex. The three p's would have been more persuasive if they had not been interspersed with tee-hees and haw-haws of the strangest kind. 'If this is love,' said Orlando to herself, looking at the Archduke on the other side of the fender, and now from the woman's point of view, 'there is something highly ridiculous about it.'

Falling on his knees, the Archduke Harry made the most passionate declaration of his suit. He told her that he had something like twenty million ducats in a strong box at his castle. He had more acres than any nobleman in England. The shooting was excellent: he could promise her a mixed bag of ptarmigan and grouse such as no English moor, or Scotch either, could rival. True, the pheasants had suffered from the gape in his absence, and the does had slipped their young, but that could be put right, and would be with her help when they lived in Roumania together.

As he spoke, enormous tears formed in his rather prominent eyes and ran down the sandy tracts of his long and lanky cheeks.

That men cry as frequently and as unreasonably as women, Orlando knew from her own experience as a man; but she was beginning to be aware that women should be shocked when men display emotion in their presence, and so, shocked she was.

The Archduke apologized. He commanded himself sufficiently to say that he would leave her now, but would return on the following day for his answer.

That was a Tuesday. He came on Wednesday; he came on Thursday; he came on Friday; and he came on Saturday. It is true that each visit began, continued, or concluded with a declaration of love, but in between there was much room for silence. They sat on either side of the fireplace and sometimes the Archduke knocked over the fire-irons and Orlando picked them up again. Then the Archduke would bethink him how he had shot an elk in Sweden, and Orlando would ask, was it a very big elk, and the Archduke would say that it was not as big as the reindeer which he shot in Norway; and Orlando would ask, had he ever shot a tiger, and the Archduke would say he had shot an albatross, and Orlando would say (half hiding her yawn) was an albatross as big as an elephant, and the Archduke would say – something very sensible, no doubt, but Orlando heard it not, for she was looking at her writing-table, out of the window, at the door. Upon which the Archduke would say, 'I adore you', at the very same moment that Orlando said 'Look, it's beginning to rain', at which they were both much embarrassed, and blushed scarlet, and could neither of them think what to say next. Indeed, Orlando was at her wit's end what to talk about and had she not bethought her of a game called Fly Loo, at which great sums of money can be lost with very little expense of spirit, she would have had to marry him, she supposed; for how else to get rid of him she knew not. By this device, however, and it was a simple one, needing only three lumps of sugar and a sufficiency of flies, the embarrassment of conversation was overcome and the necessity of marriage avoided. For now, the Archduke would bet her five hundred pounds to a tester that a fly would settle on this lump and not on that. Thus, they would have occupation for a whole morning watching the flies (who were naturally sluggish at this season and often spent an hour or so circling round the ceiling) until at length some fine blue-bottle made his choice and the match was won. Many hundreds of pounds changed hands between them at this game, which the Archduke, who was a born gambler, swore was every bit as good as horse racing, and vowed he could play at for ever. But Orlando soon began to weary.

'What's the good of being a fine young woman in the prime of life', she asked, 'if I have to pass all my mornings watching blue-bottles with an Archduke?'

She began to detest the sight of sugar; flies made her dizzy. Some way out of the difficulty there must be, she supposed, but she was still awkward in the arts of her sex, and as she could no longer knock a man over the head or run him through the body with a rapier, she could think of no better method than this. She caught a blue-bottle, gently pressed the life out of it (it was half dead already, or her kindness for the dumb creatures would not have permitted it) and secured it by a drop of gum arabic to a lump of sugar. While the Archduke was gazing at the ceiling, she deftly substituted this lump for the one she had laid her money on, and crying 'Loo Loo!' declared that she had won her bet. Her reckoning was that the Archduke, with all his knowledge of sport and horseracing, would detect the fraud and, as to cheat at Loo is the most heinous of crimes, and men have been banished from the society of mankind to that of apes in the tropics for ever because of it, she calculated that he would be manly enough to refuse to have anything further to do with her. But she misjudged the simplicity of the amiable nobleman. He was no nice judge of flies. A dead fly looked to him much the same as a living one. She played the trick twenty times on him and he paid her over £17,250 (which is about £40,885:6:8 of our own money) before Orlando cheated so grossly that even he could be deceived no longer. When he realized the truth at last, a painful scene ensued. The Archduke rose to his full height. He coloured scarlet. Tears rolled down his cheeks one by one. That she had won a fortune from him was nothing – she was welcome to it; that she had deceived him was something – it hurt him to think her capable of it; but that she had cheated at Loo was everything. To love a woman who cheated at play was, he said, impossible. Here he broke down completely. Happily, he said, recovering slightly, there were no witnesses. She was, after all, only a woman, he said. In short, he was preparing in the chivalry of his heart to forgive her and had bent to ask her pardon for the violence of his language, when she cut the matter short, as he stooped his proud head, by dropping a small toad between his skin and his shirt.

In justice to her, it must be said that she would infinitely have preferred a rapier. Toads are clammy things to conceal about one's person a whole morning. But if rapiers are forbidden, one must have recourse to toads. Moreover toads and laughter between them sometimes do what cold steel cannot. She laughed. The Archduke blushed. She laughed. The Archduke cursed. She laughed. The Archduke slammed the door.

'Heaven be praised!' cried Orlando still laughing. She heard the sound of chariot wheels driven at a furious pace down the court-yard. She heard them rattle along the road. Fainter and fainter the sound became. Now it faded away altogether.

'I am alone,' said Orlando, aloud since there was no one to hear.

That silence is more profound after noise still wants the confirmation of science. But that loneliness is more apparent directly after one has been made love to, many women would take their oath. As the sound of the Archduke's chariot wheels died away, Orlando felt drawing further from her and further from her an Archduke (she did not mind that), a fortune (she did not mind that), a title (she did not mind that), the safety and circumstance of married life (she did not mind that), but life she heard, going from her, and a lover, 'Life and a lover,' she murmured; and going to her writing-table she dipped her pen in the ink and wrote:

'Life and a lover' – a line which did not scan and made no sense with what went before – something about the proper way of dipping sheep to avoid the scab. Reading it over she blushed and repeated:

'Life and a lover.' Then laying her pen aside she went into her bedroom, stood in front of her mirror, and arranged her pearls about her neck. Then since pearls do not show to advantage against a morning gown of sprigged cotton, she changed to a dove grey taffeta; thence to one of peach bloom; thence to a wine-coloured brocade. Perhaps a dash of powder was needed, and if her hair were disposed – so – about her brow, it might become her. Then she slipped her feet into pointed slippers, and drew an emerald ring upon her finger. 'Now,' she said when all was ready and lit the silver sconces on either side of the mirror. What woman would not have kindled to see what Orlando saw then burning in the snow – for all about the looking-glass were snowy lawns, and she was like a fire, a burning bush, and the candle flames about her head were silver leaves; or again, the glass was green water, and she a mermaid, slung with pearls, a siren in a cave, singing so that oarsmen leant from their boats and fell down, down to embrace her; so dark, so bright, so hard, so soft, was she, so astonishingly seductive that it was a thousand pities that there was no one there to put it in plain English, and say outright, 'Damn it, Madam, you are loveliness incarnate,' which was the truth. Even Orlando (who had no conceit of her person) knew it, for she smiled the involuntary smile which women smile when their own beauty, which seems not their own, forms like a drop falling or a fountain rising and confronts them all of a sudden in the glass – this smile she smiled and then she listened for a moment and heard only the leaves blowing and the sparrows twittering, and then she sighed, 'Life, a lover,' and then she turned on her heel with extra-ordinary rapidity; whipped her pearls from her neck, stripped the satins from her back, stood erect in the neat black silk knicker-bockers of an ordinary nobleman, and rang the bell. When the servant came, she told him to order a coach and six to be in readi-ness instantly. She was summoned by urgent affairs to London. Within an hour of the Archduke's departure, off she drove.

JEAN RHYS

From *Wide Sargasso Sea*

Jean Rhys, who was born Ellen Rhys Williams on the island of Dominica in 1894, was the daughter of a Welsh doctor who had married a Dominican Creole woman. She was a quiet child, educated in a strong Catholic tradition at a convent school. She spent her early years wanting to be black, she said, because the black women attended Mass in the most beautiful dresses. She learned the native hymns, spent more time with the black servants than with the white employers and felt alienated from local white culture.

As a teenager she went to Europe, where she attended the Royal Academy of Dramatic Arts. Her father died and, having no more money, she began working on bit parts in films and dance halls. In 1919 she married a Frenchman and moved to Paris, where she met the American novelist Ford Maddox Ford who became her lover and patron.

Encouraged by him, she continued to write and, in 1927 The Left Bank, her first work, was published. Much of her writing describes unconscious and alienated central female characters, powerless underdogs who live in a cruel world, dominated by heartless men but, nevertheless, cleave to these men for moments of temporary comfort. Given that this was her world, she was naturally drawn to the story of the 'madwoman in the attic' – the first wife of Rochester, the hero of Charlotte Brontë's novel Jane Eyre. *Abandoned and alone, the first Mrs Rochester is locked up in the attic by a man who no longer loves her and who wishes to move on to fresh and younger pastures. Jean Rhys created her best-known novel around her interpretation of this marginalized fictional character and invented the detail of the character's early life by drawing on her own in the Caribbean.*

IN THE LATE afternoon when the water was warmer she bathed with me. She'd spend some time throwing pebbles at a flat stone in the middle of the pool. 'I've seen him. He hasn't died or gone to any other river. He's still there. The land crabs are harmless. People *say* they are harmless. I wouldn't like to – '

'Nor would I. Horrible looking creatures.'

She was undecided, uncertain about facts – any fact. When I asked her if the snakes we sometimes saw were poisonous, she said, 'Not those. The *fer de lance* of course, but there are none here,' and added, 'but how can they be sure? Do you think they know?' Then, 'Our snakes are not poisonous. Of course not.'

However, she was certain about the monster crab and one afternoon when I was watching her, hardly able to believe she was the pale silent creature I had married, watching her in her blue chemise, blue with white spots, hitched up far above her knees, she stopped laughing, called a warning and threw a large pebble. She threw like a boy, with a sure graceful movement, and looked down at very long pincer claws, jagged-edged and sharp, vanishing.

'He won't come after you if you keep away from that stone. He lives there. Oh it's another sort of crab. I don't know the name in English. Very big, very old.'

As we were walking home I asked her who had taught her to aim so well. 'Oh, Sandi taught me, a boy you never met.'

Every evening we saw the sun go down from the thatched shelter she called the *ajoupa*, I the summer house. We watched the sky and the distant sea on fire – all colours were in that fire and the huge clouds fringed and shot with flame. But I soon tired of the display. I was waiting for the scent of the flowers by the river – they opened when darkness came and it came quickly. Not night or darkness as I knew it but night with blazing stars, an alien moon – night full of strange noises. Still night, not day.

'The man who owns Consolation Estate is a hermit,' she was saying. 'He never sees anyone – hardly ever speaks, they say.'

'A hermit neighbour suits me. Very well indeed.'

'There are four hermits in this island,' she said. 'Four real ones. Others pretend but they leave when the rainy season comes. Or else they are drunk all the time. That's when sad things happen.'

'So this place is as lonely as it feels?' I asked her.

'Yes it is lonely. Are you happy here?'

'Who wouldn't be?'

'I love it more than anywhere in the world. As if it were a person. More than a person.'

'But you don't know the world,' I teased her.

'No, only here, and Jamaica of course. Coulibri, Spanish Town. I don't know the other islands at all. Is the world more beautiful, then?'

And how to answer that? 'It's different,' I said.

She told me that for a long time they had not known what was happening at Granbois. 'When Mr Mason came' (she always called her stepfather Mr Mason) 'the forest was swallowing it up.' The overseer drank, the house was dilapidated, all the furniture had been stolen, then Baptiste was discovered. A butler. In St Kitts. But born in this island and willing to come back. 'He's a very good overseer,' she'd say, and I'd agree, keeping my opinions of Baptiste, Christophine and all the others to myself. 'Baptiste says . . . Christophine wants . . .'

She trusted them and I did not. But I could hardly say so. Not yet.

We did not see a great deal of them. The kitchen and the swarming kitchen life were some way off. As for the money which she handed out so carelessly, not counting it, not knowing how much she gave, or the unfamiliar faces that appeared then disappeared, though never without a large meal eaten and a shot of rum I discovered – sisters, cousins, aunts and uncles – if she asked no questions how could I?

The house was swept and dusted very early, usually before I woke. Hilda brought coffee and there were always two roses on the tray. Sometimes she'd smile a sweet childish smile, sometimes she would giggle very loudly and rudely, bang the tray down and run away.

'Stupid little girl,' I'd say.

'No, no. She is shy. The girls here are very shy.'

After breakfast at noon there'd be silence till the evening meal which was served much later than in England. Christophine's whims and fancies, I was sure. Then we were left alone. Sometimes a sidelong look or a sly knowing glance disturbed me, but it was never for long. 'Not now,' I would think. 'Not yet.'

It was often raining when I woke during the night, a light capricious shower, dancing playful rain, or hushed, muted, growing louder, more persistent, more powerful, an inexorable sound. But always music, a music I had never heard before.

Then I would look at her for long minutes by candlelight, wonder why she seemed sad asleep, and curse the fever or the caution that had made me so blind, so feeble, so hesitating. I'd remember her effort to escape. (*No, I am sorry, I do not wish to marry you.*) Had she given way to that man Richard's arguments, threats probably, I wouldn't trust him far, or to my half-serious blandishments and promises? In any case she had given way, but coldly, unwillingly, trying to protect herself with silence and a blank face. Poor weapons, and they had not served her well or lasted long. If I have forgotten caution, she has forgotten silence and coldness.

Shall I wake her up and listen to the things she says, whispers, in darkness. Not by day.

'I never wished to live before I knew you. I always thought it would be better if I died. Such a long time to wait before it's over.'

'And did you ever tell anyone this?'

'There was no one to tell, no one to listen. Oh you can't imagine Coulibri.'

'But after Coulibri?'

'After Coulibri it was too late. I did not change.'

All day she'd be like any other girl, smile at herself in the looking-glass (*do you like this scent?*), try to teach me her songs, for they haunted me.

Adieu foulard, adieu madras, or *Ma belle ka di maman li*. My beautiful girl said to her mother (*No it is not like that. Now listen. It is this way*). She'd be silent, or angry for no reason, and chatter to Christophine in patois.

'Why do you hug and kiss Christophine?' I'd say.

'Why not?'

'*I* wouldn't hug and kiss them,' I'd say, 'I couldn't.'

At this she'd laugh for a long time and never tell me why she laughed.

But at night how different, even her voice was changed. Always this talk of death. (Is she trying to tell me that is the secret of this place? That there is no other way? She knows. She knows.)

'Why did you make me want to live? Why did you do that to me?'

'Because I wished it. Isn't that enough?'

'Yes, it is enough. But if one day you didn't wish it. What should I do then? Suppose you took this happiness away when I wasn't looking . . .'

'And lose my own? Who'd be so foolish?'

'I am not used to happiness,' she said. 'It makes me afraid.'

'Never be afraid. Or if you are tell no one.'

'I understand. But trying does not help me.'

'What would?' She did not answer that, then one night whispered, 'If I could die. Now, when I am happy. Would you do that? You wouldn't have to kill me. Say die and I will die. You don't believe me? Then try, try, say die and watch me die.'

'Die then! Die!' I watched her die many times. In my way, not in hers. In sunlight, in shadow, by moonlight, by candlelight. In the long afternoons when the house was empty. Only the sun was there to keep us company. We shut him out. And why not? Very soon she was as eager for what's called loving as I was – more lost and drowned afterwards.

She said, 'Here I can do as I like,' not I, and then I said it too. It seemed right in that lonely place. 'Here I can do as I like.'

We seldom met anyone when we left the house. If we did they'd greet us and go on their way.

I grew to like these mountain people, silent, reserved, never servile, never curious (or so I thought), not knowing that their quick sideways looks saw everything they wished to see.

It was at night that I felt danger and would try to forget it and push it away.

'You are safe,' I'd say. She'd liked that – to be told 'you are safe.' Or I'd touch her face gently and touch tears. Tears – nothing! Words – less than nothing. As for the happiness I gave her, that was worse than nothing. I did not love her. I was thirsty for her, but that is not love. I felt very little tenderness for her, she was a stranger to me, a stranger who did not think or feel as I did.

One afternoon the sight of a dress which she'd left lying on her bedroom floor made me breathless and savage with desire. When I was exhausted I turned away from her and slept, still without a word or caress. I woke and she was kissing me – soft light kisses. 'It is late,' she said and smiled. 'You must let me cover you up – the land breeze can be cold.'

'And you, aren't you cold?'

'Oh I will be ready quickly. I'll wear the dress you like tonight.'

'Yes, do wear it.'

The floor was strewn with garments, hers and mine. She stepped over them carelessly as she walked to her clothes press. 'I was thinking, I'll have another made exactly like it,' she promised happily. 'Will you be pleased?'

'Very pleased.'

If she was a child she was not a stupid child but an obstinate one. She often questioned me about England and listened attentively to my answers, but I was certain that nothing I said made much difference. Her mind was already made up. Some romantic novel, a stray remark never forgotten, a sketch, a picture, a song, a waltz, some note of music, and her ideas were fixed. About England and about Europe. I could not change them and probably nothing would. Reality might disconcert her, bewilder her, hurt her, but it would not be reality. It would be only a mistake, a misfortune, a wrong path taken, her fixed ideas would never change.

Nothing that I told her influenced her at all.

Die then. Sleep. It is all that I can give you . . . wonder if she ever guessed how near she came to dying. In her way, not in mine. It was not a safe game to play – in that place. Desire, Hatred, Life, Death came very close in the darkness. Better not know how close. Better not think, never for a moment. Not close. The same . . . 'You are safe,' I'd say to her and to myself. 'Shut your eyes. Rest.'

Then I'd listen to the rain, a sleepy tune that seemed as if it would go one for ever . . . Rain, for ever raining. Drown me in sleep. And soon.

Next morning there would be very little sign of these showers. If some of the flowers were battered, the others smelt sweeter, the air was bluer and sparkling fresh. Only the clay path outside my window was muddy. Little shallow pools of water glinted in the hot sun, red earth does not dry quickly.

KATHY ACKER

From *Kathy Goes to Haiti*

Kathy Acker published her first novel Blood and Guts in
Highschool *in 1984 and lives in San Francisco.*

*The almost instantaneous meeting and coupling with
a local man whom Kathy, the central character, has just
met whilst on some kind of unexplained and aimless
holiday in Haiti, merely serves to heighten her sense of
alienation from her environment.*

KATHY OPENS the white door and walks in. She turns around and sees Roger about six inches away from her. They kiss passionately. Tongues slither down throats. Roger pushes Kathy they topple on the bed.

'Draw your curtains.'

Kathy tries to draw the curtains and fails.

Kathy lies down next to Roger so their faces are only a few inches apart. Kathy and Roger look at each other for a long time. They reach out to each other and Roger moves down on her.

They start doing the same things at the same time without thinking about it.

Roger kisses Kathy's lips and eyes. His tongue sticks up her nostrils. His hand reaches down, under her halter, and rubs her nipples

'Do you ever come from this?' Roger asks.

'From what?'

'From having your titties played with?'

'Once I did.'

Roger bends his head, lifts the halter, and places his mouth on the brown aureole. While he licks and sucks the nipple, his hand rubs the other breast.

Kathy's so open she can't believe it.

Roger and Kathy take off their clothes. They're glad to get their clothes off cause now they can touch each other all over.

They lie on their sides so all of their front presses, and rub, and slip, shove against each other. They're constantly kissing.

Roger's upper legs thrust down between Kathy's thighs so that Roger's lying practically on top of Kathy. Kathy's dying to fuck.

Kathy's in agony. She knows this is going to be a good fuck. Roger rubs his cock-head up and down Kathy's clit and the skin around her clit. Kathy knows that Roger's playing with her but she's too hot to care.

She opens her legs wider and thrusts upward. The right part of her body rises higher than her left. Roger moves slightly backward so the back part of his cock rubs roughly against the skin at the back of Kathy's cunt. Then he moves forward so he's lying fully on top of Kathy. Kathy wants to come so badly she's thrusting and shoving and bouncing too much every which way.

Roger and Kathy roll to their sides and Kathy's left leg bends so her knee's near Roger's face. He's using his hands to push her back and forth. Kathy swings her left leg over Roger's thigh so his cock presses against the back and left side of her cunt. They begin to fuck a little bit faster.

Kathy's about to come.

Roger slips on top of Kathy. He continues fucking at the same pace. Kathy feels spasms run up and down his cock and at the same time she feels all her muscles relax, a force like a warm fire an exploding bomb and all the wants in the world, these three things together rise up her cunt muscles and then slowly into her whole body. She shakes and relaxes in Roger's arms.

'That fuck was good, but it wasn't as terrific as the buildup had promised. I've got to try harder the second time so that the fuck'll be as good as we've kind of promised each other.'

He slides down her body with his face upraised so she watches his large brown eyes. When his face reaches her cunt, he stops and his fingers open her nether lips.

'You don't have to do that.'

'I love to suck women. Sometimes I come in my pants when I'm sucking a woman I like it so much.'

Roger opens Kathy's lips and sticks his tongue into her. Kathy wants to tell Roger he's hurting her, but she doesn't because she's scared she'll hurt his feelings and he'll stop sucking her. She tries to relax to him and open herself up to him. 'If Roger likes to suck, I don't have to worry about making myself come as soon as possible. I must taste terrible cause of the dysentery.'

Kathy feels Roger's tongue move up to the extra sensitive spot where her cunt lips meet. Roger's tonguing hurts and makes Kathy feel good. The hurt increases the pleasure. The hurt disappears. Kathy feels the beginning of the rising that always comes when she relaxes.

Kathy's amazed that the rising's beginning so fast. All of her cunt skin begins to tingle. The trick is your cunt membrane has to get more and more sensitive but not so fast that you tense up cause the more you relax the more you feel. You want to feel everything. Roger touches Kathy's clit with his tongue and her clit swells. The tingling increases strength and speed. Then Roger blows on her cunt so Kathy feels almost nothing. Instantaneously she wants him to touch her even harder. By the time his tongue returns to her clit, her clit feels like a three inch long raw desirous nerve.

'Follow Roger's tongue, follow Roger's tongue. Don't let the feeling carry you away. Don't go too fast.'

The vibrations move around Kathy's cunt like a snake. Are what Roger's doing. As the vibrations run up and down, they grow fiercer and sharper so at the extreme there are these peaks of fire, tiny explosions everywhere, and nothing.

Kathy's cunt is silent, ready, nothing. Roger's tongue is the explosions, the fires, the desire. The explosions the fires the desire come faster and harder they become simultaneous and infinite.

Roger's tongue draws Kathy out of herself, makes her quiver, and puts her back, slightly changed, into herself.

'Oh my God,' Kathy says. She's in love with Roger.

Roger rises up and sticks his cock in Kathy. As soon as he moves back and forth about three times, she comes. She spreads her legs as wide as possible. She feels like she's ready for anything. He continues moving his cock slowly back and forth in her cunt. Her cunt is sensitive to feel his cock. She can feel every inch of that cock it's going into her.

He pulls out of her so that only his cock-head is lying in her cunt. He presses and rubs the upper ridge of his cock back and forth past the tight uterine opening.

Kathy can't come again because Roger's cock isn't in her. She's desperate. She begins to flex her cunt muscles. Soft. Tight. Around and around. Soft. Tight. He sticks his cock back in her and begins to fuck her good and hard. She comes again. She keeps on tensing her cunt muscles.

They're both a little crazy. They roll around so she's sitting on top of him.

She leans down over him so her breasts dangle in his eyes. His hands hold her breasts for dear life. Her clit catches against the edge of the bones above his cock. She arches her back so his cock razes the sides of her cunt. She bends back as far as she can, now she can move freely, and

Roger and Kathy begin fucking like maniacs. They crash against each other. They throw themselves against each other as hard as they can. They rub their genitals against each other like they're trying to grind each other to bits. They're too out of it to do anything but want more. Kathy comes again but she hardly knows what she's doing any more. The cheap pension double bed is bumping against the back wall and banging in time to the fucking movements. Roger rolls over Kathy so he's partially on his side and partially over Kathy. His hands hold Kathy's thighs. He moves his cock in and out of Kathy and his thighs up and down on Kathy steadily and hard. Kathy comes so much she no longer knows what coming means. Roger's body stops moving. Only his cock moves. Kathy's cunt clearly feels his cock grow smaller and larger like an accordion and hot liquid shooting out of the end of his cock.

'I get crazy when I come too much.'

'I thought women could come indefinitely.'

'I can't. When I come too hard and too much, I can't stop anymore. My body gets out of control. I shiver and shake and go crazy cause I'm so oversensitive.'

'Do you fuck a lot of men?'

'No. Not a lot. I'm alone, you know, and I've got to get laid. I've changed a lot in the past few years though. I used to fuck around all the time just fuck anyone. I can't do that. I guess fucking's getting too important to me or too serious. I can only fuck people I really go for now, and I only go for about three or four different men a year. And sometimes these men don't go for me.'

'The only person I've slept with since I started living with my wife,' Roger says, 'was this French teacher. She was staying here at L'Overture. And she really wanted it oh boy. She came after me.'

'But you fucked her?'

'I spent the night with her. But it didn't mean anything.'

'What do you do when you go out at night?'

'I drink so much you wouldn't believe it. Last month I really drank too much.'

'That's no good. Why don't you take your wife out now and then?'

'She doesn't want to go. She wants to stay shut up in the house. You know she doesn't even like to fuck. She won't let me do anything to her but fuck her how-d-you-call-it?'

'Missionary style?'

'Yes. She's from Kansas and she's very young. She stays all alone in that house and never sees anyone.'

'I'd love to meet her. I'd love to be able to talk to an American who's been in Haiti for a while.'

'Why don't you come to Le Roi tomorrow?'

'What's Le Roi?'

'It's where all of us live. Betty, me, my two brothers and their families. It's one of my father's factories.'

'What does your father do?'

'Oh, he's into lots of things. He's got lumber rubber sugar cocoa and coffee factories and plantations. He owns Cap Haitian.'

'Oh.'

'Last year the government tried to arrest him cause they wanted to take over his money. They sent some troops up here to arrest him. All the people around here stood up for my father and protected him. My father's nice to his peasants so the peasants'll protect him. The troops had to go back to Port-au-Prince. All of us are always in danger of being arrested.'

'That's why Gerard said you're "retired".'

'I'm not retired. I work at the factory as hard as Gerard works on the mountain. But I earn much more for my work than he does for his and he resents that. Everyone in this town knows who I am and resents me cause I'm my father's son.'

'Everyone watches what you do. You have no privacy.'

'Whatever I'm doing, I have to be very careful. I live out in the country where no one can spy on me. Sometimes I can relax out there.'

He gets up to go to the bathroom. Kathy hears him piss. 'Come here.'

She walks into the bathroom and sees him sitting on the toilet.

'Sit on me.'

She sits down slowly, her back facing him. His cock slides up her asshole. His hands grab her tits.

She wonders if he's still going to the bathroom. 'Shit and piss,' she thinks to herself, 'Fuck and suck what and not.'

Everything's everything else. Kathy's crouching behind the window, watching the gray cat stalk someone she can't see. 'Let's go to bed,' Roger says.

He takes Kathy's hand and leads her to the bed.

Lays her back down on the bed. 'This bed makes too much noise.'

'It's just a lousy bed.'

'Let's move it away from the wall.'

'Do I have to get up?'

'No.' He pulls the bed away from the wall so the wood head-board doesn't bang against the wall and lies down. His head is on Kathy's cunt. He sticks his tongue in Kathy's cunt and licks. Then he raises his head. His dark brown beard hairs are rubbing the lighter brown wet cunt hairs. Roger's beard hairs are partly white from sucking Kathy.

She moans.

'Now do you like my beard?' Roger asks.

'I always liked your beard.'

'But now you see why my beard's so special.'

'Oh shit.' Kathy's heat's rising. She's about to come again. Roger doesn't want her to come again from his tongue. He rises over Kathy and sticks his cock into her cunt.

Kathy doesn't exactly know what's happening. Roger and Kathy fuck and then stop fuck and then stop fuck and then stop. They're actually fucking slowly and in a steady rhythm. Kathy's cunt is so sore that Kathy comes whenever Roger's cock is inside her. Yet they're fucking slowly enough that she's not becoming hysterical. Fucking is not fucking and not fucking is fucking. No one can tell who's coming or who's not coming. No one knows and forgets anything.

'Will you really come to Le Roi tomorrow?'

'I said I would,' laughing.

'What haven't you done in bed?'

'I don't know. If I knew, I'd do it. Oh, I've never really gotten tied up and beaten or tied up and beaten someone, though I've thought about it a lot. Have you?'

'Oh yes. I once went with a girl the only way she could get off was if I tied her up and hit her. Otherwise she didn't want it, no way. I tied her wrists behind her back. I hit her hard. When she was ready she'd be writhing and shaking and then she'd want it so bad.'

'You didn't like it?'

'It was OK. I didn't care for it that much. Did you ever ass fuck?'

'Jesus Christ we were ass fucking when we were on the toilet. Couldn't you tell?'

'I was so hot, all I could think about was getting my own. I don't even know if you've been coming.'

'I've been coming enough. I'm satisfied.'

'I want to fuck you up the ass when I know it.'

'I like to fuck women. I don't do it much anymore though I used to.'

'I like when women make love with women.'

'Have you ever made it with a man?'

'I wouldn't let a man near me. I know what I want,' Roger says.

'What do you want?'

'Are you really going to come to Le Roi?'

'I said I was going to. Jesus Christ, I'm here cause I want to see as much of Haiti as possible.'

'I'd love to have you make love to my wife. That's why I want you to come to Le Roi.'

'Wait a minute. I don't go for women all that much and I definitely only go for women I want. I don't even know Betty. I'd like to meet Betty cause she's an American and cause she sounds pretty damn lonely, but that's it.'

'Maybe you and her will get something together. I want to find a woman who'll make love to my wife. That's what Betty needs.'

'Roger, even if Betty and I do do anything, that's between me and Betty. It's none of your business. What goes on between you and Betty doesn't concern me. Jesus Christ I don't even know Betty yet.'

'I don't believe you're going to come to Le Roi tomorrow.'

'How do I get to Le Roi?'

'Everyone in town knows where Le Roi is. You can ask anyone. There's a bridge and there's a big red chimney. The big red chimney's Le Roi.'

'On the way to the airport?'

'Yes.'

'I guess I'll find it.'

'What time will you come?'

'About one o'clock.'

'I'll wait for you. My father's rebuilding the factory. He has three new rum tanks. I'll show you the rum tanks, and then I'll take you in to meet Betty.'

'Are you sure it'll be OK with Betty? I don't know if she wants to meet me.'

'The only way Betty ever meets people is when I introduce them to her.'

Roger and Kathy look at each other. Their lips meet. Roger sticks his cock into Kathy's overfucked cunt. Roger comes. Kathy feels every inch of his cock spasm back and forth as clearly as she sees the white ceiling above her. Kathy's orgasm makes Kathy hot.

They stop fucking. Roger's cock is hard again. Roger wets his finger and sticks it into Kathy's ass. His finger moves around easily. He sloshes some saliva on the asshole and eases his cock into Kathy's ass. Kathy doesn't feel any pain at all.

Roger's moving his cock back and forth rapidly. Kathy's coming like a maniac. All of her ass and intestinal muscles are shaking. 'Oh oh oh,' Kathy cries. Kathy stops coming. Roger's still shaking away. Kathy feels a little pain. Kathy and Roger both come again.

JANE BOWLES

From *Two Serious Ladies*

It is the independence of spirit implicit when women feel alienated during sex that makes this state of affairs so threatening to men, and, since the great majority of Jane Bowles's work is concerned with this theme, it is no surprise that her work has been relatively ignored for fifty years whilst that of her husband, Paul Bowles, goes from celebrated strength to strength.

Born in New York, in 1917, Jane was left lame in her teens by a riding accident and married the author Paul Bowles at the age of twenty. They went to live in a Brooklyn Heights apartment block also occupied by, amongst others, W. H. Auden, Benjamin Britten and Carson McCullers. She wrote her only completed novel Two Serious Ladies *at the age of twenty-four and after many nomadic years during which they travelled all over the world, she and her husband settled in Tangiers. At the age of forty she suffered a cerebral haemorrhage following which she could no longer read or write. She died in a convent hospital in Spain in 1973.*

Two Serious Ladies *chronicles the decline and fall of two initially solid and respectable New York women (Miss Goering and Mrs Copperfield) in terms alternately hilarious and tragic. That these two central characters' quest for some late-life independence involves their solitude and social downfall seems inevitable. The women turn to the pleasures of the flesh as symbols of independence without appearing actually to enjoy a single moment of the experience. Sex is merely a political*

assertion but one which can, ironically, afford no satis-
faction beyond the spiritual.

Whilst male characters are addressed by their first
names, the female characters never get beyond the titles
by which they are known to the outside world. Here
Miss Goering is a spectator in a scene in which she is
about to lose her virginity. Whilst the male character
considers this to be of the utmost importance, Miss
Goering's mind is on more pressing issues.

SHE NOTICED with a faint heart that the man had lifted his drink from the bar and was coming towards her. He stopped about a foot away from her table and stood holding his glass in mid-air.

'You will have a drink with me, won't you?' he asked her without looking particularly cordial.

'I'm sorry,' said Frank from behind the bar, 'but we're going to close up now. No more drinks served, I'm afraid.'

Andy said nothing, but he went out the door and slammed it behind him. They could hear him walking up and down outside of the saloon.

'He's going to have his own way again,' said Frank, 'damn it all.'

'Oh, dear,' said Miss Goering, 'are you afraid of him?'

'Sure I'm not,' said Frank, 'but he's disagreeable – that's the only word I can think up for him – disagreeable; and after it's all said and done, life is too short.'

'Well,' said Miss Goering, 'is he dangerous?'

Frank shrugged his shoulders. Soon Andy came back.

'The moon and the stars are out now,' he said, 'and I could almost see clear to the edge of the town. There are no policemen in sight, so I think we can have our drink.'

He slid in, onto the bench opposite Miss Goering.

'It's cold and lifeless without a living thing on the street,' he began, 'but that's the way I like it nowadays; you'll forgive me if I sound morose to a gay woman like yourself, but I have a habit of never paying attention to whoever I am talking to. I think people would say, about me: 'Lacking in respect for other human beings.' *You* have great respect for your friends, I'm sure, but that is only because you respect yourself, which is always the starting-off point for everything: yourself.'

Miss Goering did not feel very much more at ease now that he was talking to her than she had before he had sat down. He seemed to grow more intense and almost angry as he talked, and his way of attributing qualities to her which were not in any way true to her nature gave his conversation an eerie quality and at the same time made Miss Goering feel inconsequential.

'Do you live in this town,' Miss Goering asked him.

'I do, indeed,' said Andy. 'I have three furnished rooms in a new apartment house. It is the only apartment house in this town. I pay rent every month and I live there all alone. In the afternoon the sun shines into my apartment, which is one of the finest ironies, in my opinion, because of all the apartments in the building, mine is the sunniest and I sleep there all day with my shades drawn down. I didn't always live there. I lived before in the city with my mother. But this is the nearest thing I could find to a penal island, so it suits me; it suits me fine.'

He fumbled with some cigarettes for a few minutes and kept his eyes purposely averted from Miss Goering's face. He reminded her of certain comedians who are at last given a secondary tragic role and execute it rather well. She also had a very definite impression that one thing was cleaving his simple mind in two, causing him to twist between his sheets instead of sleeping, and to lead an altogether wretched existence. She had no doubt that she would soon find out what it was.

'You have a very special type of beauty,' he said to her; 'a bad nose, but beautiful eyes and hair. It would please me in the midst of all this horror to go to bed with you. But in order to do this we'll have to leave this bar and go to my apartment.'

'Well, I can't promise you anything, but I will be glad to go to your apartment,' said Miss Goering.

Andy told Frank to call the hackstand and tell a certain man who was on duty all night to come over and get them.

The taxi drove down the main street very slowly. It was very old and consequently it rattled a good deal. Andy stuck his head out of the window.

'How do you do, ladies and gentlemen?' he shouted at the empty street, trying to approximate an English accent. 'I hope, I certainly hope that each and every one of you is having a fine time in this great town of ours.' He leaned back against his seat again and smiled in such a horrid manner that Miss Goering felt frightened again.

'You could roll a hoop down this street, naked, at midnight and no one would ever know it,' he said to her.

'Well, if you think it is such a dismal place,' said Miss

Goering, 'why don't you move somewhere else, bag and baggage?'

'Oh, no,' he said gloomily, 'I'll never do that. There's no use in my doing that.'

'Is it that your business ties you down here?' Miss Goering asked him, although she knew perfectly well he was speaking of something spiritual and far more important.

'Don't call me a business man,' he said to her.

'Then you are an artist?'

He shook his head vaguely as though not quite sure what an artist was.

'Well, all right,' said Miss Goering, 'I've had two guesses; now won't you tell me what you are?'

'A bum!' he said stentoriously, sliding lower in his seat. 'You knew that all the time, didn't you, being an intelligent woman?'

The taxicab drew up in front of the apartment house, which stood between an empty lot and a string of stores only one story high.

'You see, I get the afternoon sun all day long,' he said, 'because I have no obstructions. I look out over this empty lot.'

'There is a tree growing in the empty lot,' said Miss Goering. 'I suppose that you are able to see it from your window?'

'Yes,' said Andy. 'Weird, isn't it?'

The apartment house was very new and very small. They stood together in the lobby while Andy searched his pockets for the keys. The floor was of imitation marble, yellow in colour except in the centre where the architect had set in a blue peacock in mosaic, surrounded by various long-stemmed flowers. It was hard to distinguish the peacock in the dim light, but Miss Goering crouched down on her heels to examine it better.

'I think those are water lilies around that peacock,' said Andy, 'But a peacock is supposed to have thousands of colours in him, isn't he? Multicoloured, isn't that the point of a peacock? This one's all blue.'

'Well,' said Miss Goering, 'perhaps it is nicer this way.'

They left the lobby and went up some ugly iron steps. Andy lived on the first floor. There was a terrible odor in the hall, which he told her never went away.

'They're cooking in there for ten people,' he said, 'all day long.

They all work at different hours of the day; half of them don't see the other half at all, except on Sundays and holidays.'

Andy's apartment was very hot and stuffy. The furniture was brown and none of the cushions appeared to fit the chairs properly.

'Here's journey's end,' said Andy. 'Make yourself at home. I'm going to take off some of my clothes.' He returned in a minute wearing a bathrobe made of some very cheap material. Both ends of his bathrobe cords had been partially chewed away.

'What happened to your bathrobe cords?' Miss Goering asked him.

'My dog chewed them away.'

'Oh, have you a dog?' she asked him

'Once upon a time I had a dog and a future, and a girl,' he said, 'but that is no longer so.'

'Well, what happened?' Miss Goering asked, throwing her shawl off her shoulders and mopping her forehead with her handkerchief. The steam heat had already begun to make her sweat, particularly as she had not been used to central heating for some time.

'Let's not talk about my life,' said Andy, putting his hand up like a traffic officer. 'Let's have some drinks instead.'

'All right, but I certainly think we should talk about your life sooner or later,' said Miss Goering. All the while she was thinking that she would allow herself to go home within an hour. 'I consider,' she said to herself, 'that I have done quite well for my first night.' Andy was standing up and pulling his bathrobe cord tighter around the waist.

'I was,' he said, 'engaged to be married to a very nice girl who worked. I loved her as much as a man can love a woman. She had a smooth forehead, beautiful blue eyes, and not so good teeth. Her legs were something to take pictures of. Her name was Mary and she got along with my mother. She was a plain girl with an ordinary mind and she used to get a tremendous kick out of life. Sometimes we used to have dinner at midnight just for the hell of it and she used to say to me: "Imagine us, walking down the street at midnight to have our dinner. Just two ordinary people. Maybe there isn't any sanity." Naturally, I didn't tell her that there were plenty of people like the people who live down the hall in 5D who eat dinner at midnight, not because they are crazy, but because they've got jobs that cause them to do so, because then maybe she wouldn't have got so much fun out of it. I wasn't going to spoil it and tell her that the world wasn't crazy, that the world was medium fair; and I didn't know either that a couple of months later her sweetheart was going to become one of the craziest people in it.'

The veins in Andy's forehead were beginning to bulge, his face was redder, and the wings of his nostrils were sweaty.

'All this must really mean something to him,' thought Miss Goering.

'Often I used to go into an Italian restaurant for dinner; it was right around the corner from my house; I knew mostly all the people that ate there, and the atmosphere was very convivial. There were a few of us who always ate together. I always bought the wine because I was better fixed than most of them. Then there were a couple of old men who ate there, but we never bothered with them. There was one man too who wasn't so old, but he was solitary and didn't mix in with the others. We knew he used to be in the circus, but we never found out what kind of a job he had there or anything. Then one night, the night before he brought her in, I happened to be gazing at him for no reason on earth and I saw him stand up and fold his newspaper into his pocket, which was peculiar-looking because he hadn't finished his dinner yet. Then he turned towards us and coughed like he was clearing his throat.

' "Gentlemen," he said, "I have an announcement to make." I had to quiet the boys because he had such a thin little voice you could hardly hear what he was saying.

' "I am not going to take much of your time," he continued, like someone talking at a big banquet, "but I just want to tell you and you'll understand why in a minute. I just want to tell you that I'm bringing a young lady here tomorrow night and without any reservations I want you all to love her: This lady, gentleman, is like a broken doll. She has neither arms nor legs." Then he sat down very quietly and started right in eating again.'

'How terribly embarrassing!' said Miss Goering. 'Dear me, what did you answer to that?'

'I don't remember,' said Andy, 'I just remember that it was

embarrassing like you say and we didn't feel that he had to make the announcement anyway.

'She was already in her chair the next night when we got there; nicely made up and wearing a very pretty, clean blouse pinned in front with a brooch shaped like a butterfly. Her hair was marcelled too and she was a natural blonde. I kept my ear cocked and I heard her telling the little man that her appetite got better all the time and that she could sleep fourteen hours a day. After that I began to notice her mouth. It was like a rose petal or a heart or some kind of a little shell. It was really beautiful. Then right away I started to wonder what she would be like; the rest of her, you understand – without any legs.' He stopped talking and walked around the room once, looking up at his walls.

'It came into my mind like an ugly snake, this idea, and curled there to stay. I looked at her head so little and so delicate against the dark grimy wall and it was the apple of sin that I was eating for the first time.'

'Really for the first time?' said Miss Goering. She looked bewildered and was lost in thought for a moment.

'From then on I thought of nothing else but finding out; every other thought left my head.'

'And before what were your thoughts like?' Miss Goering asked him a little maliciously. He didn't seem to hear her.

'Well, this went on for some time – the way I felt about her. I was seeing Belle, who came to the restaurant often, after that first night, and I was seeing Mary too. I got friendly with Belle. There was nothing special about her. She loved wine and I actually used to pour it down her throat for her. She talked a little bit too much about her family and was a little good. Not exactly religious, but a little too full of the milk of human kindness sort of thing. It grew and grew, this terrible curiosity or desire of mine until finally my mind started to wander when I was with Mary and I couldn't sleep with her any more. She was swell all the way through it, though, patient as a lamb. She was much too young to have such a thing happen to her. I was like a horrible old man or one of those impotent kings with a history of syphilis behind him.'

'Did you tell your sweetheart what was getting on your nerves?' asked Miss Goering, trying to hurry him up a bit.

'I didn't tell her because I wanted the buildings to stay in place for her and I wanted the stars to be over her head and not cockeyed – I wanted her to be able to walk in the park and feed the birdies in years to come with some other fine human being hanging onto her arm. I didn't want her to have to lock something up inside of her and look out at the world through a nailed window. It was not long before I went to bed with Belle and got myself a beautiful case of syphilis, which I spent the next two years curing. I took to bowling along about then and I finally left my mother's house and my work and came out to No-man's Land. I can live in this apartment all right on a little money that I get from a building I own down in the slums of the city.'

He sat down in a chair opposite Miss Goering and put his face in his hands. Miss Goering judged that he had finished and she was just about to thank him for his hospitality and wish him good-night when he uncovered his face and began again.

'The worst of all I remember clearly; more and more I couldn't face my mother. I'd stay out bowling all day long and half the night. Then on the fourth day of July I decided that I would make a very special effort to spend the day with her. There was a big parade supposed to go by our window at three in the afternoon. Very near to that time I was standing in the parlour with a pressed suit on, and Mother was sitting as close to the window as she could get. It was a sunny day out and just right for a parade. The parade was punctual because about a quarter to three we began to hear some faint music in the distance. Then soon after that my country's red, white, and blue flag went by, held up by some fine-looking boys. The band was playing *Yankee Doodle*. All of a sudden I hid my face in my hands; I couldn't look at my country's flag. Then I knew, once and for all, that I hated myself. Since then I have accepted my status as a skunk. "Citizen Skunk" happens to be a little private name I have for myself. You can have some fun in the mud, though, you know, if you just accept a seat in it instead of trying to squirm around.'

'Well,' said Miss Goering, 'I certainly think you could pull yourself together with a bit of an effort. I wouldn't put much stock in the flag episode either.'

He looked at her vaguely. 'You talk like a society lady,' he said to her.

'I am a society lady,' said Miss Goering. 'I am also rich, but I have purposely reduced my living standards. I have left my lovely home and I have moved out to a little house on the island. The house is in very bad shape and costs me practically nothing. What do you think of that?'

'I think you're cuckoo,' said Andy, and not at all in a friendly tone. He was frowning darkly. 'People like you shouldn't be allowed to have money.'

Miss Goering was surprised to hear him making such a show of righteous indignation.

'Please,' she said, 'could you possible open the window?'

'There will be an awfully cold wind blowing through here if I do,' said Andy.

'Nevertheless,' said Miss Goering, 'I think I would prefer it.'

'I'll tell you,' said Andy, moving uncomfortably around his chair. 'I just put in a bad spell of grippe and I'm dead afraid of getting into a draft.' He bit his lip and looked terribly worried. 'I could go and stand in the next room if you want while you get your breath of fresh air,' he added, brightening up a bit.

'That's a jolly good idea,' said Miss Goering.

He left and closed the bedroom door softly behind him. She was delighted with the chance to get some cool air, and after she had opened the window she placed her two hands on the sill far apart from each other and leaned out. She would have enjoyed this far more had she not been certain that Andy was standing still in his room consumed with boredom and impatience. He still frightened her a little and at the same time she felt that he was a terrible burden. There was a gas station opposite the apartment house. Although the office was deserted at the moment, it was brightly lighted and a radio on the desk had been left on. There was a folk-song coming over the air. Soon there was a short rap at the bedroom door, which was just what she had been expecting to hear. She closed the window regretfully before the tune had finished.

'Come in,' she called to him, 'come in.' She was dismayed to see when Andy opened the door that he had removed all of his clothing with the exception of his socks and his underdrawers. He did not seem to be embarrassed, but behaved as though they had both tacitly understood that he was to appear dressed in this fashion.

He walked with her to the couch and made her sit down beside him. Then he flung his arm around her and crossed his legs. His legs were terribly thin, and on the whole he looked inconsequential now that he had removed his clothing. He pressed his cheek to Miss Goering's.

'Do you think you could make me a little happy?' he asked her.

'For heaven's sake,' said Miss Goering, sitting bolt upright, 'I thought you were beyond that.'

'Well, no man can really look into the future, you know.' He narrowed his eyes and attempted to kiss her.

'Now, about that woman,' she said, 'Belle, who had neither arms nor legs?'

'Please, darling, let's not discuss her now. Will you do me that favour?' His tone was a little sneering, but there was an undercurrent of excitement in his voice. He said: 'Now tell me whatever it is that you like. You know . . . I haven't lost all my time these two years. There are a few little things I pride myself on.'

Miss Goering looked very solemn. She was thinking of this very seriously, because she suspected that were she to accept Andy's offer it would be far more difficult for her to put a stop to her excursions, should she feel so disposed. Until recently she had never followed too dangerously far in action any course which she had decided upon as being the morally correct one. She scarcely approved of this weakness in herself, but she was to a certain extent sensible and happy enough to protect herself automatically. She was feeling a little tipsy, however, and Andy's suggestion rather appealed to her. 'One must allow that a certain amount of carelessness in one's nature often accomplishes what the will is incapable of doing,' she said to herself.

Andy looked towards the bedroom door. His mood seemed to have changed very suddenly and he seemed confused. 'This does not mean that he is not lecherous,' thought Miss Goering. He got up and wandered around the room. Finally he pulled an old gramophone out from behind the couch. He took up a good deal of time dusting it off and collecting some needles that were scattered around and underneath the turntable. As he knelt over the instrument he became quite absorbed in what he was doing and his face took on an almost sympathetic aspect.

'It's a very old machine,' he mumbled. 'I got it a long, long time ago.'

The machine was very small and terribly out of date, and had Miss Goering been sentimental, she would have felt a little sad watching him; however, she was growing impatient.

'I can't hear a word that you are saying,' she shouted at him in an unnecessarily loud voice.

He got up without answering her and went into his room. When he returned he was again wearing his bathrobe and holding a record in his hand.

'You'll think I'm silly,' he said, 'bothering with that machine so long, when all I've got to play for you is this one record. It's a march; here.' He handed it to her in order that she might read the title of the piece and the name of the band that was executing it.

'Maybe,' he said, 'you'd rather not hear it. A lot of people don't like march music.'

'No, do play it,' said Miss Goering. 'I'll be delighted, really.'

He put the record on and sat on the edge of a very uncomfortable chair at quite a distance from Miss Goering. The needle was too loud and the march was the *Washington Post*. Miss Goering felt as uneasy as one can feel listening to parade music in a quiet room. Andy seemed to be enjoying it and he kept time with his feet during the entire length of the record. But when it was over he seemed to be in an even worse state of confusion than before.

'Would you like to see the apartment?' he asked her.

Miss Goering leaped up from the couch quickly lest he should change his mind.

'A woman who made dresses had this apartment before me, so my bedroom is kind of sissyish for a man.'

She followed him into the bedroom. He had turned the bed down rather badly and the slips of the two pillows were gray and wrinkled. On his dresser were pictures of several girls, all of them terribly unattractive and plain. They looked more to Miss Goering like the church-going type of young woman than like the mistresses of a bachelor.

'They're nice-looking girls, aren't they?' said Andy to Miss Goering.

'Lovely-looking,' she said, 'lovely.'

'None of these girls live in this town,' he said. 'They live in different towns in the vicinity. The girls here are guarded and they don't like bachelors my age. I don't blame them. I go take one of these girls in the pictures out now and then when I feel like it. I even sit in their living-rooms of an evening with them, with their parents right in the house. But they don't see much of me, I can tell you that.'

Miss Goering was growing more and more puzzled, but she didn't ask him any more questions because she was suddenly feeling weary.

'I think I'll be on my way now,' she said, swaying a little on her feet. She realized immediately how rude and unkind she was being and she saw Andy tightening up. He put his fists into his pockets.

'Well, you can't go now,' he said to her. 'Stay a little longer and I'll make you some coffee.'

'No, no, I don't want any coffee. Anyway, they'll be worrying about me at home.'

'Who's they?' Andy asked her.

'Arnold and Arnold's father and Miss Gamelon.'

'It sounds like a terrible mob to me,' he said. 'I couldn't stand living with a crowd like that.'

'I love it,' said Miss Goering.

He put his arms around her and tried to kiss her, but she pulled away, 'No, honestly, I'm much too tired.'

'All right,' he said, 'all right!' His brow was deeply furrowed and he looked completely miserable. He took his bathrobe off and got into his bed. He lay there with the sheet up to his neck, threshing his feet about and looking up at the ceiling like someone with a fever. There was a small light burning on the table beside the bed which shone directly into his face, so that Miss Goering was able to distinguish many lines which she had not noticed before. She went over to his bed and leaned over him.

'What *is* the matter?' she asked him. 'Now it's been a very pleasant evening and we all need some sleep.'

He laughed in her face. 'You're some lunatic,' he said to her, 'and you sure don't know anything about people. I'm all right here, though.' He pulled the sheet up farther and lay there breathing heavily. 'There's a five o'clock ferry that leaves in about a half hour. Will you come back tomorrow evening? I'll be where I was tonight at that bar.'

She promised him that she would return on the following evening, and after he had explained to her how to get to the dock, she opened his window for him and left.

JENNY DISKI

From *Nothing Natural*

Jenny Diski was born in London in 1947 where she lives with her daughter. Nothing Natural was her first novel. Her books set out to challenge the arbitrary nature of socially accepted norms.

[Two]

THREE YEARS before, just after Michael had moved out, Rachel met Joshua at a dinner party. They had been invited so that they could meet. Molly Cassel, an old school friend of Rachel's, liked throwing people together and when she heard that Rachel and Michael had separated was immediately on the phone.

'Rachel,' Molly had enthused. 'You must come and meet my friend Joshua.'

'Why? I'm not really in the mood for meeting men. What's so special?'

'Well, he's a strange bloke. Very clever, but a bit odd. Not someone to get involved with, but interesting.'

'So far it sounds like I could live without him. Why isn't he someone to get involved with? Not,' she added hurriedly, 'that I'm a candidate for involvement.'

'Oh, he screws around a lot, but never more than once with any one woman. He really messes people up. He's got two kids from an ex-marriage he sees all the time, but he's a bit weird about women.'

'Molly, you're doing a lousy selling job. I don't need a one-night stand; I don't need anything actually. Anyway, what's his problem with women?' This wasn't genuine curiosity, just conversation.

'I don't know. He's really a friend of Tom's. I suppose he gets bored easily.'

'Very easily. This is the least enticing invitation I've had in weeks. Thanks all the same but I'll skip it. He probably can't get it up more than once. Low sex drive type. Woman hater.'

'Mm . . . I gather that's pretty much it, about not getting it up, I mean. But he's terribly clever, you'd enjoy talking to him.'

'No!'

Three weeks later, the telephone conversation forgotten, Molly had invited her to dinner. Rachel, having just seen off her current lover and thereby what remained of her social life, went with a minimum of enthusiasm. She arrived late to find Molly, Tom and

Joshua already seated at the refectory table dipping into the houmous. She glared briefly at Molly as she was introduced to Joshua, and sitting at the table prepared to jolly her way through another pointless evening. She recollected what a waste of time socializing was and how much she liked spending the evenings alone in her flat. She longed to be there.

Joshua smiled at her. He directed a beam of gleaming white teeth and knowing amusement straight towards her; he shone himself at her.

Oh shit, she thought, I've seen this one before. The Charmer.

Joshua gave her his full and undivided attention, smiling all the while. The questions came thick and fast, impudently personal while the shining white grin rubbed the edge of rudeness off them. The act was excellent, but it *was* one she had seen before, and she found herself watching his technique with some admiration. She answered his questions as frankly as he put them as if she were being interviewed. So she had split up with her husband? Yes, well they'd never found a way of introducing each other at parties – my husband, my wife, never slipped comfortably from their lips, so they had decided that my ex-husband etc. came much more easily. Relations were cordial, she added. But why had they broken up? Well, they'd been leading separate lives sexually for some time and it had got harder and harder to organize what with living in the same place, so Michael had bought a flat just round the corner. Hadn't they been jealous of each others' affairs? Yes and no, but mostly no.

And so on. All the time smiling and polite. Her life history was requested and given with some major omissions. She had been adopted? And had she known Molly for long? A teacher? And what did she enjoy doing?

'Dancing, reading and fucking,' Rachel replied with a polite social smile on her face.

Molly choked on her fruit salad while Tom, a dour individual, examined his spoon carefully to check he had eaten everything on it with the last mouthful. Joshua's grin, improbably, doubled. There had been all along a collusion between himself and Rachel; they looked each other squarely in the eyes as they spoke, each knowing that the other knew precisely what the game was. The act was good, total attention with just a touch of superiority;

enough to flatter Rachel while at the same time making her feel uneasy, slightly attacked. She was to be hypnotized by his dark, intent eyes and the paradoxically enchanting, easy smile. She was to be thrown off balance but feel that somehow he was really interested in her, just her. A fascinated rabbit dying to be gobbled up.

Except, she thought, that I see through you, sunshine. You're just a little too calculating, or I'm a little too smart.

At the end of the evening he stood up and offered her a lift home. She looked at him in his tweed suit: the clothes were good, not too smart. He was a large man, plump actually, but tall enough not to look absurd. She liked large – fat – men; small thin ones left her cold, literally. He looked grown up, confident, his wide fleshy face made massive by the deep furrows that outlined his mouth and ran seriously across his spacious brow; his beard was one of those carefully contrived to seem no more than a reluctance to shave but was in fact a permanent face-altering feature, his short grey hair was shot through with its original black. He didn't look like a sexual incompetent, but you never could tell. More often than not the confidence was all exterior and once the clothes were off it broke apart to reveal, yet again, a little boy. But it might be interesting to see what was what. She wasn't committed one way or another and at worst she was in for a single boring night, if Molly was right. She didn't feel in any way threatened by this man, on the contrary, she felt that she controlled the situation. She had loaned her car to Michael who had Carrie for the night, so she accepted the lift.

She was relieved to be back in her own territory, as she turned on the living room lights. Joshua prowled around reading book titles on her shelves, investigating the kitchen which opened out from the living room. It was a good, comfortable place; an old sofa covered with a North African rug, an armchair, stripped wooden chests acting as surfaces for rocks and shells gathered from various seashores, and bookshelves filling the alcoves. Rachel's small rural longings were catered for by masses of plants which flourished wherever light and available space permitted. She turned on the kitchen light to make coffee; Joshua turned it off.

'I don't want anything. Put on some music.'

Oh dear, Rachel thought, and began to feel a little gloomy. When it came to it even one boring night seemed too much. She imagined herself, as she put on a tape of vintage Fred Astaire, lying awake beside a sleeping post-coital man, the hours dragging slowly by. He would certainly snore, and she would lie gazing into the darkness wishing him away, wishing him never there in the first place, wanting her bed to herself, remembering that mediocre sex wasn't better than none at all.

Maybe, she mused, I'd better send him home now, he's not even all that attractive. There certainly wasn't that ache deep in her abdomen that made him necessary to her. But he held her now and moved slowly to the music with her in his arms. He had turned off all the other lights so that the room was in darkness and as they rocked softly together she knew it was too late to tell him to go. She decided that she'd just have to put up with the night ahead; she didn't want a scene, and in any case, it wasn't unpleasant, swaying in the darkness. Joshua kissed her slowly and then led her by the hand next door into the unlit bedroom. He undressed her efficiently while she stood passive, watching his face as his fingers undid the buttons of the teeshirt she normally just pulled over her head. When she was naked he ran his hands down her back and slowly over her buttocks, then lay her on the bed while he took off his own clothes carefully, unhurriedly. She lay watching him, and sensing his extraordinary confidence began to feel what she had been supposed to feel at dinner – impressed, excited, uncertain. Now she wanted him.

Joshua got on to the bed beside her, on his side, resting on his elbow. His hand moved across her belly and up to stroke each breast, then, as his hand moved down towards her vulva he ducked his head and sucked for a moment at each nipple. Lifting his head he looked carefully at her face, watching; a long, cold stare. He kept his eyes on her all the time, his face impassive, observing, as his fingers found her vulva. He parted the labia and began expertly to massage her clitoris, all the time keeping his eyes on her face, observing her reactions, like a technician working on a new model of a machine he had spent a lifetime servicing. The long, slow strokes gave way, as she got wetter, to a circular motion, and she began to breathe deeper and faster as he increased the pressure and speed. Her eyes became vague and distant, focusing on the waves rising from her wet, excited cunt and the sudden overwhelming need to be penetrated, filled. He slipped a finger deep inside her and she gasped, breathing heavier, beginning to moan softly as thumb rubbed clitoris and finger moved slowly inside. Joshua watched unblinking as she started to move her pelvis rhythmically up and down against the movement of his hand to increase the pressure and dropped her knees against the bed so that she was wide open. She came with small sharp cries, lifting her hips off the bed, arching her back and grasping the arm that still worked on her between her thighs, pressing hard against the heel of his hand to the rhythm of the contractions pulsing inside her.

'Please . . . please . . .' she sobbed, then holding her breath for a long moment relaxed down beside him, releasing the air in her lungs and feeling her heart pounding. Joshua pulled her on top of him and she saw his face beneath her, the eyes still watching, cold, but glistening icily with excitement. He put her hand onto his penis so that she could guide it into her, and then with his hands on her hips moved her very slowly up and down. As she began to come again she felt and heard him slapping her, quite gently, on the bottom, almost tentatively, and when he saw that she continued to move, a little harder not so that it hurt but so that the sound of each slap rang around the room.

Christ, she thought, this is new. What is this?

Then the feeling of his penis inside her, the sound, and the smarting on her buttocks made her come with long deep moans and she heard and felt him coming in grunting spasms.

She lay sprawled on his chest for a long while, catching her breath and feeling her body gradually quieten. She wondered in the silence about the smacking. She had never been with anyone who was into spanking – she supposed that was what it was. She was curious and a little embarrassed, but also excited by it.

'Fancy a fuck?' Joshua spoke jauntily into her ear in his rich acquired Oxbridge tones.

'What did you say your name was? Never mind, let's do it!'

He rolled over so that she was underneath him and this time fucked her hard and fast, whispering, 'Can you feel me deep inside you? Suck me into you.'

His eyes remained open all the time still looking angrily at her and when they had both come he pulled out of her almost immediately so that Rachel had to catch her breath at the suddenness of his absence. Then he lay still with one arm around her, his eyes finally closed.

Rachel lay in the dark room next to the sleeping man who breathed heavily.

Well, that wasn't what I'd been led to expect, she thought. It was, on the whole, worth a sleepless night, she decided. She dozed off and on, waking often with sudden starts. Once Joshua woke as she jerked awake and whispered to her, 'It's all right, darling, it's me, Joshua, don't be frightened.'

They both woke early, she a little before him, and as he opened his eyes and oriented himself she saw him stare sharply at her before he realized that she was awake too. He was out of bed instantly.

'I've got to go. Taking the kids to the country today. No, I don't want tea. Thanks.'

He was dressed within seconds, glanced at her briefly and nodded a curt, unsmiling ''Bye' as he left barely five minutes after he had woken.

'Jesus,' Rachel whispered to the icy cloud that hung heavily in her bedroom. 'Jesus Christ.'

MARY McCARTHY

From *The Group*

Mary McCarthy was born in Seattle, Washington and educated during the 1930s at Vassar, a leading liberal ladies' college of the time. After graduating she worked as an editorial assistant, an editor, a theatre critic and a teacher. Her second husband was the well-known American critic, Edmund Wilson. She had one child and wrote a large number of novels, travel books and an autobiography. She died in 1989.

The Group, published in 1963 and by far her best known work, is the story of eight young women who graduate from Vassar in 1933 and the choices that they are allowed to make in their lives. In this extract Dottie has sex for the first time with a man she barely knows and though she realizes that she enjoys the experience, she is nevertheless extremely embarrassed to have felt such enjoyment. Just as in Two Serious Ladies, *Dottie sees the experience as one in which she is somehow a spectator rather than a participant and, thus alienated, and though she calls the man with whom she has sex 'Dick', Dottie herself is impersonally referred to as 'Boston' – not even a surname but a nickname derived from the place she comes from and what she represents.*

[Chapter 2]

JUST AT FIRST, in the dark hallway, it had given Dottie rather a funny feeling to be tiptoeing up the stairs only two nights after Kay's wedding to a room right across from Harald's old room, where the same thing had happened to Kay. An awesome feeling, really, like when the group all got the curse at the same time; it filled you with strange ideas about being a woman, with the moon compelling you like the tides. All sorts of weird, irrelevant ideas floated through Dottie's head as the key turned in the lock and she found herself, for the first time, alone with a man in his flat. Tonight was midsummer's night, the summer solstice, when maids had given up their treasure to fructify the crops; she had that in background reading for *A Midsummer Night's Dream*. Her Shakespeare teacher had been awfully keen on anthropology and had had them study in Frazer about the ancient fertility rites and how the peasants in Europe, till quite recent times, had lit big bonfires in honour of the Corn Maiden and then lain together in the fields. College, reflected Dottie as the lamp clicked on, had been almost *too* rich an experience. She felt stuffed with interesting thoughts that she could only confide in Mother, not in a man, certainly, who would probably suppose you were barmy if you started telling him about the Corn Maiden when you were just about to lose your virginity. Even the group would laugh if Dottie confessed that she was exactly in the mood for a long, comfy discussion with Dick, who was so frightfully attractive and unhappy and had to much to give.

But the group would never believe, never in a million years, that Dottie Renfrew would come here, to this attic room that smelled of cooking-fat, with a man she hardly knew, who made no secret of his intentions, who had been drinking heavily, and who was evidently not in love with her. When she put it that way, crudely, she could scarcely believe it herself, and the side of her that wanted to talk was still hoping, probably, to gain a little time, the way, she had noticed, she always started a discussion of current events with the dentist to keep him from turning on the drill.

Dottie's dimple twinkled. What an odd comparison! If the group could hear that!

And yet when It happened, it was not at all what the group or even Mother would have imagined, not a bit sordid or messy, in spite of Dick's being tight. He had been most considerate, undressing her slowly, in a matter-of-fact way, as if he were helping her off with her outdoor things. He took her hat and furs and put them in the closet and then unfastened her dress, bending over the snaps with a funny, concentrated scowl, rather like Daddy's when he was hooking Mother up for a party. Lifting the dress carefully off her, he had glanced at the label and then back at Dottie, as though to match the two, before he carried it, walking very steadily to the closet and arranged it on a wooden hanger. After that, he folded each garment as he removed it and set it ceremoniously on the armchair, looking each time at the label with a frown between his brows. When her dress was gone, she felt rather faint for a minutes, but he left her in her slip, just as they did in the doctor's office, while he took off her shoes and stockings and undid her brassière and girdle and step-ins, so that finally, when he drew her slip over her head, with great pains so as not to muss her hairdo, she was hardly trembling when she stood there in front of him with nothing on but her pearls. Perhaps it was going to the doctor so much or perhaps it was Dick himself, so detached and impersonal, the way they were supposed to be in art class with the model, that made Dottie brave. He had not touched her once, all the time he was undressing her, except by accident, grazing her skin. Then he pinched each of her full breasts lightly and told her to relax, in just the tone Dr Perry used when he was going to give her a treatment for her sciatica.

He handed her a book of drawings to look at, while he went into the closet, and Dottie sat there in the armchair, trying not to listen. With the book on her lap, she studied the room conscientiously, in order to know Dick better. Rooms told a lot about a person. It had a skylight and a big north window and was surprisingly neat for a man; there was a drawing-board with some work on it which she longed to peek at, a long plain table, like an ironing-table, monk's-cloth curtains, and a monk's-cloth spread on the single bed. On the chest of drawers was a framed photograph of a blonde woman, very striking, with a short, severe haircut; that must be 'Betty', the wife. Tacked up on the wall there was a snapshot that looked like her in a bathing-suit and a number of sketches from the nude, and Dottie had the sinking feeling that they might be of Betty too. She had been doing her very best not to let herself think about love or let her emotions get entangled, for she knew that Dick would not like it. It was just a physical attraction, she had been telling herself over and over, while trying to remain cool and collected despite the pounding of her blood, but now, suddenly, when it was too late to retreat, she had lost her sang-froid and was jealous. Worse than that, even, the idea came to her that Dick was, well, *peculiar*. She opened the book of drawings on her lap and found more nudes, signed by some modern artist she had never heard of! She did not know, a second later, just what she had been expecting, but Dick's return was, by contrast, less bad.

He came in wearing a pair of white shorts and carrying a towel, with a hotel's name on it, which he stretched out on the bed, having turned back the covers. He took the book away from her and put it on a table. Then he made Dottie lie down on the towel, telling her to relax again, in a friendly, instructive voice; while he stood for a minute, looking down at her and smiling, with his hands on his hips, she tried to breathe naturally, reminding herself that she had a good figure, and forced a wan, answering smile to her lips. '*Nothing will happen unless you want it, baby.*' The words, lightly stressed, told her how scared and mistrustful she must be looking. 'I know, Dick,' she answered, in a small, weak, grateful voice, making herself use his name aloud for the first time. 'Would you like a cigarette?' Dottie shook her head and let it drop back on the pillow. 'All right, then?' 'All right.' As he moved to turn out the light, she felt a sudden harsh thump of excitement, right in *there*, like what had happened to her in the Italian restaurant when he said 'Do you want to come home with me?' and fastened his deep, shadowed eyes on her. Now he turned and looked at her steadily again, his hand on the bridge lamp; her own eyes, widening with amazement at the funny feeling she noticed, as if she were on fire, in the place her thighs were shielding, stared at him, seeking confirmation; she swallowed. In reply, he switched off the lamp and came towards her in the dark, unbuttoning his shorts.

This shift gave her an instant in which to be afraid. She had never seen *that* part of a man, except in statuary and once, at the age of six, when she had interrupted Daddy in his bath, but she had a suspicion that it would be something ugly and darkly inflamed, surrounded by coarse hair. Hence, she had been very grateful for being spared the sight of it, which she did not think could have borne, and she held her breath as the strange body climbed on hers, shrinking. 'Open your legs,' he commanded, and her legs obediently fell apart. His hand squeezed her down there, rubbing and stroking; her legs fell farther apart, and she started to make weak, moaning noises, almost as if she wanted him to stop. He took his hand away, thank heaven, and fumbled for a second; then she felt it, the thing she feared, being guided into her as she braced herself and stiffened. 'Relax,' he whispered. 'You're ready.' It was surprisingly warm and smooth, but it hurt terribly, pushing and stabbing. 'Damn it,' he said. 'Relax. You're making it harder.' Just then, Dottie screamed faintly; it had gone all the way in. He put his hand over her mouth and then settled her legs around him and commenced to move it back and forth inside her. At first, it hurt so that she flinched at each stroke and tried to pull back, but this only seemed to make him more determined. Then, while she was still praying for it to be over, surprise of surprises, she started to like it a little. She got the idea, and her body began to move too in answer, as he pressed *that* home in her slowly, over and over, and slowly drew it back, as if repeating a question. Her breath came quicker. Each lingering stroke, like a violin bow, made her palpitate for the next. Then, all of a sudden, she seemed to explode in a series of long, uncontrollable contractions that embarrassed her, like the hiccups, the moment they were over, for it was as if she had forgotten Dick as a person; and he, as if he sensed this, pulled quickly away from her and thrust that part of himself onto her stomach, where it pushed and pounded at her flesh. Then he too jerked and moaned, and Dottie felt something damp and sticky running down the hill of her belly.

Minutes passed; the room was absolutely still; through the skylight Dottie could see the moon. She lay there, with Dick's weight still on her, suspecting that something had gone wrong – probably her fault. His face was turned sideward so that she could not look into it, and his chest was squashing her breasts so that she could hardly breathe. Both their bodies were wet, and the cold perspiration from him ran down her face and matted her side hair and made a little rivulet between her breasts; on her lips it had a salty sting that reminded her forlornly of tears. She was ashamed of the happiness she had felt. Evidently, he had not found her satisfactory as a partner or else he would say something. Perhaps the woman was not supposed to move? 'Damn it,' he had said to her, when he was hurting her, in such a testy voice, like a man saying 'Damn it, why can't we have dinner on time?' or something unromantic like that. Was it her screaming out that had spoiled everything? Or had she made a *faux pas* at the end somehow? She wished that books were a little more explicit; Krafft-Ebing, which Kay and Helena had found at a secondhand bookstore and kept reading aloud from, as if it were very funny, mostly described nasty things like men making love to hens, and even then did not explain how it was done. The thought of the blonde on the bureau filled her with hopeless envy; probably Dick at this moment was making bitter comparisons. She could feel his breathing and smell the stale alcohol that came from him in gusts. In the bed, there was a peculiar pungent odour, and she feared that it might come from her.

The horrible idea occurred to her that he had fallen asleep, and she made a few gentle movements to try to extricate herself from under him. Their damp skins, stuck together, made a little sucking noise when she pulled away, but she could not roll his weight off her. Then she knew that he was asleep. Probably he was tired, she said to herself forgivingly; he had those dark rings under his eyes. But down in her heart she knew that he ought not to have gone to sleep like a ton of bricks on top of her; it was the final proof, if she still needed one, that she meant nothing to him. When he woke up tomorrow morning and found her gone, he would probably be glad. Or perhaps he would not even remember who had been there with him; she could not guess how much he had had to drink before he met her for dinner. What had happened, she feared, was that he had simply passed out. She saw that her only hope of saving her own dignity was to dress in the dark and steal away.

But she would have to find the bathroom somewhere outside in that unlit hall. Dick began to snore. The sticky liquid had dried and was crusting on her stomach; she felt she could not go back to the Vassar Club without washing it off. Then the worst thought, almost, of all struck her. Supposing he had started to have an emission while he was still inside her? Or if he used one of the rubber things and it had broken when she had jerked like that and that was why he had pulled so sharply away? She had heard of the rubber things breaking or leaking and how a woman could get pregnant from just a single drop. Full of determination, Dottie heaved and squirmed to free herself, until Dick raised his head in the moonlight and stared at her, without recognition. It was all true then, Dottie thought miserably; he had just gone to sleep and forgotten her. She tried to slide out of the bed.

Dick sat up and rubbed his eyes. 'Oh, it's you, Boston,' he muttered, putting an arm around her waist. 'Forgive me for dropping off.' He got up and turned on the bridge lamp. Dottie hurriedly covered herself with the sheet and averted her face; she was still timorous of seeing him in the altogether. 'I must go home, Dick,' she said soberly, stealing a sideward look at her clothes folded on the armchair. '*Must* you?' he inquired in a mocking tone; she could imagine his reddish eyebrows shooting up. 'You needn't trouble to dress and see me downstairs,' she went on quickly and firmly, her eyes fixed on the rug where his bare handsome feet were planted. He stooped and picked up his shorts; she watched his feet clamber into them. Then her eyes slowly rose and met his searching gaze. 'What's the matter, Boston?' he said kindly. 'Girls don't run home, you know, on their first night. Did it hurt you much?' Dottie shook her head. 'Are you bleeding?' he demanded. 'Come on, let me look.' He lifted her up and moved her down on the bed, the sheet trailing along with her; there was a small bloodstain on the towel. 'The very bluest,' he said, 'but only a minute quantity. Betty bled like a pig.' Dottie said nothing. 'Out with it, Boston,' he said brusquely, jerking a thumb towards the framed photograph. 'Does *she* put your nose out of joint?' Dottie made a brave negative sign. There was one thing she had to say. 'Dick,' and she shut her eyes in shame, 'do you think I should take a douche?' 'A douche?' he repeated in a mystified tone. 'Why? What for?' 'Well, in case . . . *you* know . . . birth control,' murmured Dottie. Dick stared at her and suddenly burst out laughing; he dropped on to a straight chair and threw his handsome head back. 'My dear girl,' he said, 'we just employed the most ancient form of birth control. *Coitus interruptus,* the old Romans called it, and a horrid nuisance it is.' 'I thought perhaps . . .?' said Dottie. 'Don't think. What did you think? I promise you, there isn't a single sperm swimming up to fertilize your irreproachable ovum. Like the man in the Bible, I spilled my seed on the ground, or, rather, on your very fine belly.' With a swift motion, he pulled the sheet back before she could stop him. 'Now,' he said, 'lay bare your thoughts.' Dottie shook her head and blushed. Wild horses could not make her, for the words embarrassed her frightfully; she had nearly choked on 'douche' and 'birth control', as it was. 'We must get you cleaned up,' he decreed after a moment's silence. He put on a robe and slippers and disappeared to the bathroom. It seemed a long time before he came back, bringing a dampened towel, with which he swabbed off her stomach. Then he dried her, rubbing hard with the dry end of it, sitting down beside her on the bed. He himself appeared much fresher, as though he had washed, and he smelled of mouthwash and tooth powder. He lit two cigarettes and gave her one and settled an ashtray between them.

'You *came*, Boston,' he remarked, with the air of a satisfied instructor. Dottie glanced uncertainly at him; could he mean that thing she had done that she did not like to think about? 'I beg your pardon,' she murmured. 'I mean you had an orgasm.' Dottie made a vague, still-inquiring noise in her throat; she was pretty sure, now, she understood, but the new word discombobulated her. 'A climax,' he added, more sharply. 'Do they teach that word at Vassar?' 'Oh,' said Dottie, almost disappointed that that was all there was to it. 'Was that . . .?' She could not finish the question. 'That was it,' he nodded. 'That is, if I am a judge.' 'It's normal then?' she wanted to know, beginning to feel better. Dick shrugged. 'Not for girls of your upbringing. Not the first time, usually. Appearances to the contrary, you're probably highly sexed.'

Dottie turned even redder. According to Kay, a climax was something very unusual, something the husband brought about by carefully studying his wife's desires and by patient manual stimu-

lation. The terms made Dottie shudder, even in memory; there
was a horrid bit, all in Latin, in Krafft-Ebing, about the Empress
Maria Theresa and what the court doctor told her consort to do
that Dottie had glanced at quickly and then tried to forget. Yet
even Mother hinted that satisfaction was something that came
after a good deal of time and experience and that love made a big
difference. But when Mother talked about satisfaction, it was not
clear exactly what she meant, and Kay was not clear either, except
when she quoted from books. Polly Andrews once asked her
whether it was the same as feeling passionate when you were
necking (that was when Polly was engaged), and Kay said yes,
pretty much, but Dottie now thought that Kay had been mistaken
or else trying to hide the truth from Polly for some reason. Dottie
had felt passionate, quite a few times, when she was dancing with
someone terribly attractive, but that was quite different from the
thing Dick meant. You would almost think that Kay did not know
what she was talking about. Or else that Kay and Mother meant
something else altogether and this thing with Dick *was* abnormal.
And yet he seemed so pleased, sitting there, blowing out smoke
rings; probably, having lived abroad, he knew more than Mother
and Kay.

'What are you frowning over now, Boston?' Dottie gave a start.
'To be highly sexed,' he said gently, 'is an excellent thing in a
woman. You mustn't be ashamed.' He took her cigarette and put
it out and laid his hands on her shoulders. 'Buck up,' he said.
'What you're feeling is natural. "*Post coitum, omne animal triste
est*," as the Roman poet said.' He slipped his hand down the slope
of her shoulder and lightly touched her nipple. 'Your body
surprised you tonight. You must learn to know it.' Dottie nodded.
'Soft,' he murmured, pressing the nipple between his thumb and
forefinger. 'Detumescence, that's what you're experiencing.'
Dottie drew a quick breath, fascinated; her doubts slid away. As
he continued to squeeze it, her nipple stood up. 'Erectile tissue,' he
said informatively and touched the other breast. 'See,' he said, and
they both looked downward. The two nipples were hard and full,
with a pink aureole of goose pimples around them; on her breasts
were a few dark hairs. Dottie waited tensely. A great relief had
surged through her; these were the very terms Kay cited from the
marriage handbooks. Down there, she felt a quick new tremor.

Her lips parted. Dick smiled. 'You feel something?' he said. Dottie nodded. 'You'd like it again?' he said, assaying her with his hand. Dottie stiffened; she pressed her thighs together. She was ashamed of the violent sensation his exploring fingers had discovered. But he held his hand there, between her clasped thighs, and grasped her right hand in his other, guiding it downward to the opening of his robe and pressed it over that part of himself, which was soft and limp, rather sweet, really, all curled up on itself like a fat worm. Sitting beside her, he looked into her face as he stroked her down there and tightened her hand on him. 'There's a little ridge there,' he whispered. 'Run your fingers up and down it.' Dottie obeyed, wonderingly; she felt his organ stiffen a little, which gave her a strange sense of power. She struggled against the excitement his tickling thumb was producing in her own external part; but as she felt him watching her, her eyes closed and her thighs spread open. He disengaged her hand, and she fell back on the bed, gasping. His thumb continued its play and she let herself yield to what it was doing, her whole attention concentrated on a tense pinpoint of sensation, which suddenly discharged itself in a nervous, fluttering spasm; her body arched and heaved and then lay still. When his hand returned to touch her, she struck it feebly away. 'Don't,' she moaned, rolling over on her stomach. This second climax, which she now recognized from the first one, though it was different, left her jumpy and disconcerted; it was something less thrilling and more like being tickled relentlessly or having to go to the bathroom. 'Didn't you like that?' he demanded, turning her head over on the pillow, so that she could not hide herself from him. She hated to think of his having watched her eyes while he brought *that* about. Slowly, Dottie opened her eyes and resolved to tell the truth. 'Not quite so much as the other, Dick.' Dick laughed. 'A nice normal girl. Some of your sex prefer that.' Dottie shivered; she could not deny that it had been exciting but it seemed to her almost perverted. He appeared to read her thoughts. 'Have you ever done it with a girl, Boston?' He tilted her face so he could scan it. Dottie reddened. 'Heavens, no.' 'You come like a house afire. How do you account for that?' Dottie said nothing. 'Have you ever done it with yourself?' Dottie shook her head violently; the suggestion wounded her. 'In your dreams?' Dottie reluctantly nodded. 'A little. Not the whole thing.' 'Rich erotic fantasies of a Chestnut Street virgin,' remarked Dick, stretching. He got up and went to the chest of drawers and took out two pairs of pyjamas and tossed one of them to Dottie. 'Put them on now and go to the bathroom. Tonight's lesson is concluded.'

DOROTHY PARKER

From *Big Blonde*

Born in New Jersey in 1893, Dorothy Parker grew up in New York and attended a Catholic convent school. In 1926 she sold some poetry to Vogue *magazine and was given a job there. Subsequently she became the theatre critic of* Vanity Fair *and the central figure of the Algonquin Hotel Round Table, one of the leading literary lunching clubs of its day. Her collection of poems,* Enough Rope, *became a bestseller and she gained celebrity status. Best known for her biting wit, she wrote a large number of short stories as well as more poetry and had two Broadway plays written about her. She was married twice, her second husband being an actor-writer called Alan Campbell with whom she went to Hollywood to write screenplays. After he died in 1963, Parker returned to New York where she died in 1967, most members of the public having assumed that she had already been dead for years.*

She left a large body of work behind her, the titles of which – 'Lament for the Living', 'After Such Pleasures' and 'Here Lies' for example – all refer consciously or unconsciously to the themes of death and loss. Pleasures are fleeting and temporary and life, though tempered by humorous outbursts, is a desperately sad experience. In this extract from 'Big Blonde', probably her best known work, the central character, Hazel Morse, demonstrates a desperate and passive acceptance of her situation.

'Men liked you because you were fun, and when they liked you they took you out and there you were.' Herbie Morse asks her to marry him and so she does. He gets

bored, they both begin to drink. He leaves and, without really questioning her situation, she carries on through life with the guy who happens to live down the hall. And, once again, the women are distanced and alienated characters watching their own lives played out before them (only in this case in a painful drunken haze) – the men are Boys called Ed and Herbie, whereas the central character and her best friend are Mrs Morse and Mrs Miller. Only the black maid, who can never contemplate having power or individual destiny of her own and is thus no threat, is allowed the dignity of a first name, Nettie.

E D WAS ONE of The Boys. He lived in Utica – had 'his own business' there, was the awed report – but he came to New York almost every week. He was married. He showed Mrs Morse the then current photographs of Junior and Sister, and she praised them abundantly and sincerely. Soon it was accepted by the others that Ed was her particular friend.

He staked her when they all played poker; sat next her and occasionally rubbed his knee against hers during the game. She was rather lucky. Frequently she went home with a twenty-dollar bill or a ten-dollar bill or a handful of crumpled dollars. She was glad of them. Herbie was getting, in her words, something awful about money. To ask him for it brought an instant row.

'What the hell do you do with it?' he would say. 'Shoot it all on Scotch?'

'I try to run this house half-way decent,' she would retort. 'Never thought of that, did you? Oh, no, his lordship couldn't be bothered with that.'

Again, she could not find a definite day, to fix the beginning of Ed's proprietorship. It became his custom to kiss her on the mouth when he came in, as well as for farewell, and he gave her little quick kisses of approval all through the evening. She liked this rather more than she disliked it. She never thought of his kisses when she was not with him.

He would run his hand lingeringly over her back and shoulders. 'Some dizzy blonde, eh?' he would say. 'Some doll.'

One afternoon she came home from Mrs Martin's to find Herbie in the bedroom. He had been away for several nights, evidently on a prolonged drinking bout. His face was gray, his hands jerked as if they were on wires. On the bed were two old suitcases, packed high. Only her photograph remained on his bureau, and the wide doors of his closet disclosed nothing but coat-hangers.

'I'm blowing,' he said. 'I'm through with the whole works. I got a job in Detroit.'

She sat down on the edge of the bed. She had drunk much the night before, and the four Scotches she had had with Mrs Martin had only increased her fogginess.

'Good job?' she said.

'Oh, yeah,' he said. 'Looks all right.'

He closed a suitcase with difficulty, swearing at it in whispers.

'There's some dough in the bank,' he said. 'The bank book's in your top drawer. You can have the furniture and stuff.'

He looked at her, and his forehead twitched.

'God damn it, I'm through, I'm telling you,' he cried. 'I'm through.'

'All right, all right,' she said. 'I heard you, didn't I?'

She saw him as if he were at one end of a cannon and she at the other. Her head was beginning to ache bumpingly, and her voice had a dreary, tiresome tone. She could not have raised it.

'Like a drink before you go?' she asked.

Again he looked at her, and a corner of his mouth jerked up.

'Cockeyed again for a change, aren't you?' he said. 'That's nice. Sure, get a couple of shots, will you?'

She went to the pantry, mixed him a stiff highball, poured herself a couple of inches of whisky and drank it. Then she gave herself another portion and brought the glasses into the bedroom. He had strapped both suitcases and had put on his hat and overcoat.

He took his highball.

'Well,' he said, and he gave a sudden, uncertain laugh. 'Here's mud in your eye.'

'Mud in your eye,' she said.

They drank. He put down his glass and took up the heavy suitcases.

'Got to get a train around six,' he said.

She followed him down the hall. There was a song, a song that Mrs Martin played doggedly on the phonograph, running loudly through her mind. She had never liked the thing.

> 'Night and daytime,
> Always playtime.
> Ain't we got fun?'

At the door he put down the bags and faced her.

'Well,' he said. 'Well, take care of yourself. You'll be all right, will you?'

'Oh, sure,' she said.

He opened the door, then came back to her, holding out his hand.

''By, Haze,' he said. 'Good luck to you.'

She took his hand and shook it.

'Pardon my wet glove,' she said.

When the door had closed behind him, she went back to the pantry.

She was flushed and lively when she went in to Mrs Martin's that evening. The Boys were there, Ed among them. He was glad to be in town, frisky and loud and full of jokes. But she spoke quietly to him for a minute.

'Herbie blew today,' she said. 'Going to live out west.'

'That so?' he said. He looked at her and played with the fountain pen clipped to his waistcoat pocket.

'Think he's gone for good, do you?' he asked.

'Yeah,' she said. 'I know he is. I know. Yeah.'

'You going to live on across the hall just the same?' he said. 'Know what you're going to do?'

'Gee, I don't know,' she said. 'I don't give much of a damn.'

'Oh, come on, that's no way to talk,' he told her. 'What you need – you need a little snifter. How about it?'

'Yeah,' she said. 'Just straight.'

She won forty-three dollars at poker. When the game broke up, Ed took her back to her apartment.

'Got a little kiss for me?' he asked.

He wrapped her in his big arms and kissed her violently. She was entirely passive. He held her away and looked at her.

'Little tight, honey?' he asked, anxiously. 'Not going to be sick, are you?'

'Me?' she said. 'I'm swell.'

[II]

When Ed left in the morning, he took her photograph with him. He said he wanted her picture to look at, up in Utica. 'You can have that one on the bureau,' she said.

She put Herbie's picture in a drawer, out of her sight. When she could look at it, she meant to tear it up. She was fairly successful in keeping her mind from racing around him. Whisky slowed it for her. She was almost peaceful, in her mist.

She accepted her relationship with Ed without question or enthusiasm. When he was away, she seldom thought definitely of him. He was good to her; he gave her frequent presents and a regular allowance. She was even able to save. She did not plan ahead of any day, but her wants were few, and you might as well put money in the bank as have it lying around.

When the lease of her apartment neared its end, it was Ed who suggested moving. His friendship with Mrs Martin and Joe had become strained over a dispute at poker; a feud was impending.

'Let's get the hell out of here,' Ed said. 'What I want you to have is a place near the Grand Central. Make it easier for me.'

So she took a little flat in the Forties. A colored maid came in every day to clean and to make the coffee for her – she was 'through with that housekeeping stuff,' she said, and Ed, twenty years married to a passionately domestic woman, admired this romantic uselessness and felt doubly a man of the world in abetting it.

The coffee was all she had until she went out to dinner, but alcohol kept her fat. Prohibition she regarded only as a basis for jokes. You could always get all you wanted. She was never noticeably drunk and seldom nearly sober. It required a larger daily allowance to keep her misty-minded. Too little, and she was achingly melancholy.

Ed brought her to Jimmy's. He was proud, with the pride of the transient who would be mistaken for a native, in his knowledge of small, recent restaurants occupying the lower floors of shabby brownstone houses; places where, upon mentioning the name of an habitué friend, might be obtained strange whisky and fresh gin in many of their ramifications. Jimmy's place was the favorite of his acquaintants.

There, through Ed, Mrs Morse met many men and women, formed quick friendships. The men often took her out when Ed was in Utica. He was proud of her popularity.

She fell into the habit of going to Jimmy's alone when she had no engagement. She was certain to meet some people she knew, and join them. It was a club for her friends, both men and women.

The women at Jimmy's looked remarkably alike, and this was

curious, for, through feuds, removals, and opportunities of more
profitable contacts, the personnel of the group changed
constantly. Yet always the newcomers resembled those whom
they replaced. They were all big women and stout, broad of
shoulder and abundantly breasted, with faces thickly clothed in
soft, high-colored flesh. They laughed out loud and often,
showing opaque and lusterless teeth like squares of crockery.
There was about them the health of the big, yet a slight, unwhole-
some suggestion of stubborn preservation. They might have been
thirty-six or forty-five or anywhere between.

They composed their titles of their own first names with their
husbands' surnames – Mrs Florence Miller, Mrs Vera Riley, Mrs
Lilian Block. This gave at the same time the solidity of marriage
and the glamour of freedom. Yet only one or two were actually
divorced. Most of them never referred to their dimmed spouses;
some a shorter time separated, described them in terms of great
biological interest. Several were mothers, each of an only child – a
boy at school somewhere, or a girl being cared for by a grandmother. Often, well on toward morning, there would be displays
of kodak portraits and of tears.

They were comfortable women, cordial and friendly and irre-
pressibly matronly. Theirs was the quality of ease. Become fatal-
istic, especially about money matters, they unworried. Whenever
their funds dropped alarmingly, a new donor appeared; this had
always happened. The aim of each was to have one man, permanently, to pay all her bills, in return for which she would have
immediately given up other admirers and probably would have
become exceedingly fond of him; for the affections of all of them
were, by now, unexacting, tranquil, and easily arranged. This end,
however, grew increasingly difficult yearly. Mrs Morse was
regarded as fortunate.

Ed had a good year, increased her allowance and gave her a
sealskin coat. But she had to be careful of her moods with him. He
insisted upon gaiety. He would not listen to admissions of aches
or weariness.

'Hey, listen,' he would say, 'I got worries of my own, and
plenty. Nobody wants to hear other people's troubles, sweetie.
What you got to do, you got to be a sport and forget it. See? Well,
slip us a little smile, then. That's my girl.'

She never had enough interest to quarrel with him as she had with Herbie, but she wanted the privilege of occasional admitted sadness. It was strange. The other women she saw did not have to fight their moods. There was Mrs Florence Miller who got regular crying jags, and the men sought only to cheer and comfort her. The others spent whole evenings in grieved recital of worries and ills; their escorts paid them deep sympathy. But she was instantly undesirable when she was low in spirits. Once, at Jimmy's when she could not make herself lively, Ed had walked out and left her.

'Why the hell don't you stay home and not go spoiling every-body's evening?' he had roared.

Even her slightest acquaintances seemed irritated if she were not conspicuously light-hearted.

'What's the matter with you, anyway?' they would say. 'Be your age, why don't you? Have a little drink and snap out of it.'

When her relationship with Ed had continued nearly three years, he moved to Florida to live. He hated leaving her; he gave her a large check and some shares of a sound stock, and his pale eyes were wet when he said good-by. She did not miss him. He came to New York infrequently, perhaps two or three times a year, and hurried directly from the train to see her. She was always pleased to have him come and never sorry to see him go.

Charley, an acquaintance of Ed's that she had met at Jimmy's, had long admired her. He had always made opportunities of touching her and leaning close to talk to her. He asked repeatedly of all their friends if they had ever heard such a fine laugh as she had. After Ed left, Charley became the main figure in her life. She classified him and spoke of him as 'not so bad.' There was nearly a year of Charley; then she divided her time between him and Sydney, another frequenter of Jimmy's; then Charley slipped away altogether.

Sydney was a little, brightly dressed, clever Jew. She was perhaps nearest contentment with him. He amused her always; her laughter was not forced.

He admired her completely. Her softness and size delighted him. And he thought she was great, he often told her, because she kept gay and lively when she was drunk.

'Once I had a gal,' he said, 'used to try and throw herself out of

the window every time she got a can on. Jee-*zuss*,' he added, feel-
ingly.

Then Sydney married a rich and watchful bride, and then there
was Billy. No – after Sydney came Fred, then Billy. In her haze, she
never recalled how men entered her life and left it. There were no
surprises. She had no thrill at their advent, nor woe at their departure. She seemed to be always able to attract men. There was
never another as rich as Ed, but they were all generous to her, in
their means.

SUBMISSION

She was not in the least teaching Mr Casaubon to ask if he were good enough for her, but merely asking herself anxiously how she could be good enough for Mr Casaubon.

Geroge Eliot, *Middlemarch* (Chapter 5)

BARBARA GOWDY

Ninety-Three Million Miles Away

Barbara Gowdy is the author of two novels and a short story collection. She lives in Toronto.

AT LEAST PART of the reason Ali married Claude, a cosmetic surgeon with a growing practice, was so that she could quit her boring government job. Claude was all for it. 'You only have one life to live,' he said. 'You only have one kick at the can.' He gave her a generous allowance and told her to do what she wanted.

She wasn't sure what that was, aside from trying on clothes in expensive stores. Claude suggested something musical – she loved music – so she took dance classes and piano lessons and discovered that she had a tin ear and no sense of rhythm. She fell into a mild depression during which she peevishly questioned Claude about the ethics of cosmetic surgery.

'It all depends on what light you're looking at it in,' Claude said. He was not easily riled. What Ali needed to do, he said, was take the wider view.

She agreed. She decided to devote herself to learning, and she began a regime of reading and studying, five days a week, five to six hours a day. She read novels, plays, biographies, essays, magazine articles, almanacs, the New Testament, *The Concise Oxford Dictionary*, *The Harper Anthology of Poetry*.

But after a year of this, although she became known as the person at dinner parties who could supply the name or date that somebody was snapping around for, she wasn't particularly happy, and she didn't even feel smart. Far from it, she felt stupid, a machine, an idiot savant whose one talent was memorization. If she had any *creative* talent, which was the only kind she really admired, she wasn't going to find it by armoring herself with facts. She grew slightly paranoid that Claude wanted her to settle down and have a baby.

A few days before their second wedding anniversary she and Claude bought a condominium apartment with floor-to-ceiling windows, and Ali decided to abandon her reading regime and to take up painting. Since she didn't know the first thing about painting or even drawing, she studied pictures from art books. She did know what her first subject was going to be – herself in the nude. Several months earlier she'd had a dream about spotting her signature in the corner of a painting, and realizing from the conversation of the men who were admiring it (and blocking her view) that it was an extraordinary rendition of her naked self. She took the dream to be a sign. For several weeks she studied the proportions, skin tones and muscle definitions of the nudes in her books, then she went out and bought art supplies and a self-standing, full-length mirror.

She set up her work area in the middle of the living room. Here she had light without being directly in front of the window. When she was all ready to begin, she stood before the mirror and slipped off her white terry-cloth housecoat and her pink flannelette pajamas, letting them fall to the floor. It aroused her a little to witness her careless shedding of clothes. She tried a pose: hands folded and resting loosely under her stomach, feet buried in the drift of her housecoat.

For some reason, however, she couldn't get a fix on what she looked like. Her face and body seemed indistinct, secretive in a way, as if they were actually well-defined, but not to her, or not from where she was looking.

She decided that she should simply start, and see what happened. She did a pencil drawing of herself sitting in a chair and stretching. It struck her as being very good, not that she could really judge, but the out-of-kilter proportions seemed slyly deliberate, and there was a pleasing simplicity to the reaching arms and the elongated curve of the neck. Because flattery hadn't been her intention, Ali felt that at last she may have wrenched a vision out of her soul.

The next morning she got out of bed unusually early, not long after Claude had left the apartment, and discovered sunlight streaming obliquely into the living room through a gap between their building and the apartment house next door. As far as she knew, and in spite of the plate-glass windows, this was the only direct light they got. Deciding to make use of it while it lasted, she moved her easel, chair, and mirror closer to the window. Then she took off her housecoat and pajamas.

For a few moments she stood there looking at herself, wondering what it was that had inspired the sketch. Today she was disposed to seeing herself as not bad, overall. As far as certain specifics went, though, as to whether her breasts were small, for instance, or her eyes close together, she remained in the dark.

Did other people find her looks ambiguous? Claude was always calling her beautiful, except that the way he put it – 'You're beautiful to me,' or 'I think you're beautiful' – made it sound as if she should understand that his taste in women was unconventional. Her only boyfriend before Claude, a guy called Roger, told her she was great but never said how exactly. When they had sex, Roger liked to hold the base of his penis and watch it going in and out of her. Once, he said that there were days he got so horny at the office, his pencil turned him on. She thought it should have been his pencil sharpener.

She covered her breasts with her hands. Down her cleavage a drop of sweat slid haltingly, a sensation like the tip of a tongue. She circled her palms until her nipples hardened, and imagined a man's hands . . . not Claude's – a man's hands not attached to any particular man. She looked out the window.

In the apartment across from her she saw a man.

She leapt to one side, behind the drapes. Her heart pounded violently, but only for a moment, as if something had thundered by, dangerously close. She wiped her forehead on the drapes, then, without looking at the window, walked back to her easel, picked up her palette and brush, and began to mix paint. She gave herself a glance in the mirror, but she had no intention of trying to duplicate her own skin tone. She wanted something purer. White with just a hint of rose, like the glance of color in a soap bubble.

Her strokes were short and light to control dripping. She liked the effect, though . . . how it made the woman appear as if she were covered in feathers. Paint splashed on her own skin, but she resisted putting her smock on. The room seemed preternaturally white and airy; the windows beyond the mirror gleamed. Being so close to the windows gave her the tranced sensation of standing on the edge of a cliff.

A few minutes before she lost the direct sun, she finished the woman's skin. She set down her palette and put her brush in turpentine, then wet a rag in the turpentine and wiped paint off her hands and where it had dripped on her thighs and feet. She thought about the sun. She thought that it is ninety-three million miles away and that its fuel supply will last another five billion years. Instead of thinking about the man who was watching her, she tried to recall a solar chart she had memorized a couple of years ago.

The surface temperature is six thousand degrees Fahrenheit, she told herself. Double that number, and you have how many times bigger the surface of the sun is compared to the surface of the earth. Except that because the sun is a ball of hot gas, it actually has no surface.

When she had rubbed the paint off herself, she went into the kitchen to wash away the turpentine with soap and water. The man's eyes tracked her. She didn't have to glance at the window for confirmation. She switched on the light above the sink, soaped the dishcloth, and began to wipe her skin. There was no reason to clean her arms, but she lifted each one and wiped the cloth over it. She wiped her breasts. She seemed to share in his scrutiny, as if she were looking at herself through his eyes. From his perspective she was able to see her physical self very clearly – her shiny, red-high-lighted hair, her small waist and heart-shaped bottom, the dreamy tilt to her head.

She began to shiver. She wrung out the cloth and folded it over the faucet, then patted herself dry with a dish towel. Then, pretending to be examining her fingernails, she turned and walked over to the window. She looked up.

There he was. Her glance of a quarter of an hour ago had regis-tered dark hair and a white shirt. Now she saw a long, older face . . . a man in his fifties maybe. A green tie. She had seen him before this morning – quick, disinterested (or so she had thought) sight-ings of a man in his kitchen, watching television, going from room to room. A bachelor living next door. She pressed the palms of her hands on the window, and he stepped back into the shadow.

The pane clouded from her breath. She leaned her body into it, flattening her breasts against the cool glass. Right at the window she was visible to his apartment and the one below, which had closed vertical blinds. 'Each window like a pillory appears,' she thought. Vaguely appropriate lines from the poems she had read last year were always occurring to her. She felt that he was still watching, but she yearned for proof.

When it became evident that he wasn't going to show himself, she went into the bedroom. The bedroom windows didn't face the apartment house, but she closed them anyway, then got into bed under the covers. Between her legs there was such a tender throbbing that she had to push a pillow into her crotch. Sex addicts must feel like this, she thought. Rapists, child molesters.

She said to herself, 'You are a certifiable exhibitionist.' She let out an amazed, almost exultant laugh, but instantly fell into a darker amazement as it dawned on her that she really was . . . she really was an exhibitionist. And what's more, she had been one for years, or at least she had been working up to being one for years.

Why, for instance, did she and Claude live here, in this vulgar low-rise? Wasn't it because of the floor-to-ceiling windows that faced the windows of the house next door?

And what about when she was twelve and became so obsessed with the idea of urinating on people's lawns that one night she crept out of the house after everyone was asleep and did it, peed on the lawn of the townhouses next door . . . right under a streetlight, in fact.

What about two years ago, when she didn't wear underpants the entire summer? She'd had a minor yeast infection and had read that it was a good idea not to wear underpants at home, if you could help it, but she had stopped wearing them in public as well, beneath skirts and dresses, at parties, on buses, and she must have known that this was taking it a bit far, because she had kept it from Claude.

'Oh, my God,' she said wretchedly.

She went still, alerted by how theatrical that had sounded. Her heart was beating in her throat. She touched a finger to it. So fragile, a throat. She imagined the man being excited by her hands on her throat.

What was going on? What was the matter with her? Maybe she was too aroused to be shocked at herself. She moved her hips, rubbing her crotch against the pillow. No, she didn't want to masturbate. That would ruin it.

Ruin what?

She closed her eyes, and the man appeared to her. She experienced a rush of wild longing. It was as if, all her life, she had been waiting for a long-faced, middle-aged man in a white shirt and green tie. He was probably still standing in his living room, watching her window.

She sat up, threw off the covers.

Dropped back down on the bed.

This was crazy. This was really crazy. What if he was a rapist? What if, right this minute, he was downstairs, finding out her name from the mailbox? Or what if he was just some lonely, normal man who took her display as an invitation to phone her up and ask her for a date? It's not as if she wanted to go out with him. She wasn't looking for an affair.

For an hour or so she fretted, and then she drifted off to sleep. When she woke up, shortly after noon, she was quite calm. The state she had worked herself into earlier struck her as over-wrought. So, she gave some guy a thrill, so what? She was a bit of an exhibitionist . . . most women were, she bet. It was instinctive, a side effect of being the receptor in the sex act.

She decided to have lunch and go for a walk. While she was making herself a sandwich she avoided glancing at the window, but as soon as she sat at the table, she couldn't resist looking over.

He wasn't there, and yet she felt that he was watching her, standing out of sight. She ran a hand through her hair. 'For Christ's sake,' she reproached herself, but she was already with him. Again it was as if her eyes were in his head, although not replacing his eyes. She knew that he wanted her to slip her hand down her sweatpants. She did this. Watching his window, she removed her hand and licked her wet fingers. At that instant she would have paid money for some sign that he was watching.

After a few minutes she began to chew on her fingernails. She was suddenly depressed. She reached over and pulled the curtain across the window and ate her sandwich. Her mouth, biting into the bread, trembled like an old lady's. 'Trembled like a guilty thing surprised,' she quoted to herself. It wasn't guilt, though, it wasn't frustration, either, not sexual frustration. She was acquainted with this bleached sadness – it came upon her at the height of sensation . . . after orgasms, after a day of trying on clothes in stores.

She finished her sandwich and went for a walk in her new toreador pants and her tight, black, turtleneck sweater. By the time she returned, Claude was home. He asked her if she had worked in the nude again.

'Of course,' she said absently. 'I have to.' She was looking past him at the man's closed drapes. 'Claude,' she said, suddenly, 'am I beautiful? I mean not just to you. Am I empirically beautiful?'

Claude looked surprised. 'Well, yeah,' he said. 'Sure you are. Hell, I married you, didn't I? Hey!' He stepped back. 'Whoa!'

She was removing her clothes. When she was naked, she said, 'Don't think of me as your wife. Just as a woman. One of your patients. Am I beautiful or not?'

He made a show of eyeing her up and down. 'Not bad,' he said. 'Of course, it depends on what you mean by "beautiful".' He laughed. 'What's going on?'

'I'm serious. You don't think I'm kind of . . . normal? You know, plain?'

'Of course not,' he said lovingly. He reached for her and drew her into his arms. 'You want hard evidence?' he said.

They went into the bedroom. It was dark because the curtains were still drawn. She switched on the bedside lamp, but once he was undressed, he switched it off again.

'No,' she said from the bed, 'leave it on.'

'What? You want it on?'

'For a change.'

The next morning she got up before he did. She had hardly slept. During breakfast she kept looking over at the apartment house, but there was no sign of the man. Which didn't necessarily mean that he wasn't there. She couldn't wait for Claude to leave so that she could stop pretending she wasn't keyed up. It was gnawing at her that she had overestimated or somehow misread the man's interest. How did she know? He might be gay. He might be so devoted to a certain woman that all other women repelled him. He might be puritanical . . . a priest, a born-again Christian. He might be out of his mind.

The minute Claude was out the door, she undressed and began work on the painting. She stood in the sunlight mixing colors, then sat on the chair in her stretching pose, looking at herself in the mirror, then stood up and – without paying much attention, glancing every few seconds at his window – painted ribs and uplifted breasts.

An hour went by before she thought, he's not going to show up. She dropped into the chair, weak with disappointment, even though she knew that, very likely, he had simply been obliged to go to work, that his being home yesterday was a fluke. Forlornly she gazed at her painting. To her surprise she had accomplished something rather interesting: breasts like Picasso eyes. It is possible, she thought dully, that I am a natural talent.

She put her brush in the turpentine, and her face in her hands. She felt the sun on her hair. In a few minutes the sun would disappear behind his house, and after that, if she wanted him to get a good look at her, she would have to stand right at the window. She envisioned herself stationed there all day. You are ridiculous, she told herself. You are unhinged.

She glanced up at the window again.

He was there.

She sat up straight. Slowly she came to her feet. Stay, she prayed. He did. She walked over to the window, her fingertips brushing her thighs. She held her breath. When she was at the window, she stood perfectly still. He had on a white shirt again, but no tie. He was close enough that she could make out the darkness around his eyes, although she couldn't tell exactly where he was looking. But his eyes seemed to enter her head like a drug, and she felt herself aligned with his perspective. She saw herself – surprisingly slender, composed but apprehensive – through the glass and against the backdrop of the room's white walls.

After a minute or two she walked over to the chair, picked it up, and carried it to the window. She sat facing him, her knees apart. He was as still as a picture. So was she, because she had suddenly remembered that he might be gay or crazy. She tried to give him a hard look. She observed his age and his sad, respectable appearance . . . and the fact that he remained at the window, revealing his interest.

No, he was the man she had imagined. I am a gift to him, she thought, opening her legs wider. I am his dream come true. She began to rotate her hips. With the fingers of both hands she spread her labia.

One small part of her mind, clinging to the person she had been until yesterday morning, tried to pull her back. She felt it as a presence behind the chair, a tableau of sensational, irrelevant warnings that she was obviously not about to turn around for. She kept her eyes on the man. Moving her left hand up to her breasts, she began to rub and squeeze and to circle her fingers on the nipples.

The middle finger of her right hand slipped into her vagina, as the palm massaged her clitoris.

He was motionless.

You are kissing me, she thought. She seemed to feel his lips, cool, soft, sliding, and sucking down her stomach. You are kissing me. She imagined his hands under her, lifting her like a bowl to his lips.

She was coming.

Her body jolted. Her legs shook. She had never experienced anything like it. Seeing what he saw, she witnessed an act of shocking vulnerability. It went on and on. She saw the charity of her display, her lavish recklessness and submission. It inspired her to the tenderest self-love. The man did not move, not until she had finally stopped moving, and then he reached up one hand – to signal, she thought, but it was to close the drapes.

She stayed sprawled in the chair. She was astonished. She couldn't believe herself. She couldn't believe him. How did he know to stay so still, to simply watch her? She avoided the thought that right at this moment he was probably masturbating. She absorbed herself only with what she had seen, which was a dead-still man whose eyes she had sensed roving over her body the way that eyes in certain portraits seem to follow you around a room.

The next three mornings everything was the same. He had on his white shirt, she masturbated in the chair, he watched without moving, she came spectacularly, he closed the drapes.

Afterward she went out clothes shopping or visiting people. Everyone told her how great she looked. At night she was passionate in bed, prompting Claude to ask several times, 'What the hell's come over you?' but he asked it happily, he didn't look a gift horse in the mouth. She felt very loving toward Claude, not out of guilt but out of high spirits. She knew better than to confess, of course, and yet she didn't believe that she was betraying him with the man next door. A man who hadn't touched her or spoken to her, who, as far as she was concerned, only existed from the waist up and who never moved except to pull his drapes, how could that man be counted as a lover?

The fourth day, Friday, the man didn't appear. For two hours she waited in the chair. Finally she moved to the couch and watched television, keeping one eye on his window. She told herself that he must have had an urgent appointment, or that he had to go to work early. She was worried, though. At some point, late in the afternoon when she wasn't looking, he closed his drapes.

Saturday and Sunday he didn't seem to be home – the drapes were drawn and the lights off . . . not that she could have done anything anyway, not with Claude there. On Monday morning she was in her chair, naked, as soon as Claude left the house. She waited until 10:30, then put on her toreador pants and white, push-up halter top and went for a walk. A consoling line from *Romeo and Juliet* played in her head: 'He that is stricken blind cannot forget the precious treasure of his eyesight lost.' She was angry with the man for not being as keen as she was. If he was at his window tomorrow, she vowed she would shut her drapes on him.

But how would she replace him, what would she do? Become a table dancer? She had to laugh. Aside from the fact that she was a respectably married woman and could not dance to save her life and was probably ten years too old, the last thing she wanted was a bunch of slack-jawed flat-eyed drunks grabbing at her breasts. She wanted one man, and she wanted him to have a sad, intelligent demeanor and the control to watch her without moving a muscle. She wanted him to wear a white shirt.

On the way home, passing his place, she stopped. The building was a mansion turned into luxury apartments. He must have money, she realized . . . an obvious conclusion, but until now she'd had no interest whatsoever in who he was.

She climbed the stairs and tried the door. Found it open. Walked in.

The mailboxes were numbered one to four. His would be four. She read the name in the little window: 'Dr Andrew Halsey.'

Back at her apartment she looked him up under 'Physicians' in the phone book and found that, like Claude, he was a surgeon. A general surgeon, though, a remover of tumors and diseased organs. Presumably on call. Presumably dedicated, as a general surgeon had to be.

She guessed she would forgive his absences.

The next morning and the next, Andrew (as she now thought of him) was at the window. Thursday he wasn't. She tried not to be disappointed. She imagined him saving people's lives, drawing his scalpel along skin in beautifully precise cuts. For something to do she worked on her painting. She painted fishlike eyes, a hooked nose, a mouth full of teeth. She worked fast.

Andrew was there Friday morning. When Ali saw him she rose to her feet and pressed her body against the window, as she had done the first morning. Then she walked to the chair, turned it around and leaned over it, her back to him. She masturbated stroking herself from behind.

That afternoon she bought him a pair of binoculars, an expensive, powerful pair, which she wrapped in brown paper, addressed, and left on the floor in front of his mailbox. All weekend she was preoccupied with wondering whether he would understand that she had given them to him and whether he would use them. She had considered including a message! 'For our mornings' or something like that, but such direct communication seemed like a violation of a pact between them. The binoculars alone were a risk.

Monday, before she even had her housecoat off, he walked from the rear of the room to the window, the binoculars at his eyes. Because most of his face was covered by the binoculars and his hands, she had the impression that he was masked. Her legs shook. When she opened her legs and spread her labia, his eyes crawled up her. She masturbated but didn't come and didn't try to, although she put on a show of coming. She was so devoted to his appreciation that her pleasure seemed like a siphoning of his, an early, childish indulgence that she would never return to.

It was later, with Claude, that she came. After supper she pulled him onto the bed. She pretended that he was Andrew, or rather she imagined a dark, long-faced, silent man who made love with his eyes open but who smelled and felt like Claude and whom she loved and trusted as she did Claude. With this hybrid partner she was able to relax enough to encourage the kind of kissing and movement she needed but had never had the confidence to insist upon. The next morning, masturbating for Andrew, she reached the height of ecstasy, as if her orgasms with him had been the fantasy, and her pretenses of orgasm were the real thing. Not coming released her completely into his dream of her. The whole show was for him – cunt, ass, mouth, throat offered to his magnified vision.

For several weeks Andrew turned up regularly, five mornings a week, and she lived in a state of elation. In the afternoons she worked on her painting, without much concentration though, since finishing it didn't seem to matter anymore in spite of how well it was turning out. Claude insisted that it was still very much a self-portrait, a statement Ali was insulted by, given the woman's obvious primitivism and her flat, distant eyes.

There was no reason for her to continue working in the nude, but she did, out of habit and comfort, and on the outside chance that Andrew might be peeking through his drapes. While she painted she wondered about her exhibitionism, what it was about her that craved to have a strange man look at her. Of course, everyone and everything liked to be looked at to a certain degree, she thought. Flowers, cats, anything that preened or shone, children crying, 'Look at me!' Some mornings her episodes with Andrew seemed to have nothing at all to do with lust; they were completely display, wholehearted surrender to what felt like the most inaugural and genuine of all desires, which was not sex but which happened to be expressed through a sexual act.

One night she dreamed that Andrew was operating on her. Above the surgical mask his eyes were expressionless. He had very long arms. She was also able to see, as if through his eyes, the vertical incision that went from between her breasts to her navel, and the skin on either side of the incision folded back like a scroll. Her heart was brilliant red and perfectly heart-shaped. All of her other organs were glistening yellows and oranges. Somebody should take a picture of this, she thought. Andrew's gloved hands barely appeared to move as they wielded long, silver instruments. There was no blood on his hands. Very carefully, so that she hardly felt it, he prodded her organs and plucked at her veins and tendons, occasionally drawing a tendon out and dropping it into a petri dish. It was as if he were weeding a garden. Her heart throbbed. A tendon encircled her heart, and when he pulled on it she could feel that its other end encircled her vagina, and the uncoiling there was the most exquisite sensation she had ever experienced. She worried that she would come and that her trembling and spasms would cause him to accidentally stab her. She woke up coming.

All day the dream obsessed her. It *could* happen, she reasoned. She could have a gall bladder or an appendicitis attack and be rushed to the hospital and, just as she was going under, see that the surgeon was Andrew. It could happen.

When she woke up the next morning, the dream was her first thought. She looked down at the gentle swell of her stomach and felt sentimental and excited. She found it impossible to shake the dream, even while she was masturbating for Andrew, so that instead of entering *his* dream of her, instead of seeing a naked woman sitting in a pool of morning sun, she saw her sliced-open chest in the shaft of his surgeon's light. Her heart was what she focused on, its fragile pulsing, but she also saw the slower rise and fall of her lungs, and the quivering of her other organs. Between her organs were tantalizing crevices and entwined swirls of blue and red – her veins and arteries. Her tendons were seashell pink threaded tight as guitar strings.

Of course she realized that she had the physiology all wrong and that in a real operation there would be blood and pain and she would be anesthetized. It was an impossible, mad fantasy; she didn't expect it to last. But every day it became more enticing as she authenticated it with hard data, such as the name of the hospital he operated out of (she called his number in the phone book and asked his nurse) and the name of the surgical instruments he would use (she consulted one of Claude's medical texts), and as she smoothed out the rough edges by imagining, for instance, minuscule suction tubes planted here and there in the incision to remove every last drop of blood.

In the mornings, during her real encounters with Andrew, she became increasingly frustrated until it was all she could do not to quit in the middle, close the drapes, or walk out of the room. And yet if he failed to show up, she was desperate. She started to drink gin and tonics before lunch and to sunbathe at the edge of the driveway between her building and his, knowing he wasn't home from ten o'clock on, but laying there for hours, just in case.

One afternoon, lightheaded from gin and sun, restless with worry because he hadn't turned up the last three mornings, she changed out of her bikini and into a strapless, cotton dress and went for a walk. She walked past the park she had been heading for, past the stores she had thought she might browse in. The sun bore down. Strutting by men who eyed her bare shoulders, she felt voluptuous, sweetly rounded. But at the pit of her stomach was a filament of anxiety, evidence that despite telling herself otherwise, she knew where she was going.

She entered the hospital by the Emergency doors and wandered the corridors for what seemed like half an hour before discovering Andrew's office. By this time she was holding her stomach and half believing that the feeling of anxiety might actually be a symptom of something very serious.

'Dr Halsey isn't seeing patients,' his nurse said. She slit open a manila envelope with a lion's head letter opener. 'They'll take care of you at Emergency.'

'I have to see Dr Halsey,' Ali said, her voice cracking. 'I'm a friend.'

The nurse sighed. 'Just a minute.' She stood and went down a hall, opening a door at the end after a quick knock.

Ali pressed her fists into her stomach. For some reason she no longer felt a thing. She pressed harder. What a miracle if she burst her appendix! She should stab herself with the letter opener. She should at least break her fingers, slam them in a drawer like a draft dodger.

'Would you like to come in?' a high, nasal voice said. Ali spun around. It was Andrew, standing at the door.

'The doctor will see you,' the nurse said impatiently, sitting back behind her desk.

Ali's heart began to pound. She felt as if a pair of hands were cupping and uncupping her ears. His shirt was blue. She went down the hall, squeezing past him without looking up, and sat in the green plastic chair beside his desk. He shut the door and walked over to the window. It was a big room; there was a long expanse of old green and yellow floor tiles between them. Leaning his hip against a filing cabinet, he just stood there, hands in his trouser pockets, regarding her with such a polite, impersonal expression that she asked him if he recognized her.

'Of course I do,' he said quietly.

'Well – ' Suddenly she was mortified. She felt like a woman about to sob that she couldn't afford the abortion. She touched her fingers to her hot face.

'I don't know your name,' he said.

'Oh. Ali. Ali Perrin.'

'What do you want, Ali?'

Her eyes fluttered down to his shoes – black, shabby loafers. She hated his adenoidal voice. What did she want? What she wanted was to bolt from the room like the mad woman she suspected she was. She glanced up at him again. Because he was standing with his back to the window, he was outlined in light. It made him seem unreal, like a film image superimposed against a screen. She tried to look away, but his eyes held her. Out in the waiting room the telephone was ringing. What do *you* want, she thought, capitulating to the pull of her perspective over to his, seeing now, from across the room, a charming woman with tanned, bare shoulders and blushing cheeks.

The light blinked on his phone. Both of them glanced over at it, but he stayed standing where he was. After a moment she murmured, 'I have no idea what I'm doing here.'

He was silent. She kept her eyes on the phone, waiting for him to speak. When he didn't, she said, 'I had a dream . . .' She let out a disbelieving laugh. 'God.' She shook her head.

'You are very lovely,' he said in a speculative tone. She glanced up at him, and he turned away. Pressing his hands together, he took a few steps along the window. 'I have very much enjoyed our . . . our encounters,' he said.

'Oh, don't worry,' she said. 'I'm not here to – '

'However,' he cut in, 'I should tell you that I am moving into another building.'

She looked straight at him.

'This weekend, as a matter of fact.' He frowned at his wall of framed diplomas.

'This weekend?' she said.

'Yes.'

'So,' she murmured. 'It's over then.'

'Regrettably.'

She stared at his profile. In profile he was a stranger – beak-nosed, round-shouldered. She hated his shoes, his floor, his formal way of speaking, his voice, his profile, and yet her eyes filled and she longed for him to look at her again.

Abruptly he turned his back to her and said that his apartment was in the east end, near the beach. He gestured out the window. Did she know where the yacht club was?

'No,' she whispered.

'Not that I am a member,' he said with a mild laugh.

'Listen,' she said, wiping her eyes. 'I'm sorry.' She came to her feet. 'I guess I just wanted to see you.'

He strode like an obliging host over to the door.

'Well, good-bye,' she said, looking up into his face.

He had garlic breath and five o'clock shadow. His eyes grazed hers. 'I wouldn't feel too badly about anything,' he said affably.

When she got back to the apartment the first thing she did was take her clothes off and go over to the full-length mirror, which was still standing next to the easel. Her eyes filled again because without Andrew's appreciation or the hope of it (and despite how repellent she had found him) what she saw was a pathetic little woman with pasty skin and short legs.

She looked at the painting. If *that* was her, as Claude claimed, then she also had flat eyes and crude, wild proportions.

What on earth did Claude see in her?

What had Andrew seen? 'You are very lovely,' Andrew had said, but maybe he'd been reminding himself. Maybe he'd meant, 'lovely when I'm in the next building.'

After supper that evening she asked Claude to lie with her on the couch, and the two of them watched TV. She held his hand against her breast. 'Let this be enough,' she prayed.

But she didn't believe it ever would be. The world was too full of surprises, it frightened her. As Claude was always saying, things looked different from different angles, and in different lights. What this meant to her was that everything hinged on where you happened to be standing at a given moment, or even on who you imagined you were. It meant that in certain lights, desire sprang up out of nowhere.

MARGARET ATWOOD

From *Surfacing*

Canada's most eminent novelist, Margaret Atwood won the country's top literary prize – the Governor-General's Award, when she was only twenty-seven years old. She was born in 1939 in Ottawa and received no formal education until the age of twelve, though she has received numerous academic accolades since. After living on a farm in Ontario for many years and then spending periods in London and New York, Atwood now lives in Toronto with her second husband and daughter.

In the UK and the US, she is best known for powerful novels about states of female (dis)empowerment, including The Handmaid's Tale *(1985). In Canada, however, she is primarily considered as a poet and one who is concerned with the primal forces of nature and the half of the population who have rarely achieved any element of self-definition. Because of this interest her work often takes the central characters back to situations where they retreat into a universe without imposed social constructs and where people, and more particularly women, can thus become their 'whole' selves again.*

In Surfacing *(1972), the nameless 'I' character takes her boyfriend, Joe, and another couple, David and Anna, on a journey to the house on a remote and isolated island on which her father used to live. He has mysteriously disappeared and she is searching both for him and for the meaning of his vanishing. As the four characters remain on the island, their artificial barriers come down and they revert to 'natural' instincts. David refuses to understand why the narrator will not have sex with him. Her rejection of him can only have one meaning in his terms – she is 'a third-rate cold tail'. She will not submit to his requests and is thus considered the abnormal one.*

She is in a camp of her own, even including the other female of the group. They are all named individuals; she is out on a limb – an isolated 'I'. She realizes that, 'it wasn't the men I hated, it was the Americans, the human beings, men and women both.' To them she must be the 'inhuman' one since her questioning of their sexual and moral values forces them to question their own. If they club together and reject her as 'abnormal' then the threat to their world is instantaneously eliminated. But to her, it is the Americans who are the enemy and Joe, Anna and David, through their attempted bulldozing of her personality, are equated with these more generally destructive Americans – forces of violence who carelessly reject the natural environment of her cherished childhood world.

[Chapter 18]

THERE WAS no one in the cabin. It was different, larger, as though I hadn't been there for a long time: the half of me that had begun to return was not yet used to it. I went back outside and unhooked the gate of the fenced oblong and sat down on the swing, carefully, the ropes still held my weight; I swayed myself gently back and forth, keeping my feet on the ground. Rocks, trees, sandbox where I had made houses with stones for windows. The birds were there, chickadees and jays; but they were wary of me, they weren't trained.

I turned the ring on my left-hand finger, souvenir: he gave it to me, plain gold, he said he didn't like ostentation, it got us into the motels easier, opener of doors; in the intervening time I wore it on a chain around my neck. The cold bathrooms, interchangeable, feel of tile on footsoles, walking into them wrapped in someone else's towel in the days of rubber sex, precautions. He would prop his watch on the night-tables to be sure he wasn't late.

For him I could have been anyone but for me he was unique, the first, that's where I learned. I worshipped him, non-child-bride, idolater, I kept the scraps of his handwriting like saints' relics, he never wrote letters, all I had was the criticisms in red pencil he paperclipped to my drawings. CS and DS, he was an idealist, he said he didn't want out relationship as he called it to influence his aesthetic judgment. He didn't want our relationship to influence anything; it was to be kept separate from life. A certificate framed on the wall, his proof that he was still young.

He did say he loved me though, that part was true; I didn't make it up. It was the night I locked myself in and turned on the water in the bathtub and he cried on the other side of the door. When I gave up and came out he showed me snapshots of his wife and children, his reasons, his stuffed and mounted family, they had names, he said I should be mature.

I heard the thin dentist's-drill sound of a powerboat approaching, more Americans; I got off the swing and went half-way down the steps where I would be shielded by the trees. They slowed their motor and curved into the bay. I crouched and watched, at first I thought they were going to land: but they were only gazing, surveying, planning the attack and the takeover. They pointed up at the cabin and talked, flash of binoculars. Then they accelerated and headed off towards the cliff where the gods lived. But they wouldn't catch anything, they wouldn't be allowed. It was dangerous for them to go there without knowing about the power; they might hurt themselves, a false move, metal hooks lowered into the sacred water, that could touch it off like electricity or a grenade. I had endured it only because I had a talisman, my father had left me the guides, the man-animals and the maze of numbers.

It would be right for my mother to have left something for me also, a legacy. His was complicated, tangled, but hers would be simple as a hand, it would be final. I was not completed yet; there had to be a gift from each of them.

I wanted to search for it but David was jogging down the path from the outhouse. 'Hi,' he called, 'you seen Anna?'

'No,' I said. If I went back to the house or into the garden he would follow me and talk. I stood up and walked down the rest of the steps and ducked into the trail entrance through the long grass.

In the cool green among the trees, new trees and stumps, the stumps with charcoal crusts on them, scabby and crippled, survivors of an old disaster. Sight flowing ahead of me over the ground, eyes filtering the shapes, the names of things fading but their forms and uses remaining, the animals learned what to eat without nouns. Six leaves, three leaves, the root of this is crisp. White stems curved like question marks, fish-coloured in the dim light, corpse plants, inedible. Finger-shaped yellow fungi, unclassified, I never memorized all of them; and further along a mushroom with cup and ring and chalk gills and a name: Death Angel, deadly poison. Beneath it the invisible part, threadlike underground network of which this was the solid flower, temporary as an icicle, growth frozen; tomorrow it would be melted but the roots would stay. If our bodies lived in the earth with only the hair sprouting up through the leafmould it would seem as if that was all we were, filament plants.

The reason they invented coffins, to lock the dead in, preserve them, they put makeup on them; they didn't want them spreading or changing into anything else. The stone with the name and the date was on them to weight them down. She would have hated it, that box, she would have tried to get out; I ought to have stolen her out of that room and brought her here and let her go away by herself into the forest, she would have died anyway but quicker, lucidly, not in that glass case.

It sprang up from the earth, pure joy, pure death, burning white like snow.

The dry leaves shuffled behind me: he had shadowed me along the trail. 'Hi, whatcha doin'?' he said.

I didn't turn or speak but he didn't wait for an answer, he sat down beside me and said, 'What's that?'

I had to concentrate in order to talk to him, the English words seemed important, foreign; it was like trying to listen to two separate conversations, each interrupting the other. 'A mushroom,' I said. That wouldn't be enough, he would want a specific term. My mouth jumped like a stutterer's and the Latin appeared. 'Amanita.'

'Neat,' he said, but he wasn't interested. I willed him to go away but he didn't; after a while he put his hand on my knee.

'Well?' he said.

I looked at him. His smile was like a benevolent uncle's; under his forehead there was a plan, it corrugated the skin. I pushed his hand off and he put it back again.

'How about it?' he said. 'You wanted me to follow you.'

His fingers were squeezing, he was drawing away some of the power, I would lose it and come apart again, the lies would recapture. 'Please don't,' I said.

'Come on now, don't give me hassle,' he said. 'You're a groovy chick, you know the score, you aren't married.' He reached his arm around me, invading, and pulled me over towards him; his neck was creased and freckled, soon he would have jowls, he smelled like scalp. His moustache whisked my face.

I twisted away and stood up. 'Why are you doing this?' I said. 'You're interfering.' I wiped at my arm where he had touched it.

He didn't understand what I meant, he smiled even harder. 'Don't get uptight,' he said, 'I won't tell Joe. It'll be great, it's good for you, keeps you healthy.' Then he went 'Yuk, yuk' like Goofy.

He was speaking about it as though it was an exercising programme, athletic demonstration, ornamental swimming in a chlorine swimming pool noplace in California. 'It wouldn't keep me healthy,' I said, 'I'd get pregnant.'

He lifted his eyebrows, incredulous. 'You're putting me on,' he said, 'this is the twentieth century.'

'No it isn't,' I said. 'Not here.'

He stood up also and took a step towards me. I backed away. He was turning mottled pink, turkey neck, but his voice was still rational. 'Listen,' he said, 'I realize you walk around in never-never land but don't tell me you don't know where Joe is; he's not so noble, he's off in the bushes somewhere with that cunt on four legs, right about now he's shoving it into her.' He glanced quickly at his wristwatch as though timing them; he seemed elated by what he'd said, his eyes gleamed like test-tubes.

'Oh,' I said; I thought about it for a minute. 'Maybe they love each other.' It would be logical, they were the ones who could. 'Do you love me,' I asked in case I hadn't understood him, 'is that why you want me to?'

He thought I was being either smart or stupid and said 'Christ.' Then he paused, aiming. 'You aren't going to let him get away with it, are you?' he said. 'Tit for tat as they say.' He folded his arms, resting his case, retaliation was his ultimate argument: he must have felt it was a duty, an obligation on my part, it would be justice. Geometrical sex, he needed me for an abstract principle; it would be enough for him if our genitals could be detached like two kitchen appliances and copulate in mid-air, that would complete his equation.

His wristwatch glittered, glass and silver: perhaps it was his dial, the key that wound him, the switch. There must be a phrase, a vocabulary that would work. 'I'm sorry,' I said, 'but you don't turn me on.'

'You,' he said, searching for words, not controlled any more, 'tight-ass bitch.'

The power flowed into my eyes, I could see into him, he was an imposter, a pastiche, layers of political handbills, pages from magazines, *affiches*, verbs and nouns glued on to him and shredding away, the original surface littered with fragments and tatters.

In a black suit knocking on doors, young once, even that had been a costume, a uniform; now his hair was falling off and he didn't know what language to use, he'd forgotten his own, he had to copy. Second-hand American was spreading over him in patches, like mange or lichen. He was infested, garbled, and I couldn't help him: it would take such time to heal, unearth him, scrape down to where he was true.

'Keep it to yourself then,' he said, 'I'm not going to sit up and beg for a little third-rate cold tail.'

I detoured around past him, back towards the cabin. More than ever I needed to find it, the thing she had hidden; the power from my father's intercession wasn't enough to protect me, it gave only knowledge and there were more gods than his, his were the gods of the head, antlers rooted in the brain. Not only how to see but how to act.

I thought he would stay there, at least till I was out of range, but he followed along behind me. 'Sorry I blew my cool,' he said. His voice had changed again, now it was deferential. 'It's between us, okay? No need to mention it to Anna, right?' If he'd succeeded he would have told her as soon as he could. 'I respect you for it, I really do.'

'That's all right,' I said; I knew he was lying.

They sat around the table in the regular places and I served dinner. There hadn't been any lunch but no one mentioned that.

'What time is Evans coming tomorrow?' I said.

'Ten, ten-thirty,' David said. 'Have a nice afternoon?' he said to Anna. Joe stuck a new potato with his fork and put it into his mouth.

'Fantastic,' Anna said. 'I got some sun and finished my book, then I had a long talk with Joe and went for a stroll.' Joe chewed, his closed mouth moving, silent refutation. 'And you?'

'Great,' David said, his voice buoyant, inflated. He bent his arm onto the table, his hand brushing mine casually, as though by accident, for her to see. I flinched away, he was lying about me, the animals don't lie.

Anna smiled mournfully at him. I watched him, he wasn't laughing, he was staring at her, the lines in his face deepening and sagging. They know everything about each other, I thought, that's

why they're so sad; but Anna was more than sad, she was
desperate, her body her only weapon and she was fighting for her
life, he was her life, her life was the fight: she was fighting him
because if she ever surrendered the balance of power would be
broken and he would go elsewhere. To continue the war.

I didn't want to join. 'It's not what you think,' I said to Anna.
'He asked me to but I wouldn't.' I wanted to tell her I hadn't acted
against her.

Her eyes flicked from him to me. 'That was pure of you,' she
said. I'd made a mistake, she resented me because I hadn't given
in, it commented on her.

'She's pure all right,' David said, 'she's a little purist.'

'Joe told me she won't put out for him any more,' Anna said,
still looking at me. Joe didn't say anything; he was eating another
potato.

'She hates men,' David said lightly. 'Either that or she wants to
be one. Right?'

A ring of eyes, tribunal; in a minute they would join hands and
dance around me, and after that the rope and the pyre, cure for
heresy.

Maybe it was true, I leafed through all the men I had known to
see whether or not I hated them. But then I realized it wasn't the
men I hated, it was the Americans, the human beings, men and
women both. They'd had their chance but they had turned against
the gods, and it was time for me to choose sides. I wanted there to
be a machine that could make them vanish, a button I could press
that would evaporate them without disturbing anything else, that
way there would be more room for the animals, they would be
rescued.

'Aren't you going to answer?' Anna said, taunting.

'No,' I said.

Anna said, 'God, she really is inhuman,' and they both laughed
a little, sorrowfully.

ANNE RADCLIFFE

From *The Mysteries of Udolpho*

Anne Radcliffe (1764–1823) was born to professional but not literary parents. In 1787 she married William Radcliffe who became the editor of a newsletter called the English Chronicle. *She wrote* The Mysteries of Udolpho *and* The Italian *and although these were two of the most popular books of the late eighteenth century she did not mix in literary circles and preferred to stay at home. She suffered severely from asthma.*

In the work of Mrs Radcliffe, the gothic romantic novel reached its apogee. In any self-respecting example of the genre a beautiful, virginal and innocent heroine would be forced by brutish circumstance to enter some kind of dangerous and enclosed area (the symbolism could not have been much clearer) and then proceed to be threatened sexually by an overpowering male. Eventually she would be rescued, her virginity happily intact, most probably to marry a handsome and morally upright nobleman. This kind of fiction also heralded an interest in the supernatural, though Mrs Radcliffe herself bucked the trend by incorporating its thrilling elements but refusing to give them credence. The novel is perhaps, however, today most notable for being mocked in Jane Austen's Northanger Abbey *as utterly ridiculous.*

And yet Emily, Anne Radcliffe's heroine, though she is extremely partial to all the same manifestations of 'sensibility' as any nice girl of the period (she faints and blushes with impeccable regularity for example), still manages to show a remarkable rationality of thought

*and refuses to indulge in her servants' preposterous
terror of ghosts and phantoms. The plot itself is, to a
large extent, irrelevant and entirely predictable. Emily is
in love with a young man called Valancourt but has
been separated from him, kidnapped and is, at this
point, incarcerated in a mountain castle, somewhere in
deepest Italy, her virginity entirely at the mercy of her
violent male captors. Whilst unwilling to allow her
heroine to appear silly, Mrs Radcliffe still manages to
thrill her contemporary readership by shamelessly incorporating every gothic device known to her and then
giving it a rational explanation. By working on both
levels she became the unchallenged mistress of the genre
and was massively popular, read by both cynical males
and credulous women.*

ANNETTE, HOWEVER, returned without satisfactory intelligence, for the servants, among whom she had been, were
either entirely ignorant, or affected to be so, concerning the
Count's intended stay at the castle. They could talk only of the
steep and broken road they had just passed, and of the numerous
dangers they had escaped and express wonder how their lord
could choose to encounter all these, in the darkness of night; for
they scarcely allowed, that the torches had served for any other
purpose but that of showing the dreariness of the mountains.
Annette, finding she could gain no information, left them, making
noisy petitions, for more wood on the fire and more supper on the
table.

'And now, ma'amselle,' added she, 'I am so sleepy! – I am sure,
if you was so sleepy, you would not desire me to sit up with you.'

Emily, indeed, began to think it was cruel to wish it; she had
also waited so long, without receiving a summons from Montoni,
that it appeared he did not mean to disturb her, at this late hour,
and she determined to dismiss Annette. But, when she again
looked round her gloomy chamber, and recollected certain
circumstances, fear seized her spirits, and she hesitated.

'And yet it were cruel of me to ask you to stay, till I am asleep,
Annette,' said she, 'for I fear it will be very long before I forget
myself in sleep.'

'I dare say it will be very long, ma'amselle,' said Annette.

'But, before you go,' rejoined Emily, 'let me ask you – Had
Signor Montoni left Count Morano, when you quitted the hall?'

'O no, ma'am, they were alone together.'

'Have you been in my aunt's dressing-room, since you left me?'

'No, ma'amselle, I called at the door as I passed, but it was
fastened; so I thought my lady was gone to bed.'

'Who, then, was with your lady just now?' said Emily, forgetting, in surprise, her usual prudence.

'Nobody, I believe, ma'am,' replied Annette, 'nobody has been
with her, I believe, since I left you.'

Emily took no further notice of the subject, and, after some
struggle with imaginary fears, her good nature prevailed over

them so far, that she dismissed Annette for the night. She then sat, musing upon her own circumstances and those of Madame Montoni, till her eye rested on the miniature picture, which she had found, after her father's death, among the papers he had enjoined her to destroy. It was open upon the table, before her, among some loose drawings, having, with them, been taken out of a little box by Emily, some hours before. The sight of it called up many interesting reflections, but the melancholy sweetness of the countenance soothed the emotions, which these had occasioned. It was the same style of countenance as that of her late father, and while she gazed on it with fondness on this account, she even fancied a resemblance in the features. But this tranquillity was suddenly interrupted, when she recollected the words in the manuscript, that had been found with this picture, and which had formerly occasioned her so much doubt and horror. At length, she roused herself from the deep reverie, into which this remembrance had thrown her; but, when she rose to undress, the silence and solitude, to which she was left, at this midnight hour, for not even a distant sound was now heard, conspired with the impression the subject she had been considering had given to her mind, to appall her. Annette's hints, too, concerning this chamber, simple as they were, had not failed to affect her, since they followed a circumstance of peculiar horror, which she herself had witnessed, and since the scene of this was a chamber nearly adjoining her own.

The door of the stair-case was, perhaps a subject of more reasonable alarm, and she now began to apprehend, such was the aptitude of her fears, that this stair-case had some private communication with the apartment, which she shuddered even to remember. Determined not to undress, she lay down to sleep in her clothes, with her late father's dog, the faithful *Manchon*, at the foot of the bed, whom she considered as a kind of guard.

Thus circumstanced, she tried to banish reflection, but her busy fancy would still hover over the subjects of her interest, and she heard the clock of the castle strike two, before she closed her eyes.

From the disturbed slumber, into which she then sunk, she was soon awakened by a noise, which seemed to arise within her chamber; but the silence, that prevailed, as she fearfully listened, inclined her to believe, that she had been alarmed by such sounds as sometimes occur in dreams, and she laid her head again upon the pillow.

A return of the noise again disturbed her; it seemed to come from that part of the room, which communicated with the private stair-case, and she instantly remembered the odd circumstance of the door having been fastened, during the preceding night, by some unknown hand. Her late alarming suspicion, concerning its communication, also occurred to her. Her heart became faint with terror. Half raising herself from the bed, and gently drawing aside the curtain, she looked towards the door of the stair-case, but the lamp, that burnt on the hearth, spread so feeble a light through the apartment, that the remote parts of it were lost in shadow. The noise, however, which, she was convinced, came from the door, continued. It seemed like that made by the undrawing of rusty bolts, and often ceased, and was then renewed more gently, as if the hand, that occasioned it, was restrained by a fear of discovery. While Emily kept her eyes fixed on the spot, she saw the door move, and then slowly open, and perceived something enter the room, but the extreme duskiness prevented her distinguishing what it was. Almost fainting with terror, she had yet sufficient command over herself, to check the shriek, that was escaping from her lips, and, letting the curtain drop from her hand, continued to observe in silence the motions of the mysterious form she saw. It seemed to glide along the remote obscurity of the apartment, then paused, and, as it approached the hearth, she perceived, in the stronger light, what appeared to be a human figure. Certain remembrances now struck upon her heart, and almost subdued the feeble remains of her spirits; she continued, however, to watch the figure, which remained for some time motionless, but then, advancing slowly towards the bed, stood silently at the feet, where the curtains, being a little open, allowed her still to see it; terror, however, had now deprived her of the power of discrimination, as well as of that of utterance.

Having continued there a moment, the form retreated towards the hearth, when it took the lamp, held it up, surveyed the chamber, for a few moments, and then again advanced towards the bed. The light at that instant awakening the dog, that had slept at Emily's feet, he barked loudly, and, jumping to the floor, flew at the stranger, who struck the animal smartly with a sheathed sword, and, springing towards the bed, Emily discovered – Count Morano!

She gazed at him for a moment in speechless affright, while he, throwing himself on his knee at the bed-side, besought her to fear nothing, and, having thrown down his sword, would have taken her hand, when the faculties, that terror had suspended, suddenly returned, and she sprung from the bed, in the dress, which surely a kind of prophetic apprehension had prevented her, on this night, from throwing aside.

Morano rose, followed her to the door, through which he had entered, and caught her hand, as she reached the top of the stair-case, but not before she had discovered, by the gleam of a lamp, another man half-way down the steps. She now screamed in despair, and, believing herself given up by Montoni, saw, indeed, no possibility of escape.

The Count, who still held her hand, led her back into the chamber.

'Why all this terror?' said he, in a tremulous voice. 'Hear me, Emily: I come not to alarm you; no, by Heaven! I love you too well – too well for my own peace.'

Emily looked at him for a moment, in fearful doubt.

'Then leave me, sir,' said she, 'leave me instantly.'

'Hear me, Emily,' resumed Morano, 'hear me! I love, and am in despair – yes – in despair. How can I gaze upon you, and know, that it is, perhaps, for the last time, without suffering all the phrensy of despair? But it shall not be so; you shall be mine, in spite of Montoni and all his villainy.'

'In spite of Montoni!' cried Emily eagerly: 'what is it I hear?'

'You hear, that Montoni is a villain,' exclaimed Morano with vehemence, – 'a villain who would have sold you to my love! – Who – '

'And is he less, who would have bought me?' said Emily, fixing on the Count an eye of calm contempt. 'Leave the room, sir, instantly,' she continued in a voice, trembling between joy and fear, 'or I will alarm the family, and you may receive that from Signor Montoni's vengeance, which I have vainly supplicated from his pity.' But Emily knew, that she was beyond the hearing of those, who might protect her.

'You can never hope any thing from his pity,' said Morano, 'he has used me infamously, and my vengeance shall pursue him. And for you, Emily, for you, he has new plans more profitable than the last, no doubt.' The gleam of hope, which the Count's former speech had revived, was now nearly extinguished by the latter; and, while Emily's countenance betrayed the emotions of her mind, he endeavoured to take advantage of the discovery.

'I lose time,' said he: 'I came not to exclaim against Montoni; I came to solicit, to plead – to Emily; to tell her all I suffer, to entreat her to save me from despair, and herself from destruction. Emily! the schemes of Montoni are insearchable, but, I warn you, they are terrible; he has no principle, when interest, or ambition leads. Can I love you, and abandon you to his power? Fly, then, fly from this gloomy prison, with a lover, who adores you! I have bribed a servant of the castle to open the gates, and, before tomorrow's dawn, you shall be far on the way to Venice.'

Emily, overcome by the sudden shock she had received, at the moment, too, when she had begun to hope for better days, now thought she saw destruction surround her on every side. Unable to reply, and almost to think, she threw herself into a chair, pale and breathless. That Montoni had formerly sold her to Morano, was very probable; that he had now withdrawn his consent to the marriage, was evident from the Count's present conduct; and it was nearly certain, that a scheme of stronger interest only could have induced the selfish Montoni to forego a plan, which he had hitherto so strenuously pursued. These reflections made her tremble at the hints, which Morano had just given, which she no longer hesitated to believe; and, while she shrunk from the new scenes of misery and oppression, that might await her in the castle of Udolpho, she was compelled to observe, that almost her only means of escaping them was by submitting herself to the protection of this man, with whom evils more certain and not less terrible appeared, – evils, upon which she could not endure to pause for an instant.

Her silence, though it was that of agony, encouraged the hopes of Morano, who watched her countenance with impatience, took again the resisting hand she had withdrawn, and, as he pressed it to his heart, again conjured her to determine immediately. 'Every moment we lose, will make our departure more dangerous,' said he: 'these few moments lost may enable Montoni to overtake us.'

'I beseech you, sir, be silent,' said Emily faintly: 'I am indeed very wretched, and wretched I must remain. Leave me – I command you, leave me to my fate.'

'Never!' cried the Count vehemently: 'let me perish first! But forgive my violence! the thought of losing you is madness. You cannot be ignorant of Montoni's character, you may be ignorant of his schemes – nay, you must be so, or you would not hesitate between my love and his power.'

'Nor do I hesitate,' said Emily.

'Let us go, then,' said Morano, eagerly kissing her hand, and rising, 'my carriage waits, below the castle walls.'

'You mistake me, sir,' said Emily. 'Allow me to thank you for the interest you express in my welfare, and to decide by my own choice. I shall remain under the protection of Signor Montoni.'

'Under his protection!' exclaimed Morano, proudly, 'his *protection*! Emily, why will you suffer yourself to be thus deluded? I have already told you what you have to expect from his *protection*.'

'And pardon me, sir, if, in this instance, I doubt mere assertion, and, to be convinced, require something approaching to proof.'

'I have now neither the time, or the means of adducing proof,' replied the Count.

'Nor have I, sir, the inclination to listen to it, if you had.'

'But you trifle with my patience and my distress,' continued Morano. 'Is a marriage with a man, who adores you, so very terrible in your eyes, that you would prefer to it all the misery, to which Montoni may condemn you in this remote prison? Some wretch must have stolen those affections, which ought to be mine, or you could not thus obstinately persist in refusing an offer, that would place you beyond the reach of oppression.' Morano walked about the room, with quick steps, and a disturbed air.

'This discourse, Count Morano, sufficiently proves, that my affections ought not to be yours,' said Emily, mildly, 'and this conduct, that I should not be placed beyond the reach of oppression, so long as I remained in your power. If you wish me to believe otherwise, cease to oppress me any longer by your presence. If you refuse this, you will compel me to expose you to the resentment of Signor Montoni.'

'Yes, let him come,' cried Morano furiously, 'and brave *my* resentment! let him dare to face once more the man he has so courageously injured; danger shall teach him morality, and vengeance justice – let him come, and receive my sword in his heart!'

The vehemence, with which this was uttered, gave Emily new cause of alarm, who arose from her chair, but her trembling frame refused to support her, and she resumed her seat; – the words died on her lips, and when she looked wistfully towards the door of the corridor, which was locked, she considered it was impossible for her to leave the apartment, before Morano would be apprised of, and able to counteract, her intention.

Without observing her agitation, he continued to pace the room in the utmost perturbation of spirits. His darkened countenance expressed all the rage of jealousy and revenge; and a person, who had seen his features under the smile of ineffable tenderness, which he so lately assumed, would now scarcely have believed them to be the same.

'Count Morano,' said Emily, at length recovering her voice, 'calm, I entreat you, these transports and listen to reason, if you will not to pity. You have equally misplaced your love, and your hatred – I never could have returned the affection, with which you honour me, and certainly have never encouraged it; neither has Signor Montoni injured you, for you must have known, that he had no right to dispose of my hand, had he even possessed the power do to so. Leave, then, leave the castle, while you may with safety. Spare yourself the dreadful consequences of an unjust revenge, and the remorse of having prolonged to me these moments of suffering.'

'Is it for mine, or for Montoni's safety, that you are thus alarmed?' said Morano, coldly, and turning towards her with a look of acrimony.

'For both,' replied Emily, in a trembling voice.

'Unjust revenge!' cried the Count, resuming the abrupt tones of passion. 'Who, that looks upon that face, can imagine a punishment adequate to the injury he would have done me? Yes, I will leave the castle; but it shall not be alone. I have trifled too long. Since my prayers and my sufferings cannot prevail, force shall. I have people in waiting, who shall convey you to my carriage. Your voice will bring no succour; it cannot be heard from this remote part of the castle; submit, therefore, in silence, to go with me.'

This was an unnecessary injunction, at present; for Emily was too certain, that her call would avail her nothing; and terror had so entirely disordered her thoughts, that she knew not how to plead to Morano, but sat, mute and trembling, in her chair, till he advanced to lift her from it, when she suddenly raised herself, and, with a repulsive gesture, and a countenance of forced serenity, said, 'Count Morano! I am now in your power; but you will observe, that this is not the conduct which can win the esteem you appear so solicitous to obtain, and that you are preparing for yourself a load of remorse, in the miseries of a friendless orphan, which can never leave you. Do you believe your heart to be, indeed, so hardened, that you can look without emotion on the suffering, to which you would condemn me?' –

Emily was interrupted by the growling of the dog, who now came again from the bed, and Morano looked towards the door of the stair-case, where no person appearing, he called aloud, 'Cesario!'

'Emily,' said the Count, 'why will you reduce me to adopt this conduct? How much more willingly would I persuade, than compel you to become my wife! but, by Heaven! I will not leave you to be sold by Montoni. Yet a thought glances across my mind, that brings madness with it. I know not how to name it. It is preposterous – it cannot be. – Yet you tremble – you grow pale! It is! it is so; – you – you – love Montoni!' cried Morano, grasping Emily's wrist, and stamping his foot on the floor.

An involuntary air of surprise appeared on her countenance. 'If you have indeed believed so,' said she, 'believe so still.'

'That look, those words confirm it,' exclaimed Morano, furiously. 'No, no, no, Montoni had a richer prize in view, than gold. But he shall not live to triumph over me! – This very instant – '

He was interrupted by the loud barking of the dog.

'Stay, Count Morano,' said Emily, terrified by his words, and by the fury expressed in his eyes, 'I will save you from this error. – Of all men, Signor Montoni is not your rival; though, if I find all other means of saving myself vain, I will try whether my voice may not arouse his servants to my succour.'

'Assertion,' replied Morano, 'at such a moment, is not to be depended upon. How could I suffer to myself to doubt, even for an instant, that he could see you, and not love? – But my first care shall be to convey you from the castle. Cesario! ho, – Cesario!'

A man now appeared at the door of the stair-case, and other steps were heard ascending. Emily uttered a loud shriek, as Morano hurried her across the chamber, and, at the same moment, she heard a noise at the door, that opened upon the corridor. The Count paused an instant, as if his mind was suspended between love and the desire of vengeance; and, in that instant, the door gave way, and Montoni, followed by the old steward and several other persons, burst into the room.

'Draw!' cried Montoni to the Count, who did not pause for a second bidding, but, giving Emily into the hands of the people, that appeared from the stair-case, turned fiercely round. 'This in thine heart, villain!' said he, as he made a thrust at Montoni with his sword, who parried the blow, and aimed another, while some of the persons, who had followed him into the room, endeavoured to part the combatants, and others rescued Emily from the hands of Morano's servants.

'Was it for this, Count Morano,' said Montoni, in a cool sarcastic tone of voice, 'that I received you under my roof, and permitted you, though my declared enemy, to remain under it for the night? Was it, that you might repay my hospitality with the treachery of a fiend, and rob me of my niece?'

'Who talks of treachery?' said Morano, in a tone of unrestrained vehemence. 'Let him that does, shew an unblushing face of innocence. Montoni, you are a villain! If there is treachery in this affair, look to yourself as the author of it. If – do I say? I – whom you have wronged with unexampled baseness, whom you have injured almost beyond redress! But why do I use words? – Come on, coward, and receive justice at my hands!'

'Coward!' cried Montoni, bursting from the people who held him, and rushing on the Count, when they both retreated into the corridor, where the fight continued so desperately, that none of the spectators dared approach them, Montoni swearing, that the first who interfered, should fall by his sword.

Jealousy and revenge lent all their fury to Morano, while the superior skill and the temperance of Montoni enabled him to wound his adversary, whom his servants now attempted to seize, but he would not be restrained, and, regardless of his wound, continued to fight. He seemed to be insensible both of pain and loss of blood, and alive only to the energy of his passions. Montoni, on the contrary, persevered in the combat, with a fierce, yet wary, valour; he received the point of Morano's sword on his arm, but, almost in the same instant, severely wounded and disarmed him. The Count then fell back into the arms of his servant, while Montoni held his sword over him, and bade him ask for his life. Morano, sinking under the anguish of his wound, had scarcely replied by a gesture, and by a few words, feebly articulated, that he would not – when he fainted; and Montoni was then going to have plunged the sword into his breast, as he lay senseless, but his arm was arrested by Cavigni. To the interruption he yielded without much difficulty, but his complexion changed almost to blackness, as he looked upon his fallen adversary, and ordered, that he should be carried instantly from the castle.

In the mean time, Emily, who had been with-held from leaving the chamber during the affray, now came forward into the corridor, and pleaded a cause of common humanity, with the feelings of the warmest benevolence, when she entreated Montoni to allow Morano the assistance in the castle, which his situation required. But Montoni, who had seldom listened to pity, now seemed rapacious of vengeance, and, with a monster's cruelty, again ordered his defeated enemy to be taken from the castle, in his present state, though there were only the woods, or a solitary neighbouring cottage, to shelter him from the night.

The Count's servants having declared, that they would not move him till he revived, Montoni's stood inactive, Cavigni remonstrating, and Emily, superior to Montoni's menaces, giving water to Morano, and directing the attendants to bind up his wound. At length, Montoni had leisure to feel pain from his own hurt, and he withdrew to examine it.

The Count, meanwhile, having slowly recovered, the first object he saw, on raising his eyes, was Emily, bending over him with a countenance strongly expressive of solicitude. He surveyed her with a look of anguish.

'I have deserved this,' said he, 'but not from Montoni. It is from you, Emily, that I have deserved punishment, yet I receive only pity!' He paused, for he had spoken with difficulty. After a moment, he proceeded, 'I must resign you, but not to Montoni. Forgive me the sufferings I have already occasioned you! But for *that* villain – his infamy shall not go unpunished. Carry me from this place,' said he to his servants. 'I am in no condition to travel: you must, therefore, take me to the nearest cottage, for I will not pass the night under his roof, although I may expire on the way from it.'

Cesario proposed to go out, and enquire for a cottage, that might receive his master, before he attempted to remove him: but Morano was impatient to be gone; the anguish of his mind seemed to be even greater than that of his wound, and he rejected, with disdain, the offer of Cavigni to entreat Montoni, that he might be suffered to pass the night in the castle. Cesario was now going to call up the carriage to the great gate, but the Count forbade him. 'I cannot bear the motion of a carriage,' said he: 'Call some others of my people, that they may assist in bearing me in their arms.'

At length, however, Morano submitted to reason, and consented, that Cesario should first prepare some cottage to receive him. Emily, now that he had recovered his senses, was about to withdraw from the corridor, when a message from Montoni commanded her to do so, and also that the Count, if he was not already gone, should quit the castle immediately. Indignation flashed from Morano's eyes, and flushed his cheeks.

'Tell Montoni,' said he, 'that I shall go when it suits my own convenience; that I quit the castle, he dare to call his, as I would the nest of a serpent, and that this is not the last he shall hear from me. Tell him, I will not leave *another* murder on his conscience, if I can help it.'

'Count Morano! do you know what you say?' said Cavigni.

'Yes, Signor, I know well what I say, and he will understand well what I mean. His conscience will assist his understanding, on this occasion.'

'Count Morano,' said Verezzi, who had hitherto silently observed him, 'dare again to insult my friend, and I will plunge this sword in your body.'

'It would be an action worthy the friend of a villain!' said Morano, as the strong impulse of his indignation enabled him to raise himself from the arms of his servants; but the energy was momentary, and he sunk back, exhausted by the effort. Montoni's people, meanwhile, held Verezzi, who seemed inclined, even in this instant, to execute his threat; and Cavigni, who was not so depraved as to abet the cowardly malignity of Verezzi, endeavoured to withdraw him from the corridor; and Emily, whom a compassionate interest had thus long detained, was now quitting it in new terror, when the supplicating voice of Morano arrested her, and, by a feeble gesture, he beckoned her to draw nearer. She advanced with timid steps, but the fainting languor of his countenance again awakened her pity, and overcame her terror.

'I am going from hence for ever,' said he: 'perhaps, I shall never see you again. I would carry with me your forgiveness, Emily; nay more – I would also carry your good wishes.'

'You have my forgiveness, then,' said Emily, 'and my sincere wishes for your recovery.'

'And only for my recovery?' said Morano, with a sigh. 'For your general welfare,' added Emily.

'Perhaps I ought to be contented with this,' he resumed; 'I certainly have not deserved more; but I would ask you, Emily, sometimes to think of me, and, forgetting my offence, to remember only the passion which occasioned it. I would ask, alas! impossibilities: I would ask you to love me! At this moment, when I am about to part with you, and that, perhaps, for ever, I am scarcely myself. Emily – may you never know the torture of a passion like mine! What do I say? O, that, for me, you might be sensible of such a passion!'

Emily looked impatient to be gone. 'I entreat you, Count, to consult your own safety,' said she, 'and linger here no longer. I tremble for the consequences of Signor Verezzi's passion, and of Montoni's resentment, should he learn that you are still here.'

Morano's face was overspread with a momentary crimson, his eyes sparkled, but he seemed endeavouring to conquer his emotion, and replied in a calm voice, 'Since you are interested for my safety, I will regard it, and be gone. But, before I go, let me again hear you say, that you wish me well,' said he, fixing on her an earnest and mournful look.

Emily repeated her assurances. He took her hand, which she scarcely attempted to withdraw, and put it to his lips. 'Farewell, Count Morano!' said Emily; and she turned to go, when a second message arrived from Montoni, and she again conjured Morano, as he valued his life, to quit the castle immediately. He regarded her in silence, with a look of fixed despair. But she had no time to enforce her compassionate entreaties, and, not daring to disobey the second command of Montoni, she left the corridor to attend him.

He was in the cedar parlour, that adjoined the great hall, laid upon a couch, and suffering a degree of anguish from his wound, which few persons could have disguised, as he did. His countenance, which was stern, but calm, expressed the dark passion of revenge, but no symptom of pain; bodily pain, indeed, he had always despised, and had yielded only to the strong and terrible energies of the soul. He was attended by old Carlo and by Signor Bertolini, but Madame Montoni was not with him.

Emily trembled, as she approached and received his severe rebuke, for not having obeyed his first summons; and perceived, also, that he attributed her stay in the corridor to a motive, that had not even occurred to her artless mind.

'This is an instance of female caprice,' said he, 'which I ought to have foreseen. Count Morano, whose suit you obstinately rejected, so long as it was countenanced by me, you favour, it seems, since you find I have dismissed him.'

Emily look astonished. 'I do not comprehend you, sir,' said she: 'You certainly do not mean to imply, that the design of the Count to visit the double-chamber, was founded upon any approbation of mine.'

'To that I reply nothing,' said Montoni; 'but it must certainly be a more than common interest, that made you plead so warmly in his cause, and that could detain you thus long in his presence, contrary to my express order – in the presence of a man, whom you have hitherto, on all occasions, most scrupulously shunned!'

'I fear, sir, it was a more than common interest, that detained me,' said Emily calmly; 'for of late I have been inclined to think, that of compassion is an uncommon one. But how could I, could *you*, sir, witness Count Morano's deplorable condition, and not wish to relieve it?'

'You add hypocrisy to caprice,' said Montoni, frowning, 'and an attempt at satire, to both; but, before you undertake to regulate the morals of other persons, you should learn and practise the virtues, which are indispensable to a woman – sincerity, uniformity of conduct and obedience.'

Emily, who had always endeavoured to regulate her conduct by the nicest laws, and whose mind was finely sensible, not only of what is just in morals, but of whatever is beautiful in the female character, was shocked by these words; yet, in the next moment, her heart swelled with the consciousness of having deserved praise, instead of censure, and she was proudly silent. Montoni, acquainted with the delicacy of her mind, knew how keenly she would feel his rebuke; but he was a stranger to the luxury of conscious worth, and, therefore, did not foresee the energy of that sentiment, which now repelled his satire. Turning to a servant who had lately entered the room, he asked whether Morano had quitted the castle. The man answered, that his servants were then removing him, on a couch, to a neighbouring cottage. Montoni seemed somewhat appeased, on hearing this; and, when Ludovico appeared, a few moments after, and said, that Morano was gone, he told Emily she might retire to her apartment.

She withdrew willingly from his presence; but the thought of passing the remainder of the night in a chamber, which the door from the stair-case made liable to the intrusion of any person, now alarmed her more than ever, and she determined to call at Madame Montoni's room, and request, that Annette might be permitted to be with her.

On reaching the great gallery, she heard voices seemingly in dispute, and, her spirits now apt to take alarm, she paused, but soon distinguished some words of Cavigni and Verezzi, and went towards them, in the hope of conciliating their difference. They were alone. Verezzi's face was still flushed with rage; and, as the first object of it was now removed from him, he appeared willing to transfer his resentment to Cavigni, who seemed to be expostulating, rather than disputing, with him.

Verezzi was protesting, that he would instantly inform Montoni of the insult, which Morano had thrown out against him, and above all that, wherein he had accused him of murder.

'There is no answering,' said Cavigni, 'for the words of a man in a passion; little serious regard ought to be paid to them. If you persist in your resolution, the consequences may be fatal to both

We have now more serious interests to pursue, than those of a petty revenge.'

Emily joined her entreaties to Cavigni's arguments, and they, at length, prevailed so far, as that Verezzi consented to retire, without seeing Montoni.

On calling at her aunt's apartment, she found it fastened. In a few minutes, however, it was opened by Madame Montoni herself.

It may be remembered, that it was by a door leading into the bedroom from a back passage, that Emily had secretly entered a few hours preceding. She now conjectured, by the calmness of Madam Montoni's air, that she was not apprised of the accident, which had befallen her husband, and was beginning to inform her of it, in the tenderest manner she could, when her aunt interrupted her, by saying, she was acquainted with the whole affair.

Emily knew indeed, that she had little reason to love Montoni, but could scarcely have believed her capable of such perfect apathy, as she now discovered towards him; having obtained permission, however, for Annette to sleep in her chamber, she went thither immediately.

A track of blood appeared along the corridor, leading to it; and on the spot, where the Count and Montoni had fought, the whole floor was stained. Emily shuddered, and leaned on Annette, as she passed. When she reached her apartment, she instantly determined, since the door of the stair-case had been left open, and that Annette was now with her, to explore whither it led – a circumstance now materially connected with her own safety. Annette accordingly, half curious and half afraid, proposed to descend the stairs; but, on approaching the door, they perceived, that it was already fastened without, and their care was then directed to the securing it on the inside also, by placing against it as much of the heavy furniture of the room, as they could lift. Emily then retired to bed, and Annette continued on a chair by the hearth, where some feeble embers remained.

PAT CALIFIA

From *The Calyx of Isis*

Pat Califia, who lives in San Francisco, is probably the best known writer of specifically lesbian erotic fiction in America. She was a key figure in the massive burgeoning market of lesbian books, coming out of small, independent publishing houses and magazines of the eighties and her short story collection Macho Sluts, *written in 1988, defined the new confidence of the market – alternatively but unapologetically pornographic.*

Califia, clearing a new way before her, clearly wishes her writing to be responsible and informative as well as arousing (she includes an appendix with information on safe sex for lesbians). Pornography, derived from the ancient Greek porne *and* graphos, *means 'writing about whores', though the term itself did not come into use until the late nineteenth century. Califia writes in the introduction that the 'anti-porn movement has done at least as much as the male system to make whores seem vile in the popular imagination. This book will certainly seem vile to many people. Therefore this book is a whore. And I wrote it, knowing that meant being a pornographer.' Califia believes that women should have the right to reclaim their sexuality and, with it, the right to be submissive sexually, on their own terms, if that is what they desire.*

'Macho sluts are supposedly a contradiction in terms, like virgins and whores,' she writes, 'a victim of male violence – woman who accepts male definitions of her sexuality. Instead, I believe that she is someone men hate because she is potentially beyond their control. If

she has to pleasure many men briefly to escape belonging permanently to one particular man, she will.'

Califia does not appear to address the problem that the woman may have no choice in the matter. It may not be a question of liberation through many men or oppression through one, it may simply be a matter of oppression through both alternatives. Or, possibly, liberation. In precisely the terms of her argument, Califia uses this particular passage in 'The Calyx of Isis', to appropriate the terminology of male pornography in order to 'free' female sexuality. Whether this is truly liberation or merely another example of oppression via the imitation of the sexual behaviour of the oppressor rather than the creation of a sexual terminology of one's own, is open to debate.

THEY ALL laughed, then turned as the door of the dungeon creaked and gaped wide. EZ, Joy and Michael (who was, indeed, in Marine Corps dress blues) came in, staggering a little under the weight of a long, leather bag bound with straps and buckles. Alex brought up the rear. Her eyes never left Roxanne's mummified form.

Tyre pulled a rope down from a ceiling pulley and opened the panic snap at the end of it. She gestured for them to bring Roxanne to her, and unzipped the bottom of the bag. Two manacled feet in spike-heeled shoes were revealed. Alex unbuckled a strap that went around the outside of the body-bag at mid-calf height, and the three other women put Roxanne on her feet. After unbuckling the thigh strap, they continued unzipping the bag, up both sides. As soon as the chained wrists were revealed, tucked into the small of the girl's back, Tyre stopped them and fastened the panic snap midpoint between Roxanne's wrists. Alex unbuckled the strap that went around the upper arms outside the bag, and EZ and Joy finished unzipping and removing it. Michael rolled it up and stowed it behind the bar.

The girl was wearing a black silk slip and stockings of the same material. Anne-Marie knelt behind her and adjusted the seams with minute hitches. Roxanne was hooded. Alex had gathered her long, curly blonde hair into a ponytail and pulled it through a hole in the hood. The only other openings in it were the nose holes. A piece of tubing, ending in an incongruous orange valve and a black rubber bulb, dangled from the mouth of the hood. Tyre cocked Roxanne's head, made sure she was breathing freely, then drew the rope down hand over hand until the girl was standing bent at the waist, her chained hands high in the air behind her back. Tyre secured the rope by winding it in a figure-eight around a cleat on the wall.

Alex had put her arm over Michael's shoulder. She was stroking the sky-blue fly of the Marine Corps uniform. 'Do you always strap it on before you come to work?' she asked.

Michael grinned. 'Well, you know who I work for,' she replied. her hips rocked in response to Alex's touch, straps pulled tight up against her cunt. She wanted Alex to take out her cock and suck it. Anne-Marie was stroking the chained girl in much the same way, but her cunt had no protection other than a pair of crotchless silk panties held together with tiny ribbons tied in bows. The rest of the pack gathered around and watched Anne-Marie pull up the girl's skirt and untie each bow, then plunge her fingers into her cleft from behind. The chains made a pleasant accompaniment, barely discernible over the music. The girl staggered, and tossed her shoulders. The rope was not long enough to let her escape. She could not lower her hands and cover her exposed vaginal lips. She was helpless. She tossed her shoulders again as Anne-Marie worked one finger into her ass.

'I think you oughta stick around,' Alex growled in Michael's ear. She had moved behind her and was massaging her butt.

'Pleasure's mine.'

'It will be,' Alex promised.

The girl in the middle of the pack didn't turn her head in response to this dialogue. Apparently the hood completely sealed off hearing as well as sight.

'You put in ear plugs?' Tyre asked Alex.

'Yes. And it already has pads over the ears. The blindfold can be unsnapped. And you can see the gag. There's a rubber insert that fits inside the mouth and gets pumped up.'

Kay went over to the girl, took the bulb that dangled from her face, and pumped it once or twice. Roxanne shook her head, and her long hair sprayed across her back.

'I already pumped that up pretty good,' Alex warned. 'Why don't you turn the valve and let some of the air out, then pump it up again? I like keeping something big in her mouth.'

Michael reached over her shoulder and touched Alex's lips. She got her fingers bitten. She gave Alex a lazy smile and put them in her own mouth, sucked the pain away. When she noticed that EZ was watching them, looking bitter and hungry, she ran her tongue around her lips and gave EZ a slack-jawed come-on so ravenous that it made EZ look away, abashed.

The hood was an alien face, insect-like, fish-like, sitting atop the body of a beautiful young woman. It depersonalized her, made her even more sexy, removed any inhibitions the assembled dominatrices might have had about getting their hands on her. Anne-

Marie had allowed Joy to take her place. The fly-whisk was in her hand, and she was dangling its scarlet horsehair tips across Roxanne's up-turned cheeks, then striking full across them. It left very thin red lines, as if it were a big paintbrush. Joy ran her fingertips across them, cooed something in dialect, then ran her tongue all over Roxanne's ass. The next strokes fell on wet skin, and Roxanne's slender heels made a staccato noise upon the planks of the dungeon floor.

'Can she keep her footing in those shoes?' Tyre asked.

'Can you?' Alex said, glancing down at the madam's boot-heels.

'Could you?' Tyre asked.

'You're trying to change the subject.'

'C'mon, answer my question.'

'Tyre, she never wears any other kind of shoes. She dances in them all day, for Chrissake. Even her bedroom slippers got high heels.'

'I see. You like girls in six-inch spikes, huh?'

'You could say that,' Alex said, rubbing Michael's neck. Michael's hands were behind her back, and she had a couple of fingers hooked under Alex's leather codpiece. The master's pubic hair was damp.

'She ever fuck you with them?' Michael asked innocently.

Alex gave her a little push and went to join the group clustered closer to Roxanne. Tyre shook her head. 'That mouth,' she whispered, putting two long fingers, tipped with sharp nails, into the orifice of which she spoke, 'is going to get you into soooo much trouble some day.'

Michael swallowed her fingers easily, arrogantly. Her eyes said she couldn't hope for a better fate.

By now, Joy had turned Roxanne's entire ass a bright red. Kay was to one side of her with a doubled-over belt, and she used it in overlapping strokes that moved from the buttocks down the thighs. Then she changed sides and repeated the maneuver. The red deepened, the ass seemed to swell. Roxanne's wet thighs, when she moved under the belt, chafed each other. EZ was kneeling in front of her, holding her by her waist, and had somehow managed to get her tongue up between her labia, and was teasing her orally while Kay strapped her.

Alex watched impassively, but inside she was flame, barely contained, so close to what she wanted that her throat and chest ached. When she saw Anne-Marie with one of her canes politely gesturing to Chris that she should use her signal whip first, Alex nudged EZ out of the way with her boot and took her lady's torso in her arms, standing to one side of her, to steady her against these new forms of pain. Chris kept shaking her head, and insisted on holding back, so it was Anne-Marie who stepped forward and gave Roxanne six cuts, close and fast. Each cane stroke left two parallel marks across both buns, and Anne-Marie was so accurate that the top edge of each blow lined up perfectly with the bottom edge of the prior stroke.

It was a good thing Alex was there, because Roxanne threw herself sideways, apparently losing track of up or down when the pain from the caning faded, then returned in shocking force. Chris waited until she was steady on her feet and in Alex's arms before she hurled the leather snake in her hand out and down toward Roxanne's tender flesh. Impact! Impact! Impact! Impact! Just four explosions, each leaving a v-shaped kiss that was already turning purple. Alex passed her hand over the marks and smiled. She crooked her index finger at Michael, who came along as if it were tied to a string around her dick.

'Gonna help me out, my man?' she asked, letting go of Roxanne and reaching for Michael's fly.

The chauffeur put her fists on her hips and stared at her insolently. 'Get it up for me and I won't be able to help myself,' she replied.

Alex extracted her cock. Kay was already at her elbow with a can of Crisco and a towel. 'Room Service,' she grinned. 'Oh, yeah, slick it up, stud, get that big fuck-pole ready to do that fine piece a favour. Gonna fuck that slut right offa those high-heeled shoes.'

Alex milked Michael, led her to Roxanne by her hard-on, and put the well-greased tip of the instrument up against, just barely inside, Roxanne's wetness. Then she got behind Michael, wiping off her hands, and once they were clean, she clamped them onto Michael's hips and humped her ass as Michael fucked Roxanne, drawing the girl smoothly and relentlessly back and forth on her thick shaft.

The pack shouted obscene encouragement. Alex's lips were

drawn back in a snarl, Michael's hands were like claws on Roxanne, and when she finally lost control and threw herself into the girl, no one could tell if Roxanne had come or not because of the gag in her mouth, but it was very clear that Michael had. Alex plucked her off Roxanne, tucked her inside her jacket, and began to kiss her, sloppy butch kisses that made everybody cheer.

Kay gave EZ a towel and sent her over to clean off Michael and put her equipment away. When EZ knelt in front of her and began to swab at her dick, Michael couldn't resist turning her hips just enough to slap the side of it into EZ's face. The look she got was hatred laced with lust and panic. As if knees weren't made to bend! She was going to remember that look and hope she saw it again sometime, when her own knees weren't so weak.

Tyre had pulled a slim blade, Damascus steel with a horn handle, from the sleeve of her jacket. She ran its edge up the back of Roxanne's legs. The girl stopped panting and immediately froze, obviously trained to mind the blade. 'I think I'm gonna wet my pants,' Kay said to Anne-Marie. 'This is too delicious.'

'I know just how you feel, dear. It's such a cleansing release. So good for the system.'

The knife travelled the inside of Roxanne's thighs. The girl had spread her feet as far apart as her manacles and chain permitted. When the tip of it probed her clit, she jumped a little, then steadied herself. Shoulders, neck, upper arms felt the fine scrape of Tyre's weapon. Then the blade disappeared between her slip and her skin, and its tip plunged up through the thin material. The silk made a grieving sound as it was cut, as if it knew it could not heal itself. Tyre let the elegant rags fall from Roxanne's body, and the girl shivered. Tiny goosebumps came out all over her. She smelled like pure sex. God, she was pretty.

Under the slip she wore a leather corset, cinched so tight that her waist was visibly compressed. Six short garters on each leg kept her stockings taut. Alex motioned everyone close, and all eight women held their hands above Roxanne, then simultaneously lowered them. She jumped when she felt herself handled by so many. The rude hands went everywhere. Obviously, much was going to be demanded from her. She shook beneath their hands, but her nipples got larger and as firm as cherries, and her pussy was already producing enough slippery stuff to pave the way for

all of them to take her in turn. And, in fact, they did just that –
hand after hand plunging as deep as it could go, turning slowly
into her, then being withdrawn to give its neighbour a turn. She
was being laid open to the pack, made equally the vessel of each of
its members.

Alex took her head between her thighs and worked on the
hood's laces. She let all the air out of the gag before peeling the
thin kid off Roxanne's face and tweaking out the ear plugs. Tyre
had unwound the rope from its cleat, and she slowly lowered her
hands. Roxanne sank until she knelt in manacles at Alex's boots.
Alex took the rubber band out of her hair and spread the long,
curly mass out with both hands.

Roxanne had freckles and a turned-up, defiant nose. Her hazel
eyes were clear and determined. She refused to look at anyone but
Alex. The girl was no coward, but she was obviously relieved to
find that her master was there. Tyre loved the look of her. She was
the ultimate bar-femme, dressed up to play the whore for her
butch. She might be a slave, but she was also tough. Try to separate her from Alex, and she'd go after you with a broken bottle. It
wasn't, Tyre realized from the set of that grim little jaw, Roxanne
who doubted the nature and the quality of their relationship. It
was Alex – who was explaining to Roxanne and all of them that
she was giving them her 'flashy piece of trash' for the evening, to
do with as they liked.

The pack stood in a small circle around the master and her
property. Of course, Roxanne had an out. 'All you have to do,'
Alex whispered, kneeling to plunge her hand between Roxanne's
corset and her breasts, 'is tell me you don't belong to me, and you
can walk.' She rubbed her nipples, producing a moan, and then
stood, and moved right up to her. Roxanne knelt over her boot
and wrapped her arms around Alex's thigh. She stared defiantly at
the women behind Alex, and openly rubbed her pussy against the
steel toe of Alex's engineer boot.

'Put rings in me now,' she said. Her voice was high and clear.
'I'm not going to change my mind. I belong to you and walking
out wouldn't change that any more than it would make water run
uphill. Beat me. Brand me. Let these bitches wear themselves out
on me if it will entertain you. But I belong to you, Daddy.'

'Well, for now you belong to them,' Alex said, and the pack

closed in as if on cue. Michael had taken her cock out again, and she finally got the blowjob she had been craving ever since Alex ran her fingertips along her inseam. She worked her entire length back and forth in Roxanne's throat until she made tears come, then pulled her off and handed her over to Anne-Marie, who shooed the girl under her latex skirts. There, Roxanne's tongue found a pair of salty, wet lips held between cool, smooth, chemical-tasting latex panties, and Anne-Marie kept her there until the taste of both was firmly imprinted in her mind. Kay made her kiss her boots, and only allowed her to rub her face over EZ's denim crotch, although EZ ground her pubic bone into Roxanne's face long enough and hard enough to reach a minor climax. Kay cuffed her shoulder and pushed Roxanne over to Joyous Day, who untied her leather-and-fur bikini and rubbed the inside of it all over Roxanne's face. Then her dark hands closed over the blonde head and pulled it between her thighs to service her. Chris, standing next to Joy, unzipped her leather pants, and Joy pushed her hand inside them. She made Roxanne lick her fingers, and used the wetness to jerk Chris off. Every time Joy got close enough to coming, she made Roxanne stop going down on her long enough to lick Chris's cream from her fingers. Then Joy rubbed the moisture into Chris's vulva, over and over again until Chris sobbed and came all over her hand. Chris had been hanging onto Joy's full, brown breasts, and now she held them up to her mouth and sucked hard on Joy's nipples while Roxanne held on to her tattooed thighs and licked her quickly and lightly to orgasm.

Tyre didn't feel like coming yet. She had Roxanne spread her legs wide and lean back, bracing herself with her hands flat on the floor. Then she put her foot up on the girl's mound, and carefully tucked the high heel of her boot into Roxanne's pussy. The chained girl was terribly excited after experiencing so many orgasms vicariously, and she tried to tilt her hips and take all of the boot-heel. Tyre knew it was at the wrong angle to go in without hurting her, so she kept Roxanne at the edge of danger and climax and surprised herself by masturbating at the spectacle until she came, relishing Roxanne's frustrated and tear-spattered face.

'So you think we're going to wear ourselves out on you?' Alex asked her.

'Yes. I want more!' Roxanne cried.

'Oh, I don't think that will be a problem,' Alex said drily. 'Next?' She helped Roxanne to her feet, untied and loosened her corset, then put her back on the floor.

Kay and EZ had moved over to the sling. EZ was perched on its edge, swinging. Kay was applying an emery board to her nails. They gave each other a quick, conspiratorial smile.

'How's the old manicure?' Kay asked EZ.

EZ stretched out her hands and examined her fingertips.

'Flawless,' she said. 'Soft as a baby's bottom. How's yours?'

'Down to the knuckles,' Kay averred. 'Where do you think they hide the grease in this establishment? It don't look to me like Mama's gonna fry much chicken in this here restaurant.'

'Why, you near-sighted fool, there's a whole fucking five-pound can of it hanging from a chain right over here.' EZ hit it with her elbow and made it swing.

Kay pretended to start at the sight of the dangling, industrial-sized tub of Crisco. 'Think that'll be enough?' she asked.

'Hell, I never bother with the stuff myself,' EZ boasted. 'I just make 'em spit on my hand. And if that don't get it wet enough I ram it down their throats.'

Kay made a little ticking noise of approval with her tongue. 'You talk like trash, girl. Cruuude.'

EZ grinned. 'That's the way they like it. I'm not responsible for the taste of trash. I'm just the garbage collector. Out of the gutter and into the sling, that's my motto.'

Kay nodded, staring off into space. She seemed to have forgotten their conversation.

'Slave!' EZ snapped. 'Look at me, fuck-face.'

Roxanne reluctantly came to her knees and barely turned her face in the direction of the sling. She did not care to be addressed in that tone of voice by someone who had not been properly introduced. Who did this punked-out boytoy think she was, smoothing the platinum stripes in her dark topknot? Alex yanked her head up. 'Look her in the eye,' she hissed. Roxanne complied. She was very pale.

'You ever been fisted in the ass?' EZ demanded.

'No, but I – ' A yank on her hair shut her up.

'Wanna bust up a virgin ass?' EZ asked Kay.

Kay shrugged. 'Feels the same to me, whether they've had it one time or twenty-two. Think she's been cleaned out?'

'You! Slave! Answer her!' bellowed EZ.

'No,' Roxanne said – almost inaudibly.

'Well, forget it,' Kay said. 'I'm not interested in slaves who are literally full of shit.' And she gave EZ a meaningful glare, which was broadly ignored.

Anne-Marie bustled over with a collar in one hand and a leash in the other. 'If I might prepare her for your ministrations, ladies?'

'Would you be so kind?' Kay said.

'Certainly. It's so nice to feel useful,' she beamed. She buckled the collar around Roxanne's neck, snapped on the leash, and slipped the wrist-strap over her hand. 'On your feet, dear,' she said. 'Do we remember how we walk on a leash?'

'Small steps, keep the chain taut, do *not* bump into the person leading you,' Roxanne repeated. 'Ma'am.'

'Shoulders up and back,' Anne-Marie added. 'Proud posture at all times, even the most humiliating.'

'Yes, of course, ma'am. I am forgetful, ma'am.'

Alex had raised one eyebrow. 'Never saw this side of her before,' she remarked to Tyre.

'Yeah, I thought you didn't know much about all that frilly Victorian stuff,' Tyre said. 'Live and learn.'

'And the penalty for forgetfulness is?' Anne-Marie prompted gently.

'A dozen of the best,' Roxanne said with resignation. 'Ma'am.'

'At least you remember your manners. I am going to miss you. Come along to the operating table, dear.'

The badgirl dancing shoes teetered after the sensible white nurse's flats, taking tiny steps. Roxanne kept the leash taut. She did not bump into the person leading her. Her shoulders stayed up and back, making her tits jut defiantly at Anne-Marie's broad shoulders. The domme walked her to the foot of the table until her hips touched it, unclipped the leash, then bent her over with a hand between her shoulderblades. Roxanne made an unhappy puppy noise when her bare flesh was plastered over the cold steel surface of the table.

'You'll stay put on your own, won't you, dear?'

'Yes, ma'am.'

'So much less fuss and muss.' Anne-Marie took the enema bag off the IV stand and opened a hitherto-invisible door in the dungeon wall. A small bathroom lay behind it. The pack sauntered over to watch and comment upon Roxanne's buttocks, twitching in anticipation as Anne-Marie turned the taps on high, filled the red rubber bag to its gills, and screwed in the stopper. She had already clipped the hose shut, and now she brought the bag back to the table and opened her doctor's bag, perched at the head of the table. Michael took the bag from her and hung it upside down. Anne-Marie took nozzle after nozzle out of the bag, and rejected each one. Finally she lubricated the bulb of the Bardex, hooked it up to the enema bag and pushed the balloon into Roxanne's ass. Then she inflated the latex sphere. Roxanne's asshole was completely sealed. Anne-Marie then emptied the swollen bag with ruthless efficiency, ignoring Roxanne's stifled cries. 'It's just nice warm water, dear, those cramps won't last long,' she said, patting her fanny. 'Now we'll just stir it up inside. A dozen of the best, I believe you said?'

Tyre knew that one of Michael's favourite things was a blowjob from someone who was being worked over. She smiled and shook her head when her chauffeur, who really was an ex-Marine, climbed up on the table and forced Roxanne to lift her head and watch her unzip her fly. Michael and Anne-Marie were also old friends, and the nurse shot Tyre a look of delight. 'Don't think you got enough of this Marine Corps meat,' Michael said, and shoved it down her throat just as the first stroke of the cane landed in the crack between Roxanne's buttock and upper thigh. Alex winced, but Roxanne held steady, her head bobbing up and down Michael's cock, as the characteristic double-weal came up, livid on her fair skin. Anne-Marie bided her time. Tyre walked over to Michael, unbuttoned the high-necked, dark-blue tunic with narrow red piping and began working on her nipples with her sharp nails. Her cruelty was passed on to Roxanne, who found herself choking on the energetic cock in her throat, and Anne-Marie chose just that moment to strike again.

'Alex,' said Joy, putting a hand on her shoulder, 'you are not used to lookin' at this from the outside. So tell me, do you like it?'

'I –'

'You mus' remember how good it make you feel to whip her

yourself, I think. How good it feels in the muscles of your arm and here.' Joy put a hand between her breasts. 'your heart is poundin' and poundin' like a drumhead that's gonna split. Feel yourself.' She took Alex's hand and put it on top of her codpiece. 'Come on, girl, half the women here playin' with themselves. Check out your stuff. She gonna hit her soon again I think – yes. You feel your clit jump? Oh, yeah, this is good for you and for her. She like it so much, Alex, see how still she hold herself out of pride for you? That's a beautiful ass she got. I mus' say I want another handful of that girl of yours all t'myself.' Joy chuckled and mock-punched Alex on the point of her chin. 'You seriously twisted, girl, I like that ver' much, just don't try to straighten out now, or you break.'

Kay was hauling EZ, who had gone AWOL to the bar, back into the circle by her ear. 'You got eight hours of music set up at the very least,' she said. 'We don't need you providin' a sound track for the rest of the fucking decade. Now park your butt here and watch this action with me or go play on the freeway.' She smacked her ass, then slid her hand into EZ's back pocket. 'I thought you said girls just played around with this shit. So far I'm in no danger of fallin' asleep. Whyncha just admit you don't know what the fuck you were talkin' about? Or do you maybe like boys better'n girls after all, dipshit?'

'Kiss my ass,' EZ hissed.

'Oh, I will, if I can beat it first,' Kay said lazily. 'Ouch! God, that has got to hurt about as much as bein' hit by a truck.'

Ten of the twelve 'best' had been administered. Anne-Marie gestured to Michael to remove herself. 'We must let her concentrate,' she said absently, adjusting her cap. Tyre released Michael's nipples and helped her off the table. They swaggered arm-in-arm over to Kay and her buddy.

'I gotta get stoned,' EZ said, and produced a joint from behind her ear.

'Why do you think they call it dope?' Kay asked, handing over her lighter. EZ gave her a guilty look, Kay gave her an amused one, and they both giggled.

The last two strokes were administered so quickly they elicited a single scream. Roxanne did not raise her torso from the table, but she kicked. Anne-Marie barely jumped out of the way in time.

'That was naughty, dear,' she said. 'Ponies prance, ladies dance. Tyre?'

Roxanne put her head back down and just listened to Tyre stalk over to the horse and unrack her cane. It was thicker and longer than Anne-Marie's favourite size, and not as flexible. Alex perked up and watched closely, curious to see how Tyre would handle this piece of equipment.

Tyre stood behind and slightly to one side of Roxanne, tapping the cane on the toe of her boot. 'What's the damage, Anne-Marie?' she asked.

'How vicious do you feel, Tyre?'

The madam considered. 'Why don't we make it just one,' she said, 'with one for practice.'

Alex was disappointed. Two strokes (one and a half, really) didn't sound like much of a show. Maybe Tyre didn't like administering corporal punishment.

Tyre folded her right arm across her chest. The cane stretched out at a right angle to her body. Then it flew toward its target, impelled by a series of three snaps, from shoulder, elbow, and wrist. It landed with an audible 'thunk', and rebounded out of the channel it had made for itself in Roxanne's thighs. Roxanne seemed to have crammed a whole fist into her mouth, but she did not scream, jump, or kick. 'That gives me the distance,' Tyre said pleasantly. 'Now for the home run.'

'Oh, these Yankee metaphors,' Anne-Marie sighed. 'Such a jarring anachronism.'

This stroke landed so hard across the middle of Roxanne's cheeks that Alex could have sworn it shoved the girl and the table forward by a good six inches. Of course, they hadn't moved at all. Only Roxanne's flesh had been displaced, and when it returned to its original contours, it bore a lovely purple welt that did not quite bleed, except for a few drops at the very end, where the tip of the cane (going faster than the body of the rod) had bitten in.

'Well caned!' Anne-Marie applauded. 'Weren't you, dear?'

'Yes, ma'am. I was, was well caned. For my fault. Jesus. Thank you, Tyre. Ma'am.'

Anne-Marie led her victim to the tiny bathroom, unchained her hands, and closed the door. 'If we do not respect their privacy,' she said to all assembled, 'how can we hope that they will ever respect ours?'

EZ snorted, and Kay elbowed her in the gut.

When Roxanne came out of the bathroom, she had refilled the enema bag and timidly offered it to Anne-Marie. 'Please,' she said 'I'm not sure I'm clean yet.'

'Certainly, dear girl. Bend over. This time we'll use a dilating nozzle.'

The dilating nozzle was the size of Michael's cock. Anne-Marie inserted it into Roxanne's cunt. 'What – ' Roxanne said, then fell silent. Anne-Marie manipulated the object, to little or no purpose. She gave the assembled dominatrices a significant look over her shoulder, then removed the nozzle and threaded the enema tube into it. As soon as the tip of it touched Roxanne's asshole, she sighed. It sank in without a snag, without need for a pause or a retreat, and the girl immediately began to wiggle as if it had pinned her to the table.

EZ nudged Kay. 'See that?'

'Oh, yeah. Mmm. I got a tingle in my elbow.'

'I got a tingle in both hands.'

Tyre took charge of the valve and dispensed the water slowly, while Anne-Marie plunged the large nozzle repeatedly into Roxanne's eager bottom. The girl's hands (still manacled, but no longer strapped behind her back) clawed at the table, and even closed into her and pounded on it, as she yielded to the hot, fat nozzle and the even hotter water that flowed continuously from it, filling her completely. She came again, and again.

Alex looked around and saw that Joy had been right, just about everybody was beating off. She undid the top three snaps of her codpiece and slid her hand down, cupped her fingers over her clit, and rubbed it from side to side. As the nozzle came out of Roxanne's ass, it drew a little bit of the thin tissue back with it, the pink, almost transparent lip of the asshole clinging to its invader. Then it would dive and tuck everything back in, making Roxanne groan, and Alex groaned, too. She grabbed one of her own nipples and pulled on it, remembering the wrestling match in Tyre's office. Then Michael was behind her, supporting her, taking over the job of twisting her tits, and she could lean back against those muscular thighs and use both her hands to make herself come at the spectacle of Roxanne being spread open and drilled. Michael's strap-on was a hard rod against her left buttock.

They separated as soon as she came. Anne-Marie was helping Roxanne up, taking off her collar, and opening the bathroom door. 'You shouldn't pass anything but water now, dear,' she said before she closed the door.

ANNA FRIEND

Heartlands

Anna Friend, who lives in London, wrote this story in 1989.

Z ACK IS preoccupied with how many. I can't remember when
he first started counting. I know he said once that one of my
predecessors – the one who worked in a burns unit and phoned
him after they'd known each other three months to tell him she'd
met a physician – well, he said on their first occasion 'She must
have taken fifty.' And Zack wondered if this was because she
worked in a burns unit. He sounded full of respect for her.

When he was telling me about her phoning him I was thinking it
must have upset him a lot, but when I asked him he just said,
talking quickly and a bit more loudly which is what he does when
he's angry with me, 'Why should I be upset? Look Ann, we'd been
seeing each other for three months, and then she calls me to
explain she's met someone else. I thought . . . well she's met this
guy.' I asked him then if he'd missed her but he got even angrier.

Well I take twenty-five. I can't remember at what stage he told
me that, and it's not always as many as that, but now he tells me
the number he's decided and counts them out loud. Except once
when I told him not to, and then I couldn't go on and caught hold
of him round his waist and he said after a bit, gently, 'Now you
see you don't know where you are.' I think I had five more to go
which I felt I couldn't get through, but I made myself lay down
again, and every one is one less to go.

I told Dr Rogers I had met this sexual pervert. I carried on talking
and in the first pause he asked quickly and quietly – he always
slips in key questions like that as if he's being very skilful – 'What
form does his perversion take?' I said spanking, and went on
calling it spanking for several sessions because I didn't like to say
beating.

Zack had called it spanking when he broached the subject on
our first occasion, or, I should say, just afterwards. 'What I really
like is spanking,' he said, then a little later reached his side of the
bed for the little whip with the leather thongs dangling.

'How frightening,' said Valerie when I told her, but I've never
been frightened of Zack. 'As long as he doesn't get carried away,'
Valerie said.

Anyway Dr Rogers pronounced that anything that ends with orgasm during normal intercourse was all right, the other was just foreplay. 'It has one advantage.' I waited. 'At least you can have sex and get punished for it at the same time.' I laughed at the joke but I've never believed in his theory about me.

That was the session after I first went to bed with Zack.

I had answered his ad, gone to his flat once to meet him, and rung him up as soon as I got home to tell him I hoped he would meet someone soon.

'Someone else,' Zack said. 'Yes. You mean someone else,' and 'Thank you for calling.'

But I loved his slight Brooklyn accent, the wryness in his voice. I remembered him looking across at me stuck on the extreme end of the sofa away from him, the sandwich on the low table in front of me, and saying 'You can eat the turkey, I killed it myself.' I remembered him pouncing with glee, 'So you go to a therapist. Which one d'you hate your father or your mother?' He said I looked like Glenda Jackson. When he said he liked the colour of my blouse it was like a muscle-bound boxer trying to be dainty, and once looking across at me he took off his glasses and rubbed his eyes as if he was trying to make himself look better to me. But he looked older than the forty-three he'd put in the ad and his cardigan had stains on it and he looked pasty, a bit ill.

I kept thinking of when he'd told me of ending his relationships because the sex was no good. He said 'You know if you've ever had good sex it's a wonderful experience. I don't want to go back. I don't want to go back.' And he said 'We don't have much time left.'

I asked him about the replies he'd got to his ad. He said he'd gone to bed with one 'But she was no good. It was lights out and that was it.'

I tried to argue in defence of the girl but he got angry with me. 'If you go into something you go into it fully. Besides I like licking, and I like to be licked, well what do you think shall we go to bed together?' He'd said it all in one piece, but there'd been an almost imperceptible snort and smile, a glance aside, just before he'd said 'well'. That was when I got frightened and left.

I deliberated for two weeks off and on, then right through one Sunday lifting the receiver to dial his number at just gone ten.

I said, 'It's Ann. I've changed my mind.'

He said, 'Ann who?'

I was to go to his flat at twelve midday the next Wednesday.

He said he wouldn't discuss about the black underwear and stockings at that stage.

I said I'd got some black tights.

He said, 'I wasn't thinking for you but for me.'

He said, 'Ann we talked a lot last time. This time no talking. Not one word. Just straight to the bedroom.'

'I should be out in the park in this sun,' I said to Valerie. 'Not having an assignation with an old Jew in a darkened room.'

I told her I thought I'd walk straight into the bedroom and take off all my clothes But perhaps I wouldn't be able to make myself.

'I've got a better body than he has. He's got a slight paunch.'

'There's nothing wrong with *your* body,' said Valerie.

I said I'd got floppy tits.

Valerie said she'd like him having a slight paunch. She'd feel more comfortable.

I said I was all right lying down. Arranged. Perhaps she'd better go instead of me.

I didn't walk straight into the bedroom.

I walked slowly along the hot pavement through lunchtime workers towards the redbrick block. I pressed the black button 6 and his voice through the grill of the intercom said, 'Come on up.' I walked down the thin maroon carpet past all the blank doors to his at the end. I stood before the closed door looking for a bell at the side, not seeing one.

He opened it.

I recognized him with a shock. His slight stoop, his yellowish, slightly bloated cheeks, and the way he'd glance sideways at me and away again. Unfriendly. He wasn't the voice I'd spoken to on the phone.

I walked into the little hall. He'd made an effort. Light coloured short sleeved shirt, newly pressed trousers, and a slight smell of a recent shower.

I said, 'Zack, I want a whisky.'

He said, 'I'll get you one. Come in, sit down.'

I sat on the end of the sofa. The other end from where I'd sat before. The curtains were drawn. The trays of jewellery were glittering. Every surface was cluttered with books, objects. There was the piano and music stand in a corner.

He handed a whisky in a pottery goblet from behind and above me. It was a large one, unwatered. I said I'd get some water myself, glad to get up and go to the kitchen. There was sunlight, trees, through the window.

I went back and sat on the sofa. He was sitting in the chair. The same one he'd sat in before.

I said, 'I'm nervous.'

He said he would have thought I'd have been smoking if I was nervous.

So I rummaged through my bag while he put the ashtray before me on the low table.

He was telling me about when someone gave him a cigarette when he was four. He was talking about being put off smoking for life. There was a white paperback *Healthy Sex* among the books on the bookshelves. I was thinking that he'd got ready to do it and I couldn't say I wouldn't. My hands were sweating.

I said, 'Look Zack. I can't just do it cold like that.'

He drew his chair beside me and tried to take one of my hands, saying, 'It'll be warm', but the phone rang and he got up and went to the hall to answer it.

I thought 'I must make a move. I must tell him. When he comes back.'

He came back.

I said, 'Zack I just don't feel like going to bed now. I really don't.'

He said, 'Well you'd better go.'

He said, 'You know you shouldn't have come in. You should have gone. You shouldn't have had a whisky.'

Suddenly I knew I was going to bed with him. He had been straight with me. I'd answered the ad and had phoned him and it would have been like a failure to leave.

I said, 'All right I will', standing up and putting the goblet down on the low table. I walked out of the room, left in the hall, right into the bedroom. There was just the double bed with a dull coloured duvet on it and a jumble of clothes and towels over a cupboard in front of the window. The curtains were drawn. He hadn't followed me in. I took off all my clothes laying them over the others on the cupboard, then lay down on the bed on my back, only my feet covered by the duvet. He came in and began undressing, but I couldn't look at him. I started struggling to get off my bracelet as he lay down and turned towards me, propped on one elbow, watching me. I managed to undo the catch, then placed the bracelet with a show of care beside the bedside lamp, placing my hands, sweating, down by my sides.

He said, 'You look very nice.'

I said, 'Zack, I'm no good in bed.'

He said, 'Well you look very nice.'

He started kissing me gently, exploratively, and I was the one wanting something. He touched the end of each nipple lightly, accurately with his tongue. He began to stroke me very, very gently, lightly, down my body. I followed his hand moving lightly down my body, very lightly, gently, surely, to where I wanted it to go. And again, unhurriedly. It was nice. I thought, I am giving in. He moved down the bed to touch me with his tongue. I was giving in, giving in, releasing. Then I was conscious again of my breathing, my heart beating as he came up the bed.

Later he turned on his back, one arm raised over his forehead, saying, 'I don't understand. You looked like you were in pain, I don't understand. Though with some women it's difficult to tell between pleasure and pain.'

He was angry with me.

'Well let's take that off anyway.' From behind I saw the dark thick hair being lifted up. 'Don't tell me you didn't know I wore a toupé.' He looked much younger, more human, healthier, without it.

I told him he was number thirteen and the only man who had ever made me come. 'Didn't you know I did?'

'No.'

'Well you were busy.'

I told him about my dismal sexual history. He had his arm under my neck. Objective, unaffectionate, but friendly. Without his toupé he fell into a definitive Jewish type. The neat patches of hair over the ears, the domed bald head. There had been something wrong about him before.

'What I really like is spanking.'

I realized without alarm, gradually as he talked, that that was what he had put the ad in for. It interested me and he answered all my questions. Why did it excite him? The redness, the submission. I asked him if he came while he was doing it. He said no, he made love afterwards, but it excited him.

'I don't have sex just for, for . . . I like foreplay,' he added emphatically.

But I said it must hurt. What about the woman?

'But you know their pleasure comes from giving pleasure, and if you are spanked it feels tingly, nice, when you are touched there afterwards, and it goes on afterwards, you feel it afterwards, a sort of glow.'

He asked me to turn over and smacked me once, quite hard. He did it again harder. 'But look', he ran his fingers lightly where he had hit. 'That feels tingly.'

So then I told him my sexual fantasy. The sexual fantasy I had when I was a little girl.

I can remember it now, standing on the grass bank that ran along the other side of the road from the council houses. I had just learned how to spell RABBIT. I remember boasting to my friends about that and telling them how my father spanked me. And I remember how important, grown up I felt as I imagined it hurting, feeling warm, deliciously, and the cool soothing ointment being smoothed on.

'What sort of ointment was it?' Zack asked.

I felt sorry my fantasy hadn't been more specific.

Zack put his hand across me and caught hold of my arm affectionately.

'Well what do you feel about the spanking then?'

I told him I wasn't really sure. I might feel differently in a couple of weeks.

As I was dressing I could hear him singing a few bars to himself as he got ready to go out.

'D'you think I look very American in this?' He was standing beside me in a peaked baseball cap admiring himself in the mirror.

Only a small semi-circle above the band at the back showed his toupéless scalp.

As we walked talking together down the busy Holborn street, he suddenly said, 'I do other things you know.'

'My God. What else?'

'We could go to the theatre, the cinema, a restaurant. I mean' – he was shouting – 'I don't just fuck and spank you know!'

Well that was our first occasion.

Dr Rogers and I had our lines crossed in the next session. Before I'd seen Zack again he had pronounced against him. He'd done that with all the men I'd proffered for inspection as prospective partners in an equal loving relationship.

I will say one thing for Dr Rogers. He always had my best interests at heart. He'd ask firstly, was it especially good in bed? Then, is he rich? Then steer straight through my romantic irrelevancies to the nub of the question, is he going to commit himself to you?

Zack got thumbs down because giving sexual pleasure and being 'probably quite rich' didn't outweigh his unattractiveness and the fact that he frightened me. I said he couldn't help being unattractive and asked why did he think Zack frightened me?

He said, 'The beating must have frightened you.'

He'd thought I'd gone along to Zack's and got beaten right away just like that.

Zack was a skilful teacher. I can see that now.

He started off gently and would monitor progress before our next session asking with gusto, 'How's your arse?' and did I fantasize about it? I would prudishly allow him some snippets of satisfaction which he'd register with a loud 'Good' or a smile to himself, but would add, 'You've got to learn to take a beating, Ann.'

I can see now too, he was puzzled about what I got out of it. Was it because I was guilty, or for the sex or for love? He tried playing on the first but I ruled that out. The last wasn't on offer, so he dismissed that too. That left him with the sex and he wasn't always too sure about that. 'You've got to enjoy it, Ann', he'd say.

I felt I must try and do better.

'Ann. How you doing?'

I'd get a thrill of pleasure at his wry Brooklyn voice popping up incongruously in the earpiece of my phone at the office. Sometimes I'd go to his flat straight from work. I'd buzz up and he'd leave his door on the latch. I'd push it open and there he'd be sitting hunched over working at his paste jewellery on the little formica top fixed to the wall of his kitchen. He'd look aside at me smiling, then quickly back again. I'd dump my coat and bag in the hall or the living room, then sit at the top watching him pick up the little sparkling pieces with eyebrow tweezers and peer over his thick lensed glasses, his nose only a few inches away from his hands, to place them in the little niches prepared with glue.

'Do you want a whisky? Help yourself.'

He never drank. But usually had drink there. The whisky I think for me and the wine for his Other Woman. She was a business associate and had taught Zack all he knew about his trade. And he would tell me about Art Deco and Art Nouveau and show me his favourite new pieces. 'I'm not taking less than one eighty for that.'

He told me the little starlike pieces of paste were called crowns, the oblong ones baguettes. 'That means little sticks in French,' I told him. I would sit down looking at his hands. I loved the back of his hands, light brown, broad, hairless, his short square-ended sturdy fingers.

'Zack. Did you put another ad in?'

'What ad?'

'Dominant male, forty-three, seeks submissive female for mutual pleasure and enjoyment. I live in central London.'

'It sounds like beating,' said Zack. 'Do you think you're submissive?'

'Yes.'

'Why don't you answer it then?'

'In case it's you. And I don't like beating.'

'But you take it.'

'Yes.'

'Why do you take it?'

I told him I didn't know.

We'd talk for a bit and Zack would jump up to go to the sink to try and get the Superglue off his fingers, 'If you got it over your whole body you'd die', then stand there scraping at his hand with a fingernail. Then he'd stop and look at me smiling, saying loudly, 'Well, my dear . . .?'

Dr Rogers was against the beating.

I stood up for Zack. I said it wasn't sadism, it wasn't the pain that gave Zack pleasure, but the redness, the submission, the sound. It was more like a fetish, I said.

Dr Rogers said Zack must hate women.

I said I didn't feel that, I didn't feel that at all.

I said I didn't like the beating but I liked the whole package, so what was wrong?

He said, 'But it's meant to be loving.'

I said, 'Yes. You are right. It's meant to be loving.'

I said I didn't find Zack attractive and I just went to his flat and that was that, and I didn't know why I wanted him to phone me so much, why I wanted to see him.

Zack liked to try things out. Manacles. Or vibrator. Standing hands against the wall legs apart, or lying trousers down across his knees telly on, I was a mechanical toy that wouldn't work. My suggestions for improvement to the mode of operation didn't do anything for Zack, so the experimental stage didn't last long.

Then we got into the groove.

But Zack would try and vary things from time to time.

'I don't get many marks tonight,' I'd say crying into my pillow.

'You do for that Oscar winning performance,' he'd say getting up to go and look in the fridge, to turn the telly on.

Dr Rogers told me Zack didn't do anything for my self-esteem. 'Cut your losses,' he said.

And I would try to imagine life without Zack.

'I could do with a little less drama,' Zack would say a week or two later when I'd give in and phone him. Or, 'I just wanted to make it different. You are a woman who always wants everything exactly the same. If the temperature is a few degrees more or a few degrees less . . .'

And I would check the ads.

'How's the good doctor?'

'He's all right. I must give him up.'

'So what did you talk about?'

'We talked about you.'

'What did he say?'

'He's against you. He says you hate women. He says it's not loving.'

'What about eroticism? You know the two don't often go together,' Zack said peering over his glasses as he dug with the point of the tweezers at the hardened glue in the niches of the brooch.

'Why do you see me then?'

'I don't know,' I said. 'I don't know. I don't know if I even like you.'

I felt gently with my fingers under my body, under the curve of my right hip. The flesh felt strange, as if it was raised in parallel strips. Corrugated. I pulled up my hand to look. There was no blood on it.

'It looks beautiful to me,' said Zack still lying beside me.

I heard the refrigerator door open and shut. The television go on.

I dressed in a rush, in a rage to leave.

Zack was sitting naked on the low sofa hunched over a bowl he held in his left hand, his forearm resting on his thigh. He was eating the dry, broken up Weetabix with his fingers, munching, staring at the television right across the other side of the room.

'Haven't you got any milk?' I said.

'I like it like this,' said Zack staring at the television.

'I can't take that,' I said. 'I can't take being cut like that.'

'Are you leaving already then?' he said, still staring at the television, his hand in the bowl.

'I can't take that. I'm going.'

'Well go,' he said.

'You want to stop? All right we'll stop. Take care,' Zack said. Then hung up.

I said I was sorry I'd said what I'd said. I said Dr Rogers had said

it wasn't loving, but it was loving enough for me. I said I didn't
know why I'd said what I'd said. I said I didn't know why I'd said
I didn't like him.

'Oh I knew you didn't mean that,' Zack said.

'How?' I asked.

'Because I'm such a lovable person,' he said.

'Do you ever see that Brooklyn man?' Valerie asked the other day.

I can see the little boy standing back from the door looking
through, his body turned slightly sideways to the door ready to
turn and run, his eyes looking sideways ready to look away. But
he stands there, one hand pulling out the front of his vest, and he
doesn't run, he doesn't look away.

The older boy inside pulls down his pants and bends over the
high mahogany framed bed, lifting his arms as he lays his head
down, one cheek turned on the counterpane. The man stands
before him muscled, tall, his legs set slightly apart. He unclips his
belt and with one movement pulls it free.

'And my brother would cry,' Zack told me.

'And my brother would just pull down his pants and bend over.
And I thought, I would never be like that. I would never do that. I
would never allow that to happen to me.'

And it never did happen to him, Zack answered my question,
his arm resting along the sofa, his fingers touching the back of my
neck.

The first stroke.

So harsh, each time the searing pain reminds my mind and body
they've forgotten it. I know I can't last out, but Zack has trained
me well. He'll give me time, a pause where he'll caress me, but he
knows, I know, he's made his terms, and I'm the one who's
buying.

PAULINE REAGE

From *The Story of O*

Almost nothing is known about the woman who wrote what is one of the most famous pornographic novels by a woman. It first appeared in Paris in mysterious circumstances in around 1954 and has been sold in massive quantities since that date. In most ways the novel concords precisely with the classic and stereo-typical male fantasy of the woman who will do anything for her man. Here the central female character has so subjugated her personality to her primary function as pleasurer of man that she not only has no name but is reduced to a mere letter – 'O'.

Submission becomes not only acceptable but positively normal, in this context, since every character is behaving, unquestioningly, according to the same rules of conduct. O is initiated into a world governed by men for men and she enjoys her acceptance of this status quo, not because it is pleasurable in itself (it is, in fact, exceptionally painful and unpleasant), but because the very acuteness of this pain merely goes to prove the exceptional qualities of O's adoration of her lover. In all of these ways the book accords precisely with male fantasy.

O's personality is gradually denuded as, in scenes of ever increasing degradation, each element which defines her as an individual is wiped away. She wears fewer and fewer clothes, she is branded as a possession and, eventually, she is led around the floor, chained up like a dog. Finally, when no part of her original identity remains, she is taken to a party wearing a mask, no longer in

possession, even, of her own face. For the very first time
in the novel, she is observed from the outside and the
external world is filled with horror and loathing.
Though the reader now senses her shame, the 'heroine'
has become immune to such sensations. She has become
a receptacle, a hollow void, an 'O'.

A ND THEN I know that they released O's hands, until that
point still tied behind her back, and told her to undress.
They were going to bathe her and make her up. But they made her
stand still; they did everything for her, they stripped her and laid
her clothes neatly away in one of the cupboards. They did not let
her do her own bathing, they washed her themselves and set her
hair just as hairdressers would have, making her sit in one of those
big chairs that tilt backwards when your hair is being washed and
then come up again when the drier is applied. That took at least
an hour. She was seated nude in the chair and they prohibited her
from either crossing her legs or pressing them together. As, on the
opposite wall, there was a mirror running from floor to ceiling
and straight ahead of her, in plain view, every time she glanced up
she caught sight of herself, of her open body.

When she was made up, her eyelids lightly shadowed, her
mouth very red, the point and halo of her nipples rouged, the
sides of the lips of her sex reddened, a lingering scent applied to
the fur of her armpits and her pubis, to the crease between her
buttocks, to beneath her breasts and the palms of her hands, she
was led into a room where a three-sided mirror and, facing it, a
fourth mirror on the opposite wall enabled, indeed obliged, her
to see her own image reflected. She was told to sit on a hassock
placed between the mirrors, and to wait. The hassock was
upholstered with prickly black fur; the rug was black, the walls
red. She wore red slippers. Set in one of the little boudoir's walls
was a casement window giving out upon a magnificent but
sombre, formal garden. The rain had stopped and the trees were
swaying in the wind while the moon raced high among the
clouds. I don't know just how long she remained in the red
boudoir, nor if she really was alone, as she thought she was, for
someone may perhaps have been watching her through a
peephole disguised somewhere in the wall. What I do know is
that when the two chambermaids returned, one was carrying a
tape-measure and the other had a basket over her arm. With
them came a man wearing a trailing violet robe with sleeves cut
wide at the shoulder and gathered in at the wrist; as he walked,

the robe showed to be open at the waist. You could make out
that he was in some kind of tights which covered his legs and
thighs but left his sex free. It was the sex that O saw first, then
the whip made of strands of leather, the whip was stuck in his
belt, then she noticed that the man was masked in a black hood
completed by a section of black gauze hiding his eyes – and
finally she noticed the fine black kid-gloves he was wearing. He
ordered her not to move, he told the women to hurry. The one
with the tape took the measure of O's neck and wrists. Although
somewhat small, her sizes were in no way out of the ordinary,
and they had no trouble selecting a suitable collar and bracelets
from the assortment contained in the basket. Both collar and
bracelets were fashioned of many layers of thin leather, the
whole being no thicker than a finger, fitted with a catch that
worked automatically, like a padlock, and which needed a key
to be opened. Next to the catch, and imbedded in the leather,
was a metal ring. They fitted snugly, but not so tightly as to
chafe or break the skin. After they had been set in place, the
man told her to rise. He himself sat on the fur-covered hassock
and made her approach until she stood against his knees. He
passed his gloved hand between her thighs and over her breast
and explained to her that she would be presented that same
evening after she had dined. Still nude, she took her meal alone
in a kind of small cabin; an unseen hand passed the plates to her
through a little window. When she had finished eating, the two
maids came for her again. In the boudoir, they had her put her
hands behind her back and secured them there by means of the
rings of her wristbands; they draped a long red cape over her
shoulders, and it was fastened to the ring set in her collar. The
cape covered her completely, but with her hands behind her
back that way she couldn't prevent it from opening when she
walked. One woman preceded her, and opened the doors; the
second followed, and shut them again. They filed through a
vestibule, through two drawing-rooms, and entered the library
where four men were at coffee. They wore the same flowing
robes as the first she had seen, but were not masked.
Nevertheless, O did not have time to observe their faces or
recognize whether her lover was there (he was), for one of the
men trained a spotlight upon her face, dazzling her. Everyone

stood in silence, the women on either side, the men in front, watching her. Then the light was switched off and the women went away, but a blindfold had been placed over O's eyes. Stumbling a bit, she was made to advance and could sense that she was standing before the fire around which the four men had been grouped. In the quiet, she could hear the soft crackling of the logs and feel the heat; she was facing the fire. Two hands lifted away her cape, two others checked the clasp on her wristbands and descended inspectingly down over her buttocks. These hands were not gloved, and one of them simultaneously penetrated her in two places – so brusquely that she let out a cry. Some voice laughed. Another said: 'Turn her around so we can see her breasts and belly.' She was turned about, and now it was on her buttocks that she felt the glow of the fire. A hand moulded itself round one of her breasts, squeezed, a mouth closed upon the nipple of her other breast. Suddenly, she lost her balance and tottered backwards into unknown arms. At the same instant, her legs were spread apart and her lips gently worked open – hair grazed the inner surfaces of her thighs. She heard a voice declare that she ought to be made to kneel, and she was. It was painful to be on her knees, seated on her heels in the position nuns take when they pray.

'You've never imposed physical restraints, for example tied her up?'

'No, never.'

'Or whipped her?'

'Never. Though, the fact is – ' It was her lover who was answering.

'The fact is,' said the other voice, 'that if you do tie her up, if you use a whip on her, and if she likes that – then no, you understand. Pleasure, we've got to move beyond that stage. We must make the tears flow.'

She was then drawn to her feet, and they were probably about to detach her hands so as to tie her to some post or other or to the wall, when someone interrupted, saying that before anything else he wanted her – immediately. She was forced down upon her knees again, but this time a hassock was placed as a support under her chest; her hands were still fixed behind her back, her haunches were higher than her torso. One of the men gripped her buttocks and sank himself into her womb. When he was done, he ceded his place to a second. The third wanted to drive his way into the narrower passage and, pushing hard, violently, wrung a scream from her lips. When at last he let go of her, moaning and tears streaming down under her blindfold, she slipped sidewise to the floor only to discover by the pressure of two knees against her face that her mouth was not to be spared either. Finally, finished with her, they moved off, leaving her, a captive in her finery, huddled, collapsed on the carpet before the fire. She heard drink being poured, glasses tinkling, chairs stirring; logs were added to the fire. Then her blindfold was suddenly snatched away. It was a large room. Bookcases lined the walls, dimly lit by a bracketed lamp and the flicker of the fire. Two of the men were standing; they were smoking. Another was seated, a riding-crop across his knees, and there was still another leaning over her, caressing her breasts; that one was her lover. All four had taken her and she had not been able to distinguish him from amongst the rest.

It was explained to her that as long as she was in this château it would always be this way: she would see the faces of those who violated and bullied her, but never at night, and in this way she would never know which ones were responsible for the worst of her sufferings. When she was whipped the same would hold true, except when it was desired that she see herself being whipped, as happened to be the case this first time; no blindfold, but the men in masks in order to be unidentifiable. Her lover had picked her up and set her, in her red cape, on the arm of a large chair in the corner by the chimney, so that she might listen to what they had to tell her and see what they wished to exhibit to her. Her hands were still pinioned behind her back. She was shown the riding-crop, black, long and slender, made of fine bamboo sheathed in leather, an article such as one finds in the display-windows of expensive saddle-makers' shops; the leather whip – the one she'd seen tucked in the first man's belt – was long, with six lashes each ending in a knot; there was a third whip whose numerous light cords were several times knotted and stiff, quite as if soaked in water, and they actually had been soaked in water, as O was able to verify when they stroked her belly with those cords and, opening her thighs, exposing her hidden parts, let the damp, cold ends trail against the tender membranes. On the console there yet remained the collection of keys and the steel chains. Midway up one of the library's walls ran a balcony supported by two pillars. In one of these, as high up as a man standing on tip-toe could reach, was sunk a hook. O, whose lover had taken her in his arms, one hand under her shoulder, the other in her womb which was burning her almost unbearably, O was informed that when, as soon they would, they unfastened her hands, it would only be to attach them to this whipping-post by means of those bracelets on her wrists and this steel chain. With the exception of her hands, which would be immobilized a little above her head, she would be able to move, to turn, to face around and see the strokes coming, they told her; by and large, they'd confine the whipping to her buttocks and thighs, to the space, that is to say, between her waist and her knees, precisely that part of her which had been prepared in the car when she had been made to sit naked on the seat; it was likely, however, that some one of the four men would want to score her with the crop, for it caused fine, long, deep welts which lasted quite some time. They'd go about it gradually, giving her ample opportunity to scream and fight and cry to her heart's content.

They'd pause to let her catch her breath, but after she'd recovered it, they'd start in again, judging the results not by her screams or her tears but by the more or less livid and durable marks traced in her flesh by the whips. It was called to her attention that these criteria for estimating the effectiveness of the whip, apart from their just impartiality and from the fact they rendered unnecessary any attempts victims might make to elicit pity by exaggerating their moans, did not by any means bar open-air whipping – there would indeed be a good deal of that in the park outside the château – or for that matter, whipping in any ordinary apartment or hotel room provided a tight gag were employed (they showed her a gag), which, while giving free rein to tears, stifles any scream and even makes moaning difficult.

They did not, however, intend to use the gag that night. To the contrary, they were eager to hear O howl, the sooner the better. Proud, she steeled herself to resist, she gritted her teeth; but not for long. They soon heard her beg to be let loose, beg them to stop, stop for a second, for just one second. So frantically did she twist and wheel to dodge the biting lashes that she almost spun in circles. The chain, although unyielding, for, after all, it was a chain, was nevertheless slack enough to allow her leeway. Owing to her excessive writhing, her belly and the front of her thighs received almost as heavy a share as her rear. They left off for a moment, deeming it better to tie her flat up against the post by means of a rope passed around her waist; the rope being cinched tight, her head necessarily angled to one side of the post and her flanks jutted to the other, thereby placing her rump in a prominent position. From then on, every deliberately aimed blow dealt her struck home. In view of the manner in which her lover had exposed her to this, O might well have supposed that an appeal to his pity would have been the surest way to increase his cruelty, so great was his pleasure in wresting or in having the others wrest these from her decisive proofs of his power over her. And it was in fact he who was the first to observe that the leather whip, with which they'd begun marked her the least (for the moistened lash had obtained strong results almost instantly, and the crop with the first blow struck), and hence, by employing no other, they could prolong the ordeal and, after brief pauses, start in again just about immediately or according to their fancy. He asked that they use only that first whip. Meanwhile, the man who liked women only for what they had in common with men, seduced by the sight of that proffered behind straining out from under the taut rope and made all the more tempting by its wrigglings to escape, requested an intermission in order to take advantage of it; he spread apart the two burning halves and penetrated, but not without difficulty, which brought him to remark that they'd have to contrive to make this thoroughfare easier of access. The thing could be done, they agreed, and decided that the proper measures would be taken.

The young woman, swaying and half fainting under her flowing red cape, was released then and, before being led away to the cell where she was to stay, they had her sit down in a chair by the fireside and listen while there were outlined to her, in detail, all the rules she was to observe during her period at the château and also during her everyday life once she'd returned home from the château (not, however, that she was going to recover her former freedom); one of the men rang. The two costumed maids who had received her now appeared, bringing the clothes she was to wear and tokens whereby those who had been guests at the château prior to her coming and after it might be able to recognize her when later on she had left. This costume was similar to the chambermaids'. Over a whalebone bodice which severely constricted the waist, and over a starched linen petticoat, was worn an ample gown, the open neck of which left the breasts, raised by the bodice, practically visible beneath a light film of gauze. The petticoat and gauze were white, the bodice and gown a seagreen satin. When O was dressed and reseated beside the fireplace, her pallor intensified by the paleness of the gown, the two girls, who had not uttered a word, made ready to leave. As they were going, one of the men stepped forward, signalled to her nearest the door to wait, and brought the other back towards O. He took her by the waist with one hand and raised her skirts with the other, making her turn, displaying the costume's practical advantages, having O admire its design, and explaining that, simply by means of a belt, the skirts could be held at any desired height, thus, which meant that all of what was exposed was very ready to hand, thus. As a matter of fact, he added, they often had the girls stroll in the garden or move about the château with their skirts hitched up behind, or – thus – hitched up in front, at the level of the midriff. He bade the girl demonstrate to O how the skirt was to be kept in the right position: how she was to take in the folds, roll them (like a lock of hair in a curler), keep them just so by means of a belt, the buckle exactly in front, so as to leave the way clear to the womb, or this other way, so, in back to expose the buttocks. In both instances, petticoat and skirt were to fall away in flowing diagonal folds. Like O, the girl's flanks bore fresh marks of the riding-crop. She went away.

This is the speech they then made to O:

'You are here to serve your masters. During the day, in connection with the maintenance of the household, you will perform whatever chores are assigned to you, such as sweeping, putting the books back in place, arranging flowers, or waiting upon table. Your tasks will not be more onerous than these. But at the first word or gesture you will stop in the middle of whatever you happen to be doing, addressing yourself to your one primary task, your only significant one duty, which is to avail yourself to be used. Your hands are not your own, neither are your breasts, nor, above all, is any one of the orifices of your body, which we are at liberty to explore and into which we may, whenever we so please, introduce ourselves. In order that you bear it constantly, or as constantly as possible, in mind that you have lost the right to withhold or deny yourself, in our presence you will at all times avoid altogether closing your labia, nor will you ever cross your legs, nor press your knees together (as, you recall, was forbidden to you directly you set out for this place), which will signify, in your view and in ours, that your mouth, your belly and your behind are constantly at our entire disposal. Before us, you must never touch your breasts; your bodice lifts them supplicatingly to us, they are ours. During the day, since you will be dressed, you will raise your skirt if ordered to, and whoever would have you will use you as he likes, undisguised; but he will not whip you. The whip will only be applied between the hours of sundown and dawn. But over and above those whippings, which you will receive from whoever desires to whip you, you will be punished, in the form of further whipping, at night for any infraction of the rules during the day: that is to say, for thoughtlessness, for insubmissiveness, for having raised your eyes upon whoever speaks to or takes you: never must you look any one of us in the face. If our night-time costume, what we are wearing now, leaves our sex uncovered, it is not for the sake of convenience, since it would be just as convenient otherwise, but for that of insolence, so that your eyes will focus themselves there and nowhere else, so that you will come finally to understand that there resides your master, your lord, to whom all of you is destined and above all your lips. In the day, when we are dressed in the usual manner and you as you are now, you will observe the same rule and when requested you will simply open our clothing and later close it again when we are finished with you. Also, at night, you will have only your lips wherewith to do us honour, and also your widespread thighs, since, at night, you will have your hands secured behind your back and you will be nude, as you were when brought here a short while ago; you will not be blindfolded save when you are to be maltreated and, now that you have seen yourself being beaten, when you are whipped. In this regard, if it were advisable that you accustom yourself to whipping – and it shall be frequent, daily, so long as you remain here – it is less for our pleasure than for your instruction. This may be stressed by the fact that, on those nights when no-one wants you, you may expect a visit from the valet who has been appointed to the job: he will enter your cell and, in the solitude, mete out to you what you need to receive and which we are not inclined to bestow. Actually, the object of these procedures, as well as of the chain which will be affixed to your collar, is to confine you to within a limited scope and more or less to your bed for several hours every day, a good deal less to make you suffer pain, scream or shed tears than, by means of this pain, to enforce upon you the idea that you are subject to constraint and to teach you that you utterly belong to something which is apart from and outside yourself. When you are dismissed from here, you will go forth wearing an iron ring on your finger; by it others will recognize you. You will then have learned to obey those who wear the same token – upon seeing it, they will know that you are constantly naked beneath your skirt, however correct or ordinary your dress and that this is on their behalf, this nudity for them. Those who find you unco-operative will bring you back here. You will now be shown to your cell.'

While these words were being uttered to O, the two women who had come to dress her were standing the whole while on either side of the post where she had been whipped; but they avoided touching it, as though it frightened them or (which was more likely) as though they had been forbidden to touch it; when the man had concluded, they moved towards O, who understood that she was to rise and follow them. And so she got to her feet, collecting her skirts to keep from stumbling, for she wasn't used to long dresses, nor to managing in these thick-soled and very high-heeled clogs which only a single broad band of satin, of the same green as her gown, prevented from slipping off. Stooping to gather her skirts, she cast a quick glance around. The women were waiting, the men had shifted their attention elsewhere. Her lover, sitting on the floor, his back

propped against the hassock over which she'd been bent earlier
in the evening, his legs drawn up and his elbows resting on his
knees, was idly toying with the leather whip. At the first step she
took to overtake the women, the edge of her skirt brushed him
and he looked up, smiling; he pronounced her name, also rose to
his feet. Gently, he caressed her hair, ran the tip of his finger
gently along her eyebrows, gently kissed her lips. He gazed at
her and, aloud, said that he loved her. Trembling, O was
terrified to hear herself say: 'I love you,' and it was true, she did.
He pressed her to him and said: 'My love, my darling,' then
kissed her chin, kissed her neck, kissed the corner of her cheek,
for she had let her head sink upon the shoulder of his violet
robe. Murmuring now, he repeated that he loved her and,
murmuring still, he said: 'Now kneel down, caress me, kiss me.'
He backed a step away from her, motioning the women back
and leaning an elbow upon the console. He was tall, but the
console was not very high, and his long legs, sheathed in the
same violet as her dress, were slightly bent at the knees over
which the open robe hung like a drapery. The top of the console,
pushing against his buttocks from behind, thrust forward the
heavy sex and the light fleece that crowned it. The three men
drew near. O knelt on the rug, her green skirt spreading round
her in a pool, her bodice holding her breasts, the nipples visible,
at the level of her lover's knees. 'A little more light,' said one of
the men. As they were directing the beam so that it would fall
upon his sex and upon the face of his mistress, who was
completely ready, and upon her hands, which were already
caressing him, René said: 'Say it once again. Say: "I love you." '
O said: 'I love you,' said it with such delight that she scarcely
dared touch her lips to the tip of his sex, still protected by its
mantlet of soft skin. The three men were smoking, commenting
upon her movements, upon the way her mouth closed over and
worked at the sex it had seized and along whose length it ran,
ran back and forth, upon how tears came to her eyes every time
the swollen member struck the back of her throat, causing her to
choke, to shudder as though from an imminent nausea. It was
with her mouth still half-gagged by the hardened flesh filling it
that she brought out, again, thickly, the words: 'I love you.' The
two women had stationed themselves one on either side of René

who, leaning his hands on their shoulders, had lowered himself towards O. She heard the remarks being made by the witnesses, but listened through them for her lover's moans, caressing him carefully, with infinite respect and slowly, in the way she knew he liked. O was aware of the splendour of her mouth, of its beauty, since her lover deigned to enter it, since he deigned to make a spectacle of its caresses, since he deigned to shed his seed in it. She received him as one receives a god, with thanksgiving heard his cry, joyously heard the others laugh, and when once she had received him, fell, unstrung, and lay with her face against the floor. The two women aided her to rise, and this time led her away.

APHRA BEHN

From *Oroonoko*

Aphra Behn was born around 1640 in Kent and in the early 1660s went to live in the colony of Surinam, which forms the setting for Oroonoko *(1688). She was employed by Charles II as a spy in Antwerp, before beginning to write poetry, plays and novels, becoming the first known professional woman writer in England; and she had a strong sympathy for Roman Catholicism and the aristocracy. She was married to a merchant who was, most likely, a much older man – many of her writings involve the thrusting of unwanted attentions by geriatric men onto young women.*

Charles II, on being restored to the throne, was keen to reopen the theatres and took active steps to encourage women to go onto the stage. In 1662 a royal warrant was issued decreeing that they must do so in place of the boys used on the Renaissance stage. Leading actresses of the day, like Nell Gwyn, gained wide repute. At this period too, women began actually to go to the theatre as members of the audience. Though there had been female playwrights, none produced anything like the output of Behn's twenty or so plays, many of which were shoddily produced commercial ventures. Her best known play, The Rover, *includes a heroine, Hellena, who demonstrates that male dress allows women the kind of freedoms generally only available to prostitutes, and, generally, the position of women is rather a dark one.*

Oronooko was published in 1688. It is often cited as the first piece of writing denouncing slavery and promoting black issues, since the black Oroonoko is cruelly killed and treated like a slave. In fact, Behn is more conservative than this, her views on female emancipation are personal rather than general and she is more concerned with class and inherent nobility of person than liberation of the dispossessed. The perceived salaciousness of her work, however, meant that she soon went out of favour, since her writing was not considered suitable for a woman.

Oronooko is a prince of Surinam who falls in love, naturally, with the woman to whom he is most suited, Imoinda, the daughter of another great leader. Oronooko's grandfather, the king, also falls in love with Imoinda and orders her to be his wife and so she and Oronooko are parted. During some festivities, Imoinda's maid, Onahal arranges a secret meeting between the two. It is implicit that hero and heroine deserve to be together since compatibility is dictated by birth and age. Once it is discovered that Imoinda and Oronooko have had sex and she is thus 'polluted' she is sent away as a slave. This is the greatest punishment for a 'maid of her quality'. It is not her sex that defines her but her aristocracy – far better to be dead than to be demeaned socially. Even so, and despite this realization, the king makes no attempt to find Imoinda again – her merits are defined in terms of her 'value'. A much more pressing need is to excuse himself in the eyes of Oronooko, since he is a man and has power and his resentment, therefore, might actually affect the king's position.

THE LADIES were still dancing, and the king, laid on a carpet, with a great deal of pleasure, was beholding them, especially Imoinda, who that day appeared more lovely than ever, being enlivened with the good tidings Onahal had brought her of the constant passion the prince had for her. The prince was laid on another carpet, at the other end of the room, with his eyes fixed on the object of his soul; and as she turned, or moved, so did they; and she alone gave his eyes and soul their motions. Nor did Imoinda employ her eyes to any other use, than in beholding with infinite pleasure the joy she produced in those of the prince. But while she was more regarding him than the steps she took, she chanced to fall, and so near him as that leaping with extreme force from the carpet, he caught her in his arms as she fell; and 'twas visible to the whole presence, the joy wherewith he received her. He clasped her close to his bosom, and quite forgot that reverence that was due to the mistress of a king, and that punishment that is the reward of a boldness of this nature; and had not the presence of mind of Imoinda (fonder of his safety, than her own) befriended him in making her spring from his arms and fall into her dance again, he had, at that instant, met his death; for the old king, jealous to the last degree, rose up in rage, broke all the diversion, and led Imoinda to her apartment, and sent out word to the prince to go immediately to the camp; and that if he were found another night in court, he should suffer the death ordained for disobedient offenders.

You may imagine how welcome this news was to Oroonoko, whose unseasonable transport and caress of Imoinda was blamed by all men that loved him; and now he perceived his fault, yet cried, that for such another moment, he would be content to die.

All the otan was in disorder about this accident; and Onahal was particularly concerned, because on the prince's stay depended her happiness, for she could no longer expect that of Aboan. So that, e'er they departed, they contrived it so that the prince and he should come both that night to the grove of the otan, which was all of oranges and citrons, and that there they should wait her orders.

They parted thus, with grief enough, till night; leaving the king in possession of the lovely maid. But nothing could appease the jealousy of the old lover. He would not be imposed on, but would have it that Imoinda made a false step on purpose to fall into Oroonoko's bosom, and that all things looked like a design on both sides, and 'twas in vain she protested her innocence. He was old and obstinate, and left her more than half assured that his fear was true.

The king going to his apartment, sent to know where the prince was, and if he intended to obey his command. The messenger returned, and told him he found the prince pensive, and altogether unpreparing for the campaign; that he lay negligently on the ground, and answered very little. This confirmed the jealousy of the king, and he commanded that they should very narrowly and privately watch his motions; and that he should not stir from his apartment, but one spy or other should be employed to watch him. So that the hour approaching, wherein he was to go to the citron grove, and taking only Aboan along with him, he leaves his apartment, and was watched to the very gate of the otan, where he was seen to enter, and where they left him, to carry back the tidings to the king.

Oroonoko and Aboan were no sooner entered but Onahal led the prince to the apartment of Imoinda, who, not knowing anything of her happiness, was laid in bed. But Onahal only left him in her chamber to make the best of his opportunity, and took her dear Aboan to her own, where he showed the height of complaisance for his prince, when, to give him an opportunity, he suffered himself to be caressed in bed by Onahal.

The prince softly wakened Imoinda, who was not a little surprised with joy to find him there, and yet she trembled with a thousand fears. I believe he omitted saying nothing to this young maid, that might persuade her to suffer him to seize his own, and take the rights of love; and I believe she was not long resisting those arms where she so longed to be; and having opportunity, night and silence, youth, love and desire, he soon prevailed; and ravished in a moment what his old grandfather had been endeavouring for so many months.

'Tis not to be imagined the satisfaction of these two young lovers; nor the vows she made him, that she remained a spotless

maid till that night; and that what she did with his grandfather
had robbed him of no part of her virgin honour, the gods in mercy
and justice having reserved that for her plighted lord, to whom of
right it belonged. And 'tis impossible to express the transports he
suffered, while he listened to a discourse so charming from her
loved lips, and clasped that body in his arms, for whom he had so
long languished; and nothing now afflicted him, but his sudden
departure from her; for he told her the necessity and his
commands; but should depart satisfied in this, that since the old
king had hitherto not been able to deprive him of those enjoyments which only belonged to him, he believed for the future he
would be less able to injure him. So that, abating the scandal of
the veil, which was no otherwise so, than that she was wife to
another, he believed her safe, even in the arms of the king, and
innocent; yet would he have ventured at the conquest of the
world, and have given it all, to have had her avoided that honour
of receiving the royal veil. 'Twas thus, between a thousand
caresses, that both bemoaned the hard fate of youth and beauty,
so liable to that cruel promotion; 'twas a glory that could well
have been spared here, though desired, and aimed at by all the
young females of that kingdom.

But while they were thus fondly employed, forgetting how time
ran on, and that the dawn must conduct him far away from his
only happiness, they heard a great noise in the otan, and unusual
voices of men; at which the prince, starting from the arms of the
frighted Imoinda, ran to a little battle-axe he used to wear by his
side; and having not so much leisure as to put on his habit, he
opposed himself against some who were already opening the
door; which they did with so much violence, that Oroonoko was
not able to defend it, but was forced to cry out with a
commanding voice, 'Whoever ye are that have the boldness to
attempt to approach this apartment thus rudely, know that I, the
Prince Oroonoko, will revenge it with the certain death of him
that first enters. Therefore stand back, and know this place is
sacred to love, and me this night; tomorrow 'tis the king's.'

This he spoke with a voice so resolved and assured, that they
soon retired from the door, but cried, ''Tis by the king's command
we are come; and being satisfied by thy voice, O Prince, as much
as if we had entered, we can report to the king the truth of all his

fears, and leave thee to provide for thy own safety, as thou art advised by thy friends.'

At these words they departed, and left the prince to take a short and sad leave of his Imoinda; who trusting in the strength of her charms, believed she should appease the fury of a jealous king by saying she was surprised, and that it was by force of arms he got into her apartment. All her concern now was for his life, and therefore she hastened him to the camp, and with much ado, prevailed on him to go. Nor was it she alone that prevailed, Aboan and Onahal both pleaded, and both assured him of a lie that should be well enough contrived to secure Imoinda. So that, at last, with a heart sad as death, dying eyes, and sighing soul, Oroonoko departed, and took his way to the camp.

It was not long after the king in person came to the otan, where beholding Imoinda with rage in his eyes, he upbraided her wickedness and perfidy, and threatening her royal lover, she fell on her face at his feet, bedewing the floor with her tears and imploring his pardon for a fault which she had not with her will committed, as Onahal, who was also prostrate with her, could testify that, unknown to her, he had broke into her apartment, and ravished her. She spoke this much against her conscience; but to save her own life, 'twas absolutely necessary she should feign this falsity. She knew it could not injure the prince, he being fled to an army that would stand by him against any injuries that should assault him. However, this last thought of Imoinda's being ravished changed the measures of his revenge, and whereas before he designed to be himself her executioner, he now resolved she should not die. But as it is the greatest crime in nature amongst them to touch a woman, after having been possessed by a son, a father, or a brother, so now he looked on Imoinda as a polluted thing, wholly unfit for his embrace; nor would be resign her to his grandson, because she had received the royal veil. He therefore removes her from the otan, with Onahal; whom he put into safe hands, with order they should be both sold off, as slaves, to another country, either Christian, or heathen; 'twas no matter where.

This cruel sentence, worse than death, they implored might be reversed; but their prayers were vain, and it was put in execution accordingly, and that with so much secrecy, that none, either

without or within the otan, knew anything of their absence, or
their destiny.

The old king, nevertheless, executed this with a great deal of
reluctance; but he believed he had made a very great conquest
over himself when he had once resolved, and had performed what
he resolved. He believed now, that his love had been unjust, and
that he could not expect the gods, or Captain of the Clouds (as
they call the unknown power) should suffer a better consequence
from so ill a cause. He now begins to hold Oroonoko excused;
and to say, he had reason for what he did; and now everybody
could assure the king, how passionately Imoinda was beloved by
the prince; even those confessed it now who said the contrary
before his flame was abated. So that the king being old and not
able to defend himself in war, and having no sons of all his race
remaining alive, but only this, to maintain him on the throne; and
looking on this as a man disobliged, first by the rape of his
mistress, or rather, wife; and now by depriving him wholly of her,
he feared, might make him desperate, and do some cruel thing,
either to himself, or his old grandfather, the offender; he began to
repent him extremely of the contempt he had, in his rage, put on
Imoinda. Besides, he considered he ought in honour to have killed
her for this offence, if it had been one. He ought to have had so
much value and consideration for a maid of her quality, as to have
nobly put her to death, and not to have sold her like a common
slave, the greatest revenge, and the most disgraceful of any, and to
which they a thousand times prefer death, and implore it as
Imoinda did, but could not obtain that honour. Seeing therefore it
was certain that Oroonoko would highly resent this affront, he
thought good to make some excuse for his rashness to him, and to
that end he sent a messenger to the camp with orders to treat with
him about the matter, to gain his pardon, and to endeavour to
mitigate his grief; but that by no means he should tell him she was
sold, but secretly put to death; for he knew he should never obtain
his pardon for the other.

LOVE

'I am certainly the most fortunate creature that ever existed!' cried Jane. 'Oh! Lizzy, why am I thus singled from my family, and blessed above them all! If I could but see you as happy! If there *were* but such another man for you!'

Jane Austen, *Pride and Prejudice* (Chapter 55)

ELIZABETH VON ARNIM

From *Love*

Elizabeth von Arnim, a cousin of Katherine Mansfield, was born in 1866 in Sydney and brought up in England. In 1889, she travelled to Italy where she met her first husband and the couple lived in Berlin. She wrote 21 books, the most famous of which are Elizabeth and her German Garden *and* Enchanted April. *She had five children, who were tutored by, amongst others, Hugh Walpole and E. M. Forster. Debt meant that the von Arnims moved back to England in 1908 and a few years later her husband died. She later married the brother of Bertrand Russell and she died in 1941.*

In Love, *published in 1925, Catherine, a late middle-aged woman, and Christopher, a young man in his twenties, fall in love with one another. Catherine has a grown-up daughter who is married to a vicar of her mother's age. Whilst this discrepancy is perfectly acceptable where the woman is younger, it is thought unspeakably ridiculous where the man is the junior of the two. It is the elder half of the couple and the female who is supposed to be the sensible one in this situation, but after many comfortable years of adequate marriage and tranquil widowhood, Catherine finds herself unable to reject the immensely powerful and irrational feelings overwhelming her.*

NOW CHRISTOPHER might have behaved quite differently if he had found Catherine wide awake in her chair, properly lit up, and reading or sewing. He had meant, in coming back, only to reason with her. He couldn't be sent away, cut short in the middle of a sentence and cast out as he had been by Stephen's entrance, and not see her again at least to finish what he had to say. If she wouldn't listen now, at least they might arrange an hour the next day when she would. He couldn't go home to just black misery. He couldn't. He was a human being. There were things a human being simply couldn't do. He would see her again that evening, if only to find out when she would let him call and talk quietly. Surely she owed him this. He hadn't done anything to offend her really, except tell her that he loved her. And was that an offence? No; it was most natural, inevitable and right, he assured his shrinking heart. For his heart did shrink; it was very fearful, because he knew she would be angry when she saw him. He could barely get the words out to Mrs Mitcham at the door, so short was he of breath because of his heart. It was behaving as if he had been tearing up six flights of stairs, instead of walking slowly up one.

Then, inside the room, instead of light, and Catherine looking up from whatever she was doing at him with surprise and reproach, he found first darkness, and presently, as he stood uncertain and his eyes grew more accustomed to it, the outline of Catherine in the dull glow of the fire, motionless on the sofa. He couldn't see if she was asleep. She said nothing and didn't move. She must be asleep. And just at that moment a flame leapt out of the coals, and he saw that she was asleep.

The most extraordinary feeling flooded his heart. All the mothers in his ancestry crowded back to life in him. She looked so little, and helpless and vulnerable. She looked so tired, with no colour at all in her face. Not for anything in the world would Christopher have disturbed that sleep. He would creep away softly, and simply bear the incertitude as to when he was to see her again. Such an immense tenderness he had never in his life felt. He knew now that he loved her beyond all things, and far beyond himself.

He turned to go away, holding his breath, feeling for the door handle, when his foot knocked against the leg of George's big chair.

Catherine woke up. 'Mrs Mitcham – ' she began, drowsily. And then as no one answered, for though he tried to he couldn't, she put out her hand and turned on the light.

They blinked at each other.

Astonishment, succeeded by indignation, spread over Catherine's face. She could hardly believe her eyes. Christopher. Back again. Got into her flat like a thief. Stealing in in the dark . . .

She sat up, leaning on her hands. 'You!' was all she could find to say.

'Yes, I had to. I had to bring you back your – '

He was going to shelter behind her cloak, and then was ashamed of such trifling.

She made a movement to get up, but the sofa was a very low one, and she rather ridiculously bumped down on it again; and before she could make another attempt he had flown across to help her.

'No, no,' said Catherine, whose indignation was greater than any she had felt in her life, pushing aside his outstretched hands.

So then he lifted her up bodily, indifferent to everything else in the world; and having set her on her feet he held her like that, tightly in his arms, and didn't care if he had to die for it.

There was a moment's complete silence. Catherine was so much amazed that for a moment she was quite still.

Then she gave a gasp – muffled, because of his coat, against which her face was pressed. '*Oh* – ' she gasped, faint and muffled, trying to push him away.

She might as well have tried to push a rock away.

'*Oh* – ' she gasped again, as Christopher, still not caring if he had to die for it, began kissing her. He kissed what he could – her hair, the tip of one ear, and she, aghast, horrified, buried her face deeper and deeper into his coat in her efforts to protect it.

Oh, the outrage – never in her life – how dared he, how

dared he – just because she was alone, and had no one to defend her –

Not a word of this came out; it was entirely muffled in his coat. Aghast and horrified, Catherine continued to have the top of her head kissed, and her aghastness and horror became overwhelming when she realized that she – no, it wasn't possible, it *couldn't* be that she – that this – that she was somehow, besides being horrified, strangely shot through by a feeling that was not unpleasant? Impossible, impossible . . .

'Let me go,' she gasped into his coat. 'Let me *go* – '

For answer he took her head in his hands and held it back and kissed her really, right on her mouth, as no one in her life before had ever kissed her.

Impossible, impossible . . .

She stood, her arms hanging by her side, her body quivering. She didn't seem able to move. She seemed as if she were becoming every instant more drawn into this, more absorbed in what was happening – as profoundly absorbed as he was, as remote from realities. The room disappeared, the relics of George disappeared, the world disappeared, and all the reminders of the facts of her life. Youth had swept down out of the skies and caught her up in its arms into a strange, warm oblivion. He and she were not any longer Christopher and Catherine – Catherine tied up in a tangle of relationships, of obligations, of increasing memories, Christopher an impetuous young man who needed tremendously to be kept in his proper place: she was simply the Beloved, and he was Love.

'I worship you,' murmured Christopher.

Through her dream she heard him murmuring, and it woke her up to consciousness.

She opened her eyes and looked up at him.

He was gazing down at her – beautiful, all light. She stared at him an instant, still held in his arms, collecting her thoughts.

What had she done? What was she doing? What was this? Oh, but it was shameful, shameful . . .

She made one immense effort, and with both her hands pushed him away; and before he could stop her, for he too was in a dream, she had run to the door and flown along the passage to her bedroom and locked herself in.

Then she rang violently for Mrs Mitcham, and told her
through the shut door to let Mr Monckton out – she was going
to bed at once – she had a terrible headache.

. . . And she sat down on her bed and cried bitterly.

MARILYN FRENCH

From *The Women's Room*

When The Women's Room *was first published in 1977, it was in the forefront of the first-generation feminist movement. As such it was shocking for the notion that men are not central to women's lives. In fact men are barely present in the daily lives of most women, particularly housewives, for whom it is the boring drudgery of their routine that keeps life going. It is possible for women to band together and form their own power groups, without men, and, more radically still, they can be happy in such sorority. Contrary to popular fictional belief, women's lives are often terrible and oppressed and marriage, in this novel, merely serves to aggravate this state of affairs.*

In the 1990s, the remorseless descriptions of the terrible state of womanhood seem rather dated, which is not to say that the situation for most women has changed very much. Mira, the central character, lives a perfectly regular life for a woman of her age. She goes to college, she gets married, she becomes a housewife and has two sons who grow up and no longer need her. She is bored and dissatisfied at home and, around her, all of her female friends are being cheated upon or beaten up by their husbands. And eventually her husband meets a younger woman and asks for a divorce.

Mira finds her release not through another man but through her female friends and education. An alternative existence is possible but it is only when she has achieved some element of self-determination that she can encounter Ben, also studying as a mature under-

graduate at Harvard, and that they can learn to appreciate each other as equals and that love can make her happy. Mira is eventually forced to choose between going to Africa with Ben or staying in the United States to finish her studies. When she chooses her studies, French insists on driving home the point that Ben fails her and will not accept this as a valid choice – where some women might have achieved a certain level of self-determination, even the most liberal of men were not yet ready for such a social change.

MIRA GOT a little high that night, and so did Ben, and somehow – later she could not remember whose suggestion it was, or if there had been no suggestion at all, but simple single purpose – he ended up in her car, driving her to her apartment and when they arrived, he got out and saw her to the door and of course she asked him in for a nightcap and of course he came.

They were laughing as they climbed the steps, and they had their arms around each other. They were designing the perfect world, trying to outdo each other in silliness, and giggling to the point of tears at their own jokes. Mira fumbled with her key, Ben took it from her, dropped it, both of them giggling, picked it up and opened the door.

She poured them brandies. Ben following her to the kitchen, leaning over the counter and gazing at her as she prepared the drinks, talking, talking. He followed her out of the kitchen and right into the bathroom, until she turned with a little surprise and he caught himself, cried 'Oh!' and laughed, and stepped out, but stood right beside the closed door talking to her through it while she peed. Then sat close beside her on the couch, talking, talking, laughing, smiling at her with shining eyes. And when he got up to get refills, she followed him into the kitchen and leaned across the counter gazing at him as he prepared the drinks, and he kept looking at her as he did it, and poured too much water in her glass. And they sat even closer this time, and there needed no forethought or calculation for the moment when they reached across and took each other's hands and it was only a few moments later that Ben was on her, leaning against her, his face searching in her face for something madly wanted that did not reside in faces, but searched, kept searching, and she too, in his. His body was lying on her now, his chest against her breasts, and the closeness of their bodies felt like completion. Her breasts were pressed flat under him: they felt soft and hard at once. Their faces stayed together, mouths searching, probing, opening as if to devour, or rubbing softly together. Their cheeks too rubbed softly like the cheeks of tiny children just trying to feel another flesh, and hard, his beard, shaved though he was, harsh and hurtful on her cheek. He had her head in his hands, and he held it firmly, possessively, and gently, all at once, and he dipped his face into hers, searching for nourishment, hungry, hungry. They rose together, like one body, and like one body walked into the bedroom, not separating even in the narrow hallway, just squeezing through together.

For Mira, Ben's lovemaking was the discovery of a new dimension. He loved her body. Her pleasure in this alone was so extreme that it felt like the discovery of a new ocean, mountain, continent. He loved it. He crowed over it as he helped her to undress, he kissed it and caressed it and exclaimed, and she was quieter, but adored his with her eyes as she helped him to undress, ran her hands over the smooth skin of his back, grabbed him from behind around the waist and kissed his back, the back of his neck, his shoulders. She was shy of his penis at first, but when he held her close and nestled against her, he pressed his penis against her body, and her hand went out to it, held it, caressed it. Then he wrapped his legs around her, covered her, holding on to her tightly, and kissed her eyes, her cheeks, her hair. She pulled away from him gently and took his hands and kissed them, and he took hers and kissed the tips of her fingers.

She lay back again as he pressed against her, and he caressed her breasts. She felt that her body was floating out to sea on a warm gentle wave that had orders not to drown her, but she didn't even care if she drowned. Then, rather suddenly, he put his mouth to her breasts and nursed at them, and quickly entered her and quickly came, silently, with only an expelled breath, and a pang of self-pity hit her, her eyes filled with tears. No, no, not again, it couldn't be the same, it wasn't fair, was there really something wrong with her? He lay on top of her, holding her closely for a long time afterward, and she had time to swallow the tears and paste a smile back on her face. She patted his back gently and reminded herself that she had at least had pleasure from it this time, and maybe that was a good sign. He had given her, if nothing else, more pleasure than she had ever had from her body before.

After a time, he leaned back and lay on his side close to her.

They lighted cigarettes and sipped their drinks. He asked her about her girlhood: what kind of child had she been? She was surprised. Women ask such things, sometimes, but not men. She was delighted. She lay back and threw herself into it, talking as if it were happening there and then. Her voice changed and curled around its subject: she was five, she was twelve, she was fourteen. She hardly noticed at first that he had begun to caress her body again. It seemed simply natural that they would touch each other. He was gently rubbing her belly and sides, her shoulders. She put her cigarette out and caressed his shoulders. Then he was leaning over her, kissing her belly, rubbing his hands on her thighs, on the insides of her thighs. Desire rose up in her more fiercely than before. She caressed his hair, then his head moved down, and she tightened up, her eyes widened, he was kissing her genitals, licking them, she was horrified, but he kept stroking her belly, her leg, he kept doing it and when she tried to tighten her legs, he held them gently apart, and she lay back again and felt the warm wet pressure and her innards felt fluid and giving, all the way to her stomach. She tried to pull him up, but he would not permit it, he turned her over, he kissed her back, her buttocks, he put his finger on her anus and rubbed it gently, and she was moaning and trying to turn over, and finally, she succeeded, and then he had her breast in his mouth and the hot shoots were climbing all the way to her throat. She wrapped her body around him, clutching him, no longer kissing or caressing, but only clinging now, trying to get him to come inside her, but he wouldn't. She surrendered her body to him, let him take control of it, and in an ecstasy of passivity let her body float out to the deepest part of the ocean. There was only body, only sensation: even the room had ceased to exist. He was rubbing her clitoris, gently, slowly, ritually, and she was making little gasps that she could hear from a distance. Then he took her breast in his mouth again and wrapped his body around her and entered her. She came almost immediately and gave a sharp cry, but he kept going, and she came over and over again in a series of sharp pleasures that were the same as pain. Her face and body were wet, so were his, she felt, and still the pangs came, less now, and she clutched him to her, holding him as if she really might drown. The orgasms subsided, but still he thrust himself into her. Her legs were aching, and the thrust no longer felt like pleasure. Her muscles were weary, and she was unable to keep the motion going. He pulled out and turned her over and propped her on a pillow so that her ass was propped up, and entered her vagina from behind. His hand stroked her breast gently, he was humped over her like a dog. It was a totally different feeling, and as he thrust more and more sharply, she gave out little cries. Her clitoris was being triggered again, and it felt sharp and fierce and hot and as full of pain as pleasure and suddenly he came and thrust fiercely and gave off a series of loud cries that were nearly sobs, and stayed drooped over her like a flower, heaving, his wet face against her back.

When he pulled out, she turned over and reached up to him and pulled him down and held him. He put his arms around her and they lay together for a long time. His wet penis was against her leg, and she could feel semen trickling out of her onto the sheets. It began to feel cold, but neither of them moved. Then they moved a few inches and looked into each other's faces. They stroked each other's faces, then began to laugh. They hugged each other hard, like friends rather than lovers, and sat up. Ben went into the bathroom and got some tissues and they dried themselves and the sheets. He went back and started water running in the tub. Mira was lying back against the pillow, smoking.

'Come on, woman, get up!' he ordered, and she looked at him startled, and he reached across and put his arms around her and lifted her from the bed, kissing her at the same time, and helped her to her feet, and they went together to the bathroom and both peed. The water was at bath level by then. Ben had put Mira's bath lotion in the water, and it was bubbly and smelled fresh, and they got in together and sat with bent knees intertwined, and gently threw water at each other and lay back enjoying the warmth and caressed each other beneath and above the water.

'I'm hungry,' she said.

'I'm famished,' he said.

Together, they pulled everything out of the refrigerator, and produced a feast of Jewish salami and feta cheese and hard-boiled eggs and tomatoes and black bread and sweet butter and half-sour pickles and big black Greek olives and raw Spanish onions and beer, and trotted all of it back to bed with them, and sat there gorging themselves and talking and drinking and laughing and touching each other with tender fingertips. And finally they set the platters and plates and beer cans on the floor and Ben nuzzled his face in her breast, but this time she pushed him down and got on top of him and, refusing to let him move, she kissed and caressed his body and slid her hands down his sides and along the insides of his thighs, held his balls gently, then slid down and took his penis in her mouth and he gasped with pleasure and she moved her hands and head slowly up and down with it, feeling the vein throb, feeling it harden and melt little drops of semen, and wouldn't let him move until suddenly she raised her head and he looked startled and she got on top of him and set her own rhythms, rubbing her clitoris against him as she moved and she came, she felt like a goddess, triumphant, riding the winds, and she kept coming and he came too then, and she bent down her chest and clutched him, both of them moaning together, and ended, finally, exhausted.

They fell back on the rumpled sheets for a while, then Mira lighted a cigarette. Ben got up and smoothed the bedclothes out, and fluffed up the pillows, and got in beside her and pulled up the sheets and blankets and took a drag of her cigarette and put his arms behind his head and just lay there smiling.

It was five o'clock, and the sky above the houses was light, lightening, a pale streak of light blue. They were not tired, they said. They turned their heads toward each other, and just smiled, kept smiling. Ben took another drag of her cigarette, then she put it out. She reached out and switched off the lamp, and together they snuggled down in the sheets. They were still turned to each other, and they twisted their bodies together. They fell immediately asleep. When they awakened in the morning, they were still intertwined.

RADCLYFFE HALL

From *The Well of Loneliness*

Radclyffe Hall was born into an upper middle-class family in Bournemouth in 1883. She was christened Marguerite Radclyffe-Hall but insisted on calling herself John. Before the First World War she began writing reams of poetry but began to consider prose after meeting Mabel Batten in 1907 and forming a relationship with her. It was through Mabel that she developed a profound interest in Catholicism and after Mabel's death in 1916 Radclyffe Hall met Una Troubridge with whom she lived until her death in 1943. During this period she published seven novels.

The Well of Loneliness, *credited with being the first novel in the English language openly to describe a lesbian relationship, was published in 1928 amidst a welter of negative publicity and was, subsequently, successfully prosecuted as an obscenity in both Britain and the UK. In the novel, Stephen Gordon, whose father gives her a boy's name since he never wished for anything but a son, realizes that she is an 'invert' – a person with a male spirit trapped inside a woman's body. Radclyffe Hall genuinely believed that lesbianism was a genetic deficiency and that she herself could not escape this terrible affliction, a state of affairs aggravated by her conversion to Catholicism. Stephen (and presumably Hall herself) is a deeply conservative character – she does not question the values of the society in which she lives. There is nothing in her nature which attracts her to the kind of 'abnormal' and marginal life which her sexuality, as she sees it, condemns her to lead.*

She must therefore bear its cross and suffer. Being a 'man' in spirit, she can only be attracted to 'real' women, who cannot possibly be permanently attracted to her: she is therefore doomed to a life of loneliness.

Since Hall shows herself to be such an innately conservative person, it is hardly surprising then, that what is credited as being the first openly lesbian novel in English literature, contains practically no scenes of romantic encounter. Prurient and contemporary readers knowing nothing of the details of lesbianism would have been sorely disappointed reading this book. This chapter, for example is one of the sexual highlights of the novel in its description of Stephen's first affair.

[Chapter 18]

O N A BEAUTIFUL evening three weeks later, Stephen took Angela over Morton. They had had tea with Anna and Puddle, and Anna had been coldly polite to this friend of her daughter's, but Puddle's manner had been rather resentful – she deeply mistrusted Angela Crossby. But now Stephen was free to show Angela Morton, and this she did gravely, as though something sacred were involved in this first introduction to her home, as though Morton itself must feel that the coming of this small, fair-haired woman was in some way momentous. Very gravely, then, they went over the house – even into Sir Philip's old study.

From the house they made their way to the stables, and still grave, Stephen told her friend about Raftery. Angela listened, assuming an interest she was very far from feeling – she was timid of horses, but she liked to hear the girl's rather gruff voice, such an earnest young voice, it intrigued her. She was thoroughly frightened when Raftery sniffed her and then blew through his nostrils as though disapproving, and she started back with a sharp exclamation, so that Stephen slapped him on his glossy grey shoulder: 'Stop it, Raftery, come up!' And Raftery, disgusted, went and blew on his oats to express his hurt feelings.

They left him and wandered away through the gardens, and quite soon poor Raftery was almost forgotten, for the gardens smelt softly of night-scented stock, and of other pale flowers that smell sweetest at evening, and Stephen was thinking that Angela Crossby resembled such flowers – very fragrant and pale she was, so Stephen said to her gently:

'You seem to belong to Morton.'

Angela smiled a slow, questioning smile: 'You think so, Stephen?'

And Stephen answered: 'I do, because Morton and I are one,' and she scarcely understood the portent of her words; but Angela, understanding, spoke quickly:

'Oh, I belong nowhere – you forget I'm the stranger.'

'I know that you're you,' said Stephen.

They walked on in silence while the light changed and deepened, growing always more golden and yet more elusive. And the
birds, who loved that strange light, sang singly and then all
together: 'We're happy, Stephen!'

And turning to Angela, Stephen answered the birds: 'Your
being here makes me so happy.'

'If that's true, then why are you so shy of my name?'

'Angela –' mumbled Stephen.

Then Angela said: 'It's just over three weeks since we met – how
quickly our friendship's happened. I suppose it was meant, I
believe in Kismet. You were awfully scared that first day at The
Grange; why were you so scared?'

Stephen answered slowly: 'I'm frightened now – I'm frightened
of you.'

'Yet you're stronger than I am –'

'Yes, that's why I'm so frightened, you make me feel strong – do
you want to do that?'

'Well – perhaps – you're so very unusual, Stephen.'

'Am I?'

'Of course, don't you know that you are? Why, you're altogether different from other people.'

Stephen trembled a little: 'Do you mind?' she faltered.

'I know that you're you,' teased Angela, smiling again, but she
reached out and took Stephen's hand.

Something in the queer, vital strength of that hand stirred her
deeply so that she tightened her fingers: 'What in the Lord's name
are you?' she murmured.

'I don't know. Go on holding like that to my hand – hold it
tighter – I like the feel of your fingers.'

'Stephen, don't be absurd!'

'Go on holding my hand, I like the feel of your fingers.'

'Stephen, you're hurting, you're crushing my rings!'

And now they were under the trees by the lakes, their feet
falling softly on the luminous carpet. Hand in hand they entered
that place of deep stillness, and only their breathing disturbed the
stillness for a moment, then it folded back over their breathing.

'Look,' said Stephen, and she pointed to the swan called Peter,
who had come drifting past on his own white reflection. 'Look,'

she said, 'this is Morton, all beauty and peace – it drifts like that swan does, on calm, deep water. And all this beauty and peace is for you, because now you're a part of Morton.'

Angela said: 'I've never known peace, it's not in me – I don't think I'd find it here, Stephen.' And as she spoke she released her hand, moving a little away from the girl.

But Stephen continued to talk on gently; her voice sounded almost like that of a dreamer: 'Lovely, oh, lovely it is, our Morton. On evenings in winter these lakes are quite frozen, and the ice looks like slabs of gold in the sunset, when you and I come and stand here in the winter. And as we walk back we can smell the log fires long before we can see them, and we love that good smell because it means home, and our home is Morton – and we're happy, happy – we're utterly contented and at peace, we're filled with the peace of this place – '

'Stephen – don't!'

'We're both filled with the old peace of Morton, because we love each other so deeply – and because we're perfect, a perfect thing, you and I – not two separate people but one. And our love has lit a great, comforting beacon, so that we need never be afraid of the dark any more – we can warm ourselves at our love, we can lie down together, and my arms will be round you – '

She broke off abruptly, and they stared at each other.

'Do you know what you're saying?' Angela whispered.

And Stephen answered: 'I know that I love you, and that nothing else matters in the world.'

Then, perhaps because of that glamorous evening, with its spirit of queer, unearthly adventure, with its urge to strange, unendurable sweetness, Angela moved a step nearer to Stephen, then another, until their hands were touching. And all that she was, and all that she had been and would be again, perhaps even tomorrow, was fused at that moment into one mighty impulse, one imperative need, and that need was Stephen. Stephen's need was now hers, by sheer force of its blind and uncomprehending will to appeasement.

Then Stephen took Angela into her arms, and she kissed her full on the lips, as a lover.

TERRY McMILLAN

From *Mama*

Terry McMillan was born in Michigan and now teaches creative writing in Tucson, Arizona where she lives with her son. Mama, published in 1987, was her first novel.

Mildred is the mama in question and, having lived her whole life satisfying the needs of inadequate husbands and children, she considers that she is entitled to some love, affection and fun also. His name is 'Spooky'.

[Seven]

SPOOKY COOPER was no good and Mildred knew it. He was quiet. Slick was a better word, according to everybody in town. And he was so handsome that even he did a double take in the mirror when he combed his hair and moustache. Though he was supposed to be black, they said his daddy was white, and he resembled Clark Gable. He talked with a southern drawl, almost as if he were trying to prove his blackness. He was also married to a bony woman who looked like she was dying of cancer. Kaye Francis. Nobody ever did figure out how she snagged Spooky in the first place, and it was hard to ascertain if her three babies had anything to do with it.

When Mildred had worked at the Shingle, Spooky had often flirted with her but never actually came right out and approached her. He wasn't one of those husbands who had offered her more than a free drink after she and Crook were divorced. Oh, she'd watched him, but he had always made her feel too fluttery inside, so she had avoided his eyes all those years. And now, here he was knocking on her front door.

Spooky was puffing on a cigarette like a gangster and pulling his pants up like a pimp so his penis bulged and so Mildred could see that his socks were silk and his pointed-toe shoes were expensive. She opened the door and tried to remain cool, especially since it was one of those rare occasions when she was alone in the house. As the saying goes, you always want what you can't have. To Mildred, there was something so mysterious about Spooky it made him damn near taboo. And his seeming off-limits only made him more desirable.

Mildred knew she looked OK. Connie James had just pressed and curled her hair and she hadn't wiped off her peach lipstick yet. She sat her plate of collard greens and ham hocks on the dining room table and went to open the screen door.

'What brings you way over here, handsome?' Mildred heard herself asking.

'Oh, I was just driving in the neighborhood, and I said to myself, Baby Franks rented that house to Mildred, didn't he, and I just wondered if you were home. Can I come in?'

'Yeah, come on in. Have a seat. Ain't got nothing in here to drink but a beer. What you know good?'

The truth of the matter was Mildred already knew Kaye Francis had put him out – everybody knew it. She had finally gotten tired of all the women calling her house, claiming Spooky was the father of their brand new baby, or had given them gonorrhea, or owed them some money. A lot of people thought Spooky had married Kaye Francis because her people had money. She was the one who had bought him that white Riviera he was driving. Didn't make any difference to Mildred one way or the other. At this moment, all she knew was that he had been curious enough to stop by to see her, and for the first time in her life, Mildred felt whorish. She didn't want to talk about anything, just do it while the kids were gone and then put him out. Her panties were already getting slippery, and when Spooky put his cigarette out and finished his beer, Mildred felt a lingering weakness inside.

It had started to rain, and the sky was growing darker and darker. She walked to the sun porch to close the windows and a flash of lightning crackled and lit up the whole sky.

'You gon' get caught in this storm, you know,' she said.

'I'm already caught in the storm,' he said.

This would be the first time Mildred wouldn't stop to think about her kids. She was just glad they were gone. She and Spooky sat on the sun porch, listening to the thunder and the rain falling in the drain pipes.

'My daddy always saying a thunderstorm is the Lord doing his work and we should be quiet,' she said, unable to think of anything else to say.

'I'm a quiet man,' Spooky said.

She offered him some greens and corn bread, but he said he wasn't hungry. At least not for food. Mildred couldn't finish hers either. She turned off the television.

'Why don't we go into the living room,' Mildred whispered.

Her heart hadn't pounded so hard since she fell in love with Crook. She had forgotten that feeling. Spooky Cooper sat beside her smiling into her eyes, and the gap in his tooth only added to his charisma and charm. He bent over and kissed her like a movie star, then led Mildred to her bedroom like he already knew where it was.

Spooky knew his power, and Mildred couldn't resist. His black eyes had hypnotized her, especially when he told her that he had always yearned for her, long before he ever married Kaye Francis, but she had married Crook. Spooky wasn't really lying, but his timing was brilliant. He knew how picky Mildred had always been when it came to men, and the only piece of a man she had had since she moved into this house was old smelly Rufus, who often stopped by to see the kids and lend her ten or twenty dollars, which he never made her pay back. Rufus had the hots for her too, and though he drank too much, a few times Mildred had let herself get loose enough to ignore his funk, his scratchy whiskers, and his unbrushed teeth. The kids liked Rufus because he was generous with his money and he was so silly. They would have never guessed in a million years, though, that their mama had actually slept with him. To Mildred, Rufus was like a spare tyre when she had a flat.

Now, she had a real man in her bedroom. And one who smelled like Aqua Velva, not Old Spice, thank God. She was so nervous that you'd have thought she was going to bed with the president of the United States.

'Make yourself comfortable,' she told him as she glided to the bathroom. Spooky had already taken off his clothes and was lying in her bed like a king. Mildred closed the bathroom door and took a quick douche, brushed her teeth and gargled, sprayed some Topaz between her legs and on the balls of her feet – like the good old days – and Q-Tipped her ears and navel. She didn't own a sexy nightgown, but it wouldn't have mattered. Spooky was so smooth and so cool that she wouldn't have had it on a minute before he would have skillfully slid the straps from her shoulders.

She turned out the bathroom light and tiptoed back to the bedroom. Before she knew it, Spooky was holding her in his arms and kissing her like she was breakable. He touched her skin in places she had forgotten could be ignited by a man. She'd never felt her body throbbing like this in all of her thirty years. She didn't even feel the house shake when the train rumbled past her bedroom window.

And Spooky took his time with her. He licked her skin in slow motion, the way a kitten licks milk from a bowl. He swirled his tongue around in her ears at 33 rpm's, until Mildred felt like she would boil over. She had never, ever, experienced this kind of passion before. And when the room grew completely black and his warm pressure amplified inside her, she screamed out his name three octaves higher than her normal voice. Spooky calmly rolled over and lit a cigarette, knowing full well his mission had been accomplished.

During the weeks that followed, Mildred made him park his car four blocks away from the house. His wife had become a reality to her. Word had already hit the streets that Mildred Peacock had made Spooky Cooper fall in love with her. And it was true. Supposedly it was impossible because there had been so many women who would have given anything to be with him and Spooky hadn't given them the time of day. Mildred hadn't asked him for a thing in return and had not posed a single question to him about his wife. She knew how to make a man feel like one: everything Spooky had done to her, she had given back to him three times over. And the first time Mildred moved her head below his waist, she gave Spooky so much pleasure that he thought she knew what she was doing. Most of her girlfriends had always said they didn't go that way. The men said they would never eat at the Y. Just about all of them were lying, and would do damn near anything behind closed doors, so long as it guaranteed some kind of pleasure.

Spooky went so far as to walk in the rain to be with Mildred, and this was something he had never done for any woman – got his shoes wet. What the hell, Mildred thought, she was fucking a dream and loving every minute of it. Spooky had been the first man to drive her far enough to bring her to a full orgasm. And Mildred got greedy. She didn't just want more of him, she wanted all of him.

But Spooky was still sneaky and no good, and when Mildred sat the kids down to tell them that he was going to be spending quite a bit of time there, they stared at her like she was crazy.

Freda, as usual, spoke for all of them. 'Mama, that's Miss Francis' husband! I know you wouldn't mess with no married man. Please don't tell us you like him, Mama. Everybody know he hang out at Carabelle's and Miss Moore's. He a ladies' man. What you got that ain't none of them got?'

'Shut up, would you,' Mildred snapped, not even bothering to correct Freda's grammar. 'I like the man and he likes me, and I don't care whose husband he *used* to be, he makes me feel damn good, better than your daddy ever did, and if you knew how long it's been since your mama felt like this, all y'all would be happy for me.'

'Happy? Everybody at school know he take money from women, and you ain't got none, so what he want with you?' Money asked.

'If y'all don't shut up, I swear . . .' and Mildred couldn't say another word. She ran some bathwater and soaked in the tub. In her mind all she could see were Spooky's black eyes. And as the bubbles burst over her brown skin, the only thing she could feel was warm air leaving his lips and penetrating every pore of her body. The hot water felt like Spooky's passion spreading like an oil slick between her legs. And at that moment, as Mildred let her shoulders slide farther into the water, she couldn't remember her children, by name or by face, and in her heart, she didn't even have any.

ANAÏS NIN

From *A Spy in the House of Love*

Anaïs Nin, whose first novel was published in the 1930s, was a mixture of Cuban, Danish, Spanish and French. She was educated in Paris until the age of eleven, at which time her family emigrated to the United States. She later returned to Paris to study psychology.

After writing a number of novels and mixing with a large number of contemporary and avant-garde artists, she wrote A Spy in the House of Love *in 1954. In the 1940s she started writing commissioned pieces of erotica for particular clients, a pursuit for which she has become famous. Another was the publication of* Henry and June, *which was an account of her relationship with the novelist Henry Miller and his wife June Mansfield. She died in Los Angeles in 1977.*

In this extract from A Spy, *the enigmatic heroine, Sabina, creeps out of the beachside hotel room, rented for her by her husband, Alan, in order to rendezvous with a young man called Philip. This exceptionally notorious work is, for us in the 1990s, extremely vague and lyrical, if not almost impenetrable.*

H E WOULD NOT believe that she wanted to return to her room to wash the sand out of her hair, to put oil over her sunburnt skin, to paint a fresh layer of polish on her nails, to relive every step of their encounter as she lay in the bath, in her habit of wanting to taste the intoxications of experience not once but twice.

To the girl she shared the room with she owed but a slight warning that she would be out that evening, but on this particular evening there was a third person staying with them for just one night, and this woman was a friend of Alan as well as hers; so her departure would be more complicated. Once more she would have to steal ecstasy and rob the night of its intoxications. She waited until they were both asleep and went silently out, but did not go towards the Main street where all her friends the artists would be walking and who might offer to join her. She leaped over the wharf's railing and slid down the wooden pole, scratching her hands and her dress against the barnacles, and leaped on to the beach. She walked along the wet sand towards the most brightly lighted of the wharves where the Dragon offered its neon lighted body to the thirsty night explorers.

None of her friends could afford to come there, where even the piano had discarded its modest covering and added the dance of its bare inner mechanism to the other motions, extending the pianist's realm from abstract notes to a disciplined ballet of reclining chess figures on agitated wires.

To reach the nightclub she had to climb large iron ladders planted on the glistening poles, on which her dress caught, and her hair. She arrived out of breath as if she had been diving from there and were returning after freeing herself from the clasp of the sea weeds. But no one noticed her except Philip, the spotlight being on the singer of cajoling blues.

A flush of pleasure showed even through the deep tan. He held a chair out for her and bent over to whisper: 'I was afraid you were not coming. When I passed by your studio at ten o'clock, I didn't see any light, so I walked up and knocked at the window, not too hard, because I don't see well at night, and I was afraid I had made a mistake. There was no answer. I stumbled about in the dark . . . waited . . .'

At the terror that Philip might have awakened her friends, at the danger that had barely been averted, she felt fever mounting, the heat of the blood set off by danger. His handsomeness at night became a drug, and the image of his night blinded self-seeking her, touched her, and disarmed her. Her eyes now turned dark and rimmed with coal dust like those of oriental women. The eyelids had a bluish tint, and her eyebrows, which she did not pluck, threw shadows which made her eyes' dark glints seem to come from a deeper source than during the day.

Her eyes absorbed the vivid modelling of his features, and the contrast between his strong head and the long-fingered hands, hairless, covered by the finest down. He not only caressed her skin along her arm, but seemed to exert a subtle musician's pressure on the concealed nerves of an instrument he knew well, saying: 'The beauty of your arm is exactly like that of your body. If I didn't know your body I would want it, just from seeing the shape of your arm.'

Desire made a volcanic island, on which they lay in a trance, feeling the subterranean whirls lying beneath them, dance floor and table and the magnetic blues uprooted by desire, the avalanches of the body's tremors. Beneath the delicate skin, the tendrils of secret hair, the indentations and valleys of flesh, the volcanic lava flowed, desire incandescent, and where it burned the voices of the blues being sung became a harsh wilderness cry, bird and animal's untamed cry of pleasure and cry of danger and cry of fear and cry of childbirth and cry of wound pain from the same hoarse delta of nature's pits.

The trembling premonitions shaking the hand, the body, made dancing unbearable, waiting unbearable, smoking and talking unbearable, soon would come the untamable seizure of sensual cannibalism, the joyous epilepsies.

They fled from the eyes of the world, the singer's prophetic, harsh, ovarian prologues. Down the rusty bars of ladders to the undergrounds of the night propitious to the first man and woman at the beginning of the world, where there were no words by which to possess each other, no music for serenades, no presents to court with, no tournaments to impress and force a yielding, no secondary instruments, no adornments, necklaces, crowns to subdue, but only one ritual, a joyous, joyous, joyous impaling of woman on a man's sensual mast.

JAYNE ANNE PHILLIPS

Home

Jayne Anne Phillips was born in West Virginia in 1952. She is the author of two collections of short stories, Fast Lanes *and* Black Tickets. Black Tickets, *in which 'Home' first appeared, was published in 1979 and won its author the Sue Kauffman Prize for first fiction. She has also written a novel called* Machine Dreams. *She now teaches at both Harvard and New York University.*

I'M AFRAID Walter Cronkite has had it, says Mom. Roger Mudd always does the news now. How would you like to have a name like that? Walter used to do the conventions and a football game now and then. I mean he would sort of appear, on the sidelines. Didn't he? But you never see him anymore. Lord. Something is going on.

Mom, I say. Maybe he's just resting. He must have made a lot of money by now. Maybe he's tired of talking about elections and mine disasters and the collapse of the franc. Maybe he's in love with a young girl.

My mother has her suspicions. She ponders. I have been home with her for two months. I ran out of money and I wasn't in love, so I have come home to my mother. She is an educational administrator. All winter long after work she watches television and knits afghans.

Come home, she said. Save money.

I can't possible do it, I said. Jesus, I'm twenty-three years old.

Don't be silly, she said. And don't use profanity.

She arranged a job for me in the school system. All day I tutor children in remedial reading. Sometimes I am so discouraged that I lie on the couch all evening and watch television with her. The shows are all alike. Their laugh tracks are conspicuously similar; I think I recognize a repetition of certain professional laughters. This laughter marks off the half hours.

Finally I make a rule: I won't watch television at night. I will watch only the news, which ends at 7:30. Then I will go to my room and do God knows what. But I feel sad that she sits there alone, knitting by the lamp. She seldom looks up.

Why don't you ever read anything? I ask.

I do, she says. I read books in my field. I read all day at work, writing those damn proposals. When I come home I want to relax

Then let's go to the movies.

I don't want to go to the movies. Why should I pay money to be upset or frightened?

But feeling something can teach you. Don't you want to learn anything?

I'm learning all the time, she says.

She keeps knitting. She folds yarn the colour of cream, the colour of snow. She works it with her long blue needles, piercing, returning, winding. Yarn cascades from her hands in long panels. A pattern appears and disappears. She stops and counts; so many stitches across, so many down. Yes, she is on the right track.

Occasionally I offer to buy my mother a subscription to something mildly informative: *Ms, Rolling Stone, Scientific American*.

I don't want to read that stuff, she says. Just save your money. Did you hear Cronkite last night? Everyone's going to need all they can get.

Often I need to look at my mother's old photographs. I see her sitting in knee-high grass with a white gardenia in her hair. I see her dressed up as the groom in a mock wedding at a sorority party, her black hair pulled back tight. I see her formally posed in her cadet nurse's uniform. The photographer has painted her lashes too lushly, too long; but her deep red mouth is correct.

The war ended too soon. She didn't finish her training. She came home to nurse only her mother and to meet my father at a dance. She married him in two weeks. It took twenty years to divorce him.

When we travelled to a neighbouring town to buy my high school clothes, my mother and I would pass a certain road that turned off the highway and wound to a place I never saw.

There it is, my mother would say. The road to Wonder Bar. That's where I met my Waterloo. I walked in and he said, 'There she is. I'm going to marry that girl.' Ha. He sure saw me coming.

Well, I asked, why did you marry him?

He was older, she said. He had a job and a car. And mother was so sick.

My mother doesn't forget her mother.

Never one bedsore, she says. I turned her every fifteen minutes. I kept her skin soft and kept her clean, even to the end.

I imagine my mother at twenty-three; her black hair, her dark eyes, her olive skin and that red lipstick. She is growing lines of tension in her mouth. Her teeth press into her lower lip as she lifts the woman in the bed. The woman weighs no more than a child. She has a smell. My mother fights it continually; bathing her, changing her sheets, carrying her to the bathroom so the smell can be contained and flushed away. My mother will try to protect them both. At night she sleeps in the room on a cot. She struggles awake feeling something press down on her and suck her breath: the smell. When my grandmother can no longer move, my mother fights it alone.

I did all I could, she sighs. And I was glad to do it. I'm glad I don't have to feel guilty.

No one has to feel guilty. I tell her.

And why not? says my mother. There's nothing wrong with guilt. If you are guilty, you should feel guilty.

My mother has often told me that I will be sorry when she is gone.

I think. And read alone at night in my room. I read those books I never read, the old classics, and detective stories. I can get them in the library here. There is only one bookstore; it sells mostly newspapers and *True Confessions* oracles. At Kroger's by the checkout counter I buy a few paperbacks, best sellers, but they are usually bad.

The television drones on downstairs.

I wonder about Walter Cronkite.

When was the last time I saw him? It's true his face was pouchy, his hair thinning. Perhaps he is only cutting it shorter. But he had that look about the eyes . . .

He was there when they stepped on the moon. He forgot he was on the air and he shouted, 'There . . . there . . . now. . . We have contact!' Contact. For those who tuned in late, for the periodic watchers, he repeated: 'One small step . . .'

I was in high school and he was there with the body count. But he said it in such a way that you knew he wanted the war to end. He looked directly at you and said the numbers quietly. Shame, yes, but sorrowful patience, as if all things had passed before his eyes. And he understood that here at home, as well as in starving India, we would pass our next lives as meagre cows.

My mother gets *Reader's Digest*. I come home from work, have a cup of coffee, and read it. I keep it beside my bed. I read it when I am too tired to read anything else. I read about Joe's kidney and Humour in Uniform. Always, there are human interest stories in

which someone survives an ordeal of primal terror. Tonight it is
Grizzly! Two teenagers camping in the mountains are attacked by
a bear. Sharon is dragged over a mile, unconscious. She is a good
student loved by her parents, an honest girl loved by her
boyfriend. Perhaps she is not a virgin; but in her heart, she is
virginal. And she lies now in the furred arms of a beast. The
grizzly drags her quietly, quietly. He will care for her all the days
of his life . . . Sharon, his rose.

But alas. Already, rescuers have organized. Mercifully her
boyfriend is not among them. He is sleeping en route to the nearest
hospital; his broken legs have excused him. In a few days, Sharon
will bring him his food on a tray. She is spared. She is not demure.
He gazes on her face, untouched but for a long thin scar near her
mouth. He thinks of the monster and wonders at its delicate mark.
Sharon says she remembers nothing of the bear. She only knows
the tent was ripped open, that its heavy canvas fell across her face.

I turn out my light when I know my mother is sleeping. By then
my eyes hurt and the streets of the town are deserted.

My father comes to me in a dream. He kneels beside me,
touches my mouth. He turns my face gently toward him.

Let me see, he says. Let me see it.

He is looking for a scar, a sign. He wears only a towel around
his waist. He presses himself against my thigh, pretending solicitude. But I know what he is doing; I turn my head in repulsion and
stiffen. He smells of a sour musk and his forearms are black with
hair. I think, it's been years since he's had an erection. . . .

Finally he stands. Cover yourself, I tell him.

I can't, he says. I'm hard.

On Saturdays I go to the Veterans of Foreign Wars rummage sales.
They are held in the drafty basement of a church, rows of collapsi-
ble tables piled with objects. Sometimes I think I recognize the pos-
sessions of old friends; a class ring, yearbooks, football sweaters
with our high school insignia. Would this one have fit Jason?

He used to spread it on the seat of the car on winter nights when
we parked by country churches and graveyards. There seemed to
be no ground, just water, a rolling, turning, building to a dull pain
between my legs.

What's wrong? What is it?

Jason, I can't . . . This pain . . .

It's only because you're afraid. If you'd let me go ahead . . .

I'm not afraid of you, I'd do anything for you. But Jason, why does it hurt like this?

We would try. But I couldn't. We made love with our hands. Our bodies were white. Out the window of the car, snow rose up in mounds across the fields. Afterwards, he looked at me peacefully.

I held him and whispered, soon, soon . . . we'll go away to school.

His sweater. He wore it that night we drove back from the football awards banquet. Jason made All State but he hated football.

I hate it, he said. So what? he said. That I'm out there puking in the heat? Screaming 'kill' at a sandbag?

I held his award in my lap, a gold man frozen in mid-leap. Don't play in college, I said. Refuse the money.

He was driving very slowly.

I can't see, he said. I can't see the edges of the road . . . Tell me if I start to fall off.

Jason, what do you mean?

He insisted I roll down the window and watch the edge. The banks of the road were gradual, sloping off in brush and trees on either side. White lines at the edge glowed in dips and turns.

We're going to crash, he said.

No, Jason. You've driven this road before. We won't crash.

We're crashing, I know it, he said. Tell me, tell me I'm OK . . .

Here on the rummage sale table, there are three football sweaters. I see they are all too small to have belonged to Jason. So I buy an old soundtrack, 'The Sound of Music'. Air, Austrian mountains. And an old robe to wear in the mornings. It upsets my mother to see me naked; she looks at me curiously, as though she didn't recognize my body.

I pay for my purchases at the cash register. Behind the desk I glimpse stacks of *Reader's Digests*. The Ladies' Auxiliary turns them inside out, stiffens and shellacs them. They make wastebaskets out of them.

I give my mother the record. She is pleased. She hugs me.

Oh, she says, I used to love the musicals. They made me happy. Then she stops and looks at me.

Didn't you do this? she says. Didn't you do this in high school?

Do what?

Your class, she says. You did 'The Sound of Music'.

Yes, I guess we did.

What a joke. I was the beautiful countess meant to marry Captain Von Trapp before innocent Maria stole his heart. Jason was a threatening Nazi colonel with a bit part. He should have sung the lead but sports practices interfered with rehearsals. Tall, blond, aged in make-up under the lights, he encouraged sympathy for the bad guys and overshadowed the star. He appeared just often enough to make the play ridiculous.

My mother sits in the blue chair my father used for years.

Come quick, she says. Look . . .

She points to the television. Flickerings of Senate chambers, men in conservative suits. A commentator drones on about tax rebates.

There, says my mother. Hubert Humphrey. Look at him.

It's true. Humphrey is different, changed from his former toady self to a desiccated old man, not unlike the discarded shell of a locust. Now he rasps into the microphone about the people of these great states.

Old Hubert's had it, says my mother. He's a death mask.

That's what he gets for sucking blood for thirty years.

No, she says. No, he's got it too. Look at him! Cancer. Oh.

For God's sake, will you think of something else for once?

I don't know what you mean, she says. She goes on knitting.

All Hubert needs, I tell her, is a good roll in the hay.

You think that's what everyone needs.

Everyone does need it.

They do not. People aren't dogs. I seem to manage perfectly well without it, don't I?'

No, I wouldn't say that you do.

Well, I do. I know your mumbo-jumbo about sexuality. Sex is for those who are married, and I wouldn't marry again if it was the Lord himself.

Now she is silent. I know what's coming.

Your attitude will make you miserable, she says. One man after another. I just want you to be happy.

I do my best.

That's right, she says, be sarcastic.

I refuse to answer. I think about my growing bank account. Graduate school, maybe in California. Hawaii. Somewhere beautiful and warm. I will wear few clothes and my skin will feel the air.

What about Jason, says my mother. I was thinking of him the other day.

Our telepathy always frightens me. Telepathy and beyond. Before her hysterectomy, our periods often came on the same day.

If he hadn't had that nervous breakdown, she says softly, do you suppose . . .

No, I don't suppose.

I wasn't surprised that it happened. When his brother was killed, that was hard. But Jason was so self-centred. He thought everyone was out to get him. You were lucky to be rid of him. Still, poor thing . . .

Silence. Then she refers in low tones to the few months Jason and I lived together before he was hospitalized.

You shouldn't have done what you did when you went off to college. He lost respect for you.

It wasn't respect for me he lost – He lost his fucking mind, if you remember –

I realize I'm shouting. And shaking. What is happening to me?

My mother stares.

We'll not discuss it, she says.

She gets up. I hear her in the bathroom. Water running into the tub. Hydrotherapy. I close my eyes and listen. Soon, this weekend. I'll get a ride to the university a few hours away and look up an old lover. I'm lucky. They always want to sleep with me. For old time's sake.

I turn down the sound of the television and watch its silent pictures. Jason's brother was a musician; he taught Jason to play the pedal steel. A sergeant in uniform delivered the message two weeks before the state playoff games. Jason appeared at my mother's kitchen door with the telegram. He looked at me, opened his mouth, backed off wordless in the dark. I pretend I hear his pedal steel; its sweet country whine might make me cry. And I recognize this silent movie . . . I've seen it four times.

Gregory Peck and his submarine crew escape fallout in Australia, but not for long. The cloud is coming. And so they run rampant in auto races and love affairs. But in the end, they close the hatch and put out to sea. They want to go home to die.

Sweetheart? My mother calls from the bathroom. Could you bring me a towel?

Her voice is quavering slightly. She is sorry. But I never know which part of it she is sorry about. I get a towel from the linen closet and open the door of the steamy bathroom. My mother stands in the rub, dripping, shivering a little. She is so small and thin; she is smaller than I. She has two long scars on her belly, operations of the womb, and one breast is misshapen, sunken, indented near the nipple.

I put the towel around her shoulders and my eyes smart. She looks at her breast.

Not too pretty is it, she says. He took out too much when he removed that lump.

Mom, it doesn't look so bad.

I dry her back, her beautiful back which is firm and unblemished. Beautiful, her skin. Again, I feel the pain in my eyes.

But you should have sued the bastard, I tell her. He didn't give a shit about your body.

We have an awkward moment with the towel when I realize I can't touch her any longer. The towel slips down and she catches it as one end dips into the water.

Sweetheart, she says. I know your beliefs are different from mine. But have patience with me. You'll just be here a few more months. And I'll always stand behind you. We'll get along.

She has clutched the towel to her chest. She is so fragile, standing there, naked, with her small shoulders. Suddenly I am horribly frightened.

Sure, I say, I know we will.

I let myself out of the room.

Sunday my mother goes to church alone. Daniel calls me from D.C. He's been living with a lover in Oregon. Now he is back east; she will join him in a few weeks. He is happy, he says. I tell him I'm glad he's found someone who appreciates him.

Come on now, he says. You weren't that bad.

I love Daniel, his white and feminine hands, his thick chestnut hair, his intelligence. And he loves me, though I don't know why. The last few weeks we were together I lay beside him like a piece of wood. I couldn't bear his touch; the moisture his penis left on my hips as he rolled against me. I was cold, cold. I huddled in blankets away from him.

I'm sorry, I said. Daniel, I'm sorry please . . . what's wrong with me? Tell me you love me anyway . . .

Yes, he said. Of course I do. I always will. I do.

Daniel says he has no car, but he will come by bus. Is there a place for him to stay?

Oh yes, I say. There's a guest room. Bring some Trojans. I'm a hermit with no use for birth control. Daniel, you don't know what it's like here.

I don't care what it's like. I want to see you.

Yes, I say. Daniel, hurry.

When he arrives the next weekend, we sit around the table with my mother and discuss medicine. Daniel was a medic in Vietnam. He smiles at my mother. She is charmed though she has reservations; I see them in her face. But she enjoys having someone else in the house, a presence: a male. Daniel's laughter is low and modulated. He talks softly, smoothly: a dignified radio announcer, an accomplished anchor man.

But when I lived with him, he threw dishes against the wall. And jerked in his sleep, mumbling. And ran out of the house with his hands across his eyes.

After we first made love, he smiled and pulled gently away from me. He put on his shirt and went to the bathroom. I followed and stepped into the shower with him. He faced me, composed, friendly, and frozen. He stood as though guarding something behind him.

Daniel, turn around. I'll soap your back.

I already did.

Then move, I'll stand in the water with you.

He stepped carefully around me.

Daniel, what's wrong? Why won't you turn around?

Why should I?

I'd never seen him with his shirt off. He'd never gone swimming with us, only wading, alone, disappearing down Point Reyes

Beach. He wore longsleeved shirts all summer in the California heat.

Daniel, I said, you've been my best friend for months. We could have talked about it.

He stepped backwards, awkwardly, out of the rub and put his shirt on.

I was loading them on copters, he told me. The last one was dead anyway; he was already dead. But I went after him, dragged him in the wind of the blades. Shrapnel and napalm caught my arms, my back. Until I fell, I thought it was the other man's blood in my hands.

They removed most of the shrapnel, did skin grafts for the burns. In three years since, Daniel made love five times; always in the dark. In San Francisco he must take off his shirt for a doctor; tumours have grown in his scars. They bleed through his shirt, round rust-coloured spots.

Face-to-face in bed, I tell him I can feel the scars with my fingers. They are small knots on his skin. Not large, not ugly. But he can't let me, he can't let anyone, look: he says he feels wild, like raging, and then he vomits. But maybe, after they removed the tumours . . . Each time they operate, they reduce the scars.

We spend hours at the Veteran's Hospital waiting for appointments. Finally they schedule the operation. I watch the black-ringer wall clock, the amputees gliding by in chairs that tick on the linoleum floor. Daniel's doctors run out of local anesthetic during the procedure and curse about lack of supplies; they bandage him with gauze and layers of Band-Aids. But it is all right. I buy some real bandages. Every night I cleanse his back with a sponge and change them.

In my mother's house, Daniel seems different. He has shaved his beard and his face is too young for him. I can grip his hands.

I show him the house, the antiques, the photographs on the walls. I tell him none of the objects move; they are all cemented in place. Now the bedrooms, my room.

This is it, I say. This is where I kept my Villager sweaters when I was seventeen, and my dried corsages. My cups from the Tastee Freez labelled with dates and boys' names.

The room is large, blue. Baseboards and wood trim are painted a spotless white. Ruffled curtains, ruffled bedspread. The bed itself is so high one must climb into it. Daniel looks at the walls, their perfect blue and white.

It's a piece of candy, he says.

Yes, I say, hugging him, wanting him.

What about your mother?

She's gone to meet friends for dinner. I don't think she believes what she says, she's only being my mother. It's all right.

We take off our clothes and press close together. But something is wrong. We keep trying. Daniel stays soft in my hands. His mouth is nervous; he seems to gasp at my lips.

He says his lover's name. He says they aren't seeing other people.

But I'm not other people. And I want you to be happy with her.

I know. She knew . . . I'd want to see you.

Then what?

This room, he says. This house. I can't breathe in here.

I tell him we have tomorrow. He'll relax. And it is so good just to see him, a person from my life.

So we only hold each other, rocking.

Later, Daniel asks about my father.

I don't see him, I say. He told me to choose.

Choose what?

Between them.

My father. When he lived in this house, he stayed in the dark with his cigarette. He sat in his blue chair with the lights and television off, smoking. He made little money; he said he was self-employed. He was sick. He grew dizzy when he looked up suddenly. He slept in the basement. All night he sat reading in the bathroom. I'd hear him walking up and down the dark steps at night. I lay in the dark and listened. I believed he would strangle my mother, then walk upstairs and strangle me. I believed we were guilty; we had done something terrible to him.

Daniel wants me to talk.

How could she live with him, I ask. She came home from work and got supper. He ate it, got up and left to sit in his chair. He watched the news. We were always sitting there, looking at his dirty plates. And I wouldn't help her. She would wash them, not me. She should make the money we lived on. I didn't want her house and his ghost with its cigarette burning in the dark like a sore. I didn't want to be guilty. So she did it. She did it all herself. She sent me to college; she paid for my safe escape.

Daniel and I go to the Rainbow, a bar and grill on Main Street. We hold hands, play country songs on the juke box, drink a lot of salted beer. We talk to the barmaid and kiss in the overstuffed booth. Twinkle lights blink on and off above us. I wore my burgundy stretch pants in here when I was twelve. A senior pinched me, then moved his hand slowly across my thigh, mystified, as though erasing the pain.

What about tonight? Daniel asks. Would your mother go out with us? A movie, a bar? He sees me in her, he likes her. He wants to know her.

Then we will have to watch television.

We pop popcorn and watch the late movies. My mother stays up with us, mixing whisky sours and laughing. She gets a high colour in her cheeks and the light in her eyes glimmers up; she is slipping, slipping back and she is beautiful, oh, in her ankle socks, her red mouth and her armour of young girl's common sense. She has a beautiful laughter. She and Daniel end by mock armwrestling; he pretends defeat and goes upstairs to bed.

My mother hears his door close. He's nice, she says. You've known some nice people, haven't you?

I want to make her back down.

Yes, he's nice, I say. And don't you think he respects me? Don't you think he truly cares for me, even though we've slept together?

He seems to, I don't know. But if you give them that, it costs them nothing to be friends with you.

Why should it cost? The only cost is what you give, and you can tell if someone is giving it back.

How? How can you tell? By going to bed with every man you take a fancy to?

I wish I took a fancy oftener, I tell her. I wish I wanted more, I can be good to a man, but I'm afraid . . . I can't be physical, not really . . .

You shouldn't.

I should. I want to, for myself as well. I don't think . . . I've ever had an orgasm.

What? she says. Never? Haven't you felt a sort of building up, and then a dropping off . . . a conclusion? Like something's over?

No, I don't think so.

You probably have, she assures me. It's not necessarily an explosion. You were just thinking too hard, you think too much.

But she pauses.

Maybe I don't remember right, she says. It's been years, fifteen years, and in the last years of the marriage I would have died if your father had touched me. But before, I know I felt something. That's partly why I haven't . . . since . . . what if I started wanting it again? Then it would be hell.

But you have to try to get what you want . . .

No, she says. Not if what you want would ruin everything. And now, anyway. Who would want me.

I stand at Daniel's door. The fear is back; it has followed me upstairs from the dead dark bottom of the house. My hands are shaking. I'm whispering . . . Daniel, don't leave me here.

I go to my room to wait. I must wait all night, or something will come in my sleep. I feel its hands on me now, dragging, pulling. I watch the lit face of the clock: three, four, five. At seven I go to Daniel. He sleeps with his pillow in his arms. The high bed creaks as I get in. Please now, yes . . . he is hard. He always woke with erections . . . inside me he feels good, real, and I tell him no, stop, wait . . . I hold the rubber, stretch its rim away from skin so it smooths on without hurting and fills with him . . . now again, here, yes but quiet, be quiet . . . oh Daniel . . . the bed is making noise . . . yes, no, but be careful, she . . . We move and turn and I forget about the sounds. We push against each other hard, he is almost there and I am almost with him and just when it is over I think I hear my mother in the room directly under us . . . But I am half dreaming. I move to get out of bed and Daniel holds me. No, he says. Stay . . .

We sleep and wake to hear the front door slam.

Daniel looks at me.

There's nothing to be done, I say. She's gone to church.

He looks at the clock. I'm going to miss that bus, he says. We put our clothes on fast and Daniel moves to dispose of the rubber . . . how? The toilet, no, the wastebasket . . . He drops it in, bends over, retrieves it. Finally he wraps it in a Kleenex and puts it in his pocket. Jesus, he swears. He looks at me and grins. When I start laughing, my eyes are wet.

I take Daniel to the bus station and watch him out of sight. I come back and strip the bed, bundle the sheets in my arms. This pressure in my chest . . . I have to clutch the sheets tight, tighter . . .

A door clicks shut. I go downstairs to my mother. She refuses to speak or let me near her. She stands by the sink and holds her small square purse with both hands. The fear comes. I hug myself, press my hands against my arms to stop shaking. My mother runs hot water, soap, takes dishes from the drainer. She immerses them, pushes them down, rubbing with a rag in a circular motion.

Those dishes are clean, I tell her. I washed them last night.

She keeps washing, rubbing. Hot water clouds her glasses, the window in front of us, our faces. We all disappear in steam. I watch the dishes bob and sink. My mother begins to sob. I move close to her and hold her. She smells as she used to smell when I was a child and slept with her.

I heard you, I heard it, she says. Here, in my own house. Please . . . how much can you expect me to take? I don't know what to do about anything . . .

She looks into the water, keeps looking. And we stand here just like this.

ELIZABETH BOWEN

From *The Death of the Heart*

Elizabeth Bowen was born in Dublin in 1899, the only child of an aristocratic landowner who apparently suffered a nervous breakdown because of his inability to have a son. Her mother died when Elizabeth was ten, leaving the child to grow up in the care of numerous relatives. She married a BBC executive called Alan Cameron and lived in both London and Ireland.

The Death of the Heart, *published in 1938, demonstrates many of Bowen's most characteristic themes – loneliness, isolation, constant migration and the relationship between children and emotionally distant adults. Portia is an orphan who is sent from Europe to live with her half-brother, Thomas, and his wife in London. She is vivacious and vibrant while they are stagnant, antique and dusty. Portia begins a furtive love affair with Eddie, a rather extravagant confidant of her sister-in-law, Anna. When Thomas and Anna go on holiday to Capri, they send Portia to board with Mrs Heccomb, Anna's former governess, at a beach resort called Seale-on-Sea where Eddie, much to the amusement of Mrs Heccomb's louche daughter, Daphne, pays her a visit. The pair appear to be genuinely attracted to one another but the sheer power of Portia's love only succeeds in emasculating Eddie, who is crushed by the force of her affection, just like his cigarettes.*

'YOU SAY YOU never love anyone.'

'How would I be such a fool? I see through all that hanky-panky. But you always make me happy – except you didn't this morning. You must never show any sign of change.'

'Yes, that's all very well, but I feel everyone waiting; everyone gets impatient; I cannot stay as I am. They will all expect something in a year or two more. At present people like Matchett and Mrs Heccomb are kind to me, and Major Brutt goes on sending me puzzles, but that can't keep on happening – suppose they're not always there? I can see there is something about me Daphne despises. And I was frightened by what you said this morning – is there something unnatural about us? Do you feel safe with me because I am bats? What did Daphne mean about ideas I hadn't got?'

'Her own, I should think. But – '

'But what ideas do you never want me to have?'

'Oh, those are still worse.'

'You fill me with such despair,' she said, lying without moving.

Eddie reached across and idly pulled her hand away from her eyes. Keeping her hand down in the grass between them, he gently bent open her fingers one by one, then felt over her palm with his finger-tip, as though he found something in Braille on it. Portia looked at the sky through the branches over their heads, then sighed impalpably, shutting her eyes again. Eddie said: 'You don't know how much I love you.'

'Then, you threaten you won't – that you won't if I grow up. Suppose I was twenty-six?'

'A dreary old thing like that?'

'Oh don't laugh: you make me despair more.'

'I have to laugh – I don't like the things you say. Don't you know how dreadful the things you say are?'

'I don't understand,' she said, very much frightened. 'Why?'

'You accuse me of being a vicious person,' said Eddie, lying racked by her on the grass.

'O, I do *not*!'

'I should have known this would happen. It always does happen; it's happening now.'

Terrified by his voice and face of iron, Portia cried, '*Oh no!*' Annihilating the space of grass between them she flung an arm across him, her weight on his body, and despairingly kissed his cheek, his mouth, his chin. 'You are perfect,' she said, sobbing. 'You are my perfect Eddie. Open your eyes. I can't bear you to look like that!'

Eddie opened his eyes, from which her own shadow completely cut the light from the sky. At the same time frantic and impervious, his eyes looked terribly up at her. To stop her looking at him he pulled her head down, so that their two faces blotted each other out, and returned on her mouth what seemed so much her own kiss that she even tasted the salt of her own tears. Then he began to push her away gently. 'Go away,' he said, 'for God's sake go away and be quiet.'

'Then don't think. I can't bear it when you do that.'

Rolling away from her, Eddie huntedly got to his feet and began to go round the thicket: she heard the tips of the hazels whipping against his coat. He paused at the mouth of every tunnel, as though each were a shut door, to stand grinding his heels into the soundless moss. Portia, lying in her form in the grass, looked at the crushed place where he had lain by her – then, turning her head the other way, detected two or three violets, which, reaching out, she picked. She held them over her head and looked at the light through them. Watching her from his distance, spying upon the movement, he said: 'Why do you pick those? To comfort yourself?'

'I don't know . . .'

'One cannot leave things alone.'

She could do nothing but look up at the violets, which now shook in her raised hand. In every pause of Eddie's movements a sea-like rustling could be heard all through the woody distance, a tidal movement under the earth. 'Wretched violets,' said Eddie. 'Why pick them for nothing? You'd better put them in my buttonhole.' He came and knelt impatiently down beside her; she knelt up, fumbling with the stalks of the flowers, her face a little below his. She drew the stalks through till the violets looked at her from against the tweed of his coat. She looked no higher till he caught both her wrists.

'I don't know how you feel,' he said, 'I daren't ask myself; I've never wanted to know. *Don't* look at me like that! And don't tremble like that – it's more than I can bear. Something awful will happen. I cannot feel what you feel: I'm shut up in myself. All I know is, you've been so sweet. It's no use holding on to me, I shall only drown you. Portia, you don't know what you are doing.'

'I do know.'

'Darling, I don't want you; I've got no place for you; I only want what you give. I don't want the whole of anyone. I haven't wanted to hurt you: I haven't wanted to touch you in any way. When I try and show you the truth I fill you with such despair. Life is so much more impossible than you think. Don't you see we're all full of horrible power, working against each other however much we may love? You agonize me by being so agonized. Oh cry out loud, if you must: cry, cry – don't just let those terrible meek tears roll down your face like that. What you want is the whole of me – isn't it, *isn't it?* – and the whole of me isn't there for anybody. In that full sense you want me I don't exist. What's started this terrible trouble in you, that you can't be happy with the truth of me that you had – however small it was, whatever might be beyond it? Ever since that evening when you gave me my hat, I've been as true to you as I've got it in me to be. Don't force me to where untruth starts. You say nothing would make you hate me. But once make me hate myself and you'd make me hate you.'

'But you do hate yourself. I wanted to comfort you.'

'But you have. Ever since you gave me my hat.'

'Why may we not kiss?'

'It's so desolating.'

'But you and me – ' she began. She stopped, then pressing her face into his coat, under the violets, twisting her wrists in his unsure grip, she said some inaudible things, and at last moaned: 'I can't bear it when you talk.' When she got her wrists free, she once more locked her arms round him, she started rocking her body with such passionless violence that, as they both knelt, he rocked in her arms. 'You stay alone in yourself, you stay alone in yourself!'

Eddie, white as a stone, said: '*You must let go of me.*'

Sitting back on her heels, Portia instinctively looked up at the oak, to see whether it were still vertical. She pressed together her hands, which, torn roughly from Eddie, had been chafed in the palms by the rough tweed of his coat. Her last tears blistered her face; beginning to lose momentum they stuck in smarting patches: she felt in her coat pocket and said: 'I have got no handkerchief.'

Eddie drew from his own pocket a yard of silk handkerchief: while he still held one corner she blew her nose on another, then diligently blotted her tears up. Like a solicitous ghost whose touch cannot be felt, Eddie, with his two forefingers, tucked her damp hair back further behind her ears. Then he gave her one sad kiss, relevant to their two eternities, not to a word that had been said now. But her fear of having assailed, injured, betrayed him was so strong that she drew back from the kiss. Her knees received from the earth a sort of chilly trembling; the walls of the thicket, shot with those light leaves, flickered beyond her eyes like woods passed in a train.

When they settled back on the grass, with about a yard between them, Eddie pulled out his twenty packet of Players. The cigarettes looked battered. 'Look what you've done, too!' he said. But he lit one: threads of smoke began to swim from his nostrils; the match he blew out sputtered cold in the moss. When he had finished the cigarette he made a grave in the moss and buried the stump alive.

JOYCE CAROL OATES

From *You Must Remember This*

Joyce Carol Oates lives in Princeton, New Jersey, where she teaches English. She is a prolific author with over twenty novels to her credit as well as many short stories, plays and critical essays. She has received numerous awards for her writing.

In You Must Remember This, *her eighteenth novel, Enid, a fifteen-year-old girl is possessed of an overwhelming but reciprocated desire for her uncle Felix, a professional boxer, in a tale reminiscent of Nabokov's Lolita. But here the narrative is seen from the point of view of the pubescent girl and not that of the bewildered but all-consumed adult male. Enid's desire for her uncle is not a mythologized, unreal one; it is an insatiable passion possessed by a young woman given a personality, thoughts and feelings.*

[6]

S O YOU WANT to love me, Felix said.

So you thought you'd kill yourself to punish me, Felix said in a voice just loud enough for Enid to hear.

In the hospital room when they were alone together he stroked her hand in secret, slowly he drew his fingers along the curve of her waist, her thigh. She felt his touch through the bedclothes, staring at him weak with love. At these times he said nothing, a kind of trance was upon them both, a languorous blood-heavy extinction of their minds. She saw he was angry with her, he was sick with desire for her, the rest of the world was distant, obliterated. Enid felt a shuddering sensation of the kind she had felt sinking into sleep, into Death. Except she had not died. They had hauled her back as one might haul a fish out of the water with a net. So you thought you could escape us!

You're never going to do that again, are you, Felix said.

Enid's lips moved numbly. No.

Are you?

No.

Are you?

No, Felix.

And they stared at each other half perplexed, trembling with anticipation, a desire so keen it must surely have charged the air in the room and anyone blundering inside would have known. Felix's colour was high, warm, his smile seemed involuntary, he was the one who had brought Enid Stevick the twelve creamy-white roses wrapped in tissue paper and smelling of cold; he was the one who had brought the Swiss chocolates in the plump red satin box there on the window-sill for Enid's visitors to sample. Of all Enid Stevick's relatives the nuns were most taken with her young Uncle Felix.

He promised her he wouldn't hurt her he wouldn't really do anything to her until he thought she was ready, no matter that Enid, crying her hot spasmodic tears, squirming eel-like and ravenous in his arms, demanded love, adult love; she *was* ready, she said, the taste of wine oddly dry in her mouth, sweat running in rivulets down her sides. Felix stroked and caressed her, he kissed and tongued and sucked her breasts, her nipples, he liked even to suck her underarms, he liked her sweat, the tastes of her body – there was nothing of her body he didn't adore! He might kiss and nuzzle the soft rather bruised flesh of the inside of her elbow, the flesh behind her knee, he kneaded her buttocks, the small of her back, her belly, always he stroked and kissed and tongued her between the legs, he loved making love to her in any way he might, rubbing his erect penis in its thin tight rubber sheath slowly between her legs, slowly slowly again again again kissing her with his tongue deep in her mouth until Enid couldn't bear the powerful waves of sensation, orgasm overcame her quick and terrible, her eyeballs rolling in their sockets and her lips drawn back in a death's-head grimace from her teeth. She heard herself cry out helplessly, crazily – the delirious words *I love you I love love love you* or no words at all, only frightened sounds like those of a small child being beaten. Their faces were hidden from each other, Felix's weight on her was profound as the very weight of the world, she wanted it never to be lifted.

Sometimes it was a glass of red wine he urged her to drink, sometimes straight vodka, he gave her only a shot glass of vodka it was such powerful stuff he warned but it should loosen her up. And it did.

He was risking jail for her, he must be crazy, he said, baring his teeth in a mirthless laugh, but what the hell: it was something they needed to do. When they weren't together he seemed to be thinking about her all the time, he'd wake in the middle of the night thinking of her, he knew what that meant, it meant this, and this, and this, *this* – he was going to teach her to like it as much as he did.

Elsewhere his life didn't interest him. The hotel at Shoal Lake was doing fairly well in its first season, better than they'd expected; he was bored with it however and had to be moving into other things, investments, he had a few ideas he was working on, he'd see. Sometimes he talked to Enid about his life, particularly about his boxing career or the prospects of Jo-Jo Pearl's boxing career, but he didn't like her to question him. There were afternoons, entire hours, when he didn't talk to her at all, he was all feeling, emotion, desire, rarely did he respond to anything she said at such times, very likely he didn't hear.

Repeatedly he cautioned her: she wasn't to expect anything from him, not anything, did she understand, yes honey but do you *understand*, he'd give her things, presents, sure, he was crazy about her wasn't he, he was paying for her piano lessons, hoping Lyle wouldn't get suspicious, that wasn't what he meant, he meant he just wasn't making any promises. It wasn't love it was just something they needed to do, he didn't intend to harm her but he wasn't making promises of any kind, did she understand, this isn't a relationship that can last. And Enid said, reckless, teasing, to show she wasn't hurt: Except I'll always be your niece, won't I.

In the beginning it worried him, their close relation, being blood kin as they were, not once did he say the word 'incest' nor did Enid allow herself to think much about it. It was just a word out of the dictionary! The main thing about being blood kin, Felix said, was of course you didn't want to have children and she wasn't going to get pregnant, that was damned sure.

Though in a few months he stopped worrying about their blood tie, or talking about it. Maybe he even liked it, he hinted, that she *was* his niece – it showed how much of a shit he was. He'd always wondered.

Still he was superstitious about seriously making love to her. Breaking her hymen, penetrating her as deeply as he could. Wouldn't it then mean too much to them both! She'd be getting married someday, he said. Enid said, hurt, I don't want to get married – I love you. Felix took such remarks lightly, he didn't really hear. He said, Sure you're going to get married someday, sweetheart – what else are you going to do?

Another time he told her he didn't want to ruin her life. And Enid said her life was already ruined, wasn't it – she had only him to make it well again.

[7]

At the start of the affair in midsummer of 1953, Felix made it a point to take Enid out of town whenever possible, to motels and tourist cabins north along the lakeshore as far away as Mattawa or Oconee, thirty miles from the Port Oriskany city limits. With the passage of weeks and then months he grew less cautious, even at times irrational: he always chose a motel beyond the city limits but he was apt to settle for one of the new motels strung out along North Decker Boulevard – the Bel-Air, the Americana, the Sleep-E-Hollow, the Great Western – not minding that the nearest of these was only a few miles from Enid's high school and from East Clinton Street. He rarely took her to a 'good' motel because he reasoned the management would be more suspicious, he tried not to return to the same place too soon, he had a dread of someone recognizing his face. Yet after one of her Saturday morning piano lessons he arranged to meet her at the Onondaga Hotel where he bought her lunch at the Café Chez Carmen – it must have been a special occasion.

Enid remembered that particular day, that lunch, she'd had to play and replay the scale of A-sharp minor for her piano instructor, he was a marvelous teacher but exacting, humorless much of the time, a former concert pianist and vain about his standards. As she and Felix sat in the crowded buzzing restaurant like niece and uncle on a holiday outing Enid's fingers secretly depressed ghost keys against the table's edge. Up and down the keyboard, the tricky scale of A-sharp minor.

Not for some time would Felix allow her to visit his apartment on Niagara Square, his concern that they might be seen together was far greater than hers, which made her laugh but also made her feel hurt, careless.

Didn't he love her? Was he ashamed of her?

Felix said, I don't know what I feel.

She would lie in his arms and bury her face in his neck and tell him of the mistake she'd made – believing Death was her friend, something of her own. But Death had no presence. No being. There

was just the body in its struggle like being drawn down by an
undertow while you were still conscious and alert, knowing you
would die not in peace but in agony, sucking water into your
lungs, dying even as you were struggling to live. No escape once
the process began unless at the very bottom of the lake there was
escape – the rich black muck, oblivion. But you couldn't reach it
unaided, that peace, you had to drown first. You had to die.

But they found you and hauled you back. A gasping thrashing
fish out of water – so ugly! You'd thought dying would be something secret and private, hidden away in your bed, but they
stripped you naked and forced a long tube down your throat and
vacuum-sucked your guts out, then stuck you with needles under
bright unwavering lights. Like being turned inside out, on display.
And all of it what you deserved.

She'd thought it was her very life she wanted to kill, but it was
only Enid Maria.

Still – she'd recovered. During her convalescence she regained the
weight she'd lost and a few pounds more, her breasts slightly
fuller, her hips, a pinch of flesh at the small of her back Felix liked
to caress. Once your pride is broken your body is a sort of sleeping
infant ravenous for nourishment from any source.

From any source.

Felix had said in the hospital. Look – promise me you won't try
it again.

Felix said, You've got guts but what's the point of it?

When he made love to her if the sensation wasn't too fierce and
sharp immediately, if she wasn't tensed against his hurting her,
she sometimes felt her mind drift free, and break: she was being
drawn down by the undertow but it had no terror for her, it
wasn't the undertow at Shoal Lake, those icy rivulets like eels or
snakes caressing her body. It was like a slightly quickened breath a
feathery accelerated heartbeat, her vision was gone though her
eyes might be open, every muscle in her body yielded and tensed,
and yielded and tensed, there was a beat not at first her own but
her lover's, a beat, a beat, an ever-increasing beat, only at the very
end was she roused to consciousness, and panic – always it was
the first time just as the beds they lay in were the same beds, the
walls enclosing them the same walls, she breathed in delirium with

the smell of disinfectant and Air-Wick, the sight of a solitary hair in a bathroom sink meant that not long before she had been grabbing and clutching at Felix, she went wild scratching at him, calling his name, hating him, wanting to draw him into her, deep into her, the orgasm was so terrible because he kept himself from her, gripping her buttocks tight, kneeling over her, cautious, straining, his forehead furrowed in sweat, he brought her slowly and then swiftly, pitilessly, to orgasm with his mouth, then trembling pumped himself to an orgasm of his own, just nudging the mouth of her womb with his stiff penis, her tight little cunt, he didn't want to hurt her he said, he thought he might injure her she was so small; still it drove him crazy, he loved it, he'd never guessed a girl her age could feel such things strong as any adult woman he had ever known. He wondered could she feel what he felt.

Enid's mind was extinguished, she wept, she did hate it; for a very long time she couldn't move, it was like waking in the hospital but knowing you were paralyzed, your muscles locked still in sleep, in stupor, while the world kept its distance. She couldn't draw a breath wholly her own, not Felix's, half asleep she imagined he was breathing her breath for her, lying heavily against her, oblivious of her, as if they had fallen together from a great height. By degrees her frantic heartbeat always calmed but this too was Felix's heartbeat. He gripped her tight, one arm awkwardly beneath her the other cradling her neck; if he slept he drew her down into sleep, the undersides of her eyes burned as she made her way through a grassy field or slope, the grass vibrantly green! so wonderfully green! and there she stood shielding her eyes against the glare of the sun on the lake, in the lake was the sky which always consoled her, Heaven and Earth in one plane. She saw in the water a shadowy reflection not her own, she stared, she stared, she began to weep with desire, a need so desperate it could scarcely be borne, like the pleasure that rose so violently between her legs that was Felix's to give or to withhold.

He had fallen asleep kissing her. But the kiss meant so little, it was one of many thousands.

Those kisses tasted of Enid's own body but also of wine or vodka or Johnnie Walker Scotch whisky Felix carried in a silver flask with the handwritten engraving *To Felix the Cat, January 1, 1948, love Irene.*

'Who is Irene?' Enid once asked.

'*Was*,' said Felix curtly. He didn't like to be questioned.

Sometimes when they woke Felix laughed softly, he felt so *good*. His body which seemed to Enid beautiful was bathed in a luminous pleasure that was sweat, he loved to sweat, he was convinced it was good for you, most things are good for you was Felix's conviction, he astonished Enid and made her laugh wildly being tickled, crazily tickled, tonguing and nuzzling her armpits, he loved the fine silky red-glinting hairs, he forbade her to shave her underarms, if you do the hair grows back rough and sort of razorish, he said. Now a woman's legs – he liked a woman's legs smooth.

Oh Jesus, already he had half a hard-on but it was getting late, he had to get her home, or did he.

Enid watched her lover aslant. Or by way of a mirror. Even a little drunk, giddy, standing naked herself, her hair disheveled, she found it difficult to face him to allow him to see her staring – it was like looking into too bright a light.

Felix's handsome face darkened with blood, hair in his eyes, the muscular beautifully formed flesh of his torso, his thighs, his springy legs, hair in uneven dark patches on his chest, belly, at his groin. He was unmindful of her and supremely confident in his body, padding naked, barefoot, genitals swinging loose like fruit.

(Like fruit! – but so delicate. She thought too of the skin of an unfledged bird. A creature fallen from its nest, its skin hardly more than a membrane, a network of tiny veins. The creature itself a sac of blood and organs, an unopened eye.)

She'd grown up in a city landscape which meant clumsy drawings or scratchings on the pavement, on walls and doors, lockers at school, *cocks, pricks*, so many thousands floating disembodied and faintly comical, there were crude attempts at female genitals as well but the symbolism was uncertain, even a girl might stare in innocent bewilderment not knowing what the circle with its harsh vertical line was supposed to mean. But the *cocks*, the *pricks* – you learned not to look to be embarrassed or ashamed or frightened, stretches of pavement your vision glazed over unseeing. But why, Enid had wondered as a child. Why were the drawings drawn, why such effort? Lizzie said it was just kids with dirty minds, not to pay any attention. And the words *fuck*, *screw*, *shit* – just kids with dirty minds, Lizzie said, assholes that don't know any better.

The Stevicks were reticent about such things, such things *were* dirty – thinking about them even involuntarily constituted a venial sin to be confessed to Father Ogden in great embarrassment. They were shy of exposing their bodies, even Enid and Lizzie growing up took care to undress with their backs to each other, Enid had only rarely glimpsed her mother in her slip and then by embarrassed chance. She would have been mortified seeing her father undressed – the very thought made her heart pound.

But Felix wasn't at all self-conscious, Felix was quite without shame, he loved his penis, his cock, Felix and his cock were one, erect and trembling with anticipation. But he hated the thin medicinal-smelling rubber contraceptives he was obliged to wear, afterward he peeled them off with disdain and Enid might find one or two in the bathroom wastebasket if there was a wastebasket, sometimes just on the floor of the bedroom kicked amid the scattered bedclothes. Still, he didn't want to get her pregnant, he worried about it more than Enid did, if he didn't wear a Trojan he'd have to come on her belly and what he liked, what he was crazy for, was pushing himself inside her as far as he could without hurting her too much, just pushing, pressing, stretching her tight little cunt, it was only a matter of an inch or two, or three, but Jesus how he loved it and Enid being so small so like a child her ass small enough to be gripped in his hands – this excited him greatly, more than he could have guessed.

Felix would penetrate her as far as he could, then a little farther, until Enid began to bite her lips to keep from screaming or maybe she did scream and he'd press the heel of his hand over her mouth but that was it, he'd stop, he'd stop, through her sticky eyelashes she could see his face in orgasm warm, rapt, dreamy, the face of a bliss she could barely imagine.

It feels good, honey, but it isn't love.

One evening at supper Mr Stevick asked Enid sharply what she was thinking about – her face showed she sure as hell wasn't listening to or thinking about *him*. And Enid blinked, seeing both her parents and Lizzie looking at her, Lizzie's sly smile; Mr Stevick had been going on in a tone difficult to interpret – comical? despairing? – about atomic bomb testing, the newest thing is H-bomb testing, H meaning *hydrogen*, meaning a lot more people killed at impact and after. Enid said in a quick embarrassed resentful voice, 'Nothing.' Mr Stevick said, hurt and cheery, '"Nothing will come of nothing" – Lear to his impudent daughter.'

She had been thinking of Felix: how she adored him, it might have been a time when she hadn't seen him or even spoken with him for some days, he called her when he could but he forbade her to call him – he gave her his telephone number but said, Don't use it! 'Nothing,' Enid said stiffly. In truth she had been thinking of her lover's face when he made love to her, she'd been thinking of his cast-off condoms, how someone would find them cleaning the room, the 'maids' in many of the motels and tourist cabins were in fact the owners' wives, even their young daughters, how like used toilet paper or Kleenex the condoms were, disgusting or maybe just the usual debris to be picked up, thrown away. Felix's milky semen bunched there heavy at the tip of the translucent rubber – picked up, thrown away.

Enid had been out of St Joseph's and was 'herself' again as everybody noted for some time when she realized the Death-panic was gone; now she'd died and the worst had happened and Felix loved her, she could recall the sensation sometimes distinctly – walking too close to a high window or a railing, glancing down the stairwell in her piano teacher's apartment building to the lobby five flights below – but it wasn't the panic itself, only its memory.

Still she couldn't bring herself to cross the canal by way of the footbridge. Not yet, Not now. Nor did she cross through the vacant lot on any errand at all – she knew the worst things that happened there didn't happen to boys. And wasn't Felix always telling her don't hitch rides, don't walk home from school alone, stay out of alleys or back streets – you look too good for something not to happen to you.

Enid's piano teacher was Mr Lesnovich, Anton Lesnovich, yes, the man was expensive and it had been difficult to get him to take her, she was only beginning, really – and at her age! – but he's the best in town, Felix said, Felix had done some inquiring, made some telephone calls, the irony was it had been his own mother, her husband rather, who'd helped – some connection or other having to do with contributions to a local chamber music group in which Lesnovich was involved. Musicians are temperamental but fair-minded, Felix thought, or anyway that's what he'd been told; also they make so little money, most of them, they're grateful for small favors. Like ex-athletes brightened by seeing their names mentioned in a sports column now and then. Lesnovich had been a solo performer at one time but only locally, he'd never made any recordings that anybody knew of but his reputation was excellent and if he charged a lot he was worth it, nothing but the best for Felix Stevick's young niece.

Felix was paying for the lessons of course – at $15 an hour nobody would expect Lyle Stevick to pay for them – and he'd also bought Enid a piano, a small trim Knabe spinet, the pretext being that the piano was secondhand, something one of Felix's friends no longer wanted, he got it at a bargain $250 while brand new it was worth ten times that much. This Lyle Stevick could appreciate, he wasn't as likely to take offence at his brother interfering with his family. Jesus, that *was* a bargain, a Knabe so cheap and it looked brand new in fact, not a scratch on it, perfectly in tune.

Felix was pleased that Lesnovich took Enid on as a pupil, that he thought she had some talent at least, but he didn't seem particularly interested in her progress, didn't ask about the lessons or what she was playing; she soon saw that that side of her life wasn't very real to him. He was more concerned that Enid's father not suspect what was going on between them.

Enid said, 'No, Daddy takes it for granted.' Rather cruelly she said, 'He tells everybody you feel guilty and you owe it to him – trying to make up for all the years you treated him like dirt.'

Okay, honey, this time we won't stop, Felix said. He'd dosed her with Johnnie Walker for which she was developing a taste and the door was bolted and chain-locked, the blind drawn down carefully past the windowsill, the shabby brown-spangled curtains yanked nearly closed, out on the highway an occasional car, the grinding of a truck changing gears. Just take it easy, honey, Felix said, and you'll be all right. But he knew to fold the towel over twice and slip it under her hips.

Oconee. Or Mattawa. Or was it Spragueville – the Bide-a-Wile Tourist Court, the Sleep-E Time Motel. Low rates, off-season rates, vacancy. Inside, the familiar stale smell of insecticide, the thin bedspread cigarette-scorched, spidery rust-coloured stains on the ceiling. Outside was Route 55 looping up from Port Oriskany how many miles to the south, running through farmland desolate in winter, running beside the enormous lake and the lake was the colour of pewter and choppy, raw this afternoon but beautiful too, saw-toothed chunks of ice at the shore. Driving up, sitting close beside Felix, saying nothing for a long time, Enid watched as snow began to fall lightly, glinting like mica. No sun, just clouds, a uniform gray like a ceiling pressing low but she was suffused with happiness like sunlight. And the air so fresh and cold and wet each breath drawn in sharply hurt, each breath felt good.

Once begun this time it wasn't to be stopped.

Felix gripped her buttocks and drew her toward him, his vision filming over as if he were going blind. With the first stab of pain Enid shut her eyes hard, not wanting to see his face.

. . . love you. Love love love love you.

Yes, she tried loving him as he'd taught: legs, knees weakly embracing him, panicked fingers on the bunched-up muscles of his back.

The pain was like nothing she'd ever felt before. A knife entering and reentering her pushing deeper each time scalding her insides but he wasn't going to stop. Her mouth was ugly with the strain of not crying out, sweat gathered in tight little beads on her forehead. A wild crazy ride. She wasn't drunk enough. Felix was fucking her half to death.

When it was over he lifted himself from her, blood on his penis, the damned condom was torn, oh Christ, he said. His breath caught in his throat, saliva gleamed at the corner of his mouth. She knew he'd loved it and she tried not to despise him.

He wanted to take her to a doctor. He knew a doctor, he said, back home. She seemed to be bleeding pretty badly, he might have torn her insides. Enid said it was all right. She thought it would be all right. It *would* be all right for Christ's sake just let her go – she

went into the bathroom shutting and locking the door behind her
if the goddamned sliding lock really worked. Her fingers felt
cramped as if she'd been lying on them. Her mouth was numb and
ashy, drained of blood, reminded her in the mirror of a fish's
mouth.

Still her eyes shone in elation, triumph. No one would ever hurt
her like that again.

Wad after wad of toilet paper, her hands shaking, then she
flushed the paper down the toilet trying not to see, the blood was a
clear thin red, not dark and clotted like mentrual blood at the start
of one of her periods. The insides of her thighs were chafed raw,
the pain was a dull throbbing burning going a little numb. So this
is it, Enid thought.

Oconee. Or was it Mattawa, Spragueville. A rust-stained toilet
bowl she'd seen many times before, stray hairs gathered in the
shower drain, strangers' voices lifting and falling away outside.
Someone starting a car in the parking lot. She waited until the
bleeding seemed to stop, then used more tissue paper, then
washed herself tenderly, awkwardly, it puzzled her that her hands
were still shaking now everything was over.

Light and teasing, vaporous, there came a dream – she knew,
dreaming, it was a dream – that she had to get home, they were
waiting for her at home but she was miles away, she didn't even
know which direction home was. What had she done, what had
been done to her! – a man's weight heavy upon her, one arm slung
across her belly in sleep. On a road somewhere nearby cars
approached, then receded, diesel trucks shifted their gears on a
long slow grade, then the country quiet again and she was half
asleep her muscles twitching her eyeballs moving jerkily in their
sockets she had to get home but she couldn't move.

In the wallpaper with its creases and wrinkles, its mysterious
hollows and ravines, footpaths, forests, floating islands – there she
was wandering utterly alone. The dime-store mirror taped to the
inside of her locker door, a reversed world over her shoulder
through which the figures of her classmates and friends passed
oblivious of her, not knowing how she observed them. And hadn't
she had a magical ring years ago? Hadn't Felix given her the ring?
Held close to her eye the glassy jewel trapped a tiny rectangle of

the world, reversed, over her shoulder, emptied of her presence. That was its extraordinary significance – it did not contain her, it knew nothing of her. She had tried to enter it once but she had failed, the crossing was too difficult.

'Enid – ?'

Felix was shaking her, she woke dazed and groggy, her heart pounding, not knowing where she was. He stood above her gripping her by the shoulder, shaking her so hard the bedsprings rattled.

He sat heavily beside her, asked was she all right? he'd showered, his hair was damp and slickly combed, a cigarette burned in his fingers and Enid even in her confusion could sense how he was trying to disguise his worry. But of course she was all right. She was always all right. Felix kissed her eyelids, her mouth, rather roughly, he said they'd better be going she'd better get dressed did she need any help?

Halfway home they stopped at a tavern. Felix had a beer and Enid needed to use the women's restroom; the bleeding had started up again, she felt it seeping hot and sullen in her loins, now there were dull intermittent cramps in the pit of her belly. Through the cheap Masonite door of the restroom a country-and-western song came twangy, sweet, insinuating, in rhythm with her pain. Again she used wads of toilet paper, again her hands were trembling. Her sensation of triumph had faded.

She was thinking of the drive up earlier that day, Felix nervous and excited but saying very little, he'd hit a patch of ice and the car went into a brief skid. Then some miles along as Felix approached an intersection a farmer in a pickup truck edged out rather incautiously – he was supposed to have stopped, Felix had the right of way – but Felix bluffed him out and sped through and the men sounded their horns, quick easy spasms of anger. 'Fucker,' Felix said to the rear-view mirror.

They spoke very little on their way to Spragueville to a shabby cinderblock motel close beside the highway advertising OFF-SEASON RATES, PRIVACY GUARANTEED, SINGLE & DOUBLE BEDS, VACANCY.

The night before Enid had read in the newspaper that Felix's boxer Jo-Jo Pearl had won a 'close' decision in Pittsburgh but when she asked Felix about it he said only that Jo-Jo had a lot to learn. Enid asked when was he going to take her to see Jo-Jo box, hadn't he promised her he would, and Felix said he'd take her sometime, maybe, if the circumstances were right. He didn't think it was a good idea for them to be seen together in public just yet, anybody who knew him would know. Know what, Enid said half tauntingly.

She'd been in the smelly unheated restroom so long waiting for the bleeding to stop, leaning against the sink, her head now aching fiercely and her eyes filled with tears, one of the waitresses came in asking was she okay? – her boyfriend was getting worried about her.

'Yes I'm okay,' Enid said. Her voice came out mocking, the word *okay* emphasized, it was a word she hated and rarely used. 'Tell him I'm *okay*. I'm coming right out.'

When she returned to the table she saw that impassive hooded look of his, that pretence that nothing was wrong he was supremely in control, Felix Stevick idly peeling a label from a beer bottle, giving her his easy smile, except he was getting worried, wasn't he just slightly worried, he was thinking maybe his girl would end up going to a doctor, not a doctor of his acquaintance, maybe she'd get through supper that night or maybe not, maybe she'd crack suddenly, Jesus was she going to crack, hysterical and crying, telling her mother first then both her mother and her father what had happened, who it was who'd fucked her, tearing up her insides so she was bleeding like a pig, yes and he'd loved it too every second of it he'd been more excited than she had ever seen him and nothing she could have said or done was going to stop him at the end, he'd raped her and he'd loved it but it wasn't going to remain a secret. Yes, Felix Stevick seemed to understand this, half rising from his chair as she sat down, he seemed to anticipate it all, looping his arm around her shoulders bringing his mouth against her ear like any lover bland and affectionate trying not to get anxious about what was coming next. Enid was going to tell her parents, she was going to tell the doctor, she was going to tell it again and again, eventually she'd be forced to tell it while a police stenographer took it all down, that was why he was beginning to look anxious, wasn't it, the arrogant son of a bitch.

She was shaking, shivering, her face burned, the skin was papery-thin waiting to be ignited, Felix hesitated then asked if she was still bleeding and Enid said quietly, 'If I'm bleeding I'm bleeding, what does it have to do with you?' Enid said in a quiet low rushing voice, 'Why do you want to know? What business is it of yours? If I'm bleeding I'm bleeding, what does it have to do with you?' She looked at him in hatred, in loathing, she was saying less quietly, 'You son of a bitch. You bastard. I know *you* – you bastard. I knew you all along. I knew you last year. I mean at Shoal Lake – I knew you then. You filthy son of a bitch, getting me drunk taking me to that place trying to fuck me standing up, then you made me – '

Felix tossed a $5 bill down on the table, Felix was walking her out of the tavern carrying their coats. Once they were in the car he made no effort to quiet her, said nothing, hardly troubled to fend off her several furious blows against his shoulder and the side of his head. As he backed out of the parking lot the white-walled tyres of his Desoto Deluxe spun and threw up gravel, then he was off on the highway, accelerating, headed for the city.

Enid fell asleep then; when she woke the sky was massive and darkening and Felix was signaling to exit the John Jamieson Expressway at Nine Mile Road, the air gritty from U.S. Steel on one side, the Goodyear Tyre smokestack rimmed in flame on the other. Now she spoke quietly. 'I don't think I want to see you again, that's all.' And Felix said after a pause, 'Yes, that's right, I think you're right, Enid.'

DELARIVIER MANLEY

From *The New Atalantis*

Delarivier Manley was born in 1663, the daughter of the royalist leader of Jersey. She wrote plays, poems, political tracts and thinly disguised novels implicating her political opponents in sex scandals, although she was also concerned with the power struggle between the two sexes themselves. She was herself (and not necessarily unwittingly) bigamously married to her cousin, John Manley in 1689. They had a son and, though polygamy was one of the many themes in which she was interested and which is discussed at some length in The New Atalantis *(since it allows for the retention of a woman's personal wealth whilst admitting sexual satisfaction), she eventually left her husband in 1694 but later lived with her printer until she died in 1724. She also collaborated with her friend, Jonathan Swift, in the production of a journal called the* Examiner.

The New Atalantis (1709), her most famous work, was a roman à clef mixing political and sexual allegory on a barely disguised basis. On its publication author, publisher and printer were all arrested. Although it is a complicated work, the main plot follows two heroines, Louisa and Zara, who are duped by a male rhetoric which claims to represent freedom but which, in fact, leads them into misadventure and ruin. Women's sexuality here is abused by men in much the same way that contemporary politicians abused members of the public for their own ends.

The novel begins from the premise that, following on from Juvenal's openly misogynist work On Women, *in which Justice (Astrea) and Chastity withdraw from the world, these two return in order to meet their mother, Virtue, and to take her on a guided tour of the island of Atalantis, where they hear tale upon tale of the sly exploitation of innocent women by calculating men. Whilst, in this extract the Duchess adores and pampers the Count, he merely satiates his lust and lies like fury to further his own ends. In order to assuage his desires he dupes the Duchess and sends her to bed with a willingly ambitious Germanicus instead. The Duchess enjoys herself immensely but, being a woman, needs to 'feign confusion'. Young Germanicus, however, is also only after what he can get 'and to merit her favour by excess of love'. Following this incident both the Count and Germanicus eventually gain peace, prosperity and lovely young wives, whilst the Duchess is treated with contempt, loses all her money and dies of vexation.*

INTELL: There was a young cavalier just then come to court (allied to a preceding favourite, which was his introduction) named Germanicus, well formed, graceful, and might very well be candidate for the manly beauties with the Count. The Duchess had seen him in the circle with approbation; as yet she had only heard of her favourite's marriage, as a thing intended, not resolved on. One day, she expostulated thus with her ingrateful, 'Is it true, Monsieur le Count, that in neglect of all my bounties, you dare to throw away a heart I esteem, and have so dearly purchased, upon a girl, who scorns to receive it at a lesser price than your perpetual slavery? Have I neglected the most agreeable monarch upon earth? have I bestowed my heart entirely upon you? and brought you in (a glorious rival) to divide with him the possession of a person, that all the world says is not unlovely? Have I called you from obscurity and want, to light and riches, thus to be rewarded? Ah ungrateful! Why am I formed of the softer passions? Why is not my soul fired, as it ought, by the rough and bold? Why has not anger and revenge the ascendant of love and joy? Why am I more tempted to embrace than kill a monster so ingrateful!' Here she cast her tempting arms about the Count's neck, and met his cheeks with drops of love (the overflowings of desire) that fell from her fine eyes. The Count overcome by the amorous pressure, took the charmer in his arms, and by reconciling himself to her resentment, made himself dearer to her pleasures. 'Twas impossible she could part with what so luxuriously gave her joys. 'No, my charming Count, we must never lose you, you must ever thus be renewing your interest in my heart, always be thus intolerably engaging. Will you leave me for another? Will you carry my rights to the detested arms of a rival?'

'Do I breathe? Do I live?' answered the Count, 'Am I insensible of beauty or of benefits? Do I possess the greatest, and can I stoop to any second? Can I be more than blessed? More than entirely happy! Would I exchange all this elysium of joys for ingratitude? Baseness, inconstancy! Never, my charming Duchess! Never believe so wrongfully of your truest votary. Jeanitin is a little thing I sometimes divert my self with at my sister's when you are otherways engaged. Vanity! (for she's a perfect coquet) has made her report (I'm sure she can't believe), that I am her conquest. She that more than suspects I am favoured by you, and must for ever despair of gaining so much as a glance from any lover that you are pleased to make happy.'

'I believe you, my dear,' answered the Duchess, overcame with transport, 'You shall live only for me, and in return, take, take, all that an over-indulgent Monarch has enriched me with! these jewels! these bills must be yours! I know nothing so valuable as your self, all my treasure is at your devotion, be you but mine. The King hunts tomorrow, and will not be in town 'till night, let us pass the afternoon at your house, in a waste of joy; let us live whilst life is pleasing, whilst there's a poignancy in the taste, desire at heighth, the blood in perfection, and all our senses fitted for those raptures you know so well how to receive and give.'

The Count would have very gladly compounded any thing (unless it were treasure) that the Duchess would abate of her fondness, but, by a relief of thought, he quickly guessed his only way to come off with honour, was to make her the aggressor, could he but fit her with a new lover, and catch her in the embrace, he should have a good pretence for his marriage with Jeanatin. He had made a strict friendship with Germanicus, from his first coming to court; as he left the Duchess's apartment, he met the young gentleman. 'Happy Count,' said he to him, 'from what joys are you come? To possess the heart and person of the finest woman of her age! What would I not do for one hour so blessed? Nay, but for one moment of inexplicable rapture!'

'You may have thousands, my lovely youth,' answered the Count, 'if they are so necessary to your quiet; I'll make you entirely easy, if you'll but rely on me.'

'Can you divide? Can you part with all that heaven of beauty?' interrupted he.

'To a friend,' replied the Count, 'I can do any thing, to a friend so much beloved as your self.'

'But how is it possible, you can give away such joys? I could never do it!'

'You speak the language of a lover,' answered the Count, 'not yet obtaining, and I that of one in full possession, and cloyed with the too luscious entertainment; there's a vast difference between desire and enjoyment; the full and vigorous light of the sun, compared with the pale glimmers of the moon, is no ill emblem of what I advance; yet though we surely know we shall be sated, we can't help desiring to eat, 'tis the law of nature, the pursuit is pleasing, and a man owes himself the satisfaction of gratifying those desires that are importunate, and important to him.'

Here they debated, and at last concluded upon a method to oblige Germanicus; the Duchess went to the Count's the next day, immediately after she had dined; she scarce allowed her self time to eat, so much more valuable in her sense were the pleasures of love. The servants were all out of the way as usual, only one gentleman, that told her, his lord was lain down upon a day-bed that joined the bathing-room, and he believed was fallen asleep, since he came out of the bath. The Duchess softly entered the little chamber of repose. The weather violently hot, the umbrellas were let down from behind the windows, the sashes open, and the jessimine, that covered 'em, blew in with a gentle fragrancy. Tuberoses set in pretty gilt and china pots, were placed advantageously upon stands; the curtains of the bed drawn back to the canopy, made of yellow velvet, embroidered with white bugles, the panels of the chamber looking-glass. Upon the bed were strewed, with a lavish profuseness, plenty of orange and lemon flowers. And to complete the scene, the young Germanicus in a dress and posture not very decent to describe. It was he that was newly risen from the bath, and in a loose gown of carnation taffety, stained with Indian figures. His beautiful long flowing hair, for then 'twas the custom to wear their own tied back with a ribbon of the same colour, he had thrown himself upon the bed, pretending to sleep, with nothing on but his shirt and nightgown, which he had so indecently disposed, that slumbering as he appeared, his whole person stood confessed to the eyes of the amorous Duchess; his limbs were exactly formed, his skin shiningly white, and the pleasure the lady's graceful entrance gave him, diffused joy and desire throughout all his form. His lovely eyes seemed to be closed, his face turned on one side (to favour the deceit) was obscured by the lace depending from the pillows on which he rested. The Duchess, who had about her all those desires she expected to employ in the embrace of the Count, was so blinded by 'em, that at first she did not perceive the mistake, so that giving her eyes time to wander over beauties so inviting, and which increased her flame, with an amorous sigh she gently threw her self on the bed, close to the desiring youth; the ribbon of his shirt-neck not tied, the bosom (adorned with the finest lace) was open, upon which she fixed her charming mouth. Impatient, and finding that he did not awake, she raised her head, and laid her lips to that part of his face that was revealed. The burning lover thought it was now time to put an end to his pretended sleep; he clasped her in his arms, grasped her to his bosom, her own desires helped the deceit; she shut her eyes with a languishing sweetness, calling him by intervals, her dear Count, her only lover, taking and giving a thousand kisses. He got the possession of her person with so much transport, that she owned all her former enjoyments were imperfect to the pleasure of this.

Still charmed and breathless with the joy, he grasped her to his ravished bosom. 'Glorious destiny,' cried he, with a transported tone, 'by what means, Fortune, hast thou made me thy happy darling? I am in possession of greater joys than mortal sense can bear!' The Duchess awaked from her amorous lethargy by a voice entirely strange, opened her languishing eyes, and seeing his charming face, which she had often admired, and perhaps secretly sighed for, stifled with his repeated kisses, and charmed with the strenuous embrace, which held her as a drowning wretch is said to grasp the last thing he has hold of, new desire for so new and lovely an object seized her; she darted back his kisses, returned his pressure, and in short, bestowed upon Germanicus, what she before in her own opinion had bestowed upon the Count.

When they had lavishingly sacrificed to love, the Duchess, with a feigned confusion, asked what was become of the Count, and whether he were such a villain to dispute another in his place? 'So far from it, Madam,' answered Germanicus, 'that I must expect to defend my life, should he know of my good fortune, for he would certainly put me to it.'

'But where is he then?' asked the inquisitive fair one.

'Did you not receive a letter from him?'

'Heavens! I receive a letter from him; for what? when he expected my self. What is the mystery of all this?'

'Ah!' returned the dissembling lover, 'the Count is possessed, he knows not what he does, his affairs called him another way; he writ you an excuse, not doubting but it would come early enough, and see if the hairbrained creature have not left it behind him; the paper that I see lie upon yonder stand, must certainly be that.' The impatient Duchess made but two steps from the bed before she got it in her hand, and finding it was really addressed to her self, she hastily broke the seal, and read these words.

Till night at ten a clock, my lovely Duchess, I can't be happy in your charms; at that hour I'll wait on you, with a heart full of impatient love, to complain to you of what has detained me from my happiness.

'The traitor's sense is degenerated, as well as his kindness,' continued the Duchess. 'But you, my fortunate lover, can, if you please, unriddle this affair. Have you the power to refuse me? Cannot my kindness triumph over your fidelity to the Count? Let it get the better of your confusion? Must I ask you twice?'

'How irresistible, and how dangerous are you, Madam,' answered Germanicus, 'I sacrifice my friend! after that, never doubt, but I would sacrifice my life. Jeanitin has sent for him.'

'How! that little creature,' interrupted the Duchess, 'Heavens! am I betrayed for so worthless a baggage? Henceforward I'll hate him more than I ever loved him. I'll be revenged, his life shall answer it. But you, how came you by the liberty of this apartment, thus undressed, thus ruinously tempting?'

'The Count sometimes makes me his bedfellow, Madam; last night I was so; the weather being extremely hot, after dinner we went into the bath; he expected your Excellence, and intended to receive you in his own bedchamber; by that means this little room of repose was left to me, where I was to suffer the killing rack of knowing the Count more happy than I could ever pretend to be. Jeanitin sent him a slight invitation to make one at ombre this afternoon; the ill-judged madman preferred the dull diversion of cards, with a worthless girl, before the most transporting joys in nature, with the most lovely of her sex. He writ that letter, and it seems, in the hurry of his thoughts (fortunately for me) forgot to send it. He went down the backstairs, and crossed the gardens to her lodgings, by which means, I suppose, the gentleman in waiting did not see him. All his other people, as expecting your Excellence after dinner, were ordered to depart the house. But how happy have I been made by his neglect? It can receive no addition, but from the assurance that my lovely Duchess does not repent the favours she has suffered me to take.'

'But what excuse does the villain intend to make me at ten a clock?' answered the lady, 'Both the King and his master are in the country, and even their service ought, in his esteem, to yield to mine. How blinded have I been?'

'Oh, Madam, that love would be propitious,' (replied Germanicus) 'and before ten a clock furnish him with a current excuse for your Excellence.'

'Never, never, will I any more hear the traitor. You shall take his place in my arms and heart.' The happy youth was dazzled at this assurance and after they had loved away three or four hours, she was preparing to depart. The new lover resolved to push for the continuation of his good fortune, and to merit her favour by excess of love, prevailed with her for more tempting embrace. The lady yielded with a pleasing willingness, surprised and charmed by a lover that then even exceeded himself. In that dangerous moment the Count (as they had agreed) with softly treading steps enters the chamber and finds the happy pair at the ultimate of all their joys. The scene was admirable; Germanicus counterfeited confusion, the Count a transport of anger. The Duchess, without counterfeiting, was really so, and, by an admirable boldness and haughtiness of nature, asked him how he durst presume to enter a place here his gentleman must tell him she was, without giving notice at the door? He indeed asked her pardon; for, knowing the warmth of her constitution, he said, he might well conclude, she could not be long in a bedchamber, with a handsome young gentleman, without consequences, favoured by his disability all tempting, the bed, and her more favourable inclination? 'Be gone, cried the Duchess, 'I banish you forever, you that can prefer Jeanitin to me!'

'I banish my self, Madam,' answered the Count, 'from the most immoderate of her sex. What, the first moment to bestow your self upon another! whilst my image yet wantoned before your eyes! whilst your blood yet mangled by those desires my idea had mingled with it! You that know how nice I am in point of amour! that for all the treasure the sea and earth can boast would not

divide the heart I adore with any other. I suffered the concurrence
of a potent monarch (who had a prior right) but with regret, and
sometimes indignation, though I never suspected that he rivalled
me in your heart, but person: but this tempting youth, this
polished Adonis, is too perfect not to have touched your heart, as
well as your desires; yet it had been modesty, as well as prudence,
to defer his joy till you had given him time to sigh after; the
blessing is too great, to be so easily obtained. I am undone by your
killing perfidy, I can never forgive it, neither can I cease to love
you. I'll this night marry Jeanitin (a creature I before contemned)
to be revenged of your infidelity. If it be true that you have any
remains of that favour you formerly honoured me with, at least I
shall pique your pride, when in your turn you shall find your self
forsaken, for a thing of not the tenth part of your value.' Here he
flung out of the chamber. The Duchess, stung with his threatening, and not yet resolved to part with him, especially to her
rival, attempted to stop him, but he broke with precipitation from
her. 'Ah, the traitor!' said she, 'how glad is his ingratitude of this
occasion! My lovely youth, what have we not to fear? He will ruin
us with Sigismund, but I shall take care to prevent him.'

What she foresaw came to pass exactly. He took his measures
so well (though his friends were sacrificed by it) that it was
Sigismund's own fault he did not twice, at her lodgings, find
Germanicus in bed with her, but he was a Prince perfectly good-
natured, full of love and inconstancy, and made strange
allowances for the frailties of flesh and blood. Thus indulgent, he
suffered a great belly of the Duchess (due to that happy amorous
rencounter of the bugle-bed) to pass in the esteem of the world (as
the rest of hers had done) for his. Indeed he got him another
mistress whom he entirely devoted himself to, without quarrelling
with the Duchess; he sometimes saw her in turn, but never after
with esteem. Thus you find how grateful the Count was to her, the
foundation of all his fortune. He immediately married Jeanitin,
and from that moment disused all conversation with the Duchess.
The new bride, well instructed by her husband and her mother,
made her court so successfully to the Princess of Inverness, before
she became her professed favourite. The young Princess had
admirable good inclinations, but without consulting them, they
had married her, according to royal custom, to the Prince of

Inverness, before she had ever seen him. Count Lofty, whose good sense was totally obscured by pride, cast his ambitious thoughts so high, as to pretend to please the Princess, whilst yet she was a maid. The favourite Countess, for so we shall call her now, no longer Jeanitin, took the alarm at his being so tenderly received by the Princess; she put his poetical declaration of love into her husband's hand; her policy suggested to her, that she ought not to suffer a rival favourite, especially one of the heart; in discharge of duty pretended, but in reality of interest, advised him to acquaint his master with it. 'Twas done as designed, the audacious lover forbid the court, and the lady immediately betrothed to the Prince of Inverness. Sometime after he arrived, and they were publicly married. The Princess has since been an example of conjugal happiness, they have loved and deserved each other; nor could there be any objection against her, but in so entirely resigning her self up to the Countess's management; who introduced the Count to her mistress with such success, that nothing was resolved on in that little court, without first consulting and having their approbation.

Thus time rolled on in an uninterrupted series of good fortune for the Count. Sigismund died, and he was, by a most advantageous remove, drawn nearer to the throne. A natural son of Sigismund pretended to succeed; but the Prince of Tameran, with the fears more than the acclamations of the people, was crowned. There was no honours that the Count and his sister might not expect in this new reign; but he immediately saw that the monarch had not the hearts of his subjects; he was a bigoted Christian, a different religion from that established in Atalantis. The Count dreaded falling (as a favourite) a sacrifice to the incensed rabble. His master, wholly guided by his too zealous priest, tottered in the throne. Young Caesario, Sigismund's natural son, was beloved. He had been vanished by his father, and was refuged in Prince Henriquez's court, who had married the new King of Atalantis's daughter. The people's wishes called aloud for him, to secure their fear against the growing tyranny of the priests. The Count had no interest in the young Caesario, a Prince of little depth, entirely in the hands and interest of a factious party. He trembled to think, if he once prevailed, himself must either fall, as a favourite of the foregoing monarch's, or waste the remainder of his life in inglorious obscurity; he therefore cast about, and with the cabal of the principal lords of Atalantis in concert sent to Prince Henriquez to invite him over to their relief, from oppression and holy fears of slavery. 'Tis true, he betrayed in this a master who tenderly loved him, but a master indiscreet and bigoted, that could not in all probability long support himself, and therefore he held it wise to evade a falling ruin. Prince Henriquez had a consummate courage, deep dissimulation, under which he concealed the most towering ambition. The Count advised that he should lend aid to Caesario, who implored it, to invade Atalantis, where the hearts and hands of the people were ready to assist him: aid not sufficient to serve, but to betray him. 'Twas done as projected. Caesario's enterprise miscarried, and his life fell a sacrifice to the laws that he had broken, after which Henriquez was considered as the successor. He came over with a much more powerful army. The Count had a tender conscience, and could not act to the prejudice of his interest; he left an indulgent master, and went to Henriquez, who was shortly after crowned with the acclamation and approbation of the major part, by the name of Henriquez the ninth.

In this warlike reign, the Count supported himself in the King's favour, and esteem, by his natural and acquired merit; he shared in all his secrets of war and government. 'Tis this Prince who is now dead, after a long and troublesome reign, turmoiled with factions, and involved in a perpetual foreign war. The Count is the only person that will be thought fit to pursue the designs Henriquez had formed; the Empress will undoubtedly make him her general. What may he not expect? What will he not perform?

Germanicus made an ample fortune by the Duchess's favour, but disliking all courtly factions, he wisely married, and retired himself from governments, remote from courts, he ended his days in a pleasing obscurity.

The Duchess by her prodigality to favourites, fell into extreme neglect: her temper was a perfect contradiction, unboundedly lavish, and sordidly covetous; the former to those who administered to her particular pleasure, the other to all the rest of the world. When love began to forsake her, and her charms were upon the turn, because she must still be a bubble, she fell into gamesters' hands, and played off that fortune Sigismund had enriched her with. She drank deep of the bitter draught of contempt; her successive amours, with mean ill formed domestics, made her abandoned by the esteem and pity of the world. Her pension was so ill paid, that she had oftentimes not a pistole at command; then she solicited the Count (whom she had raised) by his favour with the court, that her affairs might be put into a better posture; but he was deaf to all her entreaties. Nay, he carried his ingratitude much further, one night at an assembly of the best quality, where the Count tallied to 'em at basset, the Duchess lost all her money, and begged the favour of him, in a very civil manner, to lend her twenty pieces; which he absolutely refused, though he had a thousand upon the table before him, and told her coldly the bank never lent any money. Not a person upon the place but blamed him in their hearts: as to the Duchess's part, her resentment burst out into a bleeding at her nose, and breaking of her lace, without which aids, it is believed, her vexation had killed her upon the spot.

EMPOWERMENT

⚛

The following four pieces all, in different ways, describe the potential of women to reverse normal gender positions and to take power into their own hands, thereby controlling their own lives and dictating to less powerful men. That such an idea was largely unthinkable in past centuries means that three of the four pieces in the section were written in the last five years and all by relatively young women.

Monsieur Venus by Rachilde, the only exception, was published in 1884 when the author was only twenty. She formed part of the Decadent movement in Paris with its twin interests in sex and death. Whilst the heroine, Raoule de Vénérande, is a dominant sexual figure, she is also a very early example of the genre and as such, at bottom, merely a reverse fantasy dictated by the male imagination. In order to take on as much power as a man, she has to dress like a man, cause men to be subjected to her will, be a man.

In Two Girls Fat and Thin, Mary Gaitskill's heroine, Justine, learns the difference between juvenile sexual exploitation, domination and the humiliation of others. And, in Kate Pullinger's Where Does Kissing End?, Mina's dictation of pleasure to her boyfriend Stephen is associated with death, disintegration and monstrous, vampiric behaviour. But, in the final extract, from F/32 by Euridice (not surprisingly, an American), sexual power has reversed so far that woman can be separated from her genitals, just as man can give his penis names and invest it with an identity of its own in order to evade personal responsibility for his actions. So here, at last, the cunt fights back.

RACHILDE

From *Monsieur Vénus*

JACQUES WAS at a loss. After all, high society must be freer than what he was used to.

Then, emboldened, he uttered some teasing observations, asking her whether she was looking, for that of course would embarrass him . . .

He confided in her, telling her how his poor father had died in some complicated business at Lille, where he was born, one day when he had drunk a glass too many; how his mother had thrown them out to live in sin with another man. They had been very young when he and his sister had left for Paris . . . That beggarwoman of a sister knew better than he did! They had had to earn their wretched bread, stale as it was . . . He said nothing of Marie's depravities, but he made a jest of them so as to banish a mournful languor that choked his breast. Money was given to them . . . How could he know? Alas! It was all too humiliating, and as he gazed upon the claw mark of the signet ring under the water's shimmer, he forgot how Marie had urged debauchery upon him.

This came to an end with a commotion in the bathtub.

'Enough of this!' he pronounced, suddenly uneasy with the shame of being in debt to her for even the cleanness of his body.

He reached for a towel and stood there dripping, his arms akimbo. He fancied someone brushed against the curtain.

'You know, Monsieur de Vénérande,' he said sulkily, 'even between men it is unseemly . . . You are looking! I ask you, would you be happy in my place?'

And he thought this woman longed for nothing more than that he have his way with her.

'She will get more than she bargains for,' he added, in the worst of tempers, his senses now entirely dampened by the cold bath; and he put on a robe.

Prone on the floor, behind the curtain, Mademoiselle de Vénérande could see him without troubling herself in the least. The taper's softly gleaming light grazed his blond skin that was downy all over like the skin of a peach. He was facing away from the door as he played the leading role in a drama by Voltaire, as told in detail by a courtesan named Ruby-Lips.

The small of the back, where the spine's curve is drawn into a voluptuous smoothness that then rises in two adorably firm, plump contours akin to the marble of Paros with its amber trans-parencies, was worthy of a Venus Callipyge. The thighs, though somewhat less robust than those of a woman, had yet a solid rotundity that belied their sex. The calves were set high, seeming to give the torso a jutting impertinence that was all the more piquant in a body that seemed unaware of itself. The well-turned heel was so rounded that its tapering line was scarcely perceptible.

There were pink dimples in the elbows of the outstretched arms. From the armpit to a point much further down unruly golden curls stood out. Jacques Silvert had spoken in truth: he had them all over. But he would have erred had he claimed them as sole proof of his virility.

Mademoiselle de Vénérande stepped backwards towards the bed. Her hands clutched nervously at the sheets; she groaned as does the panther whom the trainer's springing whip has newly lashed.

'Oh, terrifying poetry of human nakedness, have I only now understood, I who tremble for the first time as I try to read you with indifferent eyes. Man! That is man! Not Socrates and the grandeur of his wisdom, not Christ and the majesty of martyrdom, not Raphael and the glow of genius, but a poor crea-ture stripped of his rags, the flesh of a guttersnipe. He has beauty; I fear it. He is indifferent; I tremble. He is contemptible; I admire him! And he who is there, like an infant in swaddling clothes borrowed for but a moment, in the midst of baubles that my whim will soon take back from him, I shall make my master and he will twist my soul beneath his body. I have bought him, to him I belong. It is I who have sold myself. Oh my senses, you give me a heart! Oh! Demon of love, you have taken me prisoner, unloosing my chains and leaving me more free than my jailor is. I thought to take him, he has made me his. I laughed at the thunderbolt and I am struck by it . . . When did Raoule de Vénérande, she so cold an orgy cannot warm her, when did she feel the scalding of her being before a man so weak as a young girl?'

She repeated these words: a young girl!

In a frenzy, she rushed back to the bathroom door.

'A young girl . . . ! No, no . . . Possession without delay, violence, wanton intoxication and oblivion . . . No, no, lest my unfeeling heart be a party to this sacrifice! He repelled me before he pleased me! Let him be what the rest have been, an instrument to be shattered before I become the echo of its resonance!'

She drew back the hanging with an imperious gesture. Jacques Silvert had not quite finished towelling his body.

'Child, do you know you are splendid?' she said with a cynical candour.

The youth let out a cry of amazement and pulled his robe around him. Then, woebegone and ashen from the shame of it, he let it slip loose, for the wretched creature understood. Did his sister not rear up from a corner, sneering. (Ha! Go on with you, fool, you who imagined yourself an artist. Go on with you, illicit plaything, go on with you, you bedroom toy, do your job.)

This woman had plucked him from his wreaths of artificial flowers, as a strange insect might be plucked from real flowers to be set like a jewel on a necklace.

'Go on with you, creature of the swamp! You are no playmate to a girl of noble birth. Depraved women know their own mind . . . !'

It seemed to him he heard all these insults clamour in his blushing ears, and his virginal pallor took on the same tint, such that the button tips of his breasts, quickened by the water, stood out like two Bengal flares.

'Antinous was one of your ancestors, I imagine?' murmured. Raoule as she threw her arms around his neck, compelled by her height to lean on his shoulders.

'I have never met him!' replied the humbled conqueror, bowing his head.

Ah! The wood chopped for rich houses. The crusts of bread picked up from the gutters, all his poverty valiantly borne despite the treacherous counsels of his sister . . . ! The role of hardworking woman she played so artfully, those absurd little implements whose dogged persistence became wearisome to fate, where was it all gone? And how much better it all was! Honesty did not stifle him, but he could have gone on being decent, been allowed his illusions and the time to create riches and pay her back some day . . .

'Will you love me Jacques?' Raoule asked, thrilling as she touched this naked body that was chilled to the marrow by the horror of perdition.

Jacques knelt on the train of her dress. His teeth chattered. Then he burst into sobs.

Jacques was the son of a drunkard and a whore. His honour knew naught but tears.

Mademoiselle de Vénérande raised his head; she saw the burning tears flow, felt them fall one by one on her heart, that heart she had wished to deny. All at once it seemed to her the room was filled with the dawn, she felt the enchanted air. Her being expanded, immense, together embracing all earthly sensations, all celestial aspirations, and Raoule, conquered and made proud, exclaimed:

'On your feet Jacques, on your feet! I love you!'

She pulled him away from her dress and ran to the door of the studio, saying over and over:

'I love him! I love him!'

She turned again:

'Jacques, you are the master here . . . I am leaving! Farewell for ever. You will see me no more! Your tears have made me pure and my love deserves your pardon.'

She fled, mad with a dreadful joy more voluptuous than the voluptuousness of the carnal, more painful than unappeased desire, but more complete than pleasure fulfilled; mad with that joy called heartfelt first love.

'Well,' observed Marie Silvert once she had gone, 'it looks as though the fish has taken the bait . . . It will go like clockwork, God be praised!'

MARY GAITSKILL

From *Two Girls Fat and Thin*

GREG AND DEIDRE left the room, disappearing behind a closed door. The two other boys became rougher and more demanding; one of them told Dody to make him a drink, and when she didn't move fast enough, he grabbed her hair and pulled her toward the kitchen. 'You leave my friend alone!' Justine yelled in the phony little-girl voice employed by sluts and whores the world over (and she an actual little girl!) as she leapt up to grab the boy's shirt, pummeling his back with deliberate futility. She and Dody overpowered him and pinned him to the wall, greedily savaging him with tickling fingers until his friend leapt off the couch and the girls ran screaming until they were cornered in a parental close.

'You guys are really gonna get it now,' advised the blank-eyed boy. 'You have to stay in here and wait while we decide what we're gonna do. You have to stand back to back with your hands behind you.'

The boys left the room, and they did as they were told, standing and telling each other how afraid they were in thrilled voices.

'Do you think we should try and run for it?' asked Dody.

'No, we'd better not,' Justine said. 'They'd really kill us then.'

Justine thought of her parents sitting at the table eating dinner, her mother daintily picking an errant morsel from her teeth, and for a minute she actually did feel afraid. What if she really was in another sphere and couldn't get back to the old one? Then she relaxed; but of course, it would be as simple as the times she lay in bed and, putting her hand between her legs, became a victim nailed to a wall, and then, as her body regained its tempo, became Justine once more.

The boys came back into the room. One of them said, 'Okay LaRec, follow me.'

And Dody sneering, 'Oh, I'm really scared,' followed him into the bathroom, visible at the end of a short hall, leaving Justine to stare at this pretty-eyed creature with chiseled features, peachy skin, and no human expression. Her heart pounded. She wanted to sit down. He forbade her. He told her his friend was 'going to strip Dody and finger her.' Her underwear became wet. She told him Dody was probably beating his friend's butt, but no sound of butt-beating emanated from the bathroom. They stood silently, Justine's breath getting quicker and shallower, every detail of the boy's bored, sideways-looking face becoming larger by the moment. She felt as if he were right next to her, his breath filling her pores, his smell up her nose. The longer they stood the more genuinely afraid she became. The more afraid she became, the more bolted to the floor she was, her armpits damp, her throat closed, her pelvis inflamed and disconnected from her body, her head disconnected from her neck. She heard Deidre laughing in the bedroom.

The bathroom door opened, and Dody paraded out with her boy lurking and smirking behind. Her face was red but her body exuded pride.

'Come on,' said Justine's boy, 'your turn.'

The bathroom was pink-tiled and green-rugged, the sink decorated with large, stylish shells and glass jars filled with bubble bath balls. The boy sat on the green toilet and looked at her. 'You hafta get over my lap,' he said.

Justine thrust her hip out and tried to look like she was making fun of him, but she didn't know how to do that without her friends. The music from a ballpoint pen commercial was playing in her head, and she imagined huge-eyed Cool Teens dancing to it.

'I'm not gonna do that,' she said.

'You hafta.'

Back and forth they went. Heat and tension sat between her legs: the rest of her felt cold. He grabbed her hand and pulled her face down across his lap. She tried to appear graceful, feeling heavy and fat on his slim haunches. She looked at the toilet cleaning brush in the corner as he pulled down her pants. Her breath held itself as his numb fingers pushed into her numb contracting body. He fingered her with strange mechanical movements. His hand felt far away even when his fingers were inside her, as if he were doing something someone had told him to do and was pleased because he'd succeeded in doing it, not because he liked it. His remoteness made him authoritarian and huge, like a robot in a comic book. It inflamed her. She thought of Richie whipping her at the swing set amid the red flames of her little cartoon hell. His fingers hurt her. She gripped his thighs – and, in contrast to his hand, felt him there, a quick boyish spirit in the warm, feeling body of a young human. 'It hurts,' she said.

Perfunctorily, he stopped, took his fingers out of her, wiped them on her bare ass and moved his hands so that she could stand.

She walked out of the bathroom feeling like a busty blonde on *The Man from U.N.C.L.E.*; womanly, proud, almost inert in the majesty of her dumb, fleshy body.

Then she and the D girls went to Dody's house and had ice cream and vanilla wafers.

She never saw those particular boys again but, although she had occasion to 'make out' a few times after that, the boys who kissed her and felt her tiny breasts never made her feel the way she had felt while standing in Greg Mills's house. The only person who provoked that feeling again was a girl – a girl she didn't even like much! She was Rose Loris, a mousey pretty thing with thin lips and eyebrows who wanted with fierce anemic intensity to be 'in the group' and who was tolerated on the fringes because she was Debby's friend, although it was a friendship based mainly on Rose's devotion to Debby, who was always standing Rose up at the mall.

This intent yet drooping girl with the shoulders of a rag doll and the alert, quizzical head of a bird, whose sleepy limbs seemed at odds with her straight spine, followed Justine around wanting to be her friend. This annoyed or flattered Justine, depending on her mood. Rose was always saying weird things that she thought would sound cool, and it embarrassed Justine. Still, she sometimes went to Rose's house to watch television and to look at Mr Loris's pornography collection.

Among the many magazines, postcards, and books, Mr Loris had a comic entitled *Dripping Delta Dykes* about two huge fleshy rivals who, through a strange plot with many perplexing changes of locale, battled each other in their changing lingerie ensembles. On the kitchen table, in the boxing ring, on tropical isles, in hospital rooms (where they worked as nurses), they met and settled one another's hash, the brunette, after a lot of hair pulling, arm-twisting, and tit-squeezing, generally trussing the blonde up in a variety of spreadeagled poses so she could stick different objects into her vagina.

Although Rose laughed and squealed 'Gross!' while perusing this book, Justine noticed she kept coming back to it over and over. Rose's reaction irritated Justine; it made her want to shove or slap Rose. Instead she said, 'God, this is no big deal, I've done this stuff with Debby. It's fun.'

Rose's stunned face seemed to fractionally withdraw, and for a moment Justine was embarrassed at her lie. But Rose drew near again. Then, as had happened in Greg Mills's house, they crossed a border together.

Justine went on talking, saying that not only had she and Debby done the things depicted in the comic but that everybody did this, didn't Rose know? She never knew if Rose believed her, but at the moment she also knew it didn't matter, that Rose was going to pretend she believed her. The torture feeling was roused and roaring as she wheedled and teased, moving closer to the agitated, awkward kid until she was all but cornered against the wall, pulling her hair across her lips. Justine whispering that Rose was a baby, a goody-goody, that she didn't know anything.

It took surprisingly little to get her in the basement bathroom, where they were least apt to be discovered.

It is with a mixture of incredulity, guilt, and conceit that she remembers that dreamy session in the Lysol-smelling toilet with the concrete walls of a jail cell. She was incredulous at Rose's docility; every cajolement or command elicited another trembling surrender, and every surrender filled Justine with a boiling greed that pushed her further into the violation she'd started as a game. The occasional feeble resistance – Rose's pleading hand on the arm that rampaged down her pants – only increased Justine's swelling arrogance and made her crave to rip away another flimsy layer of the hapless girl's humanity. Justine felt her eyes and face become shielded and impenetrable as Rose's became more exposed; she felt her personality filling the room like a gorging swine. Rose was unquestionably terrified and doubtless would've liked to stop, but she had been stripped of the territory on which one must stand to announce such decisions, as well as most of her clothes. For although Justine had only meant to cop a feel, within a few delirious moments Rose was placed on the closed lid of the toilet, her pants and panties in a wad on the floor. Her shirt was pulled up to reveal her tiny breast mounds, her legs splayed and tied with her own knee socks to conveniently parallel towel racks, her hands ritualistically bound behind her back with a measuring tape, her mouth stuffed with a small roll of toilet paper.

Justine stood and surveyed her victim. She was shocked at the sight of the hairless genitals; they reminded her of a fallen baby bird, blind and naked, shivering on the sidewalk. It disgusted her to think she had something like that too, and she focused the fullness of her disgust on Rose. There were no more cajoling words, the mouse had been hypnotized, she was free to strike at leisure.

Fascinated by the meek unprotected slit but too appalled to touch it, she plucked a yellowing toothbrush from its perch above the sink – pausing to glance at herself in the mirror as she did so – and stuck the narrow handle into her playmate's vagina. From the forgotten region of Rose's head came a truly pathetic sound; her face turned sideways and crumpled like an insect under a murdering wad of tissue, and tears ran from under her closed eyelids.

But it was not the tears that brought Justine to her senses, it was the stiff, horrified contraction of the violated genitals which she felt even through the ridiculous agent of the toothbrush, a resistance more adamant than any expressed so far. Suddenly she realized what she was doing.

She left the sobbing child crouched on the cold concrete floor, pulling on her clothes with trembling fingers, while she bounded up the basement stairs and out the back door yelling, 'I'm gonna tell everybody what I made you do!'

But she didn't. Out of a muddled combination of shame and barely acknowledged pity, she kept it to herself, for her own frenzied, crotch-rubbing nocturnal contemplation.

Rose was absent from school for a week and then appeared like an injured animal dragging its crushed hind legs. No one remarked how her head, previously so busy and alert, had joined the collapse of her shoulders, or how her cheerful little spine had somehow crumpled. She avoided Justine and the gang, then tentatively approached and realized no one knew. She once accompanied Justine home from school in an abject silence that Justine was too embarrassed to break except when they both mumbled 'Bye.'

KATE PULLINGER

From *Where Does the Kissing End?*

IN NEW YORK Stephen did not visit any of his ancient relatives. Instead he and Mina went up in the elevator of the Empire State Building. They walked along 42nd Street late at night trying to decide which pornogaphic cinema to visit. In their grey hotel room with its fluorescent strip-lighting they watched the nude talk shows on cable TV.

To Stephen's surprise, Mina would not have sex with him although they shared a bed and did not wear pyjamas. She said that Stephen had to tell her about himself first – had to confess something which she was unable to guess. Stephen began by reciting his boyhood ambitions from the other side of the bed. He laid on his back trying not to touch himself and said 'When I was really little I wanted to be a teacher but by the time I became a teenager I had decided to be a lawyer but my father wants me to join his business and my mother thinks psychiatry is a better option but I don't want to go back to university and I don't really like any of these ideas at all.' He described his father's business and his mother's academic career and when he thought he had probably satisfied Mina's curiosity – he believed that the reason she had asked him to speak was she did not want to sleep with a complete stranger – he rolled onto his side and in her direction. The silence informed him that she was asleep.

In the morning over coffee, eggs, pancakes and hash browns, Mina explained that she knew all those things about Stephen already from the way he dressed, spoke and behaved. He would have to confess something new. They spent the day running around skyscrapers and the sights they knew from countless movies: Mina had never been to New York before. Stephen worked hard to stay calm but had an erection all day.

That night they went to bed drunk. Mina said, 'Tell me something.' Stephen began by confessing his sexual fantasies, what he wanted to do with Mina if and when given the chance. He could tell she was asleep even before he stopped talking. He began to feel like Scheherazade in reverse, attempting to tell the right story and bring about what he knew must be his fate.

The next morning over a breakfast of muffins, waffles and orange juice, Mina said she was not really interested in what Stephen fantasized about but was much more concerned with what he would actually do. They spent the day riding back and forth on the Staten Island ferry and practising their American accents. Mina was convincing – she could already do Brooklyn, Texas and southern California – but Stephen was hopeless. He sounded like his father, Romanian, bits of Yiddish and English all rolled into one.

Later, when they were slow-dancing somewhere dark and smoky Stephen said, 'You know, sometimes I really don't feel English at all. I don't feel Romanian either. In fact sometimes I hardly feel human. I feel like I've just arrived here from nowhere and I haven't really got a clue what comes next – how to behave, how to respond to life.' He stopped abruptly, feeling as though he was sounding ridiculous.

Mina pulled Stephen closer. He felt her breathing; the smell of her hair was at once familiar and strange. She looked up and he kissed her on the lips. Apparently he had said the right thing.

The cruellest thing, Harry thought as he sat in the dark, chilly flat one night after Lucy had left, was the loss of desire. In his chair in front of the television, Harry smoked cigarettes and thought about masturbating. It was humiliating, but having a stroke was humiliating, being in the hospital was humiliating, having to be taken care of was humiliating. Harry had reached the stage where he did not really mind what anyone thought of him any more. He ignored Lucy when she came to visit. Death hung about in the eaves of the roof, waiting. Harry sat in front of the television, also waiting.

In New York, Mina had her legs wrapped around Stephen. With her hands gripping his ass she pulled him forward again and again. She had pillows behind her back; she wanted Stephen to push himself as far as possible inside her.

At first Stephen thought he would not be able to stop himself from coming even before they had taken off their clothes. He felt very hard, the skin on his cock was pulled almost too tight. Mina admired his body – he licked hers, he slid his tongue into dark places and managed not to say anything stupid. She held her body rigid when he first penetrated her; her skin felt very cool except between her legs where she felt, Stephen thought, indescribable.

In London, Harry was by himself. Lucy had not arrived yet that day. He thought about his life and felt he had accomplished nothing. He felt dissatisfaction and anger. Where was Mina these days anyway?

Falling asleep, Harry dreamed of Mina. She was coming toward him; she was naked and looked more like Lucy than usual. She had blood on her face, her hands, and there was blood spreading between her legs, on her thighs and up around her pubic hair in shapes almost like handprints. 'Are you listening, Harry?' she asked.

Harry nodded in his dream and in the dim light of the room, his head moved up an down. 'You can't help me now, Harry,' she said. 'And I can't help you.'

In New York Stephen came for the first time, arcing his pelvis into Mina's, fucking her hard, then gently, then hard again. He tried to stop himself – she had not come yet – but he could not. Mina's eyes were open, her hands sliding across his wet back. He rolled off her and curled into a ball.

Harry woke, shaking his head to chase the dream away. He sat up straight. The flat was untidy; he had not noticed before. He stood and, as he stretched, he thought he saw something out of his eye, something flashing. When he turned there was nothing. Lucy would arrive soon. He wondered what was he doing allowing her to behave like she had some stake in his illness. He took a step forward, he would show her, give her a bit of the old what-for.

Stephen slept a wide open, happy, tired sleep, his arms wrapped around Mina's tight body. She stared at the ceiling. A fly crackled with electrocution as it hit the fluorescent strip-light. Mina felt her soul twist and spin as though it was trying to tear itself free. She thought of Harry. She pushed her bum into Stephen's groin; she reached around and grabbed his thigh. As he woke he found himself with another erection.

And then Harry fell. Backwards. He split his head on the table beside his chair, he broke his arm on the chair itself and fractured some ribs when he hit the floor.

In New York when Stephen began to come again, he opened his eyes and looked at Mina. She was crouched over him, her feet on either side of his hips. Her head was turned and she was staring hard in the direction of the wall as she pushed herself against him. She cried out suddenly and said she was coming and Stephen let himself go too. Her body collapsed onto his, her breasts onto his chest, as Stephen felt hot liquid travel through his cock. Mina's eyes were closed and her lips were moving. Stephen could not hear her voice but this is what she was saying: 'May the earth not receive you, may the ground not consume you . . .Are you dead Harry? . . . Harry, are you dead? . . .'

EURUDICE

From *F/32 The Second Coming*

TWO MONTHS AGO (FLASHBACK)

*F*OR WEEKS I *was running to massage parlours, sex clubs, porno-extravaganzas, S&M shows, bondage parades, swingers' groups, sex-aerobics classes. I peered into aqua blue blow-ups in periodicals sold hermetically sealed in plastic, titled* Prude, Rapture, Squeeze, Shaved Pussy Special. *I inspected countless pussies peeking through Frederick's of Hollywood undies or wrinkle-free explorer's garbs. Like the Japanese businessmen around me, I placed $50 bills into sweaty G-strings so that dancers showed me their costly sponge-like vaginas at close range. I watched girls do all kinds of absurd things to themselves, lick their own nipples, suck their own vaginas, push their own fingers up their asses, pretending they were two people fucking. I saw girls whose vaginal muscles were stronger than my pectorals, play ping-pong with their vaginas, throw a lasso with their vaginas. I saw girls fucking with Dobermans, with clothes-lines, with a machine gun, fucking on stilts or while hanging from chandeliers. I saw hundreds of chains, metal cages, metal cocks, nameless instruments of torture. And I patiently continued to go from porno show to porno film to porno shop, anywhere I could locate an abundance of genitalia and audiences, certain that the cunt couldn't resist that combination.*

I ran into it when I least expected it, of course. I was sitting in an XXX theatre, exposed to the pervasive odours of sailors' cum and unwashed socks and to the prolonged discoloured bleating on the screen. The moment that the soundtrack picked up as if the cavalry were coming and the porno stars repeated: 'Yes', I saw the cunt.

It was sitting a few seats in front of me! I wouldn't have perceived it in the dark if it weren't for its familiar eerie glow that made it look as if it were made of sparkles. I ducked at once so that it wouldn't spot me and lurked in the shadows trying to form a plan.

I noticed then, to my astonishment, that it (or should I at this point say 'she'?) was sitting next to someone who, after some more careful examination, proved to be nothing more than a substantial dick. Yes, loose in the theatre, by itself, a circumcised American dick out on its own! Where did she meet it? Did she abduct it from its owner? Did she sever it to keep her company?

They were sharing the cracked vinyl seat and wildly imitating the fucking as it took place in the film, so that they would hurriedly change positions, and slow down or speed up or curve back in accordance with what was projected on screen as if playing at being the mirror.

The dick showed great talent: it performed the part of every changing position diligently and without for a moment losing its strong upward curve. The cunt, on the other hand, was clearly improvising, writhing when the porno star's vagina remained still, changing rhythm and confusing its ambitious partner, obviously bored by the repetitive missionary position of its movie counterparts. She pirouetted in and out of the pounding dick, spun around it as it penetrated her, undulating her belly, or hole, flirtatiously like a luminous oriental dancer.

Even though I had continuously peered at crass sexual imagery and genitals for the past few weeks, I could not control the surge of revulsion that overtook me at the sight of this terrifying obscenity, this mockery. I sat witnessing two unadorned genitals slurp and slosh in a small pool of secretion, fucking blindly on a public plastic seat!

I was surprised by how much the presence of legs,

underbellies, waists, arms and heads contributes to, and perhaps even justifies, our interests in, and our tolerance of, sexual conduct. Genitals, I realized, though necessary and even enjoyable, require some sort of seasoning, a few extra touches, to give them the appropriate look; otherwise they are alien and disgusting like obscure protozoa or wormy salivating molluscs that have crawled high up someone's clean white wall, unnoticed. Oh no, this wasn't a sight of life!

It was now clear to me that the cunt had picked up this separate duck, and perhaps was planning to start a family of similar loose genitalia jerking themselves obliviously into eternity! This time I planned my next move, making certain I wouldn't overreact and lose it.

I rose, walked down the aisle, staring only at the action on the screen as if absorbed by it, hiding my face in my coat collar, until I reached their row and stepped sideways towards them as if to sit next to the mating couple. They were rolling in and out of each other with abandon, and I lost no time: I abruptly sat on them with all my force.

Now I had them trapped! I could feel the romancing genitalia fumbling under my coat, perhaps still unaware of their change of fate, the dick pushing towards the entrance of my buttocks and tickling me. I shook off my trenchcoat, let it fall over my prey under my ass and even tucked the sides under the borders of the seat. Then, once I had made sure they were still squiggling beneath my bottom, I carefully tied my coat ends into a makeshift parcel. I jumped up and pulled my crossed coat sleeves tight. I grabbed the struggling contents of my coat in both hands, turned it upside down so the flat back was underneath and bunched up all the openings. Quickly, joyfully, I ran out.

Now I had her! She was under my bondage! They fought like live cats locked in a bag and about to be drowned. I was in ecstasy!

I stormed into a dilapidated hotel next door, got myself a room, locked the shaky door, checked the stained windows, which luckily were not broken, and threw my derelict package on the unmade bed triumphantly. I was ready to dance, swirl, shout a paean, blow-up the place!

How could I have imagined, after all my precautions, that under the scarlet lining of my coat lay only a single erect dick? Yet that was the spectacle afforded to my eyes as I untied the knot. What could I do? I checked if my coat had been torn by the exposed screws on the movie seat. No! I looked around the room even though I knew I wouldn't find her. Perhaps she had detected me all along and escaped at the very last instant just to enrage me more. Perhaps she turned liquid and trickled out of my trap. All I knew was that she had run off, slipping through my hands again. I had it and yet I didn't have it.

Meanwhile, the excited dick seemed to have no consciousness of its new circumstances. It danced a lonely number on the bed, standing on its wider base, blindly reaching around with its head right and left and upward, hoping to touch a penetrable surface. It had no idea where it was or what it looked like. I was so disappointed that my impulse was to take it out on this poor victim. I admit that I tried to strangle it. I put my hands tightly around it and pressed as hard as I could to choke it. That was a mistake, for the immediate result was a forceful arch of off-white liquid squirting out of its mouth and into my eyes. It occurred to me that I had given it pleasure instead!

Irony upon irony, faux pas *after* faux pas! I was not made for this plot! I considered, for a moment, giving up. I thought this wriggling, writhing, air-grasping tool was a clear sign. A mirror.

Maybe I could put it in a jar of water, take it to Ela and say: 'Look, use this. Forget womanhood. Be a man. You and I both will start over. With our singular looks, we only need to screw this on and we'll be perfect males too. We can get men's point of view, what they see inside a vagina, why they go mad, all those mysteries.

*Let's try both sides! Think of Tiresias: you'll be a seer.
We can both be blind seers!' I knew I could persuade
her. I have that power. That, I was made for. Perhaps
there was a moral lesson somewhere here.*

MEN'S CENTRAL JAIL PART V (CONTINUED)

In the visitors' gallery at the prison, Ela is shooting the breeze with
red-headed hairy dirty Harry through the visitors' window. By
now, having shed her cape, cap and sunglasses in the subway, she
is left in the tiny red lace dress and pink elfin boots, like a plucked
bird. Harry is six feet tall and wide like a truck in his threadbare
grey uniform.

Ela tells Harry she has come for a clue regarding a cannibal.

Harry says she's come to the right person. he discloses; 'First all
of us boys thought it was a pink plastic dildo, I mean *Pocket-
Pussy*; but high quality, man, exactly like the real thing; a killer.
Someone must have sneaked it in and it was doing the rounds. I've
got a love doll called Sheena, sells for £39.95 and has fleshlike
extra-thick wet latex labia for a lasting relationship, says the label,
but that is nothing in comparison . . . I mean totally high-tech . . .
the guys were fighting over it and everything like it was a real
broad. So it finally reached Dick, who's the big man here and has
got tattoos on his chest that look exactly like that Pocket-Pussy. It
turns out, Dick said it was a real-life woman's cunt, on its own . . .
what a find . . . and that this was a real man's job so he'd keep it to
himself . . . he wanted to sleep with it every night 'cause he said
he'd never screwed anything so tight . . . this is the best fucking
cunt in the world you jerks, he said . . . and Dick's had pussy from
all over . . . he's done hundreds of pussies from every town and
country . . . said he'd let us watch and jerk off but that was all . . .
he punched Tom's eyes out for asking to borrow it . . . he ordered
"no talk with Rosie!" That was final . . . maybe they knew each
other from before. Dick is a smart little pig, but Tom said to me
secretly this thing will ruin Dick, he'll fall, it's like a man's calling
to love one broad once for food and this was it for Dick . . . so
Dick kept it on a string all day, a wire or rope or something, I
dunno, like a bird, a chick . . . and said to us all "Rosie this" and

"Rosie that" . . . in the mornings he called out "I've got a live one here!" and laughed . . . he let it free at night to screw . . . he'd stick it in and be screaming crazy "fucking hell, I'm God!" . . . he kept the jail up . . . everyone was jerking off . . . I've never heard a man come for so long . . . we thought they'd have him removed to the madhouse or shoot him up to shut him up . . . but I guess they liked to listen too . . . until the fourth night that he had it. Now that was weird. Just dead silent all of a sudden. We couldn't get a peek because we were locked up; but this guard says Dick tried to fuck it but it was slipping out of Dick's fists like a live eel, water snake, it wouldn't stay put. It shook and squirmed like the devil, but you don't know Dick – he held it hard and went in, all the way. Then it happened. Blood and all. Dick being tough, bit his tongue off and didn't utter a sound. They found him half dead. The guard had passed out too. The creepy thing had gone off on its own, just like that, carrying along old Dick's cock.'

Ela suddenly feels as if she's ogling at a peep show on Times Square, with Harry looking more like Roseanne. She realizes: No one here has playful eyes. Harry, bringing her back to real time: 'The Doc searched the toilets and they asked us all if we saw it but Dick's cock vanished with Rosie. Who knows where! Reno, for all my guess is worth. Having a screwball. My notion is, the cops should shoot it, or else it'll put a lot of our guys out of use. You can't bite off a man's cock and run off with it like nothing happened!' Ela: 'Don't they want it alive?' Harry: 'Who can trust it? You've no idea how good it is! I'm talking heady stuff.' Ela: 'I must find it. Who is the guard who saw it? Where can I go next?' Her voice sobs.

Harry: 'The guard has been off duty since, maybe he's having nightmares or getting drunk or whatever, it shook him up. My theory is, it's killed a dick! Check out the women's. If it's a cunt, that's where they'd take it, if they caught it. But if they wait to fry it in the chair, it'll do much damage yet. Once a cunt, always a cunt, I say. They better not let it in back here, I'm telling you. We'll lynch it like they used to, give it what it deserves this time, tear that hole apart. We'll fuck that sucker, in the name of dead Dick!'

. . . .

A few hours later, the blaring TV awoke me to the grim reality of my indigestion caused by the fatal large pizza. I blinked at the screen, and, yes, trite as it may sound by now, I was shocked to see:

The cunt was on a talk-show! What degradation! So it wasn't eliminated in the hellish fires of Ray's Pizza! What a waste! Why had I gone so crazy? Was all this worth it? I just lost control . . . How? My eyes glued to the screen, my hand grasping my remote control, I messily spewed out my overflowing nausea . . . into the nearby toilet.

I watched it flirt with Johnny Carson and spread its lips open in front of the camera as if they were legs. My cunt was the new queen of the 'in'! That figured! It was the keeper of the secrets of the 'in'.

I turned up the volume. The image of Ela's cunt filled the monitor! Johnny held it on his desk with the discomfort he exhibits with all the monkeys and other obnoxious pets that visit his show.

But why was 'she' making a fool of herself? Even a severed cunt can have dignity . . . I felt disempowered, and disembowelled . . .

Johnny was asking her who she really was. She leaned back away from him, smiling flattered and mysteriously, tipped her cavity open, and shook with her mute laugh. She was not camera shy.

Johnny informed his audience that she was the latest craze on the East Coast, something like the cabbage-patch dolls (the insult flew by her unnoticed, for being called 'doll' in the past had always brought her good fun). No one knows what she or it is, he said, where she lives, where she has come from; we only know that she can come, he winked, and the audience clapped on cue. We don't know who owns her, who manages her, or how she made her way to the top, but here she is! V for Vulva! The crowd clapped again. V! Viva V!

Johnny said her name had been inspired by her winning streak, her power and mostly her suggestive shape. So the cunt had now acquired its own name and identity! She was a bona fide individual!

V *as in Vixen, I thought, Vermin, Viper, Villain,
Vomit, Virus, Vicious, Vile Vengeance. Vacuum,
Vacuity, Vacancy, Void. Vertex, Voracious Vampire . . .
sucking her lifeblood out of countless victims, leaving
behind a putrid trail of casualties; including my own
recently spilled insides.*

*Is she a vampire? I wondered. This could explain her
power, her magnetism, her sexual hunger, her restless-
ness, her indestructibility. Vampires had adjusted to the
'sexual revolution' of our times by moving their teeth
from mouth to cunt. That's why the encunted Ela had
slept in the day, sucked dry her men at night, lived
among bones and smells of decay and love, felt neither
hatred nor fear, only ennui, and fooled even her mirror,
as she had no reflection. Oh, my word!*

*I'd heard Ela publicly divulge, à la Baudelaire: 'Je suis
de mon coeur la vampire.' But I of course took nothing
of hers for granted, especially not her words. I had
always suspected that Ela's sexuality was a quest. Now I
could safely assume that she was searching for the lover
who could kill her, whose love would enable her to die
after centuries of redundant cities and crowds and long,
graceful throats and tired bloodstained teeth. And I was
that virginal lover. Was that the self-realization I have
existed for? It had to be done. Now! Now??*

*'She' comes in and out of the spotlight unpre-
dictably, Johnny told us after the commercial break;
she comes and she goes. [APPLAUSE]. But 'she'
refuses to be examined by scientists whose interest has
been aroused by this unrecognizable creature, and who
are now speculating on the existence on earth of a
new, more developed species, Johnny explained. 'If you
have any information on V, call the toll-free number
flashing on your screens now,' a commentator's voice
announced.*

*Meanwhile, the cunt started to puff, blowing perfect
rings of smoke up into the air through her hole. At first I
assumed they were the fumes she habitually produced,*

but the cameras soon zoomed in to the phallic Marlboro stub trapped in her lips. She looked sensual, serene, and almost civilized. She sucked on her cig with all her abysmal might and let out the most exquisite fragile airy circles that went up one after the other in parallel layers forming an inverse pagoda like labia sculpted in clouds. Throughout the show, she appeared fascinated by her wetted cigarettes, whose butts she bit out of shape.

Later that night Ela's cunt was also on David Letterman, literally. She was sandwiched between Voluminous Viewer Mail and Larry 'Bud' Melman.

Dave and V had a cigar-smoke-blowing contest which of course she won. He exhaled haphazardly, making nothing recognizable with his smoke, while she blew out smoke-men, smoke-women and smoke-babies, composed of a big ring for the body, a small one for the head, oblong rings for their arms and legs, with little loose hair on the heads, smiling mouths, and dots for eyes and shoes and umbrellas, and with blown-up genitals; they hovered in the air for – David timed it – nine seconds. She was an expert. She had a craft now, a performing gimmick!

Then she leapt on his head and sprawled on it like a glowing toupee. The audience cheered her gall approvingly. She dangled and swung like Tarzan from his nose. She slipped on to his lips, preventing him from speaking, then down to his crotch. The audience chanted: 'V! V!'

David explained that part of her contract for coming on the show was that no one would touch her of their own will. So as she refused to leave the set, there was nothing to do but let her spend the hour all over David who, being a good sport, revealed a boy's discomfort to get laughs, frolicked with it, made funny wrinkled faces and mispronounced her name, and allowed her to steal the show from his other guests, for the audience did not want to listen to their stories and jokes, busy watching the little clown annoy and arouse the host.

Who knows what happened after the lights went off and the cameras stopped rolling. Perhaps he had a taste

of its foremost talent first hand. Knowing Ela's cunt, I
was sure it got what it wanted.

I flicked through the channels and all I saw were ad
snipets announcing V's special appearances on
America's Most Wanted, *the resurrected* The Love Boat,
Roseanne *and* The Morton Downey Jr Show *where she*
would match lips with the host: V for Vulgar. Kitty
Kelley was writing a V hack-biography for a reported $9
million advance.

. . . .

A CUNTAMINATED CUNTRY

The entire nation is alarmed. Men feel endangered in
their homes and in the company of other men. This has
caused panic among workers in such male-dominated
industries as auto plants and the docks who are in the
high-risk category. Many of them failed to report to
work this week. Men refuse to go anywhere unaccompa-
nied by women, as women have been respected and
unharmed by the 'beasts'. Dozens of bachelors have
committed suicide in fear of a more horrendous end
awaiting them.

Yesterday at 9.20 a.m. a man in Long Island allegedly
saw his male-dominated household raided by the killer-
cunts and two of his sons murdered.

According to what the anonymous Long Island
victim, 52, a divorcé, told the reporters from his hospital
bed, he was having breakfast on Monday at 9 a.m. when
out of nowhere an army of little pink creatures broke in
through the doors and windows and swooped down at
his crotch.

Despite the pain, the victim, a National Rifle
Association member, managed to grab his gun from a
drawer with them hanging on to his flesh, and shoot at
them. It was impossible to aim well as they were terribly
small and agile. One of the bullets landed in the man's
thigh, but he didn't know it until later, for the pull at his

genitals was much more intense. He was saved by his sons, who just then walked into the kitchen. The killer-cunts dispersed to attack the boys and he fled to a neighbour's. The unfortunate father had nine sons, of whom two were dead on the spot and the remaining seven lie in critical condition in the hospital.

When the troops finally arrived, the killercunts realized they would be outnumbered and took off. But the soldiers felt defeated. 'I can't imagine what we'll do when they start hitting schools or monasteries!' a sergeant told reporters. 'I'll never forget the physical humiliation as long as I live! No man is safe on this earth any more!' the tragic father cried as he was taken away for plastic surgery.

Ela wakes up from her dream-infested nap. Does she miss me? Ela wonders, lying awake in her round bed. I made her life easier, I made it simple for her to get whom and what she craved. I had the language, I kept up the appearances, played by the rules and secured her prey. Isn't she having trouble, with her overt ways, finding mates? Does she like to be misinterpreted, to be taken for the wrong thing?

Ela is torn between two forces of equal and opposite gravity, so she can only stay still. She can give in neither to her desire to live in total isolation, nor to her urge to jump into the thick of things and change the world. She used to give in to her cunt, which at least followed one singleminded direction and kept her busy, so she did not have to choose either extreme. That is why now she can neither abandon her footloose cunt to its fate and live happily alone, nor come out into the glare of the world to demand what is hers.

DEADLY CUNTDOWN

Daily reports of more wild-running cunts coming into NY are alarming city officials. Experts claim that the runaway cunts had been repressed. So they emancipated themselves and began to hunt in packs. They are multiplying to dangerous numbers.

It is impossible to calculate how much havoc they have already caused, for many of the assaults go unreported. The killercunts mostly attack men in remote suburbs and seedy areas of the city. They 'rage and rave and rant and raise the devil', residents report. All city ambulance services and emergency rooms are on 24-hour standby.

No killercunts have been apprehended as yet. Police hounds, specially trained squads, guerrilla forces and the National Guard have pooled their resources and are hunting for them round the clock, but so far the police's only success has been to save the lives of partly devoured victims, after being called by neighbours who heard cries.

The police are distributing artists' sketches of the 'beasts' based on survivors' descriptions. They are the only pictures of them available, but the cunts do not look half as menacing as they are alleged to be. Until we know more about this menace, there is no hope.

Psychiatrists and sex specialists have offered their services to help understand the 'killers' motives' and interpret the killercunts' instincts. No pattern of the killers' preferences has emerged, however, other than gender. They attack anywhere, any male.

There is no precedent for such unbridled sexual violence. City officials have declared a state of emergency in NYC. If the city shuts down, including such nerve centres as Wall Street, the country and the rest of the world will feel the blow. Suggestions of moving business headquarters to Washington are made but the manpower required and the costs involved for such an undertaking render it impracticable.

Lunch hour protest marches are being held in NY and candlelight vigils are taking place. Gun sales are skyrocketing. Churches are overcrowded and priests work overtime to meet demands. Group memorial services are now available. The victim toll has reached the 9,000 mark.

Men fear to travel alone and go out only accompanied by police escorts and bodyguards. These precautions, however, have not reduced the number of men found dead in ditches and side roads every morning. Experts fear that, in a population as large and diversified as NY's, the cunt crisis may prove impossible to contain for some time. Killercunts are definitely mankind's new and possibly greatest scourge.

ACKNOWLEDGEMENTS

The editor and publishers wish to thank the following for permission to use copyright material:

Alyson Publications, Inc. for an extract from Pat Califia, 'The Calyx of Isis' from *Macho Sluts*, pp. 116–29. Copyright © 1988 by Pat Califia;

Dedalus Ltd on behalf of Flammarion and the translator for an extract from Rachilde, *Monsieur Venus*, 1992, pp. 30–4;

André Deutsch Ltd with Simon & Schuster, Inc. and McClelland & Stewart, Toronto, for an extract from Margaret Atwood, *Surfacing*, pp. 142–8. Copyright © 1972 by Margaret Atwood; and with Simon & Schuster, Inc. for an extract from Marilyn French, *The Women's Room*, pp. 451–57. Copyright © 1977 by Marilyn French.

Gerald Duckworth and Co. Ltd with Viking Penguin, a division of Penguin Books USA, Inc. for an extract from Dorothy Parker, 'Big Blonde' from *The Portable Dorothy Parker*, intro. Brendan Gill. Copyright © 1929, renewed 1957 by Dorothy Parker;

Faber and Faber Ltd and Delacorte Press/Seymour Lawrence, a division of Bantam Doubleday Bell Publishing Group, Inc. for Jayne Anne Phillips, 'Home' from *Black Tickets*, Faber, 1993. Copyright © 1979 by Jayne Anne Phillips;

Anna Friend for 'Heartlands' included in *Storia 2*, ed. Kate Figes, 1989;

Harcourt Brace & Company for an extract from Virginia Woolf,

Orlando, pp. 111–16. Copyright © 1928 by Virginia Woolf and renewed 1955 by Leonard Woolf;

HarperCollins Publishers Ltd and Aaron Priest Literary Agency on behalf of the author for an extract from Jane Smiley, *One Thousand Acres*, 1991, pp. 161–6;
David Higham Associates on behalf of the author for an extract from E. Arnot Robertson, *Cullum*, 1928, pp. 87–9;

Macmillan London Ltd with Dutton Signet, a division of Penguin Books USA Inc. for an extract from Joyce Carol Oates, *You Must Remember This*, pp. 181–94. Copyright © by Ontario Review;

William Morris Agency, Inc. on behalf of the author for an extract from Kathy Acker, *Kathy Goes to Haiti*, pp. 44–52. Copyright © 1978 by Kathy Acker;

Peter Owen Publishers with Farrar Straus & Giroux, Inc. for an extract from Jane Bowles, *Two Serious Ladies* from *The Collected Works*, pp. 144–57. Copyright © 1966 by Jane Bowles; and with Gunther Stuhlmann on behalf of the author for an extract from Anaïs Nin, *A Spy in the House of Love*, 1954, pp. 32–4;

Penguin Books Ltd for an extract from Jean Rhys, *Wide Sargasso Sea*, Penguin Books 1968, first published by André Deutsch, pp. 112–21. Copyright © 1966 Jean Rhys.

Random Century UK Ltd with Aaron Priest Literary Agency on behalf of the author for an extract from Terry McMillan, *Mama*, Jonathan Cape, 1987, pp. 76–81; with Pocket Books, a division of Simon & Schuster, Inc. for an extract from Mary Gaitskill, *Two Girls Fat and Thin*, Chatto & Windus, pp. 104–9. Copyright © 1992 by Mary Gaitskill; with Alfred A. Knopf, Inc. for an extract from Elizabeth Bowen, *The Death of the Heart*, Jonathan Cape, pp. 212–16. Copyright © 1938 and renewed 1966 by Elizabeth D. C. Cameron;

Reed Consumer Books with Simon & Schuster, Inc. for an extract from Jenny Diski, *Nothing Natural*, Methuen London, pp. 16–22. Copyright © 1986 by Jenny Diski;

Serpent's Tail for an extract from Kate Pullinger, *Where Does the Kissing End?*, 1992, pp. 44–9.

Virago Press with McIntosh and Otis, Inc. on behalf of the author for extracts from Eurudice, *F/32: The Second Coming*, pp. 113–18, 130–3, 166–9, *F/32* originally published by Fiction Collective Two and Illinois State University. Copyright © 1990, 1993 by Eurudice; and with McClelland & Stewart, Toronto, and Lucinda Vardey Agency on behalf of New End Inc. for an extract from Margaret Laurence, *A Jest of God*, pp. 28–38. Copyright © 1966 by Margaret Laurence;

George Weidenfeld & Nicolson Ltd with A. M. Heath & Co. Ltd on behalf of the Estate of the author for an extract by Mary McCarthy, *The Group*, 1954, pp. 30–8.

Every effort has been made to trace all the copyright holders but if any have been inadvertently overlooked the publishers will be pleased to make the necessary arrangement at the first opportunity.